The

of

The Line

Melanie V Taylor

For Ivy

|

Mary Queen of Scott, great grand father Henry VII

Henry VIII
|

| Catherine of Aragon (DIV) | Ann Bolyn (Beheaded) | Jane Seymoor (died) | Anna of Cleeves (DIV) | Katherie Howrn (beheaded) | Catherine Parr. (survived) |

Mary Tudor (died) Elizabeth Edward VI (died age 17)

Acknowledgements

My undying thanks to my friends who have encouraged and supported me throughout the gestation of this novel and for those who inspired the fictional characters. Without them this book would never have come into being.

Author's Note

When I was a teenager, Hilliard's self-portrait reminded me of Hollywood publicity photos and fuelled my desire to know more about this good looking English artist of the 16th century. However, it was not until many years later, whilst studying for my Master of Arts degree, I came to some understanding of the use of the visual message. The title of this novel is a quote from Hilliard's draft treatise dated 1598.

Trained initially as a goldsmith, it is generally accepted that Hilliard was taught the art of limning (miniature painting) by Levina Teerlinc, who had come to the Tudor Court in 1546. In my researches I identified an *'Unknown Lady'* painted by Hilliard in 1572 as Levina Teerlinc which, coincidentally, is the same year he painted the first of many miniature portraits of Elizabeth I.

First portrayed as The Virgin Queen within the P on the front sheet of the Plea Roll for the Hilary Law Term of the King's Bench for 1559, this concept continued throughout Elizabeth's reign. The Coronation Portrait in London's National Portrait Gallery is painted on Baltic oak and the dendrochronology shows this tree was felled between 1595 and 1600. Part of the terms for the renewal of the lease of his house at 30 Gutter Lane was that Hilliard paint a 'great' portrait of the queen, which he completed around 1600-2, making the age of the NPG portrait coincidental to the felling of the oak. Perhaps future research will reveal that this late 'great' portrait of Elizabeth was by Hilliard. Currently it is shown as being the work of that well known artist, Anon.

My interpretation of the messages or the symbolism contained within these portraits is sometimes different from the traditionally accepted readings made by earlier scholars. I know my ideas will be considered controversial. However we are looking at images from a time when art was loaded with symbols and arcane messages and could be read by those with a classical education. The majority of a modern Elizabethan audience sadly lacks that knowledge and so many of these arcane mottoes are a mystery to us. I merely suggest an alternative interpretation to these traditional readings and, in particular, propose a suggestion regarding the intended meaning behind the motto on the portrait known as *'Attici Amoris Ergo'* that is in the Victoria & Albert Museum, London and has puzzled scholars for years.

Whether Hilliard was present at the trial and execution of Mary Queen of Scots is unknown, but as a trusted and talented subject I have used artistic license to place him there. Likewise is his part in information gathering for Sir Francis Walsingham and Lord Burghley. Research into Walsingham's spy network is ongoing, but James Bell (also known as Jean de Beauvoir) is my invention and completely fictional. Sometimes life's experiences provides inspiration for such a character and I am sure there were many like him in the time of Elizabeth I.

The portraits, sketches, documents and their whereabouts are listed in the bibliography so you can, if you are as intrigued as I have been, go and see them 'in the vellum' or on-line. You will then be able to judge for yourself whether the portrait of the Young Man with the words *Attici Amoris Ergo*, is the illegitimate son of England's Virgin Queen and her favourite, Robert Dudley.

M. V. T.

April, 2012.

Email: melanie.v.taylor@gmail.com

Mine eye hath play'd the painter and hath stell'd
Thy beauty's form in table of my heart;
My body is the frame wherein 'tis held,
And perspective it is the painter's art.
For through the painter must you see his skill,
To find where your true image pictured lies;
Which in my bosom's shop is hanging still,
That hath his windows glazed with thine eyes.
Now see what good turns eyes for eyes have done:
Mine eyes have drawn thy shape, and thine for me
Are windows to my breast, where-through the sun
Delights to peep, to gaze therein on thee;
   Yet eyes this cunning want to grace their art;
   They draw but what they see, know not the heart.

Sonnet XXIV

William Shakespeare

1603

The morning of 24th March

The sudden tolling of the bells could mean only one thing. Queen Elizabeth I was dead. Nicholas Hillyarde raised his head and listened.

A tiny portrait of a woman rested on his desk gazing into the distance with unseeing eyes. He only needed to dribble white paint to form the lace edging of her ruff. A red enamelled locket lay over her heart and its twin lay on his workbench waiting to enclose and protect her.

Semi-frozen droplets of sleet slattered against the mullioned windows and the wind squirmed its way through the cracks making the room cold despite the fire crackling in the grate. Spring was only a few weeks away, but today the weather was letting London know that winter had not yet lost its grip.

As the bell continued tolling its gloomy message, Nicholas leaned back and stretched. He no longer had the heart to continue painting. He grunted in sad amusement. There had been so many portraits of so many people, many carrying declarations of undying love. Everyone recognised symbols of love such as the person placing their hand over their heart. He had once painted his dear wife, Alice, holding an ear of corn and a pink rosebud and looking very smug. She had just announced she was pregnant with their first child.

Other portraits had been far more arcane. Young Essex had asked him to include the words *Dat poenas laudata fides*, which, according to the young Earl meant "My praised faith procures my pain". Nicholas had no idea what faith had procured what pain. Then there had been the young man who had asked him to be painted holding a lady's hand coming from a heavenly cloud and had given him the puzzling motto, *Attici Amoris Ergo*.

As the years had passed he had created the image of Elizabeth as the perpetually young Astraea, the Just Virgin Goddess of a Golden Age

Elizabeth's death was not unexpected, but now it had happened Nicholas felt old. They were all gone, his beloved teacher Levina, Robert Dudley, Lord Burghley, Sir Francis Walsingham, Sir Francis Drake, young Robert Devereux.

Nicholas contemplated the lady lying on his bench and mused on the various lockets he had made over the years. Lockets hung on chains around a lover's neck or nestled between a lady's breasts where the gentle beat of her heart would sound to the painted ears of her lover.

Another blast of wind hurled another squall of sleet against the window and the room darkened even more. He shivered, remembering the death of another queen years before.

His gout pained him so much so that even his soft lambskin slippers were uncomfortable. He needed something hot to drink; perhaps something spicy. Crossing to the fire he thrust the mulling poker deep into the coals, picked up a silver tankard and poured himself some wine. Reaching for a silver box he sat for a long time looking at the lid and running his fingers over the engraved entwined initials, N and A, all set about with daisies, their petals made from halved creamy white oval seed pearls with small round yellow topaz middles and forget-me-nots of pale blue

3

sapphires with tiny diamond chip centres. This had been one of his wedding gifts to Alice, who made the best mulled wine he knew. The box held cloves, a couple of nutmegs, slivers of dried ginger and several cinnamon sticks. Nicholas took a small silver grater and grated nutmeg directly into the wine cup, then pounded a clove, a piece of the ginger and some cinnamon in a small pestle and mortar adding the powdered spices to the wine and stirring it with his finger. Plunging the red hot poker into the tankard, the cold liquid spluttered against the red hot metal. Nicholas sipped his drink, relishing the luscious taste of warm wine and spices, but it was not as good as when Alice made it.

Settling back into the chair and resting his aching foot on a padded footstool, Nicholas adjusted a fur rug around his knees and stared into the fire. He thought about the things he should be doing, but he did not have the heart to finish them. Later he would visit the Goldsmith's Hall, but for now he just wanted to be alone with his thoughts.

"*Ah Marcus*" he thought, "*If Thomas and I hadn't rescued you from those ruffians all those years ago, I wonder how different my life would have been? I bet it wouldn't have been as nearly as exciting!*"

Nicholas closed his eyes and let his memory glide back down the years.

1572

April

Nicholas's mouth was dry and his new boots squeezed his toes. He noticed how the black kid was almost invisible against the dark oak floor boards polished by the thousands of feet passing over them every week. His career hung in the balance. His teacher had insisted he demonstrate his talent for painting the tiny portraits Queen Elizabeth was so fond of.

"So, you are the young man that Mistress Teerlinc tells me can paint as well as she. Is this true Mr Hillyarde?" Elizabeth of England inspected the good looking young man standing before her.

"Mistress Teerlinc believes it so, your Majesty." Nicholas's voice was soft, still holding a trace of a Devon accent. Coughing to clear his throat, he suggested "If your Majesty cares to examine this portrait of Mistress Teerlinc, perhaps you will be better able to judge."

Nicholas knelt and proffered the image of his teacher. Elizabeth leant forward and, taking the locket, cradled the tiny portrait in the palm of her hand.

Struck by the slenderness and whiteness of that hand Nicholas raised his head. Elizabeth smiled. Her brown eyes twinkled with merriment and Nicholas ached to capture her expression and the way the light glinted on her hair.

Elizabeth returned her attention to the miniature portrait for some minutes, turning it this way and that.

"This is indeed a very good likeness."

"Thank you, Your Majesty. Mistress Teerlinc is a very excellent teacher."

"In style it is not unlike those likenesses I remember from my father's time, by Master Holbein." Elizabeth looked at Nicholas questioningly.

"Quite so, Ma'am. I was afforded the opportunity of studying the great master's sketchbooks and it was suggested I study both his style of painting and his notes."

Elizabeth beckoned to one of the young pages.

"Go, fetch Mistress Teerlinc" Elizabeth commanded. The young boy left at the run. "Now, Mr Hillyarde, this will be the test. How well will your likeness compare with the original?"

Just as Nicholas was struggling to form a reply that sounded neither pompous nor arrogant, Robert Dudley sauntered into the queen's private apartments.

"Ah Robert, come be my eyes." The Queen smiled endearingly as Dudley took her hand, raised it to his lips and held it there just a fraction of a second longer than was seemly. Nicholas was convinced he saw Elizabeth squeeze Dudley's hand in return.

Nicholas ached to capture the twinkle in her eye and the golden glints of her hair so that, in years to come, the whole world could share this exact moment when he had first met the glorious Queen of England. If only it were possible to catch her musical laugh in paint!

His teacher entered, her black silk skirts rustling as she curtseyed then rose to stand impassively. Elizabeth stood holding the tiny portrait next to Levina's face. Tipping her head from one side to the other in thought, as she compared his portrait to the living face.

6

"Not bad." Dudley had moved so he too could compare the sitter with Nicholas's painted image and was resting his hand lightly round the Queen's waist. Nicholas smiled at this familiarity, sensing the Earl was using his comparison as an excuse to caress the Queen's body.

Levina stood looking straight ahead apparently oblivious of their close scrutiny. Nicholas moved so he was in her direct line of sight; her face was unreadable, but on hearing a soft comment he noted the corners of her eyes crinkled minutely. That tiny movement spoke volumes, but he was unable to understand its message.

"Mistress Teerlinc, your pupil is a credit to you" Elizabeth stated so everyone could hear "and you say that he is also a Master Goldsmith." she concluded. Nicholas squirmed whilst he was discussed as if he were some sort of prize horse. Elizabeth turned, focussing her attention on the young goldsmith.

"Mr Hillyarde, my Lord Leicester believes you have made Mistress Teerlinc too dour; but I believe you have caught her likeness perfectly. This is a remarkable piece of work."

Before Nicholas could reply, the Queen continued.

"Now my Lord Leicester, how say you to a wager?" Elizabeth placed her hand on Robert Dudley's arm and smiled up at him.

"Don't tell me – let me guess" Dudley replied, laughing. "Mr Hillyarde is to paint your likeness and if it is not judged to be perfect – I pay his fee?"

"Oh, what a wonderful suggestion, Robert. I accept."

"But, my lady, who are to be the judges?" Dudley chided.

"Well, perhaps my ladies?" Elizabeth suggested, her head tilted coquettishly to one side.

"Oh no," Dudley wagged a finger at her "your ladies are far too biased. I suggest my gentlemen?"

"I think the same applies!" She retorted, frowning and poking Dudley in the chest.

A loud rap on the door broke their light hearted banter, the atmosphere losing its playful informality as Elizabeth resumed her seat.

"Come." She commanded.

Lord Burghley and Sir Nicholas Bacon entered. Burghley's fleeting expression of anger revealed his feelings at finding the Queen closeted, apparently in a cosy domestic encounter, with Dudley, .

"Ah, perfect!" Elizabeth clapped her hands in delight. "What say you Robert – are not these two perfect judges for our little wager? They neither know of what we speak or of what is wagered."

Dudley could only agree. As far as he was aware, these two men had no knowledge of young Hillyarde's talent. Elizabeth crooked her finger at Nicholas, indicating he should approach.

"Mr Hillyarde, how soon can you perform this service for me?" she asked.

As the centre of a royal wager with two of the most powerful men in the land as judges, the possibilities of success were endless; so too were the perils of failure. He glanced at his teacher, who was making her way towards the door.

Ever since Nicholas had known her, Mistress Teerlinc had lectured him of the perils of Court, stressing that he needed to think fast, offend no-one and acquire a reputation for absolute discretion. She had lectured him long and hard on how people would try and befriend him desperate for information that might be useful for promoting their own position. Sensing the political currents swirling round him, Nicholas realised why she had been so determined to drill these messages into him. He also remembered how these lectures had bored him and wished he had paid more attention because, if he were to become

Elizabeth's chosen limner, he would have to try and steer his way through these political perils. One wrong word, repetition of anything to the wrong person and his career at Court would be finished.

Nicholas grew even more uncomfortable in his new doublet and kid boots. A sudden patter of raindrops on the window provided him with an idea..

"Perhaps, should the sun shine, we could walk in the garden later. The rain will have washed the sky and the light will be purer, therefore better for our purpose."

The implication that, with the right location, they could be away from prying eyes pleased Elizabeth. This young man, with his dark curly hair and saturnine looks, had been well coached in the subtleties of Court language.

"I take my exercise at noon and you will find me in the Long Walk." Elizabeth smiled her most winning smile. It was both a command and a dismissal and Nicholas bowed low as he retreated from her presence.

Outside the Queen's chambers the Court was absorbed in its daily routine. Nicholas was far too busy to linger and gossip with the Maids of Honour who were all keen to know him better. The past half hour proffered once in a lifetime opportunities he needed to discuss with his teacher.

As he made his way to the Royal library he wondered what was happening inside in the Queen's rooms. Dudley had been standing looking out of the window apparently ignoring the conversation between the Queen, Lord Burghley and Bacon. It was common knowledge that there was no liking by these two for Dudley. Now it appeared that he himself was a pawn in a game where Elizabeth was using his talents to play Dudley off against two senior advisers. Was she doing it because she was bored, or to remind all three that she was their Queen? It excited him to think that Elizabeth considered his talent good enough to be used in this way

"Nicholas, that went well." Levina's gentle voice calmed his turbulent thoughts. "Her Majesty was much taken by your portrait of me." She handed him a tankard of her special mint water and Nicholas drank it down in one.

"What precisely was it the Queen said to Lord Leicester?" Nicholas desperately wanted to know exactly what had made his teacher smile.

"Ah, just when I thought you had learned the lesson of discretion, you disappoint me by wanting to know a private comment." Nicholas blushed at her reprimand. "Some things are best left unknown, but, trust me, it was very complimentary. Now, if you are to paint the Queen it will have to be done quickly. So go, get your paintbox and your sketchbooks."

The Afternoon

It was sunny with a cool easterly breeze ruffling the rising tide. Nicholas pulled his cloak closer. The light was as he had said it would be and the air was clear. Nicholas had returned to his lodgings to collect his painting gear and to ponder how best to paint the Queen. These tiny portraits were designed to be held in the hand and looked at by one person at a time; they were not at all like the big table portraits which hung on walls. He had studied Holbein's sketch books and style and those portraits by Lucas Horenbout, who had been Henry VIII's illuminator and first painter of miniatures. Levina had said that Lucas had taught the great Holbein the art of limning and she hoped that, like Holbein, Nicholas would be better skilled than his teacher.

Nicholas preferred Holbein's sketches because they were far more lifelike than the large oil portraits. The painted stubble on a man's cheek or the fur of a collar all told of Holbein's amazing virtuosity, but the finished portraits were solemn. It was

10

as if the twitch of a smile at the corner of a mouth, or the sparkle of the sitter's eyes had been buried deep in the oily palette. That vital something that made the preparatory sketches glitter with life disappeared when repeated as the painted image.

Nicholas wanted to capture Elizabeth's vivaciousness and, remembering how Holbein's enchanting first sketches had become stiff and boring when re-worked, was why he had decided today to paint directly on to the vellum. This way he hoped he could both capture Elizabeth's sparkle and complete the commission within a couple of days.

With his satchel slung over his shoulder Nicholas walked through the Palace gardens. The position of the sun told him the time and he did not want to keep the Queen waiting.

Elizabeth was playing bowls. A tall, dark green, yew hedge sheltered the players from the cool easterly breeze. Mistress Teerlinc was among those with the Queen and she smiled as he approached.

"Well done Nicholas." Levina whispered to him. "She has talked of nothing else this morning, but of how she is having a new 'eye' paint her likeness. She asked many questions about you. In fact, you have quite captured her imagination."

Nicholas was unsure whether this was a good or bad thing. He now realised how stupid he was to choose today to change the way he worked. His previous commissions had taken several sittings to enable him to prepare sketches to work from and then several more sittings in his studio with the sitter being patient whilst he made sure the details were all absolutely to his liking. He relished the prospect of showing off his talent, but was worried whether he would he be able to achieve the very high standards he set himself working in this new way. It was one thing to criticise the Holbein's great portraits for their stiffness, but quite another to decide to experiment with a new way of working for such an important commission. He cursed his

11

stupidity because he had nothing except the paper wrappings of the vellums on which to make notes or any sketches and so would have to rely heavily on his memory. Swallowing hard he replied:

"I won't let you down. I promise." He prayed these would not turn out to be hollow words.

"Nicholas, of that I am sure. Just be yourself. My lady hates those who try to be what they think she wants them to be and, besides, you can give her something she desires; but remember, she is your Queen." Levina smiled her encouragement. If it were not for her, he would not have this opportunity and Levina did not deserve to be repaid by failure.

Their exchange had taken only a few seconds and Nicholas waited as the Queen bowled her turn before approaching and bowing low.

"Ah, Master Hillyarde. I thought you would never stop gossiping."

Nicholas held her fingers gently and raised them to his lips. Her skin was soft and carried a hint of the scent of roses and marjoram. Lifting his eyes to her face he saw her dark eyes twinkling with merriment.

"Come now, Mr Hillyarde. Let us commence." Elizabeth turned to her ladies and clapped her hands. "Now ladies, off you go. Mr Hillyarde and I have work to do."

Elizabeth sat down on a bench in front of the dark green hedge.

"Your Majesty" he coughed and bowed again, not sure how to continue. Elizabeth was sitting in the full spring sunshine and he was unsure of where he to place himself. If he stood directly in front of her she would be looking straight into the sun, which would make her squint.

"Mr Hillyarde, do you not think it best to have me in the open light; in the Italian fashion, who shadoweth not and are the best of all nations at drawing?" she suggested.

"Indeed your Majesty, shadows in pictures are caused by the shadow of the place, or, if inside, coming in a high window the light will come in only one way and at an angle."

Elizabeth smiled. His voice was gentle and pleasant to listen to.

"The Italians are, indeed, the greatest painters in large, your Majesty," he continued "but limnings require close attention unlike the large paintings and, unlike other nations, Italians model their faces in like manner to a limner, needing no shadows."

"Quite so Mr Hillyarde, but I choose to sit here enjoying the April sun without shadow at all, save that as the heaven is lighter than the earth."

Nicholas understood Elizabeth's reference to the use of shadow as a metaphor for defects of character and, since she was casting no shadow, her observation implied she had none.

"Your Majesty, it is the truth of the line which is the important element, for in that line with no shadow, showeth all to good judgement, but shadow without line showeth nothing at all. Both line and colour give the lively likeness and the shadows the roundness and the effect or defect of the light wherein the picture was drawn." Nicholas expounded as he set up his paintbox on a small table directly in front of the Queen. The box folded out to provide a portable easel and a selection of very fine paint brushes, some being of only one or two squirrel hairs wide, and several prepared vellum's with the background washed with blue and the centre left ready for the person to be sketched in. Nicholas dipped his brush in the water and set to work mixing a suitable pale skin colour in the centre of his tiny scallop shell palette to match the queen's complexion.

"Mr Hillyarde," Elizabeth continued, "The Earl of Leicester tells me that he met you some years ago." Nicholas nodded his affirmation. " So how is it that you have not come to my notice 'til now?" Elizabeth watched as Nicholas concentrated on his first vital strokes

Elizabeth liked his face, which had an openness of expression suggesting a character to match. She thought it a young face, not yet sullied by life's lessons that made cynics of us all and added the lines and wrinkles of experience.

"Indeed it is true, Your Majesty, I met both him and Mistress Teerlinc on the same day." Nicholas replied as he worked on, his anxieties forgotten now he was absorbed in his work. He had caught Elizabeth's image in just four lines and, conscious of his omission to include a sketchbook, he committed these four lines to memory.

"I gather you made quite an impression even then?" Elizabeth stated, intending to learn more of that encounter. Dudley had never mentioned Nicholas until this morning and it intrigued her that this delightful, handsome and talented young man had remained unknown to her until today. .

"I was the ward of Mister John Bodley and we were just returned from Europe in the November of '59." Nicholas blushed at the memories of that November day long ago in 1559.

November 1559

The twelve year old Nicholas and his friend, Thomas Bodley, were exploring the streets and alleyways of the City of London. They had returned to England only the week before from five years of exile in Geneva.

Mrs Bodley, deciding the boys were more a hindrance than a help in unpacking the various boxes that had come with them from Switzerland, had shooed them out of the house with instructions not to be back until dark. The sounds of London were very much like Geneva, but bigger and smelled of the sea, suggesting far off lands, so they were making their way down to

The Pool of London. They were fascinated by the forest of ships masts and their ears were assaulted by the noise of halyards and blocks banging against these. The dockworkers and merchants shouted instructions as they supervised the unloading of exotic cargoes from the New World or the Orient, or not so exotic cargoes of coal or tin from the North of England and Cornwall. The shouts of the stevedores mingled with those of the rivermen plying their trade up and down the Thames hauling small cargoes of goods and passengers.

The River Thames was the artery that carried the wealth of the nation and was filled with all sizes of boats at all times of day. When the tide was low the beach was covered in all sorts of flotsam and jetsam. The boys had sometimes found money and then they used their foreshore bonus to buy pies from a hot pie seller because, like all boys, they were always hungry. The two were making their way down to the beach to see if fortune would smile on them before the tide rose.

Passing a small alleyway, a young lad dashed out, knocking them to one side. Four older boys pushed passed in hot pursuit.

Nicholas and Thomas looked at each other; odds of four to one were unfair and they took off after the four pursuers to even things up for the little lad. Their quarry pounced on the small boy and were punching and kicking the little fellow who had curled into a ball. The element of surprise in their favour, Nicholas and Thomas jumped the gang from behind, landing some hefty blows before their foes retaliated. Thomas and Nicholas thumped tight fists into jaws and stomachs. The tussle continued, but the well intentioned two were losing despite the element of surprise. The ball on the ground had uncurled into a boy who was now fighting hard, but the odds were not in their favour. Nicholas kicked a tall blonde lad hard on the shins and, with his fingers curled tightly into a fist, slammed it upwards into a knobbly chin as the boy doubled up clutching his leg.

Turning to help Thomas, Nicholas did not see the fist that smacked him in the left eye and he staggered back, tripping over his own victim and crashing on to the cobbles, winding himself badly. The body on the ground seized the opportunity and, rolling out from under Nicholas, rose quickly to his feet and kicked Nicholas hard in the side. The blow landed squarely on Nicholas's kidneys and he rolled around trying to get his breath and avoid further kickings.

"Oi" A loud, deep bellow stopped the action dead. An authoritative figure and his manservant were unsheathing their swords and bearing down on them. The four attackers took to their heels leaving Thomas, Nicholas and a very bruised boy lying in the muddy road. Thomas was bent over, panting hard and rubbing his jaw.

"What goes on?" The voice carried the note of command. An elegant man in his late twenties stood before them. Thomas squirmed at the thought of the probable punishment to come for brawling, as if the bruises from the first encounter were not enough. He attempted to brush the dust and muck off his clothes so he would not appear to be a rough lout. Nicholas scrambled to his feet and examined his skinned knuckles. Both were trying to work out who had won, concluding independently they had achieved a moral victory, but if it had gone on any longer they would have been thoroughly trounced. Thomas was concerned that it appeared as if they were the ones guilty of trying to mug this small boy.

"Sir," the victim snivelled, "these two came to my aid."

"Pray tell me, young Marcus, why were you being pursued?" the man enquired. His tone had softened.

The small boy gulped and wiped his bloody nose on the back of his hand Marcus's left eye was closing rapidly and would soon become black and very painful, but this and his split lip, would heal in time; the rents in his clothes were not so easily mended.

"I was returning from an errand when I was jumped outside Mr Brandon's workshop by four thugs. I took to my heels hoping to outrun them, but they caught me here. I thought I was going to be done for when these two came to my aid; then you came along and, as you saw, my attackers ran off." The boy had a slight trace of an accent. The man held out his hand and hauled young Marcus to his feet. A sleeve had torn from the lad's shoulder and he had ladders in his knitted woollen hose. The mud would brush off and the sleeve was easily sewn back, but his leather jerkin was ripped and would need some serious mending.

"And I suppose your attackers assumed that coming from Mr Brandon's you might have something worth stealing?" continued the questioner. "Did you recognise any of them?"

"I suppose so sir, but I was only delivering a note. My mother will be worried as she wanted me to return home straight away and, no, I didn't know any of them."

The stranger regarded Nicholas and Thomas. It was difficult to tell what station in life these boys held, but cleaned up and dressed in something less battle worn, their appearance might confirm Marcus's story. They looked well fed and their hair was short suggesting they were usually well groomed and they had not run off.

"Well done, you two. However, since you have taken it on yourself to be young Teerlinc's saviours, perhaps you should escort him home. Dust yourselves off a bit and take this for some pies." The stranger smiled and handed Marcus some pennies, "Scrapping always made me hungry when I was your age."

"Thank you sir." Thus dismissed and clutching the money, the three set off in search of a pie seller as they were, indeed, very hungry.

The stranger watched them walk off towards Stepney and decided he should follow at a discrete distance to ensure young Teerlinc was returned home safe and sound.

As they walked Nicholas and Thomas introduced themselves. Nicholas rubbed his ear and felt a swelling developing. He could not remember having felt that particular blow land.

"Thank you for helping me" Marcus's voice quavered, as if he were on the edge of tears.

"We don't like uneven odds" stated Thomas, who was worried about what his mother would say about the state of his clothes.

"My mother will want to thank you both. She worries if I am late." The small boy continued.

Nicholas rubbed his cheek and wiggled his jaw. No teeth had come loose so he would not have to worry about having to have a tooth pulled, which would mar his looks. His left eye hurt, but thankfully the punch had landed on his brow ridge and not squarely in his eye. It was bruised and painful, but at least his eye was not closing.

"Isn't Mr Brandon the Queen's Goldsmith?" he asked.

"My mother wanted me to deliver a note, that is all. I don't know why anyone would think I would be carrying anything of value." The boy stressed the 'I'.

"No accounting for intelligence, or lack of it." stated Thomas. "They were probably just chancing their luck."

Eventually they stopped outside a wooden gate set into a high, red brick wall. Twisting the heavy iron ring to lift the latch, the boys entered the kitchen garden and made their way through beds of clipped bushes of rosemary, lavender and other herbs, towards the open kitchen doorway.

A stout, rosy cheeked woman stood at a table stripping a boiled chicken and laying the flesh in a pastry case. She gasped as she caught sight of the three boys in their dusty clothes, their bruises and cuts all to obvious and young Marcus with his hose torn and his swollen eye darkening by the minute.

"Oh my, oh Master Marcus! What has happened and who are these ruffians?" clutching her face in shock, the woman turned and shouted into the depths of the house "Mistress, Mistress" her voice rising to a crescendo "young Marcus is back!"

There was the sound of someone running and a rustle of silk as a woman appeared in the kitchen.

"Oh Marcus!" her hands flew up to her face "What happened?" she said in a foreign language as she gathered Marcus to her, hugging him close. Thomas and Nicholas looked at each other. They understood her tone and recognised the language as Flemish even if they did not understand exactly what was said. Marcus was squirming in his mother's embrace, embarrassed to be cosseted like this in front of his new friends, but his mother would not let him go.

"Mother, Thomas and Nicholas saved me from four cutpurses" came his muffled reply (also in Flemish) from the depths of her hug. Thomas and Nicholas shuffled their feet, wishing they stayed outside the brick wall.

"Come in, come in. I'm Mistress Teerlinc." the woman had switched to heavily accented English and was waving her arms, sweeping the boys into the room. The serving woman shut the kitchen door behind them, cutting off any possibility of retreat.

"Now what happened?" she enquired of her son, this time in English. Not waiting for his answer, she turned to her servant "Martha, get some hot water and cloths and some comfrey and witch-hazel leaves so we can bathe these bruises; and some bread, cheese and milk for these boys."

She ushered them to a room at the back of the house where there was a lit fire and table, chairs and stools. Martha set a large pot of water to boil and took the various herbs from jars and bunches of twigs and placed them on the table next to a jug. Mistress Teerlinc examined each boy in turn, gently pressing each bruise and looking at their faces thoroughly to find out exactly what injuries had been received. After some minutes Martha re-appeared with some soft cloths. Mistress Teerlinc took some of the herbs, tore them up, placed them into the jug and poured the hot water on to them. A clean herby smell filled the air as the herbs released their oils.

"This will clean your cuts and bruises." Mistress Teerlinc stated, dipping a clean cloth into the hot water and bathing Marcus' eye. Martha tended to Nicholas and Thomas. The women's tone and demeanour became less tense as Marcus began to offer some explanation as to why they all looked so dishevelled.

Whilst their battered faces and cuts and bruises were bathed and tended, Marcus related just how Thomas and Nicholas had saved him from the thugs. Another serving girl appeared from the main kitchen and placed fresh bread, cheese, apples and a pitcher of fresh milk on the table. Mistress Teerlinc questioned them all closely, but since both Nicholas and Thomas were newly arrived in London they were unable to help.

"Marcus, your father will be worried that you were attacked so" Mistress Teerlinc rushed.

"Lord Robert Dudley came along." Marcus explained.

Thomas and Nicholas stopped mid-swig of their mugs of milk.

"Who?" they both chorused. They may be new to London but they had both heard of Sir Robert Dudley, Earl of Leicester.

Martha left to get some more towels.

"We were just by the Tower and he happened upon us."

Nicholas and Thomas looked at each other. This was turning out to be a very strange day. They were obviously in very august company and, if they added this to their story, Thomas's father would never believe it even though, secretly they both hoped that rubbing shoulders with a member of the Queen's Court would save them from the inevitable punishment for scrapping.

Martha ushered Robert Dudley into the room and the occupants jumped to curtsey or bow, whichever was appropriate.

"Please," Dudley smiled at the boys and addressed his speech to Mistress Teerlinc " I was just passing and thought I would ensure that all was well. I happened upon a small tussle and recognised your son at the bottom of the pile. I understand these two were helping defend him, but unfortunately the four attackers ran off."

"My Lord, thank you. As you can see my Marcus is bruised, but nothing that time will not heal. I have only just met these two young gentlemen, whom I understand are one Thomas Bodley and one Nicholas Hillyarde, newly come to London."

Thomas and Nicholas bowed as they were introduced. Dudley sat down and made himself comfortable, helping himself to an apple. Now the two scruffy boys had been cleaned up he could see that there was about two to three years age difference between them.

"Well young Mr Bodley and Mr Hillyarde, how long have you been in London?" Dudley enquired, continuing to munch on his apple. His questioning tone implied that he still thought they were not altogether as innocent as Marcus made out.

"My Lord, we arrived last week, after my father was given permission to return from Geneva, but originally we are both from Exeter and have been in Europe since '55." Thomas replied; keen to ensure that this grandee knew they were innocent of any crime whatsoever.

"So your father would be John Bodley, then?" Dudley eyed the pair, thoughtfully. He knew John Bodley so his suspicions were unfounded, but life had taught him that it was safer to be suspicious than accept anything at face value.

"Yes sir" replied Thomas nodding enthusiastically, wondering how Lord Dudley knew of his father.

"And you, Mr Hillyarde?" Dudley turned to Nicholas.

"I am Nicholas Hillyarde, Mr John Bodley's ward and with the family in Europe since '55. My father is Richard Hillyarde, goldsmith of Exeter. As his eldest son, he wished me to be safe when the late Queen started persecuting all good Protestants, so he sent me with the Bodley family when they left for Europe."

"And what think you of London?" enquired Lord Robert.

"I think it the greatest City in the world" replied Nicholas, his voice soft with awe and his dark brown eyes wide with excitement "with the greatest Queen." He added.

Dudley laughed and Thomas squirmed. Nicholas's gift for theatre was embarrassing and now he was playing to the gallery to impress.

"Well, young Hillyarde what do you wish to be when you become a man?" Dudley smiled at the boy's enthusiasm.

"I shall be a goldsmith sir, like my father. Perhaps even goldsmith to Her Majesty." Nicholas suggested.

"Do you think you have any talent for goldsmithing then?" Dudley was quite taken with the younger boy.

"I can draw and am educated. Mr Bodley ensured that I was educated with Thomas, so that we will both be gentlemen." Nicholas was determined that Sir Robert Dudley would not think him a brawling scruff.

Dudley smiled. The lad had the making of an attractive man with his dark curly hair and his open sunny countenance. If he truly had talent, he may well have a career in London.

"So how old are you, young Hillyarde?"

"I have just twelve summers, my Lord." Nicholas replied, confirming Dudley's first estimation of his age.

"Is that so? And you, Bodley?" Dudley's gaze returned to the embarrassed Thomas.

"Sir, I wish to be a scholar as I have a love of books and learning. I am just fifteen and hope to enter Oxford at the next term now that we have returned permanently to England. Please sir, neither of us is usually in trouble for fighting for we are the sons of gentlemen and know better than to indulge in common brawling."

"That you are is obvious because, out of charity for one you did not know, you came to the aid of young Teerlinc here. Since you are both so new to London, perhaps he will show you the sights, therefore keeping all three of you out of trouble, as there is safety in numbers."

Dudley smiled at the two boys and turned to his hostess.

"Now Madam, it is not just to enquire of your Marcus that I happen at your door, but I wonder if you have ready that limning I requested?"

"My Lord, if you will just wait one minute, I will fetch it for you." Levina replied and left the room.

"Excuse me my Lord, but what is a limning?" Nicholas had never heard of a limning and finding someone as important as the Earl of Leicester had one, intrigued him.

"If you promise to keep it a secret, I will show you." was Dudley's response. Nicholas promised, even more intrigued to know what it was that required such a promise.

In a little while Mistress Teerlinc reappeared and handed a small plain rectangular wooden box to the Earl.

"My Lord, I hope you find it a good likeness."

Dudley opened the lid to reveal a small rectangular portrait painted on vellum and nestling on a bed of silk. The Queen's hair cascaded in golden ripples over her shoulders and the white ermine lining of her golden Coronation robes embraced her, protecting her from the chill of her Coronation Day in January. Embroidered Tudor roses trailed across the skirt, cloak and sleeves of those robes. The Queen wore a belt of jewels emphasising her tiny waist. The crown sat easily on her head, whilst the detail of the few stray hairs added to the reality of the Queen's portrait. A sparkle caught his eye and Nicholas realised that a tiny diamond was set into the centre of the cross.

"It should be set in a magnificent gold box to set off its beauty." Nicholas suggested softly, captivated by the sheer exquisiteness of the little portrait.

Dudley looked at him askance.

"By having it in a magnificent locket invites people to ask what is inside it. By keeping it in this plain wooden box it is safe and hidden from general view. If this were in a grand setting then people would wish to see it. If they are then refused, you know how people are, the more you tell them they cannot have something, the more they want it, and so it is with these small portraits. The more you say you will not show them what is inside a locket, then the more people will want to know who is hidden away."

Nicholas nodded. He too would want to keep this beautiful portrait a secret so he could take it out and look at it in private perhaps inviting only special friends to see it.

"So these portraits are perfect as a way to capture someone's likeness so you can remember them when you are away?" asked Thomas.

"Sometimes they are for diplomatic purposes." Mistress Teerlinc interrupted, sensing the conversation was edging close to the personal. "Queen Katherine had a collection of them and

King Henry used similar likenesses of himself in various treaties. By combining his image with other images denoting peace, wisdom and knowledge he could infer he was a great peace maker and a ruler of infinite wisdom. However, it is important that they are a true and accurate likeness. Our Queen's father was captivated by the little painting Master Holbein painted of Anne of Cleeves and it was because of this likeness the King married her. It was unfortunate that Master Holbein had flattered the Lady Anne too much, or so King Henry insisted. He thought her nothing like her portrait and so divorced her. It took Master Holbein some time to get back into the King's good graces after the divorce. Our Gracious Majesty has many images of herself, which she insists her Ambassadors use in their work abroad to remind both them and those they deal with, of exactly who she is. Yes, Mr Hillyarde, these images are often very important politically as well as being personal tokens."

"Well said, Mistress Teerlinc," Dudley interjected "and this is, indeed, a very good likeness. I am well pleased. Now young gentlemen, I bid you good day." Dudley smiled and left, leaving them bowing and curtseying in his wake.

The afternoon light was fading and it had been an exciting day, but they realised they should return home soon, which they were loath to do because they have to explain all the bumps and cuts all over again. Nicholas wanted to stay and learn how to paint the miniatures and so perhaps avoid the punishment both Thomas and he were certain they would get for brawling.

The Long Walk, Whitehall

Nicholas stood back to survey his work so far. He was pleased with the way the portrait was progressing.

"Your Majesty, it was only later did I learn that it was Lord Dudley's gift to celebrate the first anniversary of your accession."

Elizabeth laughed. She too remembered Dudley's present; a reminder from her 'Eyes' that she had survived many perils to become Queen of England.

"So, how was it you became apprenticed to Mr Brandon?" she continued.

"I was to be apprenticed to my uncle John, who is also a goldsmith here in London. However, through Mistress Teerlinc's good offices she persuaded Mr Bodley that I was of sufficient talent to join Mr Brandon's workshop so my guardian wrote to my father recommending I become apprenticed to Mr Brandon instead. From that very first meeting with Mistress Teerlinc, I wanted to paint these tiny portraits. I wanted to be able set a tiny diamond like the one in the orb in your portrait as well as design and make the lockets in which to display my work." Nicholas continued filling in the details of Elizabeth's hat and hair.

"So how did you convince Mistress Teerlinc that you could paint portraits and when did you join Mr Brandon?" Elizabeth was intrigued that it appeared that Nicholas might have been involved in making many of the objects she treasured.

Nicholas blushed as he remembered his first attempt at painting a portrait.

"I first painted Mistress Teerlinc's son. I ruined my first attempt by putting the year instead of his age, so I had to do it all over again. It taught me a good lesson." Nicholas filled in the details of the Queen's brown eyes, beginning to bring the portrait to life. "I joined Mr Brandon in '62 and was apprenticed to him until '69 when I became a Master Goldsmith." Nicholas made some notes on the piece of paper he had folded around the vellums. A cloud moved across the sun creating a chill, and mindful of his sitter's comfort, he suggested:

"If it pleases you, Your Majesty, it would be useful if we could continue this on the morrow, as the light and the temperature are making it difficult for me to continue."

"How much longer would you have need of me, Master Hillyarde?" Elizabeth was impatient to have the finished result.

Nicholas gulped. He had no idea. Normally a commission took anywhere between three and five days to finish and he did not want to rush this particular one in case he made a mistake.

"Probably all day, Ma'am. I need to be able to paint the embroidery and the details of your chain." He replied, erring on the side of caution.

"Oh, if that is all you need of me, then perhaps my ladies could bring you both the chain and my apparel, if you promise to return them, that is." Elizabeth smiled at him. As Levina's protégé she knew he was trustworthy. Likewise she knew that she was unable to idle away a whole day no matter how much she wished to leave matters of State aside. It was one thing to attempt to win a bet, but her sense of duty would not let her abandon her country to the rule of others. There was no knowing what they might agree if she did not keep her councillors under close supervision.

"That would be most agreeable, your Majesty. But I will still require other sittings to ensure that I have all the details correct."

"I can spare you one more sitting of one hour. Come to my private chambers in two days time, at the same time as today."

Nicholas thanked the Queen for the loan of her garments. It would make his work very much easier. If the Queen were not there, he could relax and, he hoped, work faster than today.

As Nicholas made his way back to his workshop his mind was whirling. The Queen's questions made him realise how nurtured and protected he had been and by friends even more so than his own family.

Nicholas thought about his guardian who had been more of a father to him than his own father in Exeter. It had been

Mistress Bodley who had nursed him when he was ill and mended the cuts and tears in his clothes whilst he was growing up. Then, thanks to both John Bodley and Mistress Teerlinc, he had become apprenticed to the Queen's own goldsmith, thus ensuring an elite clientele when he became raised to the level of Master.

Nicholas was humbled by just how much he owed to Mr and Mrs Bodley and Mistress Teerlinc for his education, upbringing and the nurturing of his artistic talent. Up until now he had taken them for granted. He mused on his good fortune and was determined not to fail.

Nicholas was pleased with his afternoon's work. It had been a good idea to paint straight from life. His painted Queen was very much alive even though she was unfinished. He had a small round gold frame lying on his workbench which was the ideal size for his portrait. It had been made it for someone else, but they could wait.

Three days later

Nicholas raised his arms above his head and stretched to ease his shoulders. He was pleased with the way he had caught the Queen's expression as she had listened to his story. It was a shame he could not portray the glitter of the gems on her cap and chain more realistically. However, the burnished silver leaf he had added to the pearls gave an added sparkle to the little painting. He eased the clear rock crystal front into the gold frame and lightly wiped away a finger smear with a soft linen duster.

A gentle tapping at the door irritated him and he ignored it as he carefully placed the tiny painting inside the locket. The portrait was mounted on a Queen of Hearts playing card and Nicholas placed this Queen facing out of the crystal front. The vellum clicked into place and the portrait was secure. Nicholas gently closed the gold outer locket and polished the surface. Now he could relax.

The tapping came again.

"Come." Nicholas commanded. Levina entered the room closing the door softly behind her.

"Is it finished Nicholas?" she enquired. He could sense her anticipation.

"Just as you knocked, I was placing it in this." Nicholas handed her the little gold locket for inspection, gold side up.

He held his breath. Would it pass his teacher's scrutiny? Levina turned the locket over and smiled as the Queen of Hearts looked up at her. Then, gently pushing her thumbnail into the small depression at the side of the lid, she prised the two sides apart.

"Well done." She breathed softly. "You have done well. I see you have included a subtle reference to Calais."

"Oh, you mean the iris. Yes, I remembered the Treaty you showed me with the roses and irises in the margins symbolising England and France. I also used the crown you use on the Plea Rolls. It's the same as the Imperial crown of the Holy Roman Emperor is it not?"

"It is indeed similar to his, Nicholas. However, since very few people ever look at those records, I very much doubt anyone will appreciate my conceit of portraying a woman as an empress in her own right. Her father insisted on this crown after his break from Rome, but you are right, it is by using these subtle touches we reinforce Elizabeth's sovereignty. It is also a reminder to the French that Calais is rightly English"

Nicholas thought about these negotiations for a possible royal marriage. The Ambassadors would certainly pick up on the Imperial crown and, if Elizabeth married a Frenchman, a royal wedding could bring an heir to unite England and France. However, the Queen had been excommunicated by the Pope for following the Protestant faith and this would be a major sticking point to any European marriage negotiations.

"My cousin," Levina continued "Susannah Horenbout painted Lady Jane Grey's portrait showing a gilly flower on her bodice. It was a direct reference to her husband, Guildford Dudley. However, these flowers have also long been used as flowers signifying the nails of the True Cross, so are emblems of sacrifice. I never asked, but perhaps Lady Jane had confided her worries to Susannah who then used the gilly flower to convey a double meaning for Lady Jane; the obvious one of her husband's name, which would please both John and Guildford Dudley; but perhaps also Lady Jane's own private belief she was being nailed to the cross of John Dudley's ambition." Levina smiled, she liked the layered interpretations Nicholas had managed to include in his first portrait of the Queen. "The great Albrecht Durer had bought a 'Man of Sorrows' Susannah had painted, not long before they came to England and from then on she used the Durer 'A' on all her limnings because of his acknowledgement of her talent."

"Perhaps, Nicholas, one of the Ambassadors will be invited to inspect your image of Elizabeth. He may see the embroidered rose and iris on the sleeves as a reference to the Virgin Mary, these being flowers associated with The Passion, which might be interpreted by some as a sign that the Queen would be agreeable to reverting Catholicism should she marry."

"It is not meant as such. I meant it as the Tudor rose of England and the iris representing the Fleur de Lys of France indicating Elizabeth's sovereignty over both England and Calais." Nicholas was amazed that a simple image of a woman wearing embroidered irises and roses would have more made of it than he intended. It was also mildly amusing that such different readings could be made of something as simple as an embroidered sleeve.

"What about the fine net that covers this embroidery." Nicholas continued. "I used the white made with quicksilver that you love so much. It is the only paint fine enough to use for this." The painting of this fine mesh was a personal tour de force, but Levina had missed it. What Nicholas had failed to take into account was his teacher's age. Levina was fifty two and years of close work had taken its toll on her eyes so she was unable to make out this very fine detail. Realising this he handed her a strong magnifying glass before she had to ask. The diamond shaped mesh became clear. He knew that only another painter would examine this detail and it was something that only she would appreciate. Others would be more interested in the accuracy of the queen's features or, as he now realised, the symbolism of the details.

"You will become very much in demand when the Queen sees this." Levina continued. "Many will want you to paint their portraits and whilst painting these commissions you may hear much that is dangerous. It may be that they will wish to embroil you in their secrets. Remember, the only one the Queen truly trusts is Sir William."

"Lord Burghley?" Nicholas queried. "I would have thought she would be more likely to confide in Sir Robert? Burghley's old enough to be her father!"

"Quite so, but when she first came to the throne, within hours she had asked him to be her Chief Minister. She asked that he tell her what should be done and how to go about it, even if it were something she did not wish to hear. He was loyal to her throughout her darkest days and it is he she trusts the most, which is why she has asked him to be a judge of your work. She knows she will get an honest answer from him."

"But, from what I understand, Lord Robert is highest in her affections. Surely, she would confide in him before Burghley." Nicholas had assumed that it would be to him who held her heart

31

that the Queen would turn and was surprised to hear that
Burghley was the only one with the Queen's complete trust.
Politics did not interest him and clearly he had assumed
wrongly.

"Lord Robert may be the one whom the Queen loves, but
she recognises that he has great ambition. Remember his father,
John? He was the one who promoted Lady Jane and his own son
for his personal ambition, for which he and they, lost their
heads. I remember one occasion early in her reign, when
Elizabeth lost her temper with Dudley very publicly. He was
complaining that Lord Burghley had received all sorts of honours
and that he had not. I cannot remember exactly what he had said
or done to upset her, but she screamed that she would not make
him a peer because he was of treasonable stock. It wasn't until
1564 that Elizabeth relented and created him Earl of Leicester
and that was only because he was being proposed as a suitable
husband for Mary Stuart."

Levina paused and thought a minute. "And who is to say
that Lord Robert does not secretly wish to sit on the throne of
England and still harbours a hope that the Queen might relent on
that famous promise of hers, to remain unmarried?"

"But surely Elizabeth wants children?" Nicholas asked.

"Nicholas, whether she does, or whether she doesn't, you
must remember that the minute the Queen marries, her first
obedience is to her husband. For that reason alone, Elizabeth
will never marry, despite all these negotiations with the French.
Think on it, Nicholas, it is absurd. D'Alençon is so very much
younger than her that it is preposterous to think this is a serious
negotiation. I believe she will always put her kingdom first,
above all personal wishes. She knows the meaning of sacrifice
and, if it means that she has to be not as other women are, then,
so be it. After all, she has said it often enough despite everyone
urging her to take a husband. Elizabeth is very clever and keeps

them all dangling on a string. The trouble is, you men are so arrogant that you cannot see that she is playing a game of, what do you call it, cat and mouse, with you all. She has no intention of ever giving up her power to a husband. If you were in her position, would you?"

Nicholas was aware that various marriage negotiations had been going on for years. At the moment it was the French who were at the top of the suitor list. Nicholas prayed that this marriage would never come to pass, but until it was announced it would not happen, there was always the possibility it might.

Levina smiled. She liked the way Nicholas had struck exactly the right note of ambiguity with his symbols. Let them read into it what they will. The Queen was impatient to see her new portrait. This was not only a test of skill, it had been a test to see if he would complete his task when he said he would. Nicholas had said it would be delivered today and it was nearly noon already.

"You have done very well. What are you going to charge Lord Robert when he loses his bet?" Levina asked, deliberately ignoring Nicholas's last question.

He had given this question a bit of thought and had toyed with the idea of charging a fee of three or four pounds, but Levina's question decided him. However, he only smiled and tapped the side of his nose as if to tell her to mind her own business.

"The locket is not too ornate." she continued "That is good, it will not take away the attention from the contents. I like the engraving of the intertwined roses. Was it meant for another?"

Nicholas nodded.

"I see you have placed the Queen of Hearts on the back of the portrait. You have confined your heart within this locket, yes?"

33

Blushing to have his feelings so easily read, Nicholas hastened to explain his actions.

"I remembered something Lord Robert said that day when I first met you both. You had painted a portrait of the queen and put it in a wooden box. He told me that the portrait was a gift and because it was in a plain wooden box, no-one would examine it unless they had reason to. I asked him why not use a gold locket and he had said that a showy locket would invite people to ask what was in it. I would like people to be curious enough to ask what's in this locket, hence the crystal face showing the queen of hearts and the queen's portrait is only revealed when the locket is opened. It is only right that Elizabeth should be the Queen of all English hearts." It was a feeble attempt to deflect Levina's correct interpretation of this particular card.

"You are also showing off your skills, are you not?" Levina was impressed with his use of rock crystal. Crystal was delicate and expensive and most lockets were just made of metal. This could be worn as a pendant, but this jewel would have to be handled gently otherwise the crystal might break.

"Perhaps we should now go and show Her Majesty what you have been hidden away doing for the last few days." She commanded softly. Levina was satisfied that Nicholas was ready to take his place at Court as her successor.

He blushed; was his ambition quite so obvious he wondered? Levina leant forward and kissed him on the forehead. Nicholas felt as if his guardian angel was giving him his wings.

As they made their way through the corridors of Whitehall, Nicholas was again wishing his best black velvet doublet was not quite so tight. The locket was wrapped in a piece of white silk, nestling in a black velvet drawstring bag ready for presentation. People stepped aside for the pair as they made their way to their audience with the Queen. Levina was well known, but the good looking young man walking beside her was a stranger and many of the young women glanced his way, admiring his handsome face and fine figure.

A gay tune could be heard coming from the royal apartments. Elizabeth was playing the virginals to Robert Dudley, Sir Nicholas Bacon, Lord Burghley, the French Ambassador and the pompous little Venetian whose name Nicholas could not remember.

Several of her senior gentlewomen sat in the bay windows sewing, but they stopped when they saw who had entered. They were equally curious to see what this handsome young man, would produce. Elizabeth had questioned all of them about Nicholas, but all she had learned was that he made beautiful gold jewellery having trained with Richard Brandon and was friends with the sons of both Mistress Teerlinc and the Devon gentleman, John Bodley.

The queen was wearing a magnificent gown of midnight blue velvet embroidered with vine leaves outlined in real gold thread. Pearls were sewn across the fabric and the sleeves were slashed with the white silk lining pulled through. Pearl earrings danced from Elizabeth's ears as she moved her head. She was at her most flirtatious, lifting her hands and head coquettishly as she played. As she finished, all the men applauded and complimented her on her musicianship. The piece was one of her father's compositions and Nicholas was impressed by the subtle use of dress and music to convey Elizabeth's message of who she was.

Lord Robert smiled at the newcomers. He had watched Nicholas's progress both as a goldsmith and painter and was impressed with the high standard of work he had commissioned from him. Dudley had kept Nicholas's identity a secret when Elizabeth had asked who had made the various tokens Dudley had presented to her. He knew that by the Queen having this one portrait painted by the young artist meant anything coming from the Hillyarde workshop would command a much higher price than at present. Dudley preferred to keep his pockets full of his own gold.

He too recognised that Levina was aging, were not they all? Dudley had known Levina since she had come to England. Levina kept her once blond hair hidden under a headdress, using the excuse that it kept it tidy and stopped hair, or anything else, dropping on to her work. But Dudley thought it was really because Levina knew how Elizabeth was terrified of growing old. He recognised, and was pleased by, Levina's subtle introduction of her replacement. Novelty would distract Elizabeth from acknowledging her gentlewoman's age and failing eyesight.

Elizabeth stood and clapped her hands as the pair approached.

"Ah gentlemen," she said turning to the Ambassadors, "how privileged you are to be here at this moment. You can join my Lords Bacon and Burghley as judges."

Nicholas bowed and Levina curtsied. A waft of lavender drifted from her silk skirts as she sank to the ground next to him. Nicholas realised how reassuring that smell was; over the years it had been a subtle comfort whenever he felt threatened and needed advice. Levina gave Nicholas a gentle push in the small of his back.

"Your Majesty, I have completed it." he blurted out, bowing again to hide his red face.

"Well." Elizabeth raised her eyebrow and waited for him to approach. Levina gave him another nudge. Nicholas stepped forward and knelt. He placed the velvet bag on her outstretched hand. Elizabeth unwrapped the folds of silk, exposing the rose pattern on the back of the locket. The queen examined the engraving closely then turned the locket over. A shaft of sunlight highlighted the red of the headdress of the Queen of Hearts and

36

it looked as red as a drop of heart blood. Elizabeth smiled, she had not expected such an overt declaration from him so soon.

Elizabeth prised the locket apart as you would prise open an oyster to get to the pearl inside. Dudley peered over her shoulder to get a better look and the Ambassadors crowded forward, all desperate to see the finished image.

"My, Mr Hillyarde." Elizabeth gasped with delight.

"My Lady, are not others to be the judge of this work?" Dudley chided.

"Of course. Come Burghley, Bacon, what do you think of this?"

Nicholas scrabbled to his feet and followed the Queen to the bay window. Standing in the window where the light came from three sides, the Queen held the tiny portrait up next to her face and smiled as the two lords peered at it at length. The ambassadors peered over the shoulders of the two judges and her ladies all pressed forward trying to get a glimpse.

"Well? What is your verdict?" Elizabeth demanded, tapping her foot impatiently.

Burghley was the first to comment.

"I have to say, my Lady, this is a remarkable likeness."

"It is as if you are listening intently to something." Nicholas Bacon tendered. "If I didn't know better, I would say you were thinking very hard about what you had been told and wondering what to say when the speaker finished."

Elizabeth threw back her head, laughing with delight at their comments.

"Mr Hillyarde, it is as if you have caught your Sovereign's spirit and bound it to the vellum." offered the Frenchman. Nicholas decided to ignore his oblique suggestion of witchcraft. He wondered if the Ambassador had also caught the deliberate reference of the Imperial Crown. It was a good thing the Spanish Ambassador was not there. Philip II was not only King of Spain, but also son of the Holy Roman Emperor and this allusion to imperial ambition might just be enough to inflame the Spanish King. At present, English and Spanish diplomatic relations could best be described as strained.

Dudley clapped his hand on Nicholas's shoulder as he congratulated the young artist.

The Venetian Ambassador hurried forward. "Mr Hillyarde, I would be very much honoured if you would execute a similar image for me to take to The Doge." This immediate commission demonstrated the accuracy of his work and his heart leapt for joy. Nicholas could not see his teacher's expression, but he knew her well enough to know that she would be more than pleased.

"Well Robert, it appears that you owe young Hillyarde his fee as there is no doubt that this resembles me very well." Elizabeth smiled up Dudley

"Oh no, your Majesty" Nicholas interrupted, bowing low to cover his blushes.

"Oh no what, young man?" the Queen enquired, smiling with delight. This young man was so charming, she forgave his interrupting her.

"I couldn't take a fee. You are my inspiration. It is a gift." Nicholas bowed low to cover his blushes. Levina sighed with satisfaction, Nicholas had learnt his lessons well; this was exactly the type of flattery the Queen loved.

Nicholas blushed deeply. The matter of the fee had not come out quite as he had intended.

"In that case, if I am not to pay the fee, then I claim the image." Dudley stated. No-one could ignore the warmth of the glance between the Queen and her Master of Horse.

Nicholas realised that the Queen of Hearts had now taken on a further meaning. Dudley was making it very clear to all that

Elizabeth was the queen of his heart no matter what negotiations were taking place.

1573

The Manual of Limning

I t was a joyous summer day; not too hot and no hint of rain as Nicholas rode out to see Levina and he was enjoying the feeling of freedom.

George Teerlinc had built a comfortable (and expensive) house in Stepney. The house was a mix of Flemish and English styles, brick built with many mullioned glass windows allowing light to flood into the rooms. There was a substantial vegetable garden, an orchard with apple trees, damsons, pears and mulberry trees where a sow and her piglets rooted and some chickens scratched and a cultivated area for vegetables and a herb garden. At the front were formal beds planted with roses and edged with neatly clipped box hedges where the family could walk and enjoy themselves.

Levina had written him a note requesting he come and visit so Nicholas had decided to take a day's holiday. He found her in the garden, picking various herbs for drying. Instead of her usual black Court dress she was wearing a simple sage green gown that complimented her hazel eyes and her white hair. Nicholas kissed her warmly on her cheek.

"Ah Nicholas, it is good to see you. Tell me your news. Have you seen my Marcus? He said he was going to seek you out as it has been too long since we have seen you here." Levina plied him with questions. "Here, you carry this trugg, and save me the effort." The scent from the fragrant bundles of sage, rosemary, thyme and comfrey filled his nostrils. Nicholas linked Levina's arm linked through his.

"I have indeed. Marcus came and dined with me just the other night and I understand he is to be a father."

"That is so. I am glad I will be able to see my first grandchild before I die."

"Don't be so pessimistic, Levina. You have many years ahead of you yet." The reference to her death cut him to the quick. He did not want to contemplate life without her gentle advice and encouragement, but, if he thought about it, Levina was now fifty three, which was a good age.

"Nicholas, when are you going to find yourself a nice young woman to keep you under control?"

Nicholas had endured a lot of teasing at Marcus's wedding because he had not yet found a wife.

"I'm not ready yet. The queen and members of the Court keep me busy wanting their portraits painted. Then there're the various lockets they want for them to keep these in, not to mention the other various jewellery commissions, which all goes to keeping me very busy so there's not enough time to go courting.."

"Are you sure? Nicholas, you are as much a son to me as Marcus and I would like to see you married before I die." Levina's soft Flemish tones grew more pronounced when she was worried or passionate about something. Nicholas knew she was fond of him, but Levina did not often show emotion and her statement took him by surprise. Nicholas took her hand and held it.

"Levina, when I find her and do decide, you will be the first to know, that I promise. However, first I have to make sure I can afford a wife." He had a thriving business, but keeping up the outward appearances necessary for those visiting Court cost money.

"Yet you are able keep a horse." Levina observed.

"Oh the roan. She's on loan from the Rising Sun. I have an arrangement with the ostler and it's much easier to hire one of his than keep a horse of my own. I could have walked, but it's quicker to ride the few miles to see you and I get here all the more quickly."

"Have you asked the Queen's permission?" Nicholas realised Levina had reverted to the subject of marriage. The direct question gave him no room to give proffer any excuses.

"Unlike you, I'm not officially a member of her Court so I don't think it will be necessary. Besides, as I said, I'm too busy to get married."

"Well, don't leave it too long," Levina smiled at him "please." She did not go to Court quite as much these days, letting Nicholas bask in his success, but that was not the only reason. Her health was not as good as it had been, but only George knew about her bouts of shortness of breath. Her fingers were showing signs of stiffening and swelling of the joints, which made it difficult to hold a brush. This was much worse in damp weather with the winter months being particularly bad.

"Nicholas, come with me." Levina led the way slowly to the top of the house. The floors were polished until they shone and the oak panelling on the walls glowed gold. A Flemish tapestry of a unicorn and a maiden, a gift from Margaret of Hungary to Levina's father, covered one wall of the hall. Portraits of Levina and George by William Scrots, painted when they were in their prime, hung opposite.

Her workroom was right at the top of the house and gave a clear view north-east towards the Hackney marshes. The solid lines of trees and hedges defined a patchwork of the various different greens of wheat, barley and oats dotted with the white and brown bodies of horses, sheep and cows, and foals, lambs and calves.

A fire was laid in the grate just in case the day grew cold, and the room smelled of paint and lavender. A long parchment sheet was pinned to a drawing board, which Nicholas recognised as the front sheet of a Plea roll. Levina had almost completed illuminating a capital P with the image of a seated Elizabeth wearing her Coronation robes, holding the sword of justice in one hand and cradling the orb in the other. Here she was God's representative of mercy and justice.

"I see you're still painting the P's." Nicholas bent to examine the sketches laid next to the easel. Other sketchbooks were stacked neatly to one side, all dated and labelled. He recognised the one with the different flowers, each having an explanation of their meanings or coded significance written in Levina's neat hand. It was an old book with a well worn cover and she had made him study it closely. Another sketchbook contained studies of various beetles, bugs and insects and this book had been handed down to her by her father. Levina had made Nicholas sketch birds, flowers and insects from life and he too had a collection of pattern books just like these. He had hated drawing the insects, but loved the flowers knowing he could use these in his jewellery designs, but had thought it unlikely anyone would want a bejewelled bug or animal. Levina's training in Bruges had been as an illuminator of books and the symbolism of all of these flowers were ingrained in her psyche. Seeing these notebooks reminded him of the very different interpretation she had made of the embroidered flowers on the sleeves in his first miniature portrait of Elizabeth. Not only had

43

his own image been given a different meaning to the one he intended, Dudley had swooped to claim the locket with the very prominent Queen of Hearts on the outside, thereby sending a not so very subtle message to all those watching that Elizabeth was his Queen of Hearts. The different ways they had all interpreted this portrait had been a salutary lesson in diplomacy and what, or what not, he might include as signifiers.

Levina opened a cupboard and brought out a small package wrapped in silk tissue and tied with a blue ribbon.

"I know you have long wanted me to do this, so here are all the technical details I have ever used including how to fashion faux jewels, gold and silver looking paint as well as how to use real gold and silver leaf."

Nicholas took the package and undid the bow to reveal a small book bound in blue leather. *"A Manual on the Way to Limn"* was in tooled in gold letters on the front cover. Inside, Levina's hand-writing was beautifully even and clear; *"To Nicholas, with love."*

Nicholas did not quite know what to say. Here was a technical treatise on the mixing and application of colours for use in illuminations on both vellum or paper written, or rather printed, in English. He had given up suggesting she write down all she knew a long time ago but, now that she had done so, he was feeling strange and empty.

"Thank you, but …" he started.

"Why?" she finished his sentence for him. "George agreed with you and insisted I do it. He then organised to have it published." She paused and looked at him tilting her head to one side. "Do you know Richard Totthil?"

"Yes," he nodded "he has a book shop near St Paul's."

"Well, Richard has held a Royal Patent to print books of common law ever since I have been at Court" she continued "and now her Majesty has expanded his remit to cover all aspects of geography, cosmography and topography. George and he are great friends and now he publishes printed books on these subjects he wanted to know how to colour the woodcuts.

Printing may have replaced the hand-written book, but so far, no-one has invented a successful way of printing woodcuts in colour. To be beautiful, this needs to be done by hand and so Richard and George persuaded me to write this so anyone can prepare and mix the colours. Since you were the first to suggest I put my knowledge in a book I thought you would like a copy."

"But why is this written anonymously?" he asked.

"Because I am a woman and a member of the Court, the Queen would be most displeased if I were seen to be involved in a commercial venture. It would not be seemly."

It was a double edged comment. Nicholas could see the sense in this being published anonymously because of Levina's position at Court, but wondered why she would write it, give permission for its publication and not want the world to know who had written it. If he had written something like this he would want to have his name in gold letters on the front cover.

A bell sounded in the hall below calling the household to the mid-day meal.

"Come Nicholas. It is time we ate."

Nicholas took his leave of Levina later that afternoon, loaded with produce from her kitchen including a dozen of his favourite honey cakes.

That evening Nicholas sat and studied the little book in depth. He had been approached by many to teach young gentlemen how to paint on vellum and had always refused, suggesting they read Dürer's publication on drawing and painting. The great Durer had published his ideas, but he had not hidden his name from the public and again, he thought it was such a shame Levina had not put her name to the little manual.

45

Levina's treatise gave precise instructions on how to prepare the parchment, vellum, or paper; how to grind the colours, prepare and lay the size on which would be laid gold or silver leaf, then detailed instruction on how to lay that silver and gold leaf. There were basic instructions on how to prepare ink and what pencils to use. All the other publications on art had, so far, come from Europe and required translation, but now here was one written for the English and he felt very proud it had been his teacher who had written it. He would have appreciated a book such as this when he was learning his art.

Thinking about why Levina wanted to remain anonymous, he realised how used he was to literate women. His mentor's literacy and ability to read and write was all part of her skill. The Queen was the most educated woman in Europe and could converse in a number of languages. However, if he compared the Queen and his teacher with Mistress Bodley, whilst being a very goodly wife, he realised Mistress Bodley was typical of the majority of women of the merchant classes. They could read and write a little and were sufficiently skilled at numbers to be able to keep the household accounts. The Bible was printed in English, but few women read anything other than this. Levina and Queen Elizabeth were the exceptions; therefore for a woman to publish a technical book would be seen just as Levina had said, over-weaning pride.

Nicholas felt a certain satisfaction that, finally, England had produced a technical publication to rival those written in Italian and French, but written for an English audience. He appreciated the irony of the author being foreign, which was another reason Levina might want to remain anonymous.

Curiosity as to whether it was as Levina had said, and Totthil really had published this Treatise in order to preserve the art nagged him, but it was several days before he was able to seek out the publisher and satisfy his curiosity.

The elderly man was enjoying his evening meal.

"Well, young Nicholas, what brings you out this lovely evening?" Richard Tothill enquired, pushing his horn rimmed spectacles up his nose with an ink stained is finger. "Have you eaten, because there's far too much for me here."

"Thank you very much. That lamb smells delicious"

Richard rang a bell and his serving girl brought another place setting. "Come, Nicholas, tell me all your news; I hear good things about you from George. I gather you delighted the Queen with your limning of her."

Nicholas drew up a stool and sat down at the table.

"That's true. I have members of the Court lining up to have their portraits painted. How Levina has the time to do these and everything else she has to do for the Royal library, is a mystery."

Nicholas poured himself some ale, carved himself a slice of the roast lamb and helped himself to some turnips blanketed in a white sauce. The juices ran down the knife blade and dripped onto the wooden plate. The lamb was delicately flavoured with rosemary and roasted so it was just pink in the middle.

"Richard, your wife is an excellent cook. I must ask my cook if she can do turnips this way and if she can't, may I send her to your wife for lessons?" Taking some bread Nicholas mopped up the last of the juices. Richard smiled at his guest's obvious enjoyment.

"Thank you, Nicholas. I'm sure my wife will be most flattered, but actually, it was our maidservant as my wife is with our son William, today. But come, tell me your news and that of young Bodley."

"Young Thomas is now a diplomat. He is away at present and I have absolutely no idea where."

"Anyone in the diplomatic service will never have a dull moment. However, I would prefer to be in London and safe. I understand it can be costly, and not just in monetary terms." Richard observed.

"I have to admit I haven't seen Tom for some time. Both of us have been busy." Nicholas admitted. He had been far too engrossed in building his clientele to think of what Thomas did. Whilst they had been close in Geneva, Thomas had gone to Oxford University shortly after they had returned to England and since then they had only seen each other occasionally.

"Never mind young man. Perhaps it's better because I can look forward to hearing about Thomas's travels directly from him when he returns. I see his father often. No doubt Thomas will be full of tales and will have added to his book collection. But come, I want to know about what you are up to. You are the talk of the Court, and I gather, very busy, so what can I do for you?"

"I've been given a present" Nicholas reached into his pocket and brought out the slim leather bound volume.

"I suppose you now want to know why?" Richard enquired. Nicholas nodded. "As you know, George has many fingers in many pies, and has long felt it would be a good idea to have a manual which set out how to prepare pigments for illuminations. He first persuaded Levina to write down all she knew and then persuaded me to publish it. As you know, apart from printing paper books with woodcut illustrations, I also produce maps, and for many customers they wish these to be coloured."

"Ah, I see. You wanted to know the limners' secrets in order to be able to produce hand coloured woodcuts in printed volumes. Plus, not only do you learn the art of preparing the various colours, you can sell this book allowing others to do the same. I agree sometimes it's better to prepare your own colours rather than buy them from the apothecaries, especially the blues:

ultramarine in particular. It's so expensive, so why pay someone else to prepare it when you can do it yourself and so keep the cost down."

"Quite so." Richard continued. "Illustrations using wood-cuts are fine, but now I can provide a more luxurious book with coloured pictures. Publishing this Treatise is a way of preserving your art as well as providing me with the instructions for colouring illustrations by hand."

Nicholas nodded. Levina had said just that.

"However, Nicholas, are you not concerned that your place as a portrait painter may be usurped?"

Nicholas laughed. The idea was preposterous.

"Why? Do you think that just by reading this volume anyone can paint? I've spent years learning the art. From this book, you may well be able to employ people to colour your woodcuts, but to paint portraits, now that's a different matter."

"Perhaps you would consider writing a treatise to compliment this one?" Richard expanded a random thought, spurred on by Nicholas's acceptance of Levina's book. The question surprised the young artist.

"I've never thought of that. You can teach someone the technicalities, but first of all they have to have talent and the time, which means they must be of a certain class and of means." As Nicholas talked, he realised he was not keen to commit his own secrets to paper at the moment, but it was something he might do later.

"First of all, you have to be able to draw and to draw, you have to be able to observe. And to paint portraits of the Queen – well you have to be in her presence and this is not always easy, even for gentlemen!"

Richard laughed at Nicholas' arrogant reply, born of both youth and talent. His own son, William, had gone into the law and was doing very well. Watching the likes of his son William,

Thomas Bodley and young Nicholas developing their careers gave Richard Totthil a pleasing sense of continuity. Teerlinc had commented on just the same feeling now that his Marcus was involved in the family business.

"Well, if I can't persuade you to write a treatise, perhaps you would do a limning of William for me instead?" Richard asked. Nicholas smiled. Tothill's request did not come as a surprise as many of his merchant clients wanted to show their friends they were sufficiently well acquainted with Court circles to be able to commission a Hillyarde miniature. He found it amusing the way he had been wooed into painting a portrait of William Tothill on the suggestion he write a book.

"Of course, Richard. It would give me great pleasure."

"Excellent Nicholas. William is coming to see me tomorrow, so I shall tell him to come and see you?" Richard was ecstatic. His wife would be overjoyed at having such a portrait. "And will you also make a suitable locket for it?"

Nicholas rose to take his leave.

"Richard, I shall indeed. It will be a pleasure. Perhaps William would let me know when he has time during the day to meet with me. The morning light is best, I find." Nicholas replied. "Thank you also for such a delicious dinner."

The two men shook hands and Nicholas stepped into the street. His lodgings were only a few streets away and he walked quickly as the air was damp and he did not want to catch a chill.

Nicholas thought on this latest commission as he walked home and wondered whether Richard would have asked him directly if he had not gone round to visit him.

The Phoenix

"Nicholas?" Levina called up the stairs "Nicholas!" she called again, this time with a sharpness to her voice. "I am not climbing all the way to the top of your house so you will have to come down to me."

Nicholas was in his workroom which, like Levina's, was right at the top of his lodgings. He was concentrating on filling in the background to William Totthill's portrait and had not heard her first call. He laid down his brush and clattered down the stairs to find his teacher sitting in his parlour.

"Finally, you hear me. You think I have all day to wait until you decide to clean out your ears?"

"I'm sorry, Levina. I was concentrating on the curls of a beard, and you know how difficult that can be ...." Nicholas let the sentence trail off, using technical difficulty as an excuse for his apparent deafness.

"Let me get you some honey cakes and buttermilk." he proffered as his portly Cook appeared, puffing from her climb from the kitchen. Nicholas hoped there was fresh buttermilk and it would be cool. Levina was sparing in her drinking, preferring milk or water boiled with mint to wine or ale. He too drank little. It was so easy enough to make a mistake sober, so he only drank wine or ale in the evening or dining with friends.

"That would be nice. At least you haven't forgotten your manners even if you are becoming hard of hearing." she chided.

Levina was excited and wanted to be the one to tell Nicholas her news and not some anonymous Court official. Finding him hard at work had been good, but she had been waiting for some minutes. It was not so much that Nicholas had kept her waiting that made her gruff, but her excitement, which was almost overwhelming. Levina prided herself in never showing emotion, but what she had to tell Nicholas was so exciting, that her normal cool, calm and collected demeanour was churned into a turmoil of expectation. She breathed deeply trying to compose herself and smoothed imaginary creases from the skirt of her dress. Small beads of sweat gathered on her forehead and taking a small piece of linen from a pocket, she patted her brow. Nicholas noted she wore the locket he had made her containing portraits of George and Marcus pinned to her bodice. The small rose cut diamonds and sapphires formed sprays of forget-me-nots, whilst the stems and leaves were chased into the gold background.

Nicholas removed his silk painting smock protecting his lawn shirt from accidental paint splashes. The day was pleasantly warm but his north-east facing study did not get any direct sun. Here in the parlour, the heat came in through the windows opening on to the small south facing garden, which was a riot of herbs. The smell from the hot rosemary and honeysuckle drifted in through the window making sitting in this room very pleasant.

"I wish you would move out of London during the summer, Nicholas. You know how I worry how you might catch the sweating sickness. "

"Yes, I suppose it would be a good idea, but where do you suggest I go?"

"Well, for this year, that is decided."

"And where is that to be?" Nicholas played her game. It was giving her pleasure to draw out whatever it was she had to tell him. His housekeeper entered puffing from the exertion of carrying a tray heavy with a plate of honey cakes, a pitcher of cool, fresh buttermilk and two good quality earthenware mugs, all the way up from the ground floor.

"Richmond, or Nonsuch " Levina paused for her announcement to sink in "or possibly Enfield."

"And why would the Queen want me with her this summer?" Nicholas was intrigued. He knew Whitehall was being cleaned whilst Elizabeth was away and, this year, it was rumoured she might not return there until December, but instead stay at Richmond or Hampton Court until Christmas. He had a full order book of jewellery commissions to keep him busy throughout the summer and a great many portraits, which was satisfying as the merchants were much better payers than Courtiers.

Nicholas waited, poured her a mug of buttermilk and offered her a honey cake. Levina sipped the creamy liquid and nibbled her cake. A bee buzzed in through the open window and circled the tray attracted by the smell of honey.

"Well, aren't you going to ask me what it is?" Levina finally said.

"No."

"Why not?"

"Because it's giving you so much pleasure to make me wait." he teased.

Levina harrumphed in part acknowledgement that this was so, and partly because he was being so difficult. If he had still been a child he would have been nagging her to tell him and part of her longed for the return of that youthful, impatient, Nicholas. Now he had grown up and sat before her secure in his own talents. This mature young man, now showing the patience of Job, had such an opportunity that she wanted him to know immediately, but because he was being so patient, she would test him (and herself) to see how long he would wait.

More minutes passed. Levina finished her buttermilk and nibbled another cake. Nicholas poured them both another mug of buttermilk then finally Levina gave in; her excitement too great to contain any longer

"Elizabeth wants you to do a big portrait of her."

"Ah" came Nicholas's reply.

"Ah – is that all you have to say? Ah!!" Levina snorted, her patience worn to breaking point by his silence. "This is very specific. Because you trained with Richard Brandon, she wants you to paint her wearing the Phoenix brooch he made for her."

"Ah" came Nicholas' response, again.

"Is 'Ah' all you can say today!! Aren't you even the slightest bit excited? You are sitting there as though you were completely disinterested" Levina was now genuinely irritated. "Have you even been listening to me?"

"No, stop. Levina, I'm amazed. Why me? You know I've never painted anything larger than a miniature, so why do you think I will be able to paint a big portrait."

"Don't be so silly, Nicholas. It is not to be life-size. Elizabeth will never pay for anything that big, but she doesn't want anyone else to paint her. It's not only because of your ability to capture her likeness, but also because of your connection with Brandon that she wants you to paint her wearing his jewels."

"But why didn't she ask you to paint her wearing these?" It was an innocent enough question.

"I can't paint anything that big" came Levina's quiet response "and who knows the mind of Elizabeth?" she added softly.

"I don't know if I can do it either. Oil is a totally different technique!" Nicholas replied.

"You will have to practise then. Just try sketching larger and if you can't manage something passable, then you will have to explain why not. However, you had better be prepared for the consequences if you really cannot do it. She may decide not to use you again! For anything." Levina had not expected her protégé to be so hesitant.

Nicholas stretched to ease his aching shoulder muscles thinking how he must remember to sit up straighter when painting. He knew he hunched over his easel which meant he might end up bent and stooped. He thought about this challenge. It was not as if he had not been experimenting with oil paints, but he did not want to be known as a painter of large portraits. Levina was an illuminator for the Royal Library and a

54

prominent member of the Queen's Household as one of her Gentlewoman. However, he had no Court appointment even though, at the moment, he seemed to be secure in his post as Levina's successor and he was a master goldsmith, entered as such in the records of the Guild of Goldsmith, not a member of the inferior Painter and Stainer's Guild.

Life was all to do with what you were seen to be.

Miniature painting was done by gentleman. Long ago he had decided he would acknowledge the great Hans Holbein as his inspiration because of the great man's ability to capture likenesses and because the great Holbein had first trained as goldsmith. Nicholas knew that if he were to secure an appointment within the Royal Household, it would be a stupid to refuse the Queen's request.

"How much bigger do you think this portrait would have to be?" Nicholas was hopeful that if he could keep the increased size to a minimum, it would not be too much of a challenge. The larger size would mean he would be able to portray Brandon's jewellery properly, plus there were some advantages to using oil. If you made a mistake with water colour and it was a big one, then the whole project was ruined; mistakes made using oil glazes could be easily remedied.

"Do you think that she would agree to being painted completely in private?" Nicholas looked at his teacher imploringly. It would be so much easier to draw the Queen without the whole Court peering over his shoulder wanting to know what was going on.

"Don't be ridiculous. The Queen couldn't be unchaperoned!" Levina was shocked by his request.

"Well, do you think she could keep her retinue to a trusted few, then?"

"Why? You can do what I do and sketch her at the Palace. I've been doing it for years, so that is a silly question."

"I know, Levina, but it is different for you. You are a member of her Court and a woman. If I'm there sketching, then everyone knows it's for a specific purpose and will be curious. My clients come here where we can be alone. Sometimes they bring musicians with them to relieve the boredom of sitting for hours, or a friend who reads poetry or something. I'm only able to concentrate provided there is no gaggle of onlookers, all offering their 'advice'. It's not such a silly request. Too much nosing and chattering irritates both me and those who I paint, and this will show." Nicholas stood up and went to the window. He was frustrated that he might have to refuse this commission because of a lack of privacy. Nicholas ran his hands through his hair. "My sitters need to relax so I can capture that special spark which is what everyone wants. It takes much longer to paint a bigger portrait and I don't want half the world passing comment every time I pick up a brush or add some detail."

Levina sat thinking. True, her position gave her privileged access to members of the Court allowing her to sketch anyone without anybody raising an eyebrow. Nicholas was right, he would be a novelty. She looked at him as he leaned against the window sill. He had grown into a very good looking young man so the Maids of Honour would never leave him alone. She was always being asked by one or another of these young women when he was next coming to Whitehall. When he did appear, they fluttered their eyelashes and flirted outrageously with him. Nicholas did little to encourage them, which made him all the more attractive.

"Do you think she would come here?" Nicholas knew this was only an outside chance. "Hmm…." Levina's response made him hopeful his request might not be so preposterous.

"With perhaps either you, or some one else in attendance," he continued "rather than a whole gaggle of women?"

"That might not be so impossible, provided the intent was known, then there would be no reason for gossip. You must come and see her Nicholas and put your request to her yourself. You know how difficult she becomes if she is not getting her own way. Don't make life awkward for us Gentlewomen; we have to put up with the moods and temper whilst you can come back here and get away from it, so now would be not soon enough!"

Nicholas sighed. He could not afford to ignore the royal summons, neither could he afford to keep his current customers waiting. He would have to trust his apprentices to get on with the jewellery work and he was sure he could balance working at one of the Royal palaces and his City workshop. Another random thought flitted across his mind, now the Queen wanted him to paint bigger and more public portraits of her, he might be able to afford taking a wife in the not too distant future.

"Now I'm thinking about it, it would be interesting to try something new."

The audience with Elizabeth was as private as it could be with all her attendants, courtiers and servants milling around. She was sitting writing and, as he approached, she lay down the quill pen and leaned back in her chair. She was dressed in a simple emerald green silk riding dress. The sunlight streamed through the mullioned window behind her making it appears as if she wore a halo of polished copper round her head. Pearl drops hung from her ears, but apart from these only an emerald and diamond ring graced her hand. Nicholas realised that the Queen had most likely been hunting and had sent Levina to fetch him by royal barge so he would be there before, or shortly after, she returned from the chase.

He bowed low and took her proffered hand, raising it to his lips and kissing it in a the required manner, suffering a tinge of

57

conscience that he was breaking his self-imposed rule not to be overawed by her presence. He had still not decided whether this was because she was the Queen, or because he was emotionally drawn to her. Perhaps it was a bit of both? She flirted with him, and she loved it when he flirted back, but he did not do this often because he knew someone, somewhere, would be watching and acid tongues were always quick to wag.

Was she filling the place of the sister he might have had?

"Well, young Hillyarde. Will you paint my portrait a little larger than usual?" Elizabeth smiled at him. It was not so much a request as a command. Elizabeth looked him up and down.

"I see from your apparel, you appear eager to commence."

To emphasise the point that he was busy, Nicholas had not bothered to change. When he had sat down with Levina, he had been dressed in a clean, but old, lawn shirt.

"Your Majesty, your wish is my command and, as you can see from my humble working apparel, I hesitated not a second to obey your summons." Nicholas swept another low bow.

"So I see!" Elizabeth swept a glance from his head to his toe. A twitch of her left eyebrow indicated she expected more formal dress in her presence, but a smile still played around the corners of her mouth indicating that, for today, he was forgiven.

"Come." She rose and led the way to a bay window where she sat down and patted the space next to her, indicating that he sit. Her green silk gown rustled as she moved . When they met she always tried to distance herself and Nicholas from those around her so they had a semblance of privacy, but Nicholas knew that this was a complete nonsense as their every movement was watched. Whilst he knew that not everything could be heard, you never knew who might be watching and trying to lip read.

"Now young Nicholas, I suppose Mistress Teerlinc has told you what I want?"

"Yes ma'am " Nicholas paused "and I have a request."

"Well, request on. I can only say no and, unless you ask, you will never know what I would answer; and sit down next to me." Elizabeth patted the window seat, turned and looked out of the window contemplating the park. The oak trees were a haze of greeny bronze contrasting against the lime green of the willows now in full leaf on the river bank. Nicholas studied Elizabeth's profile wondering whether or not to try a classical profile of her. That way he could portray her as a classical ruler, just like those of Rome.

Nicholas lowered his voice and adjusted his seat so he too faced more towards the window making life really difficult for those who might attempt to read their lips.

"Ma'am, it would be a very special privilege to paint you on a panel, but you must appreciate that painting in oils is not my normal field of expertise." He paused. Elizabeth nodded and waited for him to continue.

"I have painted you often, but this is not just a simple matter of making a larger image. Painting on wood is a different process and one that I have only experimented with."

"Quite so Mr Hillyarde, but surely you would not refuse your Queen?" Elizabeth smiled her most beguiling smile.

Nicholas looked down at his hands, noticing blue pigment under his left thumbnail. The Queen was obviously determined to have him paint her and he could not refuse her.

"No Ma'am, indeed not, but it would help considerably if we were to be as private as possible. It is difficult to concentrate when half your Court are peering over my shoulder and you are being approached by all who want your favour."

"Well, that is not so difficult. You will come here and we shall find you a room. That way you will be able to finish quickly. Perhaps you would like to start today?" Elizabeth's tone made it clear that this was not so much a request as a statement of intent.

Nicholas sighed. "Ma'am, that is very short notice ..."

"Well then, tomorrow at the latest."

Nicholas could only acquiesce to such a command. It would be as he thought and he would have to leave his workshop in charge of his lead apprentice, who was quite competent. Richmond was not so far away from the City by river should he need to return to his workshop for any reason.

Nicholas looked around him and nodded with pleasure. His allotted rooms faced north with large windows overlooking the hunting park. He was not so vain as to think it was because he was the Queen's favoured artist that he was given such accommodation. The Queen would be spending some considerable time with him and she could not be expected to sit in a pokey attic. It was gratifying to know there were some benefits for being at the beck and call of his sovereign.

The jewellery had been sent to him to study. Nicholas sighed, no doubt Levina would be quizzing him on the traditional symbolism of the mythical bird. He sat cradling the jewel in his hand. The phoenix was rising, reborn from the centre of gold next alight with red enamelled flames. Within the heart of the flames was a perfect triangular cabochon ruby. As he rubbed his thumb over the ruby's smooth surface the ruby heart of the fire appeared warm to his touch.

The bird's body was a large black pearl and Nicholas smiled remembering a lecture on how since there was only ever one phoenix it was perpetually virginal. Therefore the pearl, being the symbol of virginity, was the only precious stone that could be used for the bird's body. A heart shaped diamond was set as the bird's heart as a symbol of its constancy and steadfastness. The underside of the raised wings were of white, red and black enamel. Black and white were the queen's colours, whilst the red symbolised the flames of sacrifice and rebirth. The message was clear - like the phoenix, there was only one Elizabeth. For those who were not listening to her various speeches regarding marriage, this was a visual statement of her intention to remain single.

Whilst this brooch was not to his taste, he was quietly pleased Elizabeth had sufficient faith in him to paint a larger portrait of her, even if he was not totally confident about using oil paints. It also gave him the chance to pay tribute to his master's work. Brandon's use of coral confused him because women often wore coral as a protection against death and evil during pregnancy and childbirth. Examining these fabulous pieces very closely, he realised the coral was to protect the new phoenix as it was born in the sacred fire.

Elizabeth had agreed that there would only be one other person present at the sittings and that person would be Levina. Nicholas was looking forward to this time despite his misgivings about leaving his own workshop. He wondered what they would talk about. Their conversations during the previous year had ranged from poetry to philosophy and often they would converse in French and sometimes Italian. His Italian was adequate, but he found it very difficult to concentrate on both sketching and talking in a foreign language. He dreaded Elizabeth reading anything by Dante, or Boccaccio in the original Latin, but he had read an English translation of Boccaccio's Decameron, which helped him make informed comments on this book. However, he had been taking lessons to improve his Italian because he flattered himself that Elizabeth enjoyed their conversations and he wanted to please her.

The door opened and Elizabeth swept in followed by several ladies-in-waiting all eager to see who it was that the Queen was going to see. Nicholas's heart sank. He bowed low to hide his disappointment at the appearance of this crowd of chattering women. He had made it quite clear he did not want an audience and had thought Elizabeth had understood his reasons. Now, not only was the room full of irritating brainless women, the dress she was wearing was going to be a nightmare to paint.

"Good morning, your Majesty." He bowed again, feeling slightly preposterous doing so wearing his painter's smock.

"Ah Mr Hillyarde, you are ready. I hope I've not kept you waiting." she replied, then turned and waved her hand at her ladies. "Off you all go. Mr Hillyarde and I have things to do and this room is far too small for all of us."

Her ladies tutted and chattered like disturbed starlings. Elizabeth smiled.

"If it offends you all so much that I should be with our young painter alone, then Mistress Teerlinc will stay and chaperone. If he doesn't behave then he will have to answer not only to me, but also to her."

Their mutterings faded as the murmurration of women disappeared through the door leaving the three of them in peace.

"Now where do you want me to sit, Mr Hillyarde. I can spare you no more than an hour or two, but that should be sufficient for you to make a start."

Nicholas had set a chair where the light would fall directly onto Elizabeth's face. After their conversation regarding shadow and her comment that shadow might be a reference to shady elements of someone's character, he had decided to paint her face in the softest and palest of tones. Her complexion was very pale with the absence of shadows turning her face into a mask so he decided he would create a mask of royalty hiding the woman beneath.

"I think it might be better if you painted me standing, like this." Elizabeth stood, bringing her left hand across next to her heart. In her right, she held a white ostrich feather fan. Nicholas recognised the Earl of Leicester's symbols of the ragged bear and staff on one side of the handle, noting that on the other the lion of England had a muzzled white bear at his feet.

Levina sat on a stool next to the cold fire place. The fire was unlit as the day was warm. She had brought her own work books and it was evident that she too would be sketching. He looked forward to discussing the complexities of the day's work with her.

"So have you had time to study my Phoenix?"

"Your Majesty, I feel as if I've been reunited with an old friend."

"How so?"

Nicholas explained how he had been involved in the production and design of this piece, which seemed to please her. Nicholas retrieved the jewels and handed them to his teacher. Levina placed the collar across Elizabeth's shoulders and the head-dress and choker completed the magnificent display. The phoenix hung from the an enamelled Tudor rose whose centre was a huge diamond.

"Your Majesty, you may find it quite tiresome to stand for so long, so I will leave the chair behind you." Levina said as she moved around the Queen, coaxing the heavy fabric into even folds.

Nicholas stood sketching as fast as he could. Getting the stance absolutely right was important. Details of the gown and jewels could always be put in later especially if he could persuade Elizabeth to lend him the gown. He could either set it on a wooden stand, or better still, find a girl who would not mind standing whilst he concentrated on getting the details exactly right. It did not matter if they swooned from standing still for hours. However, it would be embarrassing if the Queen fainted. It was not as if this were an uncommon occurrence because she was often unwell with one malady or another, but it would be better if she stayed well in his presence and did not give the gossips any ammunition for their far too easily wagging tongues.

"Tell me Nicholas. It must have been very difficult for you being so far from your family when you were in Geneva." Elizabeth's question was unexpected. "Did you have much news from England?" Nicholas had thought she would be far too busy thinking of affairs of state to ask him about his childhood again.

"Not really, ma'am. We'd always been great friends with the Bodley family and I knew his son Thomas quite well before we left England." He continued to sketch, his metal point slipping over the paper as he made small detailed studies of her eyes, the curls around her face and her nose.

"How old were you when you left England?" Elizabeth continued her enquiry.

"Nearly eight, but that is not so different as when a boy is sent to be a page in another household."

"Eight is still young, and you were all exiles in a foreign country." Elizabeth turned away and went to the window. "It must have been hard for your parents: particularly your mother." she finished softly.

Nicholas let the silence continue. Elizabeth appeared lost in her thoughts. He continued working, capturing more details of her dress.

"Did you miss your mother?" she asked at length. Elizabeth's voice was soft and low. Anyone was listening outside the door would be very hard pressed to hear anything said inside.

"Yes, at first I did." Nicholas responded in similarly soft tones. "I've only seen her twice since we returned, but I've seen my father more often when he has come to London."

Nicholas paused, finding it distracting being asked questions about himself.

"So what was it like being so far away from home?" Elizabeth seemed determined to pursue a greater knowledge of Nicholas's childhood. He sighed. Elizabeth's questions were raising memories of feeling lost and very alone, despite Thomas's company.

"Mr and Mrs Bodley were very kind and it was good being with Thomas and his brothers. It might have been very different if the Bodleys hadn't been so kind."

Elizabeth was inviting confidences and Nicholas was providing them. Levina remembered a similar time when she had first painted Elizabeth and she too had been asked her about her own upbringing in Bruges. Elizabeth had been a girl of thirteen and had told Levina how she envied her. Elizabeth had her father's colouring, but unlike her father, the young princess had been very quiet. Knowing Henry's treatment of his daughters Levina had realised how alien her own upbringing must have seemed to the young princess. She had watched Elizabeth survive the years of her sister Mary's reign, surrounded always by people who were quick to report her every word or move and others who proffered friendship, but whose loyalty was dubious.

Mary's reign had been difficult years for Levina as she had come to England sympathetic to the Protestant religion and happy to serve under a Protestant monarch., but there had been terrible purgings of devout Protestants during Mary's reign, which had reminded Levina of just why she had been so glad to leave Bruges and the domination of the Spanish.

Elizabeth's soft voice cut across Levina's memories.

"You and I are very similar Mr Hillyarde, having to bear the pain of separation at such a young age. It is not a wound that heals well. It is the sacrifices that mothers make for their children, which are the greatest of all."

Levina smiled. Elizabeth knew much about self-sacrifice

"With the people of England being your children, your Majesty, must be why you have chosen the Phoenix as one of your symbols?" Nicholas turned the conversation away from anything personal he might have to think about.

"You're correct." Elizabeth's tone was no longer soft and confiding. "Now tell me, what size are you going to paint this picture?"

Nicholas had neatly switched the conversation so he could concentrate on what he was doing. However, Levina was surprised by the Queen's confidences. She never talked about her mother and Levina wondered whether Elizabeth had recognised something akin to her own childhood in his story. It was as if Elizabeth had briefly exposed wounds that were too raw to bear close examination, but had to be revealed as a sign of mutual understanding.

"Perhaps this size?" Nicholas held his hands about eighteen inches apart to indicate the width of the painting and again, vertically, at approximately twenty four inches.

"So how long do you think you will need and how often will I need to come and sit for you?" It was another loaded question, but Nicholas was prepared.

"Ma'am, I know how your time is precious and affairs are always pressing so I have devised a way of working so you are able to come and go at will. I will be able to do much of the work using either a stand or a model, and when you are able to visit, I will be able to work from life. Thus the portrait will be finished sooner than if I were to work from life alone, which would take up much of your valuable time."

"If you feel that is proper, then so be it. Now, Mr Hillyarde, as much as I would like to stay and while away the day with idle chatter, as you so rightly observe, affairs of state demand my presence. However, I shall send you my dress, and you already have my jewels. Come, Mistress Teerlinc, we must leave this young man to his painting."

Nicholas bowed low at the dismissal. The Queen had been closeted with him for at least two hours and swept from the room with as much energy as she had swept in. He now had to

66

create an actual size detailed sketch on paper for the Queen's approval, which he would then use to transfer the outlines on to the final surface for painting. Unfortunately, Elizabeth's questions had disturbed him and Nicholas needed to clear his mind before continuing, otherwise it would show in his work.

Exhausted, he sat down and slaked his thirst. The elegant Venetian glass held a pale green liquid that he recognised as the same as that prepared and drunk by Levina. She collected rain water in a tank, which was boiled and poured over crushed mint leaves. After letting the mint infuse she would then sweeten it with a little honey. Levina drank it because she said it helped her digestion and so she kept a clear head.

He sat, unable to remember his mother's face or voice, but at least she was alive, whereas Elizabeth had lost her mother when she was only three. He wondered how Henry could have been so callous, beheading his wife just because the poor woman had not produced a boy. The story that Anne Boleyn had been found guilty of adulterous incest was well known, but most people who cared to think about it, believed the charges were false and the king had just wanted to replace his current queen for one who could produce an male heir.

Nicholas continued working on the paper sketch. The paper was roughly the same size as he had described with his hands, but now he had the composition planned out. He sat back, and stretched to ease his muscles. The evening light was soft and Nicholas looked out across the river. The distant pall of smoke was the City of London, where his house and workshop lay.

Nicholas wondered what he was going to eat for supper and, more to the point, where. He had finished the plate of sweetmeats and just as he was about to go exploring to find the main hall, Levina returned.

"Hmm." She said as she examined the larger scale sketch. "It went well this morning." Levina picked up Nicholas's sketchbook and flicked through his morning's work. "I believe you have her trust."

"She made me think." Nicholas was glad to be able to talk through the morning's events. "When I first painted her, she wanted to know all about me and that was the first time I had thought about why I'd gone to Europe."

Mistress and former pupil stood looking at the full sized paper layout.

"Levina, if it hadn't been for you and the Bodleys I would not be here now. Thank you."

Levina patted his shoulder.

"Nicholas, Elizabeth never talks about her mother, but don't let that fool you into believing she never thinks about her. She was only three when her father had her mother beheaded. That sort of behaviour makes you very wary about who to trust."

"I know, Levina. You have seen much in your time here. What was it like when you first came to Court? Has Elizabeth recreated Henry's glittering Court?"

"In some ways." Levina moved to make sure that the outer door to Nicholas's rooms was firmly shut. "The King was an old man and married to Katherine Parr when I first came to Court. Elizabeth and Edward were young, but old at the same time and both so good looking. Mary was so much older and I believe she hated her brother and sister."

"So is Elizabeth's Court as exciting as Henry's?" Nicholas pressed.

"It has had its moments, especially now that Elizabeth is excommunicated. Some Catholics haven't learned the lessons of the Ridolfi plot, even though the Duke of Norfolk was beheaded, but don't worry, they are being watched. Sometimes it is difficult being at Court, so I hope you take care when your sitters want to tell you their secrets."

"You should know better than to worry, Levina." It was Nicholas's turn to reassure. "I learnt a very hard lesson with the Queen of Hearts and the embroidery on my first miniature. I'm not likely to engage anyone in dangerous conversation. Let others gossip in my hearing, I'm too busy drawing and I can't do both. However, gossip relaxes people and they forget I'm drawing them. I'm sure you've found the same?"

Levina smiled, but refrained from replying, preferring to examine the paper portrait.

"The Queen is sending over her dress tomorrow morning and I am not prepared to squash myself into that hot and heavy gown for anyone, so I shall find you a stand."

Whenever and however he tried to find out if Levina had passed on any snippets of gossip to anyone, she would just ignore him and he wondered if he would ever find out just how much she knew about what went on at Court. He wanted to know who to tell if anything important was ever said in his presence. Nothing, so far, had been revealed involving anything dangerous, unless you considered knowing who was sleeping with whom as important. As far as that sort of gossip was concerned Nicholas kept his own counsel believing a person had to answer to their own conscience and to God, not to Nicholas Hillyarde.

The stand arrived the following day together with the Queen's gown so they were able to arrange the dress so it looked as if someone was wearing it then Levina left Nicholas to his day's work. He examined the gown intently. The dark velvet was an intense midnight blue and embroidered all over with vine leaves and pearls. If Elizabeth was trying to give a message of legendary virginity he wondered why she had chosen a gown embroidered with symbols of fertility. He remembered the queen had been wearing the same gown the day he had delivered his first miniature of her and she had been with the French and Venetian Ambassadors.

Every day the jewels were unlocked from the Queen's jewel chest and brought to the workroom by Levina and two soldiers, not that Levina thought anyone would try and steal them, but it was better to be sure.

Nicholas found using oil paints a great deal easier than the watercolour he used for limning and mastered them with ease. Each day Levina advised Elizabeth on Nicholas's progress and ten days later the Queen arrived to inspect Nicholas's work and announced she would be able to sit for him for a further two hours the following day in order for him to complete the final touches.

Nicholas sat for a long time studying his finished portrait. Master Holbein's large oil paintings were amazing likenesses but stiff and lifeless. His own portrait of the queen was stiff in just such a similar way and he wondered if it was because it was because he had worked in oil paint rather than watercolour.

The Queen moved to stand beside him and inspect the finished likeness.

"You have done well, Mr Hillyarde. It is exactly what I hoped for."

Nicholas blushed as he wiped his brushes clean and the Queen continued her examination of his work. Outside, the June evening was thick with the shreep, shreep of the swifts as they danced their way across the skies. They were flying low, which meant it was probably going to rain.

Levina too stood looking at the painting. Nicholas had done well, but, she thought, he was better at painting the tiny images the queen loved so much.

An Accession Day gift.

Nicholas had thought long and hard about what would be a suitable gift to celebrate Elizabeth's Accession Day. Finally, he had settled on a ring and now the rubies and diamonds of the finished jewel glinted in the candle light. He did not want to broadcast to the whole Court exactly what his gift was. The how of his giving was proving a difficult problem.

Inspired by their conversations, he had designed a ring. A single pearl represented her singular purity as England's Virgin Mother, the diamonds were for constancy and faithfulness and the red rubies symbolic of her sacrifice. It was an expensive gift, but he was quietly confident that Elizabeth would love it, so the cost was immaterial.

The Accession Day celebrations and revelry were set to start later that week. He did not want to be caught up in any of the preparations for the celebrations and hoped he could persuade Levina to let him privately into the Queen's presence. Whilst he knew Elizabeth liked his miniatures, but he was not part of the Court and it was not always easy to get to within a room's length of the Queen, let alone a private audience. He had some items to deliver to Lord Burghley, so it would not be a wasted journey if he did not manage to see the Queen. He could always ask Levina to pass his gift to the Queen secretly, but Nicholas really wanted to present it himself.

Dressed in his best black velvet doublet he kept for Court visits, Nicholas swirled his winter cape, lined with white rabbit fur, around his shoulders to keep out the November chill. His newly oiled boots would keep out the wet and finely knitted black woollen hose kept his legs warm. Nicholas loved the richness of the fabrics and the softness of the leather, but one thing he hated was the ruff. It rubbed his neck and he wondered how people tolerated wearing them every day. What he was wearing was quietly discreet compared to others. He hated November, when the wind seemed to find its way through every crack in his house. Now the gale was trying to tug his cloak from his shoulders and he was glad it would not take him long to walk to Whitehall.

Levina was working in her private room in the Royal library. Despite being alone, she covered her work as he entered.

"Nicholas what a lovely surprise. What can I do for you? I did not know you were coming?" Levina wiped her brushes and locked away the vellum she had been working on. It was very nearly finished but she did not want anyone, even Nicholas, to know what it was. The Queen's Accession day celebrations meant there was great competition as to who could give the most preferred gift.

" I have some deliveries to make and I have a gift for the Queen." Nicholas raised his eyebrows in an unasked question.

"Do you want me to give it to her?" Levina was not sure what he wanted of her, but guessed it might be something he wished passed on in private.

"Only if I can't get to see her."

Levina laughed. "That is not going to be a problem. Only earlier today she was asking after you. If you have a gift, she will be delighted to see you."

"I do and yes, privately would be preferable."

"Hmm. She's in the Great Hall, but, as for a private audience, you will be very lucky indeed if you manage that. I shall come with you as I've done all I can for today. What is it you have for her?"

"It's a secret … but I was inspired when I painted the Phoenix."

It was Levina's turn to raise her eyebrows. She remembered how Elizabeth had been almost transparent when they had talked about his childhood. Levina hoped Nicholas had not misread what had been said and was about to make a serious blunder.

As if sensing her anxiety, Nicholas put his hand on her arm.

"Don't worry. I know she will love it and if you don't know what it is, it will be a surprise for you too, if she chooses to show it to you."

Levina took off her painting smock, hung it on the back of the door and together they went in search of the Queen.

His presence in the cloisters and passages of Whitehall no longer caused the intense interest among the women as it used to. The younger serving girls still fluttered their eyelashes at him, but he ignored them. He found their attentions rather embarrassing and thought them far too bold. The older ladies of the Court also smiled when they saw him. Some had tried to find out any gossip he might have been told, but they soon gave up, finding him a closed shell. Others had tried for sexual favours under the guise of having their miniature portrait painted. The higher the social class, the more overt they were. They were far from subtle if they got him alone and several times he had been propositioned by a noble born lady when he had been painting her likeness. She would dismiss her musicians or companions and then he knew he was in trouble. Being alone with someone's wife was not his favourite pastime as it would be his word against theirs if they decided to make up a story about his behaviour. He had devised a way of being kind but firm, suggesting that he found them attractive, but purely from an academic point of view. At one point, one of the spurned had even asked if he preferred men because he was so completely oblivious of her charms. He had laughed and explained that he was a dreadful swordsman whereas her husband had a certain reputation and he had no wish to ruin his promising career by having it cut short at the end of her husband's blade. She would still pat his bottom discreetly to let him know that she was available if he ever changed his mind. Nicholas spotted her in the crowd talking with her husband. He had learnt from another of his sitters, that this lady was pursuing someone else and Nicholas felt very much relieved that he was no longer her sexual quarry.

A firm, but kindly, refusal of any invitations to gossip or indulge in anything more intimate was developing into a reputation of being someone to trust. Now his clients were asking him to paint their lovers, safe in the knowledge that he would never reveal their secrets. Fathers were happy for their daughters to sit for Nicholas as he had the reputation of being a perfectly chivalrous gentleman and any woman would be safe alone in his company.

Lord Burghley was standing just inside the door to the Great Hall talking to Sir Francis Walsingham and the two of them, dressed in their long black clerical robes, were a stark contrast to the rest of those attending this audience, who were all decked out in their best finery and on their best behaviour.

Elizabeth was seated at the end of the hall, her throne placed on the slightly raised dais, resplendent in a gold silk dress, her face framed by her highly starched ruff, and looking faintly bored. Nicholas approached the two men, bowed, and addressed Lord Burghley.

"My Lord, I have the commissions finished and ready for delivery if you would tell me when I can come to your rooms."

"Ah, Nicholas, that's very good. Sir Francis and I were just considering withdrawing. Perhaps you would like to come now?" Lord Burghley replied.

Elizabeth clapped her hands and the whole Court paused, waiting, watching, wondering what had diverted the Queen.

"Come Mister Hillyarde," she beckoned him to come closer " approach and tell me why you have not been to see us?"

Lord Burghley smiled.

"Don't worry Nicholas, come after you have seen the Queen. She is obviously wanting some diversion from her job in hand. I shall be in my rooms." With that, Lord Burghley and Sir Francis nodded their goodbyes and left.

Nicholas walked the length of the hall, the crowd parting to let him pass. It was raining outside making the room dark despite it being only eleven of the clock. The Queen was lit by candles held in a floor standing wrought iron candelabra. The gold of her gown glittered as the candle flames flickered in the drafts.

Nicholas approached, bowed, took her hand and kissed it. Her hand cream was scented with attar of roses. He wished he could hold her hand longer and take great deep breaths of that lovely scent of summer. The smell reminded him of the time the Ottoman Ambassador had arrived. A gilded box had been delivered by a young boy dressed in exotic silks. Elizabeth had been as fascinated by the boy's golden coloured skin as she had been intrigued by his costume and his curled slippers. The ornately carved wooden box had yielded an exquisite Venetian cut glass jar banded with gold and with a lid set with precious stones. The jar was filled with the hand cream used by the Sultana of Constantinople and the scent of roses had filled the room. The recipe for the hand cream had been included in a letter together with another Venetian glass bottle containing the extract of Attar of Roses, the expensive rose scent needed to finish the hand cream. The Sultana had written how this cream kept her hands white and soft and hoped the English Queen would find it did the same for her. Elizabeth had been very touched by the Sultana's kind thought, which was so delightfully feminine. She had confided to Nicholas that this present was one of the best she had ever received because it came from another woman and no man would have ever thought of something so feminine.

At the time Nicholas had been worried in case the cream had contained poison and had been assured that it would be tested before the Queen would use it.

"Well then, Mr Hillyarde." Nicholas jumped, the queen's voice reminded him of where he was and why. He rose and met the Queen's gaze.

"Where have you been?" she continued "It has been far too long since you were at Court?" Elizabeth was bored and his appearance was proving a timely diversion. This morning's audience had been particularly tedious. She had guessed rightly that he had something for her. She was like a jackdaw when it came to presents. Nicholas was always a welcome distraction and his appearance gave her the perfect excuse to finish the session.

"Madam, I could not let the matter of your anniversary go unmarked." His voice was low so only she could hear. "I hope you will accept this small token in celebration of your Accession Day anniversary and as a token of my love and loyalty." Nicholas flipped open the small box concealed in his palm. The Queen leaned forward to see the detail more closely. Their heads were very nearly touching.

The intertwined ER glinted in the candle light. The diamond E sat atop the R, which was flooded with blue enamelling. Rubies formed the shoulders of the gold shank and a pearl filled the gap between end of the short middle arm of the E and the outer edge.

"Oh, Mr Hillyarde, this is very fine." Elizabeth, still leaning forward, took the open box from him to have a closer look, managing to exclude those who were curious to see what was being given and Elizabeth handed the box back to him and asked softly,

"Perhaps you would put this on my finger, to better test the fit?"

Nicholas smiled. He had rehearsed just how he would do this should he be given the chance.

Taking her right hand he slipped the entwined ER onto the ring finger of her right hand. It fitted perfectly, and then he pressed the pearl. The lid flipped lid back to reveal the enamelled portraits of mother and daughter, Anne Boleyn and Elizabeth.

"Oh" exclaimed Elizabeth, with delight. "It fits perfectly." she said quickly, to cover her surprise. She slipped the cover closed and, smiling, she leant back and raised her hand to inspect the way the jewels caught the candlelight.

"Mr Hillyarde, this ring is indeed delightful and I thank you."

Nicholas took the proffered royal hand, this time kissing the diamond E. It was his turn to be surprised as she squeezed his hand.

"I wish you happiness for your joyous day Ma'am and am pleased that you like my gift." Nicholas withdrew leaving Elizabeth showing her gift to those pressing about her, noting she kept the lid closed.

That night Dudley commented on her new diamond and ruby ring. Elizabeth smiled and told him someone had given her something no-one had ever thought of. Dudley was intrigued and Elizabeth had finally shown him the ring's secret and telling him Nicholas had been the maker. Dudley was impressed with Nicholas's skill and ingenuity, noting Elizabeth replaced it on her finger rather than placing it in her jewellery chest.

The Pelican

"Do you know what gown she wishes to wear for this one?" Nicholas asked. "It was very evident she had taken a great deal of time and thought about what to wear for the Phoenix. All that symbolism! There is only so much purity one can show in oils! At least this painting won't take as long." Nicholas picked out the original sketch for the previous portrait. "See, by turning over the paper and transferring the same outline to the prepared surface everything will be much quicker. Not only will the portraits be identical, the wood for this one is from the same panel on which I painted the Phoenix. "

"Now that I like." Levina approved of his idea.

"Was it really necessary for the Queen to be so obvious with that portrait, Levina? Like the phoenix, there can be only one queen?" Nicholas disliked the lack of subtlety.

"Yes, you know it was and now you will have the perfect balance; The Pelican Queen facing the Phoenix Monarch. The phoenix, being both male and female, to compliment what will be the very definitely female Pelican. These portraits can be viewed as a marriage diptych of a queen to her nation, who will be so beautifully identically portrayed from the same basic sketch. Very subtle."

"Possibly so much so that your reading will go straight over the heads of those who are determined she should marry." Nicholas replied grumpily, not convinced that this combination would be read as easily as Levina seemed to imply.

Nicholas was out of sorts because he had been summoned to paint another large portrait and yet again had had to leave his workshop in the hands of young Lockey. Levina had warned him that Elizabeth would want another portrait and he wondered if she wanted him to paint these because she had enjoyed their conversations about childhood. It also crossed his mind that she would expect another gift.

He had yet to deliver a ring to Dudley who had been very specific about the design, wanting it to contain two tiny portraits of himself and Elizabeth, also to be painted by Nicholas. Elizabeth had clearly shown Dudley the secret of his own Accession gift. The Earl had paled at the cost of enamelled portraits, and the comprise was two tiny portraits on vellum.

Nicholas had designed and made the ring before painting the portraits, so the settings had been immediately available once the portraits were finished. Because Dudley's gift had occupied a lot of Nicholas's time, he had ignored the various hints Levina had given him regarding Elizabeth's desire for another large portrait. He hoped Dudley would pay for the ring when it was delivered. Not only was Dudley slow at paying for his commissions, so was Elizabeth and he had been too occupied with their commissions which had resulted in a cash flow problem.

Everyone was asking if he would paint large portraits of themselves and he was uncomfortable with this. Even Lord Burghley had spoken to him about the possibility of painting an even larger portrait of the queen, but Nicholas was not so sure. These oil paintings were not his best work, neither were they what he wanted to be remembered for. However, Burghley always settled his account immediately. Even so, was he prepared to prostitute his talent for his need for a steady income? Nicholas had considered Burghley's request for a long time and come to the conclusion that if Burghley still wanted a large portrait, he might suggest Steven Meulen or William Segar instead since they were doing these all the time and he did not want to upset the members of the Painters and Stainers Guild.

Levina and Nicholas were waiting in the rooms in Greenwich set aside as his workroom. The Queen was rarely late for sittings, but if she were, she would arrive all breathless, as if she had been running.

The door opened and Elizabeth swept in, turned and told whoever was with her that she was not to be disturbed at any cost and that nothing was so important that it could not wait for an hour.

Nicholas and Levina made the appropriate obsequies. Nicholas had ensured that Elizabeth's favourite sweetmeats, Levina's favourite honey cakes and a large ewer of the chilled mint infusion sweetened with sugar loaf were ready. The tray was set with three delicate glass goblets and the sweetmeats and honey cakes sat on a silver platter with roses twined round the edge and two silver bees settled on the flowers.

"At last, some privacy. Tell me, Mr Hillyarde, what ideas have you for this image?" Elizabeth seated herself in the large chair, reached for a sweetmeat having little ability to resist these edible temptations. Today she was in a very good mood. He noted she was wearing his ring.

Nicholas explained his idea of reversing the original image. "Because that way, your Majesty, these two can sit side by side as if they are a marriage pair."

Elizabeth nodded her understanding and acceptance of his suggestion.

"Will you use a model, or a stand?"

"I hope so to do, in order to speed up the finishing of it." came Nicholas's reply.

"Your Majesty." Levina intervened "I think the daughter of your goldsmith, young Alice Brandon, would be a suitable choice. She is a good girl with a silent tongue in her head. I have asked her father, who, because young Alice is still mourning her mother, hopes being with Nicholas will cheer her up."

"You may remember Master Brandon was my teacher for all things goldsmithing, your Majesty and I have known her since she was six years old." Nicholas added.

"Poor child. It's over a year now since her mother died, is it not?" Elizabeth paused reflecting on Alice, her sympathy for the girl's loss written on her face. "It would be nice to know who is wearing my clothes." Elizabeth stated.

Nicholas and Levina both smiled at Elizabeth's question.

"That seems admirable and well thought through. I look forward to seeing your work. Don't worry, Mr Hillyarde, I won't clutter up your rooms with onlookers. I like to keep my

Courtiers guessing at what it is you are going to produce next!"

Elizabeth left as she had entered, in a swirl of skirts, leaving both of them pleased with her unmitigated approval.

Levina turned to her young protégé.

"Nicholas, Alice is being allowed to come on the clear understanding that she is not to be exposed to the Court 'entertainments'."

Nicholas nodded. He was pleased Levina had put the idea of using a model in the Queen's mind. It would be nice to see Alice again. Nicholas remembered her as a friendly child of six years old and she had become like a little sister during his time as an apprentice. Like any older brother, he felt protective of her agreeing that the Court was far too dangerous a place for a girl of tender years. He had no wish to have to answer to Brandon for allowing any lecherous wolf to prey on his precious daughter.

Levina smiled. "Alice will be here tomorrow, and the Queen's dress and jewels will be here early. Now, if you want to come to my rooms and have supper with George and me tonight, rather than join the rest of the household, we would be very happy to see you."

Nicholas started work at first light transferring the reversed image on to the prepared wooden panel. He had pricked his sketch for the first portrait, so this time it was easy just to lay the paper over the prepared surface, clipping it firmly to the top edge. Taking his bag of pounce Nicholas patted this around the pricked edges. Tiny amounts of black powder transferred through the holes leaving the outline of the queen on the white gesso surface. He was just removing the paper when there was a gentle knocking at the door.

"Come." He was concentrating too hard to leave what he was doing. He heard the door open, then close and soft footsteps enter the room.

"Nicholas?" Alice asked softly.

Nichols put down his bag of pounce and turned to greet his visitor.

"Alice?" he replied quizzically, not believing his own eyes. Somehow, plump little Alice had turned into a tall, poised, slim young woman, a little pale and perhaps a little too slender.

"Come, sit down."

"Thank you. Is Levina not yet here?" she enquired sitting down on one of the chairs neatly arranging her skirts around her knees.

"Er, no. I thought you would be coming together?" was his croaky response.

Alice smoothed an imaginary crease from the fold of her skirt with an immaculately manicured hand. She looked up and smiled shyly.

Nicholas noticed how the blue of her gown matched the blue of her eyes and set off the soft pale gold of her hair. Soft curls tumbled down her back and wisps of hair softened the outline of her face.

"She said she was going to collect the Queen's dress and jewels and would meet me here."

"You weren't wandering around the palace on your own, were you?" Nicholas was concerned he would have to explain why Alice had been wandering the Palace alone.

"No, Levina made sure that I was escorted here by a page. By the way, my father sends his best wishes." Alice sat looking demurely at her hands. The reference to Brandon only succeeded in heightening Nicholas's awareness of Alice's loveliness and her vulnerability.

"I, er, we have given your father our undertaking that we will not let you …, er, that you won't be led astray by the more er, um, adventurous members of the Court." he ventured by way of explanation.

82

Alice leant forward and put her hand on his.

"Thank you Nicholas. I don't want to go dancing or feasting just yet. My father seems to have forgotten my mother already, but I can't. I love him dearly, but ...." Tears welled up in Alice's eyes and Nicholas put his arm around her shoulders to comfort her. Her hair smelt of rosemary.

"Alice, this grief will pass, but your mother would not want you to grieve so. She would hate to see you suffering like this." Nicholas had liked Mrs Brandon. "I see you are still wearing my bracelet." he said seeking to divert Alice from the sad subject of her mother's death.

"Oh yes, but it is a little tight." Alice twisted the two solid gold half circles set with seed pearls enclosing her wrist. She had been eight years old when Nicholas had given it to her and he had made it very loose so she could wear it until she was grown up.

"Give it to me and I will expand it for you."

Alice held out her wrist.

"The minute I get back to my workroom, I will make this larger so you can wear it again, comfortably." Nicholas looked around and found a piece of string. He took Alice's hand in his, and looped the string loosely round her wrist tying a knot so he knew how much bigger he had to make it.

"Would this be about the correct size, or would you like it a bit looser?"

Alice looked up at him and smiled a shy little smile.

"Nicholas, thank you. That is perfect."

The outer door opened again, this time no one had knocked.

"Come, bring the box here and put it on this table. Mind that fabric, don't let it drag on the floor otherwise I shall make sure the cost of cleaning is taken from your wages. Lay it down over there." Levina was issuing orders to a series of men and women carrying the Queen's personal jewel box and the gown Elizabeth had decided on.

Nicholas and Alice watched the entourage lay their various pieces down on the tables and chairs and place the chest on the chair next to the fire, then leave the room. They were all ushered out by Levina and the door closed firmly behind them.

"Ah, good Alice, you're here. Now, the Queen has been very insistent that it is this dress she wishes to be portrayed. It is one of her most impressive and expensive, so we must be careful with it. You are not to eat or drink whilst you are wearing it just in case you spill anything on it."

"And how is she supposed to get through the day, if she doesn't have some sustenance?" asked Nicholas. He did not want Alice fainting or becoming ill whilst she was in his care.

"Well, Nicholas, if anything happens to this dress, you will have to explain it to the Queen" came Levina's irascible response.

Alice moved to where the various components of this gown were laid over a chest. She lifted the fabric and ran her fingers across the embroidery.

"Oh, it's so beautiful. It's so soft and such a rich red." Alice whispered. She lifted the fabric to her lips and gently rubbed it across them. "This is so soft. I would love a dress like this." Alice stroked the fabric gently.

"And when do you intend we should start?" asked Nicholas. Now the gown and the jewels had arrived he wanted to get on with some work. It would take some time for Alice to be fastened into the gown and it looked as if it were going to rain, which would make the light difficult.

Levina opened the inlaid wooden box revealing the pelican brooch lying on top of a cushion of red velvet. It was three inches high and four across. Like the phoenix, the bird had its wings outstretched and was standing on a nest fashioned from gold twigs. Tiny pearl fledglings peered up at their mother, whose breast dripped with tiny drops of blood. According to legend, the mother pelican pecked her own breast to feed her chicks. In this instance the pearls stood for purity, diamonds for eternity, gold for constancy and the rubies being droplets of sacrificial blood rather than a sacred fire.

Nicholas sighed. Elizabeth would be standing in exactly the same pose as before, her hand over her heart declaring her fidelity and holding the rose that is England. This time she had sent a fan with symbolically coloured feathers that were the white of faith, the green of hope and the red of love. Nicholas shook his head at the thought of all that red paint. This portrait was going to be a truly sacrificial tome.

"What is Elizabeth trying to say?" he mused silently, fully absorbed in his observation of this jewel, remembering how challenging Brandon had found it to set the tiny rubies into the large baroque pearl of the pelican's body, to form the drops of blood. The pearl had first been sliced in half then drilled with holes into which the tiny rubies would be glued. Just as Brandon was drilling the final hole he had applied just a little bit too much pressure and the pearl had cracked. Brandon had taken himself off to regain his composure, but when he returned he had handed the drill to Nicholas. Instead of declining the invitation and leaving it to his master, Nicholas had taken the drill and drilled all three holes on the other half of the pearl. Not a word had been said between master and his pupil. He wondered if he dared tell the Queen about the problems that had beset the making of this brooch.

The pelican was a showy piece, but if his client wanted to be painted wearing it, then he would comply. Unlike the phoenix's declaration of the queen's singularity, this was to be a portrait declaring her personal sacrifices on behalf of her people. It was a relatively subtle statement of the mother of the nation sacrificing the pleasures of being a wife and mother in order to succour her chicks, in this case these being the people of England. She had said it often enough, but sometimes a statement, like this portrait, would reinforce her message. No doubt the portrait would be copied, so even the illiterate would accept her desire to remain unmarried. Placed together these two portraits were Elizabeth's visual statements of her divine right to rule and of the sacrifice she was making because she was a queen rather than a king. Nicholas sat back totally absorbed in his contemplation of the significance of the two portraits.

"Nicholas," Levina's call distracted him from his thoughts. Alice was finally dressed and standing waiting patiently for his instructions, but Nicholas was too surprised to issue any. Who was this goddess?

"Alice!" he said finally, his voice coming out as a low croak; he coughed. "Sit down. No – sorry, can you stand like this." He thrust the paper sketch under her nose, then quickly snatched it back before she had a chance to see anything. "Sorry, we mustn't get pounce on the gown, the Queen would never forgive me. Er, stand like this." Nicholas demonstrated how he wanted her to stand.

Alice giggled.

"Nicholas, why don't you just turn the easel round, then I can see what you mean. You look like a constipated duck standing like that."

Alice mimicked the outlined pose already on the surface of the oak panel and Nicholas handed her the ostrich fan and a rose.

Levina was pleased to see the effect Alice was having on the young artist. Nicholas was no longer the confident painter, but was stumbling over his own feet and anything else that might be in his way. The phoenix had taken a mere ten days to paint and Levina wondered how long it would take to paint this portrait.

The queen's red gown was magnificent and had white silk sleeves embroidered with blackwork embroidery and gathered into the ruff. Rolls of fabric held the sleeve at the shoulder and her right arm had an armlet half way between her elbow and her shoulder. There were further bands of the red fabric just below the elbows. These bands, the outer bodice and the shoulder rolls were embroidered with precious jewels and slashed with the white silk lining pulled through. A heavily starched ruff edged with fine bobbin lace sat under her chin and similar ruffs encircled her wrists. The kirtle was embroidered with red Tudor roses and the whole of the outer dress was embroidered and beaded with pearls and diamonds. It was a work of art in itself and worth a king's ransom.

It was not an easy job pinning the pelican brooch to the bodice. Levina looped the string of pearls behind the bird and then pinned these to the top of the bodice to form more loops. Pearls, rubies and diamonds formed headdress and a necklace.

Alice picked up the fan. "Nicholas," Alice paused, "what's this feather?"

"It is the feather of an ostrich."

"What's an ostrich?"

Nicholas sat back, thinking.

"Er, I believe it's a bird," pausing trying to visualise the bird that had provided these feathers "and probably, from the size of the feathers, a very big one."

Alice waved the fan against her cheek

"It's feathers are so very, very soft and they float so beautifully in the air, I wondered if it were the feather from an angel's wing?" Alice paused, examining the feather more closely. "If this is a bird's feather, then how does it fly? This isn't like a gull's feather, which is stiff, but look" and she waved it gently in front of her face "see how it floats and bends."

He had no idea what an ostrich looked like, let alone where it came from. Alice continued to waft the feather gently against her cheek.

Levina came to his rescue.

"The bird comes from Africa. As for what an ostrich looks like, I'm told that it stands as high as a man, can run as fast as a horse and sticks its head in the sand when it's threatened, working on the principle that if it can't see its enemies, then they can't see it."

They all laughed. Alice was seemingly unaware of the effect she was having on Nicholas.

A week later Elizabeth arrived to see how the painting was coming on. Her arrival was unannounced and she found Nicholas alone, completely lost in his own thoughts and totally unaware that he was no longer alone. The gown was laid on the chest and he was apparently peering intently at the jewelled collar, which lay beside him on his drawing board and drawing. He was actually doodling an elegant AB, with long flourishes next to a simple sketch of a girl peering provocatively over an ostrich fan.

Elizabeth stood looking at her latest portrait on the easel.

"My, Nicholas, you have been busy." she said, finally breaking the silence.

Nicholas jumped up off his high stool knocking it to the floor, stumbled, attempted to bow deeply, lost his balance and sat down on the floor with a bump.

"Your Majesty, I am so sorry, I never heard you enter. What must you think? Please, I cannot apologise enough." Nicholas struggled to his feet and this time, bowed properly.

"My, Mr Hillyarde, I never knew you had clowning as one of your talents. If ever I have need of a tumbler, I will call on you." Elizabeth laughed heartily at his acrobatics.

Nicholas blushed, pulled the chair to the middle of the room and poured his guest a glass of mint tisane. Elizabeth took the proffered drink and sat down.

"You are not on as far as I would have thought." Elizabeth observed.

"Ma'am, you are correct. The light has been difficult, with so much rain, but perhaps the weather will improve and my pace will increase."

"Nicholas, I have missed sitting for you. Perhaps it was not such a good idea using a model"

"Ma'am, it would be a pleasure if you feel you can spare the time. I too miss your presence, but now you are here perhaps I can do some work, as it is always better to work from life than from sketches." Nicholas reached for his brushes and began filling in the detail on the Queen's face.

Elizabeth sat and watched him as he worked. She had noted the way he had been lost in his private world and wondered who it was that had so captured his attention. She was jealous, not because she was in love with, or found Nicholas sexually attractive. She was jealous because she felt something precious was being taken from her. Similar memories of another 'theft' stirred, even though she had buried that memory a long time ago.

"This time, have me holding a prayer book instead of a rose. " she suggested, breaking the silence. "And I want a statement of empire, so add the imperial crown and the Tudor rose, as you did in the first portrait you ever did of me."

Nicholas turned around and made some notes in his sketchbook.

"As you wish, Ma'am." Nicholas had recovered his poise.

"I believe if symbols are to be used, then we should emphasise them, especially as this will be seen by the Court and all foreign visitors." Elizabeth added.

Nicholas continued working whilst the Queen sat with her thoughts. Being alone was extremely rare for her and she was determined to take full advantage of every moment however painful that self-examination might be.

Elizabeth watched him work. Nicholas had filled a void she never acknowledged to anyone. His lack of progress suggested his attention was diverted. If he had found someone then she would be happy for him and wish him well. Perhaps they would name their first daughter after her. That would be nice, she thought. If they asked her to be godmother that might be the nearest she would ever come to being a grandmother. She was godmother to other children, but she felt an affection for Nicholas which she did not understand and was difficult to explain.

It was nearly a full hour later before there was a knocking on the door. Nicholas waited for the Queen to invite whoever it was, to enter.

"Come." Elizabeth finally commanded. Lord Burghley entered and made a small bow.

"Ah, My Lady, I thought I might find you here." he offered by way of explaining his presence.

Nicholas bowed and continued painting, turning his attention to the background.

Burghley closed the door behind him.

"I was curious to find out what it is you're painting, Nicholas and came to the conclusion that here was also probably where our Sovereign was hiding." Burghley continued, moving over to inspect the painting. "Ah, the other side of the Phoenix. I have to say I much admired the way you portrayed the gown with the vine leaves and pearls. I wasn't quite so sure about the veil."

"Oh, Spirit, is it that obvious?" Elizabeth used the nickname she had for her elder statesman and Nicholas could see the great affection she had for the older man.

"Only to those with eyes to see," came Lord Burghley's reply. "I hate to end this haven of peace, but you are needed."

Nicholas remained as still as possible pretending he was invisible and wondering why Burghley had not sent a page to find out if the queen were in his rooms. Perhaps the older man was, as he said, just curious to see this latest portrait.

"Ah well," Elizabeth sighed, "Nicholas, thank you for your haven. Perhaps I will be able to come again tomorrow - if my Secretary of State will allow."

Nicholas bowed as they left. It had been a very productive afternoon and Elizabeth's presence had stopped him mooning over doodles of Alice like some love sick swain. He chose not to tell either Alice or Levina of the visit and Elizabeth did not visit again.

Alice sat patiently roasting in the thick heavy gown, using the ostrich fan to keep herself cool. There was much laughter and merriment and soon she had a sparkle in her eyes. He was tongue tied and shy in her presence, except when he had a paintbrush in his hand. Levina was enjoying seeing her matchmaking bearing fruit.

Meanwhile, the Queen became bad-tempered and irascible and Levina wondered if she had got wind of Nicholas's burgeoning relationship with the young, beautiful Alice Brandon.

Alice returned to her father's house two weeks later leaving Nicholas to give the portrait its final coat of varnish

Setting the portraits side by side on two separate easels, the sacrificing Pelican Mother faced the self-reproducing, virginal Phoenix Levina stood admiring his work.

"Yes, Nicholas, it works. It is, as you wished, a diptych of marriage."

"I hope Elizabeth is as pleased as you are. I hate them both!" he snapped "It's as if she has no life."

91

"They are not supposed to be lifelike, but symbols of divinity, power and status and this you have captured perfectly." Levina reassured him. "They are to provide an image of the Elizabeth, Queen of England, not Elizabeth the woman."

"Yes I know, but that doesn't mean I have to like them. I'm tired and I want to go home. I've been away from my workshop for too long and I have things to do."

"Is that so Mr Hillyarde?" Elizabeth stated. Her tone was imperious. "I will be the judge of their merit and I will be the one who will tell you when you can leave."

Levina and Nicholas spun round and sank in curtsies and bows. Being so absorbed in their comparison of the portraits they had not heard her enter and had no idea how long she had been standing there.

Elizabeth examined the two easels very closely. Finally she stood back.

"Oh get up, both of you." she snapped. "What is it you do not like, Mr Hillyarde?" Gone was the familiarity of his first name.

"I think you appear stiff and unapproachable, your Majesty. There is no sparkle."

"I am not a gaudy gee gaw to glitter in the candle light."

"On the contrary, Ma'am, you are the jewel at the centre of Court and I believe these portraits do not do you justice." It was his honest opinion. Elizabeth smiled ruefully.

"Mr Hillyarde, there are times when, as Mistress Teerlinc so rightly says, that I have to appear distant and aloof. Not all portraits are to be realistic portrayals of the way the hair curls, or a smile changes the way the eyes look. These are perfect symbols of my status and of my calling to the throne."

"I apologise and meant no offence." Nicholas bowed low again.

Elizabeth continued to examine the two paintings. Levina glided to the edge of the room and waited. Nicholas too, waited.

Elizabeth touched the corner of the portrait discovering the varnish was still wet. She held out her hand and, taking the cleanest corner of a rag, Nicholas gently wiped the oil paint from the royal finger.

"When will this be dry?" she enquired, her tone icy.

"It would be best to leave it for at least a week or two as I have, as you see, only just finished applying the varnish."

"In that case you will leave the Court for two weeks returning in fourteen days time to present the two portraits to the whole court." Elizabeth turned sharply and left through the open door.

Nicholas sat down with a thump on top of the chest in front of the windows. He was relieved to have permission finally to leave the Court.

"Well, you are very lucky Nicholas. The Queen is angry." Levina looked worried.

"What! She's just given me permission to leave the Court."

"No, she's banished you. You are being punished."

"Oh Levina, that's absurd. She crept in and heard my opinion, which I stand by. I really don't think these portrait do her justice." Nicholas could not believe what Levina was saying.

"Quite so, but your comments have obviously hurt her and she is punishing you, so pack up and go. I will have the paintings put in my rooms so they can dry and have your clothes sent on to you."

Nicholas hoped his fall from grace had not reached the rowers so he take one of the royal barges going from the Palace to the City. It would shorten his journey home considerably and tonight he could sleep long, in his own bed.

Forgiveness

Nicholas bowed low as Elizabeth glided past. She ignored him, staring straight ahead.

It had been three weeks since she had sent him from Court and, as ordered, he had remained away for two. For the last week he had travelled to Greenwich and attended Court every day. He knew the portraits were safe in Levina's rooms and were now dry enough to present to the Court, but so far the Queen had said nothing about putting them on public display. Nicholas thought the Queen looked drawn. She had circles under her eyes as if she had been having little sleep.

Burghley nodded from across the room and Nicholas nodded back. At least Lord Burghley was not ignoring him. He still at a loss to understand whether it was his overheard remarks or something completely unconnected that had caused the change in the Queen's attitude.

The various petitioners presented their petitions and the Court continued its daily business. Nicholas could not leave until the Queen had gone, so he was stuck there. He had been commanded to attend after two weeks and every day away from his workshop was costing him money. The hours of daylight were precious and now autumn was closing in, these were growing fewer daily.

"Ah, young Nicholas," Robert Dudley observed. "how is it with you?"

Nicholas turned to respond to Dudley resplendent in green velvet and white silk, realising Dudley was dressed in the Tudor colours.

"My Lord," he murmured and sketched a bow "as ever, your servant."

"Do you have my commission?" Dudley was alluding to his ring for the Queen that he had commissioned long before the queen had requested her second portrait.

Nicholas was relieved that Dudley was not going to change his mind. Some of his clients were delaying coming for sittings and Nicholas was not so naive as to realise this was a direct result of his banishment. There had only been the three of them in that room when Elizabeth had dismissed him, but the Palace had a way of hearing things that unnerved him. The past three weeks had given him much food for thought and he was designing an alarm system to warn of people coming up the stairs. He did not want to be surprised again. Having to come to Court each day, dressed up like some stuffed turkey cock, was eating into his precious time – and his pocket.

"Don't worry, Nicholas," Dudley murmured into Nicholas's ear, "the Queen still wants you to paint her. She has other things on her mind at present which causes her bad temper."

"Thank you my lord. It is a shame that others are not so sure."

"Hmm, that is only to my good then, young Hillyarde." Robert look positively delighted at Nicholas's statement. "It means you must have finished my commission all the sooner, which would please me very much."

Nicholas started to reply, but was interrupted by the loud noise of a staff being rapped on the floor. Two pages were setting up a pair of easels and George Teerlinc and another of Elizabeth's gentlemen carrying in two panels, both covered with linen cloths.

A silence hung over the Court as they watched as the two covered panels were placed on the easels.

"I have decided that today is the most propitious to show the Court Mr Hillyarde's latest work." Elizabeth announced. "Mr

Hillyarde come forward." Elizabeth beckoned and he saw his ring still glittered on her finger.

Nicholas surreptitiously wiped his sweaty hands on the side of his breeches. He was nervous and hoped he was not going to be ridiculed. Whatever it was he had done to upset her remained a mystery. He hoped Dudley's reassurance that whatever had caused her bad temper was not his fault, was true.

Nicholas moved through the parting crowd and on reaching the dais, bowed.

"Ah, Mr Hillyarde, I thought you weren't here." Elizabeth chided. A nervous titter rippled through the crowd.

"Your Majesty, I remain in the background of your Court each day, hopeful of the time when you will see me and once more allow me to bask in your radiance." His words were designed both to flatter and show contrition.

"Well, Mr Hillyarde, show us what you've been up to. I'm sure everyone is as eager as I to see how you portray your monarch in something larger than a medal. Do you capture that essence of monarchy and leave behind the person?"

Elizabeth waved her hand signalling that Nicholas lift the cloths.

The Pelican and the Phoenix portraits were revealed facing each other, producing a universal sigh of satisfaction from the Court.

"Mr Hillyarde, we are well pleased." Elizabeth beamed her approval.

"It appears you have caught all the essentials of sovereignty necessary in a monarch." commented Lord Burghley loudly.

The crowd murmured their agreement and a ripple of applause broke out. Nicholas sighed and smiled relieved to know his clients would be back, but they would have to take their turn. He bowed his gratitude at her approval, knowing that it would be some time before he received payment, but there would be no compensation for his daily attendance at Court for these past weeks.

Nicholas tried to move away, but was surrounded by courtiers all wanting to come and see him. He suggested to one and all that they make an appointment with his workshop. He sighed with relief at having survived his apparent fall from grace just wishing he knew what had caused it. Levina seemed to think that it was Alice's presence, but Nicholas disagreed because Elizabeth had never met her. Nicholas would just have to accept that he would probably never know and, now that he was back in favour, did it really matter?

It piqued his curiosity to know who or what it was that had upset the Queen. If it were Leicester, then the commission of a ring hiding two miniature portraits of Dudley and Elizabeth might be a gift because the Earl wished to remain, or perhaps return, to Elizabeth's good books. If so, then unwittingly Nicholas's work was at the centre of the latest Court intrigue. He wondered whether Elizabeth would wear this new ring as often as his own enamelled ER. In a fit of uncharacteristic jealousy, Nicholas adjusted Dudley's ring to fit the little finger of the Queen's left hand thus ensuring his own would remain on her right.

1576

25th June

The City was sweltering under an unrelenting midsummer sun and the air was heavy. Nicholas had been supervising the grinding of expensive lapis lazuli . The resulting blue dust was being carefully stored in delicate glass phials, a cork fitted in place and the phial wrapped in linen before being placed in a wooden box. Only when the box was locked away did Nicholas allow himself to breathe a sigh of relief.

He looked out of the window and saw his maidservant Molly sitting in the sun shelling peas for their supper. Thanks to a housekeeper who answered to nothing but 'Cook' and Molly, his house ran like clockwork but he was looking forward to Alice moving in. One of the things he was especially looking forward to was Alice's honey cakes. Cook ensured there were always some cakes or sweet oat cakes, with cider, mead or ale for his guests, but Alice made particularly good honey cakes.

He had finally plucked up the courage to ask Robert Brandon for his daughter's hand in marriage and during the past few months Alice had been at his lodgings planning how she would like the rooms set out and furnished. She had found a cool dark place for storing bottles of wine. Alice now knew exactly what his important patrons liked. Lord Burghley liked weak ale and small savoury pasties. Walsingham was sparing in his tastes and rarely had anything more than half a small glass of wine. Robert Dudley might want anything and never sent word he was coming. That irritated Alice, but she recognised that unless patrons such as Dudley were pandered to, she would not have the money for her rather expensive tastes in fashion.

They had been betrothed for six months and, true to his word, the first person he had told had been Levina. She had seemed unsurprised and was delighted that he was to settle down at last. As he contemplated married life there was a thumping on the door. He let Molly answer it. She knew when to allow visitors and when not. Now he had finished grinding new lapis, he had to get on and finish the silver spice box that was to be one of his wedding gifts to Alice. He settled back to his work concentrating on setting the final topaz centre in the last pearl daisy decorating the lid.

So intent was he on the setting he missed the first soft knock at the door. A louder knock broke his concentration and he dropped the tiny topaz.

"Come." He responded crossly. Molly had better have a really good reason for disturbing him.

"Sorry to disturb you Mister Hillyarde, but ….." Molly said so softly he hardly heard her. A young clerk pushed past the girl and Nicholas recognised him as one of George Teerlinc's employees. The young man was breathing hard.

"I'm sorry to be the bearer of bad news," the clerk interrupted "but Mr Teerlinc asked me to get you to come. Mistress Teerlinc has been taken bad, sir. They think she don't 'ave long."

Nicholas stared at the boy.

"Pardon?" He could not take in what he had just been told.

"I'm sorry sir, but Mistress Teerlinc's been taken bad." the boy repeated. "They don't think she 'as long to live, sir."

"Oh my God." Nicholas felt sick. The boy turned to leave.

"Wait," Nicholas called after him "I'll come with you."

Nicholas picked up the little silver spice box and put it away.

"Molly, go to Mr Brandon's house and tell Alice." Nicholas called as he strode through to the back of the house.

"Boy, are you on horseback or did you run here?"

"Horse, sir."

"Good. Now, boy, bring Mistress Brandon with you when she is ready. I will go ahead.!" Nicholas barked, shock and fear making him very short tempered.

"Molly, tell Alice what is happening and to get to the Teerlinc's as soon as possible. If necessary she is to get a horse from the Rising Son. I'll take the horse outside." Nicholas disappeared through the door to the street, slamming it behind him.

A chestnut gelding stood outside the door and he recognised it as George's own. Nicholas climbed into the saddle and spurred the beast to a gallop.

Levina could not be dying. What would he do if she did?

The air was hot and heavy and a storm threatened. It had been like this for the past two weeks, but the threatened rain never came. Nicholas felt as if he were riding through a nightmare that he could not wake from. Clattering into the stable yard, he threw the reins to the elderly groom who held the sweating and lathered beast as Nicholas jumped to the ground. The man had wet streaks running down his tanned weather-beaten cheeks and bent his head to hide his tears.

"What news of the mistress, Sam?" Nicholas asked. He had known Sam a long time, but the old man just shook his head unable to speak and turned away, leading the animal into the cool

100

stables. Nicholas let himself into the kitchens and ran through the house. There was no-one on the ground floor, but he could hear the soft murmuring of voices upstairs.

A priest stood muttering prayers. Levina lay on the bed with her long silver hair spread over the pillows. She looked so peaceful. Marcus stood by the window, tears streaming down his face. George knelt at one side of the bed, holding her hand; his head bent and his shoulders shaking with grief.

Marcus turned to Nicholas.

"She's gone."

Nicholas knelt and took her other hand. It was still warm. He kissed the back of it, expecting her to pat his head or brush his dark curls from his forehead, just as she had done so many times before when he had presented her with a really good piece of work or when he had got angry and thrown down his brush in frustration. The realisation she would never do so again broke the dam holding back his tears. Nicholas sobbed as if his heart would break.

Sometime later the three men went downstairs. Alice was sitting with Marcus's wife watching their three year old son playing with the kittens. Alice came over to Nicholas and took his hand in hers. There was nothing she could say to assuage his grief. Alice too had known Levina all her life, but for Nicholas, Levina had been more than a teacher, she had been a mother.

George walked into the garden and sat on the bench under the rose arbour. It had been Levina's favourite place and he sat surrounded by the beauty of the flowers and the wonderful scents of the herbs, lavender and roses that she loved so much.

"Poor George" murmured Alice, as she hugged Nicholas close. He took comfort in the familiar smell of rosemary as he buried his face in her golden curls, dazed and unable to accept what had happened.

Three day later they stood at the graveside as Levina's body was committed to the ground, Nicholas heard the words, but found no comfort in them. Levina had taught him everything she knew, nurturing his talent and encouraging him to dream. Too late, he realised he had loved her as a son loves a mother and he had never told her. Now he never could.

The horizon was a dark grey mass of thunderheads and the air hotter and heavier than ever. A distant growl heralded a change in weather. As the coffin was lowered into the deep, dark rectangular hole the birds ceased singing and the insects stopped flying. The priest scattered a handful of soil on top of the wooden coffin.

"Dust to dust, ashes to ashes." Big, heavy raindrops plopped on to the wood. "in sure and certain resurrection of the dead." The priest looked skywards as he intoned the last few words of the Committal. A clap of thunder, a zap of lightening and whirl of wind and the heavens opened, torrential rain soaking all of them in a matter of minutes.

Nicholas wanted to run and hide as far away as possible.

26th July

Nicholas stood in the right hand pew in front of the altar in St Vedast's church. Alice's elder sister Rebecca and her husband Robert sat with their stepmother Elizabeth and Alice's four sisters, Sara, Mary, Martha and Lucy and young brother Edward.

The church was full of courtiers, goldsmiths and wealthy merchants. Nicholas's mother waved a sad little wave as Nicholas turned and surveyed the congregation. He waved back and smiled.

Laurance Hillyarde gazed at her eldest son. It seemed such a short while since they had sent Nicholas with the Bodley family into exile in Europe. Now here he was getting married to the daughter of the leading goldsmith in the land. She felt sad because she had not been there to look after him and it had been Mrs Bodley who had bathed his cuts and grazes and nursed him through his childhood illnesses.

Richard Hillyarde squeezed his wife's hand as they waited for the arrival of the final few guests. He was very pleased. Nicholas was rising high in Court circles and marrying well. It was more than he could have offered his eldest son had he stayed in Exeter. Richard too reflected on events and decided that, although the decision to send Nicholas off to Europe had been hard, it had been a good one and now his son was destined for greatness. Those tiny portraits he painted were so much in demand and much beloved by the Queen. Richard mused on how Nicholas could make a fortune if he were careful, but considering the groom's new wedding outfit, Richard decided that there was an extravagant streak in his oldest son that would need curbing.

George Teerlinc sat with the Bodleys, just behind Richard Hillyarde and his wife. It was just over a month since Levina's death and he sat remembering his own wedding on a cold and snowy January day in 1546. It did not seem as long as forty years since they had come to Court. He remembered how terrified Levina had been at the thought of living in a foreign country, where no-one (except him) would be able to speak to her in her own tongue. The memory of Levina walking up the aisle on her father's arm brought tears to his eyes. Then he remembered the day when Marcus had been rescued from a scrap by two scrawny adolescents called Nicholas and Thomas and how Nicholas and Marcus had become friends. It was a long time since Nicholas and Thomas had come into their lives and now the three boys had all grown up and become men. They were good boys and Levina had loved them all. It was so sad she had not lived to see Nicholas married

John Bodley leaned forward and tapped Richard on the shoulder.

"Richard, in case you're interested, I hear Drake's looking for investors in a new voyage. He's planning to explore the ocean on the other side of Panama and I'm sure would welcome another Devon investor."

Before Richard could reply, there was a bustle at the back of the Church. Nicholas recognised the Queen's laugh. As one, the congregation stood then curtsied and bowed as the Queen walked down the aisle with the Earl of Leicester. Elizabeth smiled as she took her place in the empty pew immediately in front of the Brandon family. The congregation sank back down in a soft susurration of silks and whispers.

"You would have thought it were her getting married the way she looks." Thomas whispered into Nicholas's ear. Elizabeth was radiant in yellow satin embroidered with gold thread and pearls. A stiffly starched lacy ruff framed her face, setting off her pale skin and she wore her red hair piled high on her head.

Elizabeth smiled at him, then winked conspiratorially. Nicholas blushed deeply. Theirs was a strange relationship. He was not actually part of the Court but out of courtesy had asked Elizabeth's permission to marry. He knew he had not needed this, but she was funny about people around her marrying and he did not want to jeopardise the royal favour. If Elizabeth had decided he had offended her, then the commissions would dry up and so would his livelihood.

He now had many books of sketches of Elizabeth playing the virginals, or reading, or even sewing. Occasionally he managed to catch her whilst she was deep in thought and oblivious of everyone. If she were thinking on a particularly difficult problem she would frown, which produced a little wrinkle between her dark eyes. Occasionally she spoke to him in soft whispers about certain Courtiers. He knew that he was being tested. She need not have feared, Nicholas heard much and said nothing. He would never betray any secret musing she might mutter in his presence

Nicholas felt slightly sick with nerves. He had eaten a good early breakfast with his parents and was thankful his mother had insisted he eat properly. If he had had his way he would have skipped the milk and the slice of ham, the two eggs and the thick slice of bread and just had a mug of ale, or perhaps two – or even three or four and so would now be facing his marriage with a thick head! He had sat up with his father and brother until the late hours telling them about his life and work and catching up on family news. Now he was regretting not getting an early night, but at least he did not have a headache. It was a hot day and he was grateful that the church was cool. It had not been such a good idea to wear black velvet breeches and a padded white silk doublet.

"Who would have thought it – you having the Queen as a wedding guest!" Thomas muttered softly, nudging Nicholas teasingly in the ribs.

A fanfare of trumpets heralded the bride's arrival and the congregation rose again as Robert Brandon walked his daughter down the aisle to an anthem by Thomas Tallis. Nicholas turned just as Alice looked up. He was speechless. His beautiful Alice was transformed into a goddess wearing a pale blue silk gown over a white kirtle embroidered with pink rosebuds, pale blue forget-me-nots and white marguerites with yellow centres, all with pale green leaves. Alice buried her face in her posy of pink and white roses, lily of the valley, sprays of honeysuckle and sprigs of rosemary and myrtle, ivy and bay. A wreath of pink and white rose buds held her long blonde hair in place and tiny soft curls framed her face. Sapphire and diamond earrings glistened as she moved her head. Nicholas took deep breaths to steady himself and hoped Thomas had the wedding ring safe in his pocket.

Nicholas shook his head in disbelief finally realising this radiantly beautiful woman was to be his bride. Alice and her father processed down the aisle until she stood next to him. Looking up at him Alice smiled a shy little smile. Nicholas's heart leapt as he looked into her blue eyes and hardly heard the words as the priest welcomed the congregation to the marriage of Nicholas and Alice.

Robert Brandon gave his daughter unto this man and Nicholas and Alice solemnly spoke their vows. Nicholas's heart pounded as he recited the words. He could have been reciting the recipe for white paint for all he remembered. Alice was the most beautiful girl he had ever seen and she was vowing to love, honour and obey him for the rest of his life. The cornflower blue sapphires shimmering at her ears were the exact same colour as her large eyes.

The priest pronounced them man and wife. Miss Alice Brandon, spinster of this parish was how Mistress Nicholas Hillyarde, for better or for worse, for richer or for poorer and in sickness and in health. Nicholas sighed with satisfaction and taking Alice's hand in his, raised it to his lips, whispering "I love you". Alice blushed and lowered her eyes, squeezing his hand in return.

Today was Alice's triumph. She had fallen for Nicholas the first time she had seen him when she was only six years old and had decided then that she would marry him. He had always had time for the little blonde girl who was not really supposed to talk to the apprentices. She wore the little gold bracelet set with seed pearls he had made her and which she treasured. Little did Nicholas realise that Alice had slowly reeled him in like a fish on a hook.

They led the wedding guests the short distance to the Brandon city house where his father in law had laid on a sumptuous wedding feast.   Elizabeth had insisted that protocol be set aside on this occasion and the newlyweds should sit in the place of honour at the head of the table. The Queen was a private guest at a private occasion. She insisted she dance with Nicholas who was not too sure about this because if he danced with Elizabeth, it would mean Dudley could insist he dance with Alice and he was not happy about his exquisite wife dancing with the reputedly most lecherous man at Court, even if Dudley were one of his best patrons. However, Nicholas did not have anything to worry about as Dudley behaved as a solicitous uncle would towards a favourite niece.

The guests had all brought gifts. The Queen presented them with a matching set of fine Venetian glass goblets. Two Turkey carpets came from Robert Dudley. A set of ten silver forks (a new fashion introduced from Venice) had been a gift from Robert Brandon. There was a fine silver salt cellar and set of matching serving dishes from Nicholas's father and mother and his brother John had made a complete set of pewter dishes and tankards for daily use. Marcus and his wife presented them with a pair of fine chairs made from English oak; there were fine embroidered bed hangings all worked by Alice's sisters and much, much more. These gifts were all placed on the oak wedding chest Alice had slowly been filling with various items ever since she had been old enough to sew.

An army of cooks had been hard at work and served whole stuffed pike, roast swan, jugs of claret, mountains of manchet bread, blancmange with almonds, poached porpoise, herb salads, stargazie pies, mountains of strawberries, bowls of custards and clotted cream, barrels of ales, jellies – both sweet and savoury, ribs of roast beef, haunches of ham braised in cider with onions carrots and bay leaves then skinned and the fat studded with cloves then roasted with a honey glaze; chilled white wine, rivers of red wine and jugs of mead and ale for those who preferred it.

. The centre piece of the banquet was a magnificent roasted mythical Cockatrice, which rolled in on a magnificent mechanical nest. When the mythical beast stopped in front of the newly weds it exploded in a shower of golden sparks revealing a centre cavity filled with a delicious rolled roast of the various birds and beasts that made up a cockatrice, being goose, boar, lamb and chicken roasted together with fruits and all in a delicious gravy.

The festivities went on until well after dark. The guests danced galliards and gavottes, pavanes and voltes until finally it was time to put the bride and groom to bed. The women took charge of Alice, whilst the men commandeered Nicholas and charged his tankard with more ale whilst giving him good advice as to what he should do in bed and how he should do it. Nicholas blushed to his roots and wondered what on earth Alice was being told. The gaggle of women had swept Alice off to help her prepare for her wedding night. Eventually Alice's sister Sarah leant over the rail of the minstrel's gallery to say that, finally, The Bride was ready. Needing no second bidding, Nicholas was led up to their bedchamber by his rowdy friends who had all supped far too well on Brandon's lavish supply of food and drink.

Alice was sat up in bed dressed in a fine linen night shirt embroidered with pink rosebuds. Her blonde hair had been brushed until it shone and tumbled around her shoulders in a glistening golden cloud. She clasped her knees close to her chest as the rowdy revellers burst into the room, pushing Nicholas in front of them.

Nicholas stopped, turned and, with his arms stretched sideways, marshalled them back towards the door.

"Odds, Nick," his brother slurred, ogling the beautiful Alice, whose large blue eyes had grown bigger at the rowdy entrance. "You're a lucky b…" the rest of the word was cut off as Nicholas managed to force the rabble out and shut and bolt the door. He stood bracing it against any further onslaught and closed his eyes briefly.

"Don't worry Alice, they are only playing," he reassured her. The sound of the revellers clattering down the stairs was muffled by the stout oak door.

Alice was mute. She did not know what to say. Nicholas stood looking at the angel who waited for him, and swallowed hard. He still could not believe this was not a dream. Life was being so good to him and he thanked his guardian angels for their close attention.

France

"Come" a deep voice ordered from behind the door.

Taking hold of the cold iron ring of the door handle, Nicholas turned it and entered. Lord Burghley sat behind his large desk and Walsingham next to the cold fireplace. Sir Francis looked cold and unwell well despite the hot August weather. Nicholas mused that a man of his skin tone was unlikely ever to look well in an English climate, even had he been an outdoor man with a tanned complexion.

"Ah, Nicholas. Please, sit down." Sir William beamed at him and Sir Francis nodded. "I understand you have asked permission of Her Majesty to go to Paris?"

Nicholas had thought this might be the reason for the summons.

"I wish to further my skills. The French jewellers are particularly adept at enamelling and this is something which would be new to me."

"Ah, I did wonder. We have not seen you much at Court lately." Lord Burghley replied. "we know that you were much affected by Mistress Teerlinc's death and hope your new wife brings you much comfort."

It was only two months since Levina's death, but Nicholas could not think about her without tears coming to his eyes. He could not concentrate on anything and he was well behind with the commissions for both jewellery and miniatures. All this was not news to either Lord Burghley or Sir Francis.

"Rather than making your way independently, how would you prefer to have an introduction to the French Court?" enquired the soft tones of Sir Francis.

"Very much Sir Francis, but I don't see how I can do this."

"If I am wrong, please correct me, but I believe the French Court is without a man of your talents?"

"That is true. Clouet died years ago, and I have not heard of any of his skill appearing since." Nicholas stated.

"Sir Amyas Paulet is about to become Her Majesty's Ambassador to the French Court." Walsingham continued "It would be to your advantage if you were to be part of this entourage – perhaps?"

Nicholas had never been to Paris and a link with the English Ambassador was a distinct advantage. On their own, his connections would be of no consequence compared with those of Sir Amyas Paulet's. He wondered whether Alice would mind if they upped sticks and went to Paris, on an apparent whim.

"It could not be an official post," Lord Burghley explained "but you would be sufficiently in contact with Sir Amyas and others so you would not forget how to speak English. And you would be able to observe the members of the Court very closely. I assume you would wish to cultivate a similar clientele as you do here in London?" Nicholas nodded and waited for Burghley to continue "So, as in London, it would be to our advantage if you were to encourage them in the same way as you do your English patrons." With this last statement, Burghley's purpose became clear.

"So if any gobbet of interest happened to be whispered in my ear by any Frenchman, I could pass this on to my English friends" Nicholas replied, his answer confirming his willingness to spy for Burghley. The more he thought about it, the more it appealed. Alice might even become fluent in French and then, he thought wistfully, perhaps she would understand some of the sweet nothings he whispered in her ear. The opportunity was so tempting he accepted immediately.

Sir William chuckled. "Excellent. Sir Amyas leaves the second week in September, which gives you three and half weeks to get ready." Sir William was pleased Nicholas had accepted. He would be perfect in France, and what was more, Nicholas would be self-funding.

And so Nicholas and Alice travelled to Paris. Nicholas set up a workshop and learnt the finer points of the art of enamelling. He painted many members of the French Court including Madame La Serpente, Catherine De Medici and the young Duc D'Alençon, with his deformed back and strange face. If overall beauty were a sign of virtue, the Duc was sadly lacking. However, he had honest eyes so if the eyes were the mirrors of the soul, then, conversely, the young Duc could not be so lacking in virtue.

The writer, Blaise De Vigenere introduced Nicholas to the Duc and Duchesse de Nevers and the poet Ronsard wrote verses about him.

The Hillyardes were popular and as in England, his various sitters eventually told him their secrets. Some he passed on to Sir Amyas, but some he kept to himself. As an Englishmen, particularly one who spoke virtually fluent French, he had, at first, been regarded with suspicion, but had eventually established a credible reputation for discretion. The French Court had shown itself to be worse than the English as a hotbed of rumour, counter rumour, plot and counter plot.

Huguenots were tolerated, but it was becoming increasingly unsafe to be openly Protestant. Personally, Nicholas could not see what the fuss was about. If Protestants and Catholics all worshipped the same God, then why did everyone get so agitated? In Geneva he had heard the ranting against Catholics by John Knox and others and thought it all very odd that if God were a loving God, why did everyone try and kill each other. The Catholics had the more beautiful churches than the English, with sculptures and images of the Virgin and Child, and Crucifixions and entombments. These latter images were obviously designed to terrify the faithful by illustrating the consequences of misbehaviour. The altar paintings of gruesome corpses did not seem to support the idea of a loving God at all. In order to be accepted, he and Alice worshipped in the way required to insure them a peaceful existence and their pragmatism meant they became accepted in the highest echelons of French society.

They were the perfect couple. Alice, a natural blonde beauty, kept an elegant home and a delicious table. His sitters delighted in his ability of capturing their likenesses and he quickly determined those who could afford him and those who could not, but extending a line of credit to courtiers was just as necessary in France as it was in England. It amused him that the courtiers conveniently ignored that he was English and treated him as if he were French.

The French merchant classes were not as keen on having their portraits painted in miniature and he did not have them queuing as he had in England, which led to some cash flow problems, but generally the courtiers paid eventually. It was still sometimes necessary to present a commission as a gift in the hope of further, more lucrative, ones.

In the November of 1577, Nicholas received the perfect birthday present. Alice announced she was pregnant and he decided she should return to London as soon as weather permitted since it was important their firstborn be born an Englishman. Luckily his father was staying with them so Alice would be able to travel back to England with him as chaperone. As a present for her, he set about painting his self-portrait.

He painted himself as the perfect example of an English gentleman. Anxious to show how grieved he would be alone in Paris, he set a tiny dandelion flower into his hat band. He thought it could also have a double meaning in view of his information gathering so perhaps an educated English audience would think of him as a tooth of the English lion, which was his little joke because the French for dandelions was "les dents de lions" Perhaps they would laugh so hard they would 'pis en lit', which was the side effect of eating young dandelion leaves. He had painted the dandelion so small it would need the aid of a magnifying glass to see it.

After his father and Alice had left, Nicholas was left with only her tiny portrait for company. The beautiful blonde Alice Hillyarde smiled back at him, wearing an air of smug self satisfaction. As a tribute to her he called her Prima Uxor – first amongst wives. No man had a more beautiful wife than his Alice.

In May 1578, Nicholas received word that he was now a father of a healthy son. Sir Amyas informed him that on hearing the news Elizabeth had asked Burghley to recall her limner because she was growing impatient to have the benefit of his experiences and the new techniques he must surely have acquired in Paris. So, in late summer, Nicholas returned to London.

1578

August

Nicholas sighed; Elizabeth was truly glorious as she sat bathed in the late summer sun. Her ladies were sitting on various stools and benches sewing, or reading whilst one of the Court minstrels played the lute to keep them all amused.

Knowing the Queen would be eager to know the latest French styles, Nicholas had a made a little collection of sketches of all the different ruffs, sleeves, embroidery patterns, shoes and hair styles. He had also secured sheets of music of the latest French dance compositions and had learnt the latest dances. He bowed low.

"Come, sit next to me." Elizabeth patted a place on the cushioned window seat. "Tell me all about the French Court. Is it really as decadent as they say? Is Madame La Serpente as poisonous as her reputation suggests? How are the ladies wearing their hair; did you learn any of the Court dances and what are the French fashions?"

"*Ah, it is sweet to be back at Court,*" he thought as he kissed her hand, realising just how much he associated the smell of roses with Elizabeth.

"France is a poisonous place and the Court a nest of vipers. It is good to be back, your Majesty."

Nicholas opened his satchel and produced his sketch books. Elizabeth marvelled at his attention to detail. He identified all the major members of the French Royal family and all afternoon he told Elizabeth scandalous stories of how this nest of vipers played cards and lost huge fortunes. How no one really cared about anything or anyone, except their own pet ambitions and how he had only been accepted because of his skill and his ability to tread the high wire of neutrality.

Elizabeth nodded and absorbed everything he told her.

"I understand that you now have a son and have named him Daniel. From what you say about Paris, I believe you thought you were deep in the lion's den?" Elizabeth smiled and paused before adding "And have you missed us, young Nicholas?" Elizabeth asked coquettishly.

"It has been like walking in a desert being away from you, my lady. There were times when the excesses of the Court were too appalling. They despise those not of noble birth and do not listen to the voice of the people. As a result, the Royal family are not popular with the public and neither do they deserve to be for they care not for the well being of their people. But I hope that my absence has been useful and you will be better versed in all things French now that I have returned."

To any idle watcher these appeared to be sycophantic phrases parroted by a shallow courtier pandering to the Queen's vanity.

"I understand all things French so much better now that you have shown me these drawings. Sometimes it is easier to see rather than to hear and much can be gleaned from a picture. We shall have to study these drawings and see what can be improved upon for our English ladies. After all, we would not like the ladies of the French Court to think they have things all their own way - in fashion." Elizabeth paused slightly and Nicholas smiled. Elizabeth's fractional hesitation confirmed that what he had gleaned from his sitters had been of use. It had been more difficult encouraging confidences from his French patrons than Nicholas had first thought it would be, but finally he had gained their confidence. Nicholas was gratified that the machinations of the Guises and the Bourbons had been of interest.

"Indeed, Ma'am," he continued "I can only say that nowhere is there a more beneficent Queen than here, in Whitehall."

Nicholas left his prepared sketchbooks with the Queen so that she and her ladies could enjoy the various portraits and perhaps plan the next great gown.

During the past few months he had gleaned information of great sensitivity which he had dutifully passed back to Ambassador Paulet who, in turn, had informed London. However, there was a leak within Paulet's network in Paris. Sir Amays was fairly certain where the leak was coming from and Nicholas carried a sealed letter addressed to Sir Francis informing him of the treachery

William Davidson looked up from his papers.

"Ah, Mr Hillyarde, Lord Burghley was hoping you would be coming to see him. He and Sir Francis are together and I was told that, if you did stop by, you are to go straight in."

Nicholas smiled his thanks and knocked on the inner door and entered.

"Welcome back, Nicholas." Burghley smiled, noting how the arrogant and cocksure swagger had disappeared.

"France suited you?" Burghley enquired.

"It was interesting, Sir William, but I have to say I prefer England any day. I was glad Alice came home early. I wouldn't have liked to leave Paris in a hurry with her expecting our first child."

"Sit down, lad. Sit down." Sir William waved his hand at an empty seat. "Her Majesty's wellbeing is dependent on the loyalty of people like you. You may not know it, but all those little pieces of gossip sometimes help clarify other rumours that come to our ears. My door is always open, just as it was to Levina, God rest her soul." Burghley's his last sentence confirmed what Nicholas had long suspected.

"Quite so, Lord Burghley. It's good to be back, and I look forward to being of help in the future." Nicholas replied as he made himself comfortable.

"Excellent." Burghley paused, glad Nicholas was still willing to act for him.

"Yes, Nicholas," breathed Sir Francis. He was seated next to the empty fireplace with his gown folded around him; it was as if he had not moved from that seat since the August two years previously. He was tall and thin and his dark clothes made him appear menacing. It was a look that Sir Francis liked as it encouraged people to talk. Nicholas thought that his pallor and dress well deserved Elizabeth's nickname of her 'Moor' .

"Are you glad to be home?" Sir Francis enquired. His voice was soft and low.

"I've learned all I can and there's a taint to the French Court that is difficult to determine. It's as if it is a pile of beautiful apples with rottenness hidden within it and the whole pile is balanced and about to disappear into a huge cesspit at any minute. I thought England could be dangerous, but the back stabbing and slander that goes on there is terrible. You dare say nothing in case you end up speared on a dagger. Yes, I am very glad to be back home, thank you."

Sir Francis nodded and said nothing more.

Nicholas opened his doublet, withdrew a package and handed it to Lord Burghley.

"I'm sorry this is later than it should be. I had to return via a rather circuitous route. Sir Amays asked if I could bring this to you personally."

Sir William took the small rectangular package and looked at the seal. It was the private seal of Sir Amyas, which meant it was for his and Sir Francis's eyes only. Whatever the contents, it could wait for a few more minutes.

"How was Sir Amays when you last saw him?" Walsingham enquired.

"Dancing the usual attendance on the Queen Mother. I've been away from Court as late, with the Duc D'Alençon and the Duke and Duchess of Nevers at their country estates, so I'm much out of news from Paris. However, I returned via Jersey, at Sir Amays's suggestion. He thought it would be easier to gain passage from St Malo to the island and thence to England. Many Huguenots are fleeing to Brittany with the same thought in mind."

"I gathered as much." Sir Francis added.

"Whilst I was in St Helier finding passage, I met a young man. He told me he was hoping to find his fortune in London and that he would be making himself known to you, Sir Francis, because says he has fluent French and English and is, evidently, keen to travel."

"Is there something you think I would find interesting about this man, Nicholas?" Sir Francis asked. Burghley listened intently.

"Apart from being a Jerseyman and very unlearned of the ways of the world, if he should approach you, take care because I think he is untrustworthy."

"Jersey is loyal to the English crown, so what gives you cause to make this accusation? Are you basing this on fact, or instinct?"

"Both." Nicholas replied. Both men raised their eyebrows. "He is the second child of one of the oldest families on the island. However, I've learned that he has run up some very large debts and his father has determined that he will not clear these for him, again."

"When you say large – are we talking about debts that might take some time to clear, but are not so large young man might learn a lesson by having to earn some money to clear them?"

"No, Sir Francis. Much more. I gather he will be disinherited unless he clears his debts within a year and that these amount to thousands."

"Hmm…. And what is it that makes you think he is going to seek either me, or Lord Burghley?" Walsingham raised his eyebrow in question.

"Because he told me so."

"So what is he offering exactly, apart from a fluency in language?" this time it was Lord Burghley who spoke.

"He believes he can infiltrate the French Court because he has both English and French connections." Sir Francis snorted and Lord Burghley smiled.

"What makes him think that we would be interested in what he has to offer" Sir Francis appeared to be mildly amused "and that we don't already have an exceedingly good network in place?"

"Nothing other than his own confidence, my lords" Nicholas replied, smiling.

Both men roared with laughter. They would certainly look out for a young fortune hunter with an over inflated ego presenting himself at Court expecting to be taken on because,

coming from Jersey, he must be connected with Sir Amyas
Paulet, the English Ambassador to France and late Governor of
Jersey. It showed a monumental arrogance.

"However, Sir Francis, I wouldn't be telling you about him
if this were all. I believe he is in the pay of the Spaniards and that
he knew, or was told, who I was so sought me out deliberately."

"Really." Sir Francis was baffled as to why Nicholas was
concerned about what appeared to be a trifling encounter by a
naïve adolescent.

"Before he and I met up, I was taken by his interesting and
good looking face. He had no idea who I was or that I was
observing him. His face is almost too good looking – the sort of
face which attracts attention wherever he is." Nicholas paused in
case they wanted him to stop, but both men indicated he should
continue.

"We were both in a tavern near the docks and at this point
we had not spoken. After some time a dark man of medium
height came in. He walked straight over to the young man. It
was a man I had seen often in Paris on the fringes of the Court.
From their greeting it appeared that they knew each other well,
but from where I was sitting I could only hear snatches of what
they were saying. It was later in the evening, after the Frenchman
had left, that this man came over and engaged me in
conversation."

"Did you speak to the Frenchman?"

"No, Lord Burghley. However, at one point in their
conversation he looked around the tavern. I was eating and
trying to keep an eye on both of them without being noticed.
Unfortunately I think that was when the Frenchman recognised
me. He must have said who I was and what I did."

Burghley nodded. "So tell us more about this Jerseyman."

"On the more mundane aspects of who he is, he is reputed
to be a good dancer, educated in the modern sense and I gather

120

likes to brawl if he gets in his cups."

"So if he does come a calling, Nicholas. How are we to recognise him?"

Nicholas handed over a sketch he had made of the man "He may use his Jersey name of Jean De Beauvoir, but he told me he was planning to be called James Bell whilst he was in England."

"Did George Paulet know of Mr Bell?" Sir Francis asked.

Nicholas nodded. "Governor Paulet was the one who told me about the gambling debts, the womanising and the fall out with the father. He also told me that Mr Bell had been away from the island for some time, but had no idea where, and" Nicholas paused "that Mr Bell is known to be a Catholic."

"So we have a young man who is in need of money, possibly in league with the French, but probably not as stupid as he would like you (and therefore, us) to think." Lord Burghley mused. The encounter might be serendipitous.

"And if he comes knocking on your door, Nicholas, how did you leave it with him?" Sir Francis asked.

"I suggested that perhaps I could make some introductions?"

"Good …. If he appears with letters of introduction, then we will see him. If he presents himself at your house asking for an introduction, then by all means, bring him to us. In the meantime, I have a task for you."

Nicholas sighed and waited. He had hoped he could go home and spend some time with Alice and Daniel.

"The Queen of Scots is currently the guest of Lord and Lady Shrewsbury and, on the pretext of having just returned from France, I would like you to take this to her – as soon as possible." Burghley pushed a small folded package sealed with red sealing wax, across his desk. It sat next to the one from Sir Amyas. Nicholas was surprised at Burghley's request, but took the package as affirmation of his compliance. He recognised the seal as that of the Catharine De Medici.

"Paulet intercepted it last month and it contains nothing of consequence." Sir William continued. "Mary can have it and you might hear something of interest when you deliver it. If you are also able to paint her portrait, her Majesty would be very pleased. Elizabeth has got it into her head that the Scottish Queen is very beautiful …." Burghley shrugged his shoulders and spread his hands, suggesting that, to him, the beauty of Mary Queen of Scots was irrelevant.

"Mary was much in favour with certain factions in France, but I understand the Queen Mother is not fond of her. This is her seal." Nicholas replied wondering why Catherine De Medici would be writing to the Scottish Queen.   "The French also say that Lord Shrewsbury has quite fallen under her spell."

Burghley nodded and smiled. From the few short times she had been at Court, Burghley knew that in comparison to George's harridan of a wife, any moderately pretty woman would appear attractive. It was interesting that this was the subject of rumour at the French Court.

"It would be useful if you were able to put Elizabeth's mind at rest that the Scottish queen was not captivating men she believes are loyal to her and suborning them over to the Stuart side." Burghley continued. "However, I believe it is the recent gossip from France that Mary will want. I am suspicious that she's getting information from someone and, if she is already aware of your French 'gossip', then you will be able to confirm this." Burghley sat behind his desk steepled his fingers, tapping his fingertips on his chin.

"So you see," Walsingham continued "it's your recent return from France that makes you perfect for the job. Shrewsbury is continually complaining that no one listens to what he is saying and that his guest is draining his coffers to the point of penury."

Walsingham's words prompted Lord Burghley to reach into his drawer and produce a small purse which he pushed across the desk to Nicholas.

"Give this to him from me; perhaps your visit will quieten his lady wife for a bit?"

Nicholas nodded absentmindedly and put the purse into his pocket, together with the French sealed package. He was already wondering how he could give Mary the sealed letter. Information inconspicuously delivered rather than given hand to hand would not directly implicate him in anything and he would then be able to observe and note her reaction when she came across it.

"It shall be done." Nicholas said and rose to leave.

Nicholas closed the door behind him. William Davidson was still completely absorbed scratching words on a parchment, behind a stack of papers.

Nicholas sat down on a stone bench outside Burghley's offices and sighed. He had not yet been home to see his wife, let alone said hello to his new son. Alice was not going to be pleased that he was going away again straight away, but it would not be for long. Elizabeth needed him to do a small errand, that was all.

The weighty purse and the little package Burghley had given him were safe inside his doublet. He wondered what the package contained. He was glad to be away from the machinations of the French Court and its poison, but a trifle disconcerted to find the web of intrigue spanning the channel and still entangling him within it.

"Daniel" Nicholas whispered. "Daniel Hillyarde."
Nicholas kissed his son's forehead. Daniel slept on, cradled in his father's arms.

"I think he looks just like you." Alice sat with her legs curled under her. They had spread a sheepskin on the grass and the mulberry tree cast a cool shade over them whilst Nicholas got to grips with being a father and admiring his firstborn.

"Does he have my colour eyes?" Nicholas asked realising how much he had missed since Daniel had come into the world. Now he had a family and a wife who had become so much more than his 'little Alice'.

"You are so clever, doing this all on your own." He flattered her, but Alice was distant. Daniel opened his brown eyes and yawned, then opened them wider realising he did not know who was holding him and bellowed for his mother.

"Sh, Sh, Sh, young Daniel. I'm your father ….." Nicholas crooned, but Daniel was not listening and bellowed louder.

"Here, give him to me …." Alice held out her arms for the now frantic, squirming baby. Alice undid the front of her blouse and offered her son her breast. Daniel nuzzled until he found her nipple, then guzzled as if he would never eat again. The silence between husband and wife was deafening.

Nicholas sat and watched mother and son and thought of how nice it would be if he could sample the delights of married life again and take some time to get to know his son, but instead he was leaving tomorrow and would be gone for at least a month.

"Alice" Nicholas paused, not quite knowing how to tell her that he was going away again. "Burghley wants me to go North." Nicholas lay back and watched the leaves of the mulberry tree flutter in the breeze. The fruits were ripe and he hoped there would be mulberry pie later. Alice murmured something he did not catch, then realised it was not meant for him, but Daniel. Turning his head he could see his son was

taking all of Alice's attention. One squawk and Alice saw no one
else except her son. Jealousy was not something Nicholas had
ever felt, until now.

"Do you mind that I have to leave tomorrow." He asked.

"If Lord Burghley commands, you must go." she muttered,
gently rocking back and forth "You will anyway, no matter what I
say." Alice raised her head and looked at him. There had been
many months for her to think about their relationship and she
had finally realised that, as Nicholas's wife, she took a very back
seat to the Queen. Anything to do with Elizabeth took priority
and she knew it always would.

"I assume you have already seen the Queen." She
continued. Her voice was matter of fact as if she did not care
whether he confirmed or denied this.

"I had papers to deliver." Nicholas stated flatly. He had
hoped that Alice would be pleased to see him. All he wanted was
for her to put her arms around him and welcome him home.

"And what is it Burghley wants you to do? Or is it a
secret?" she asked, her fingers caressing her son's head as he fed.
Daniel's suckling was growing slower and his eyes were closing as
he wallowed in the security of his mother's arms.

Nicholas wrinkled his brow. He was regretting going to
Whitehall before coming home. He had been sure she would
understand, but he had been wrong.

"He wants me to deliver some papers, that is all." it was
uncharacteristically indiscrete of him.

"No doubt, on your return, you will be reporting straight
back to Burghley to keep the Queen happy; so much like what
you were doing in France."

"Without Elizabeth, you wouldn't have all your fine
clothes." He retorted sharply. "She's determined to have a time
of peace so that England can grow strong. Would you like to
swap places with her? You have something she will never have –

a child, and furthermore, that child is a son – an heir. Elizabeth is England and has no heir, which means the future of England is not as certain as you may think. Your jealousy is a bit hollow, Alice – try a little humility before criticising the Queen."

Nicholas got up and went into the house, leaving Alice and Daniel together.

Mary

The weather remained warm and sunny and the fields were full of people gathering in the harvest. It would be the St Bartholomew Fair within a week and time for a holiday. Nicholas breathed the fresh country air deeply, silently rejoicing to be back in England. He rode with a group of merchants and as he neared the Sheffield Castle he left the little caravan and cantered along the road reaching the Earl of Shrewsbury's estate late in the afternoon.

That first evening he sat and talked with George Talbot and his wife, who was eager to know the Court gossip and was disappointed that Nicholas was been unable to tell her much since he was not there on a daily basis. After Lady Shrewsbury had retired for the night, he listened as his host related stories about Mary Stuart's attributes and the costs of being a royal gaoler. It was evident these were not merely monetary. Now that his wife was no longer present, George revealed that even though Mary was, in effect, his prisoner it was pleasant to have someone to talk to who was educated, witty and intelligent. Not that Lady Shrewsbury was stupid, but her intellectual capabilities lay elsewhere. Obsessed with maximising the estate income, she only ever wanted to talk about the crops, the weather and the exorbitant costs of the upkeep of the castle and the other great houses of the Talbot lands.

Nicholas nodded sympathetically. George was one of the richest landowners in England and well able to afford the expense of his royal guest. Nicholas pondered whether it had it ever crossed Lady Shrewsbury's mind that Elizabeth was actually paying them a great compliment by trusting them with Mary's person. On the other hand, Nicholas knew that the shrewish Lady Shrewsbury would not be a welcome addition to Court. Capable she may be, but her talents were best kept in the counting houses. On the surface, it appeared that George could refuse Mary nothing except her liberty. Nicholas mused on how George appeared happier with the intrigues of the Court than the tussle of commerce.

If George kept Mary amused by sometimes allowing her to ride out and to receive some visitors who had been strictly vetted, it would not be so dreadful. Talbot was playing the very difficult game of trying to keep both Queens happy. Should, God forbid, Elizabeth die without issue then Mary had a very strong claim to the English throne. George and his wife would then be the first to suffer in the ensuing onslaught of retribution if they were seen to be more gaolers than hosts. Nicholas did not envy George Talbot his current position and pitied the man. As George's long venting of his troubles slowed, Nicholas reached into his pocket and withdrew the purse of gold.

"My Lord, Lord Burghley thought this might go to some way of defraying the costs of your royal guest." Nicholas laid the small kid pouch on the table next to his host. George smiled.

"Ah, William," George smiled "ever the one to recognise how to keep my lady wife quiet. Perhaps you would give it to her and tell her it is from Burghley. It will make life so much quieter whilst you are here. This monetary recognition will soften her attitude for some time."

It was not until the following day that Nicholas saw the Scottish queen. He and Talbot walked on the battlements whilst Mary was taking her exercise in the walled rose garden below. A youth was walking with her and her ladies and he was throwing a ball for Mary's pet dog.

"Who's the lad?"

"That's young Babington. He's a member of my household."

They watched for some minutes before joining them.

"Bonjour, Majesty" Nicholas bowed before her, making a leg in the latest French manner. Mary smiled. She did not appear at all surprised at his appearance and held out her hand for him to kiss.

"Monsieur Hillyarde, n'est ce pas?" she replied. "Lord Shrewsbury 'as told me that you 'ave come all ze way from Londres." Mary spoke in heavily accented English. She had an attractive voice and was tall enough to look him straight in the face, which he found a trifle disconcerting. He was used to women looking up to him, rather than facing him eye to eye. Nicholas mused that at some point she must have been an extremely attractive woman, but now she was plump and her auburn hair had threads of grey running through it. Her coquetry reminded him of how his French lady patrons had flirted outrageously with him just because they thought it was fun. Mary did not appeal to him at all, but having spent the previous evening with Lady Shrewsbury, he could understand how George would be flattered by the flirtatious behaviour of his royal guest.

"Indeed." Nicholas replied "It was thought you might find it diverting to have your portrait painted in little."

"'ow kind; and you 'ave travelled all zis way to paint me for my seester, Eleezabette" Mary's heavily accented reply was imperceptibly tinged with sarcasm implying that she thought that Elizabeth, or perhaps her advisors, had an ulterior motive. Even though this might be true, Nicholas was neither going to confirm, or deny it. He was there to observe and to deliver a package. If George decided he had to be present during the necessary sittings then it might prove difficult to pass the package undiscovered, which might make life unnecessarily complicated. If it were found and Nicholas was suspected of planting it, then ironically, George might think Nicholas was a French spy because he had so lately returned from France.

"Indeed; the queen would very much like it if you would sit for me. Provided the light is right, then this will take but a few days; however, I believe you will find the experience diverting." Nicholas smiled as he made his offer.

"Indeed, Monsieur 'illyarde, eet will relieve ze boredom of ze everyday and per'aps you can tell me all about yourself. When can you start? But perhaps you would wait until I have decided what best to wear?" Mary fluttered her eyes at him coquettishly. He had painted more difficult subjects. Indeed, he mused that Lady Shrewsbury would be a tough assignment. He was grateful that at least Mary would not batter his ears with complaints about money.

Mary took hours before finally deciding what jewels and gown she wanted to wear and Nicholas was able to set up his portable easel in her sitting room. At first his presence produced the usual crop of onlookers from her entourage, but they soon got bored and left the pair in peace. Thankfully George Talbot did not remain.

Nicholas was quite taken aback when she asked him directly what it was like in France at the moment.

"You are well informed, your Majesty." He replied.

"There is not much that does not eventually reach my ears. I understand zat you 'ave been in Paris for ze past two years, n'est ce pas?"

Mary was inviting him to expand on his French experiences, but was this invitation for something more? Was she expecting a message?

"You are well informed."

"My 'ost has told me that you 'ave only just returned. To be sent to me straight away must be difficult for your poor wife, ne c'est pas?"

Nicholas ignored Mary's question about Alice.

"Indeed, I was able to perfect the difficult art of enamelling. As I am sure you are aware, the Parisian jewellers are masters of this art and now I can use it for my work here." Nicholas made light conversation regarding jewellery design as he worked.

Mary returned to the subject of the French Court and asked about the latest fashions and music in very much the same way Elizabeth had, but Nicholas pretended he was only superficially aware of these. Discussing the latest jewellery designs was safe even though he would never give her a gift of this nature just to please her. Giving Mary a piece of jewellery could imply loyalty or sympathy and he had neither. He might paint her portrait because he had been asked to. He thought he might even go so far as to paint Lord and Lady Shrewsbury. Lady Shrewsbury was no beauty and he wondered whether he would be able to capture her avaricious glint.

By comparison, Mary did not inspire him. She was too tall, too flirtatious, full of idle chatter and he found her too much like the women in France who were, to his mind, self-centred and boring. Then he realised he was comparing how Elizabeth's hair shone like polished copper whilst Mary's auburn tresses were dull in comparison. Mary's flirting was overtly sexual whilst Elizabeth flirted with his mind; she teased him and made him think. Their conversation continued, but it was all banal twitter. Mary was disappointed that Lady Shrewsbury only concerned herself with running the estate, which was something the Scottish Queen found totally unfitting for a woman. Poor George, she bemoaned, to be married to a woman who was clearly more merchant than noble and therefore lacking in the requisite manners and decorum necessary for aristocratic life. Nicholas smiled at the irritation the two women caused each other, but he did not think that Mary's sympathies for George were anything more than a tool by which to annoy Lady Shrewsbury.

After the main meal Nicholas worked alone in his room filling in the little details of Mary's costume, which now hung on a makeshift dummy.

The following day the morning light was good and he worked on the details of Mary's face. Mary continued to flirt outrageously and when she realised that her efforts were having no effect started grumbling about how she was no longer allowed to ride abroad and how this was so inhibiting.

"'ow am I to take any exercise if I only am allowed to walk in ze garden? The only one who gets tired is my leetle dog! It ees as eef I am being 'eld as a prisoner." Nicholas refrained from comment except to say that he had never found the chase exciting and therefore was unable to comment.

It was not until Mary's third sitting when Nicholas arrived at the appointed hour and found her sitting room empty he had the opportunity to deliver Burghley's 'French' package. His heart was pounding as he tucked it under the cloth covering the tray of refreshments. He then left the room, deciding to walk in the garden until his heart stopped pounding. Technically, this sitting would be where he would put the finishing flourishes to any portrait and the almost imperceptible details of expression which made his tiny portraits so popular and he needed a steady hand.

"Mr Hillyarde?"

Nicholas turned. One of Mary's ladies was walking across the lawn.

"Mr Hillyarde, I must apologise, but my mistress is unwell today."

"I'm sorry to hear that. Is it something she ate?"

The woman looked flushed and slightly embarrassed.

"No, but she has a headache and has taken to her bed in the hope that it will pass."

"This is a shame, but never mind. I hope the weather holds as the light is perfect and we have only the littlest of work to finish."

The woman smiled. "I'm sure she will be well tomorrow, and she is looking forward very much to seeing the finished portrait, but today she is very incapacitated. I'm sure you will forgive her."

Nicholas bowed his acquiescence. "Wish her well."

It was two days later that Mary sent word that she was not returned to health and he could attend her in order to finish what they had started.

The sitting did not take long and Mary fidgeted and was unable to settle. She flirted more than usual and whilst he waited for the watercolour to dry completely, Nicholas made further lightning sketches of the way her eyes crinkled as she laughed and the way she tilted her head when she was listening to a conversation. Finally, he decided he had done enough extra sketches in his workbook and the paint on the vellum was dry enough to present it to his sitter.

"Voila Ma'am, c'est finis." Nicholas presented the portrait in the palm of his hand.

Mary took the tiny image, held it by the edges and examined it carefully by the clear light of the midday sun.

"M'sieur 'illyarde, please 'and me my mirroire?" Mary held out her hand for her mirror then proceeded to compare her reflected image to his portrayal of her.

"Ah M'sieur 'illyarde," she purred "c'est bon, c'est tres bon. C'est merveilleux." Despite his misgivings about his sitter, he was pleased that she appeared genuinely delighted with his work.

"C'est un beauvoir, n'est ce pas?" Mary looked him directly. Her seemingly innocent comment completely destroyed any pleasure he felt in finishing the portrait. Suddenly, he was nervous that his position was compromised. Was she meaning something other than her personal pleasure? Nicholas decided to ignore her comment and pretend ignorance.

"Indeed, I think it is a good likeness." He replied gallantly. The reference to 'un beauvoir' may be coincidence. Nicholas did not want to become embroiled with any plot that might be hatching. However, he would report every detail of this conversation to Lord Burghley on his return to London.

Unfortunately, Nicholas's departure was delayed. Not to be outdone by her 'guest', Lady Shrewsbury requested Nicholas paint her and her husband. She understood that he charged £3 for his work, but, since this was a double commission would he settle for £5. She did not want lockets or boxes to hold these, she just wanted the portraits. The implication behind her suggested discounted fee was that he had enjoyed livery for his horse and his own board and lodging at their expense.

Painting Lady Shrewsbury did not take long. She was aware that time was money and said virtually nothing whilst she sat for him. As a result, her portrait was finished much faster than anything Nicholas had ever done. George was not quite so silent. George had received further news about the Protestant victimisation in France and asked how Nicholas about his first hand experiences. George speculated on whether Nicholas thought Elizabeth might declare war on France and, if so, how he was supposed to treat his guest? Regarding this question, Nicholas had no idea what would happen. He repeated Court rumours that, in some circles, it was believed that Burghley would be much happier if Mary were to disappear, but his personal opinion was this was just wicked speculation by the extreme Protestant members of the Court. In his opinion, Elizabeth was very aware of the possible consequences if Mary were to pass away in suspicious circumstances and she had no wish to aggravate Spain, Scotland, or France.

Nicholas did not envy the Shrewsbury's job of gaoler. Having seen how Mary constantly demanded everything from more logs for the fire, sweetmeats to nibble and fabric for her servants, he realised that Lady Shrewsbury had some justification for complaint. The Scottish entourage needed to be housed, fed and clothed and that was no small expense, despite the number of Mary's household having been trimmed to a more reasonable size on Elizabeth's instructions. Lady Shrewsbury was delighted with the portraits and stopped moaning about the cost of everything when Nicholas presented them as a gift.

On the question of George Talbot's loyalty, whilst it appeared he might have fallen prey to Mary's sexual allure, George's loyalty to his Queen was beyond reproach. It did not take a genius to realise that Lady Shrewsbury was, at times, difficult and to the casual eye it might appear that the Earl spent time with Mary because he wanted the company of a woman who was more subtle than his forthright wife. However, Nicholas had seen that the Earl's game was a way of making Mary believe in his devotion, which might lead to information.

He had received a message from the Earl of Leicester, asking him to call at Wanstead on his return journey to London. Nicholas was surprised Robert Dudley was not at Court and wondered how the queen's favourite knew he was in Sheffield. Dudley had been a very good and loyal patron over the years and as much as Nicholas wanted to return to Alice as soon as possible, he could not refuse Dudley's summons. It might be better to be back in England, but being part of Walsingham's spy network was causing Nicholas sleepless nights.

The road south was busy and his route took him through the centre of the Sheffield. Just outside The Drover's Arms,

Nicholas spotted Jean De Beauvoir, or as he remembered what the man would more likely be calling himself, James Bell. Mary's reference to her portrait being ' un beauvoir' did not now appear quite so coincidental.

In the meantime he had an appointment at Wanstead. This diversion would mean that he would not be back in London until October at the earliest.

Wanstead proved illuminating. He was welcomed by Dudley who then him asked to paint his new wife, the previous Lady Devereux. Nicholas was stunned. However, a commission was a commission and he duly painted the newlywed Lady Leicester. For once, Dudley paid him immediately.

Reunited.

Nicholas opened the kitchen door and quietly entered the Brandon household. He could hear everyone in the main hall and, since it was time for the main meal, made his way there.

Alice jumped up and threw her arms about his neck.

"Nick, I'm so glad you are home. Will you forgive me for being so horrid last time?" her blue eyes pleaded with him. This was his Alice; his beautiful adoring Alice.

"I'm going to have to see Burghley." Nicholas held her tightly so she could not pull away. Alice gasped.

"Oh, is it something to do with why you went North?" she had spent many hours contemplating their last reunion and regretted her jealous outburst.

"Perhaps. Burghley had a specific mission for me and it would be strange if I didn't tell him about my journey as soon as I got back, but I had to see you first."

Alice hugged her husband close and laid her head on his chest.

"I'm sorry" she whispered. "I was horrid last time you came home."

Nicholas sighed. He was forgiven.

"Ah Nicholas: come in, sit down."

Nicholas reached into his doublet and brought out a second miniature of Mary. Burghley sat cradling the image in his hand.

"And how did you find Shrewsbury?"

"My Lord, he is well and you have no need to worry. His guest tries her blandishments on him, but he is well aware of her attempts at seduction. I painted both he and Lady Shrewsbury – at her request."

"I trust she paid you?"

Nicholas laughed. "She was keen to part with her money just to say that I had painted her portrait, but instead I gave them as a gift. She is not an easy wife from what I see. Better suited to the market place than the subtleties of Court."

Burghley nodded and smiled in mild amusement.

"This is a good likeness. I hope the Queen's curiosity will be satisfied with it." Burghley observed.

"No doubt her Majesty wishes to convince herself that her guest is not as good looking as herself and I hope this will put her mind at rest on this point." Nicholas replied.

Burghley laughed at Nicholas's understanding of Elizabeth's vanity.

"I think you can take it that she will be happy."

"My Lord, there is something you should know." Nicholas paused; Burghley raised his eyebrows in question.

"I spotted the Jerseyman, Jean De Beauvoir, alias James Bell, in the Sheffield market place. It may be just coincidence, but I thought you should know."

Burghley noted the name and place on a sheet of paper on his desk. "Did you speak?"

"No, I don't think he even saw me, but because he is of a striking appearance and taller than the average man was why he was so obvious in the throng."

"He hasn't been here, if you were wondering."

"At our last sitting when I presented Mary with a copy of this miniature she asked whether I thought it was 'un beauvoir'."

"Indeed." Burghley raised his eyebrows. "so you think that Mr Bell may be in contact with Mary?"

"When she said it, I thought she was just flattering me, but seeing Bell in the market place has made me think otherwise."

"Quite so. It might explain why he has not made himself known to me, or Sir Francis. However, how did you respond to Mary's comment?"

"I ignored it. I think her comment was a test and she expected some coded reply. I had placed your package on the tray of refreshments that had been left for us, then gone and walked in the garden to await her summons. I had no wish for her to know that it was me that had placed it there. One of her women came to me and told me that unfortunately, it appeared that the Scottish Queen was suffering from a headache that day and she would be unable to sit for me, but would send word when she was better. It was not until two days later that I was able to finish the portrait."

"Hmm. Well done, Nicholas. Perhaps that letter was not as innocent as we first thought. As to her comment, I agree, in the light of events, it does not appear innocent. We will have to keep an eye on Mr Bell, or Beauvoir or whatever he calls himself. Excellent work."

"Er, thank you." Nicholas paused "My Lord, I have news concerning the Earl of Leicester."

Burghley sighed wondering if there would ever be a time when that man would cease to be a burden to him. "Continue "

Nicholas took a deep breath.

"He has married Lady Devereux."

Burghley sat back and looked at his visitor disbelievingly.

"And you know this - how?" Burghley's voice carried a note of incredulity.

"The Earl sent word to me at Sheffield to call on him at Wanstead on my way back to London. When I got there he asked for me to paint Lady Letitia … his new wife."

"God's teeth!" Burghley's expletive was squeezed through gritted teeth.

"I take it that if you had no idea, then the Queen also does not yet know?" Nicholas grimaced.

"No, by God. As you are well aware, she is overly fond of Leicester – more's the pity." Burghley's unguarded remark indicated the level of shock Elizabeth's most senior minister had received. "Tell no one, Nicholas. As far as you are concerned, it was just a straight forward commission."

Nicholas sighed and thanked the Almighty he would be spared Elizabeth's temper.

Winter came early and by Christmas Eve London was carpeted in a thick layer of snow. Nicholas loved the light of the crisp sunny days and the deep blue colours of the shadows on the snow. His memories of the Christmas the previous year, spent alone in France, were forgotten. The Hillyardes were now ensconced in their new house, The Maydenhead, 30 Gutter Lane and this year Alice wanted to entertain her whole family for the Christmas festivities.

1579

January

"Alice … Alice" Nicholas called up the stairs. "Alice! Where are you?"

Alice appeared carrying a very grumpy teething toddler.

"Up here, singing to Daniel."

Nicholas bounded up the stairs and kissed his wife and son.

"You're never going to guess who I've just seen at Court?" he teased, knowing Alice was always interested in who was at Court.

"No, you are right, I haven't got a clue." Alice's immediate acquiescence to his question peeved him. He liked their games of guess the newcomer because very often she already knew who it was and he liked testing her spy network.

"Oh, I thought you might be interested."

"If you mean that Anjou's monkey has arrived in London, Sarah told me yesterday, so that's old news."

"How did she know?" Nicholas was mystified. How would Alice's sister Sarah have known that the Duc d'Alençon's valet de chambre, Jean De Simier, had arrived at Court.

"Father told mother, who told Sarah, who told me just after you'd gone out yesterday morning. See, darling husband, it's easy." Alice kissed Nicholas gently on the cheek and Daniel

139

reached up and pulled his father's hat off. The curled feather fascinated him. Nicholas gently extricated the hat from his son's hands before the delicate feather got snapped.

"But you didn't say anything last night." Nicholas was curious as to why his wife had not seen fit to share this piece of information.

"How was I to know that it wasn't a case of mis-identity. Sarah has no idea of what De Simier looks like and until I've been told by someone who knows him or have seen him for myself, I've no intention of repeating what might be idle gossip."

Nicholas took Daniel from his mother and sat down, bouncing the child up and down on his knee.

"Nick, you might want to be a bit less energetic. Daniel's only just been fed and he's extremely grisly. He might just …" Alice had been going to say 'vomit', but Daniel performed before the warning was finished. Nicholas grimaced as Daniel deposited most of his supper down the front of his father's doublet. Alice snatched the child and took him away, calling for Molly to come and help the master. Nicholas gingerly removed his doublet and handed it to the girl. Molly was having difficulty suppressing a smirk and Nicholas realised it had been idiotic to bounce a small child around just after it had been fed. Nicholas sent a small prayer of thanks heavenwards that it was not his new velvet doublet and sat down again to wait for Alice to return.

The fire had banished the January cold from the room and Alice had thick hangings across the shuttered window which helped to keep out the draughts. The table was covered with one of Dudley's wedding presents. The rich reds of the silk and wool carpet glowed in the firelight. Finally Alice returned with a clean and sleepy Daniel.

"Alice, what do you think De Simier's here for?"

"Well, father thinks that the Queen wants to re-open the marriage negotiations with le Duc D'Alençon and now you're going to ask me why?" Alice looked at her husband to see if she needed to give her reasons. Nicholas nodded. "Because father thinks that now Philip of Spain is occupying the Low Countries, England will have the Spanish right on our doorstep and he is convinced that it won't be long before Philip will set his sights on England, so he can stop the raids on his treasure ships."

"That sounds a pretty solid theory. However, if Elizabeth were to marry Alençon, then she would have to convert to Catholicism because Alençon is Catholic? And remember, it's only last year that the French King had le Duc arrested when he tried to leave the Court," he paused briefly "but I forgot, that happened after you left Paris. Anyway, evidently Alençon escaped by climbing out of his sister's window and climbing down a rope and then fled to Belgium."

"Was that before or after you left Paris?" Alice asked.

"Hmm" he paused to collect his thoughts "after you returned home, life became a bit disjointed." Alice, raised an eyebrow as if asking what he had been up to. "but" he continued, trying to mollify her "life in France wasn't the same without you. The Court became more and more poisonous. However, if he is here to open negotiations, I can't help thinking that we might be able to exploit De Simier's presence here to our advantage. He and Alençon always liked my work."

"Nick, they also didn't pay their bills!" Alice remembered both Frenchmen well, particularly the graceful and good looking De Simier. Always dressed in the latest fashion, desiring the latest accessory, both were less speedy with their coin and still owed Nicholas a fair amount of money. "Perhaps, before you rush after De Simier, you might get him to pay his account." she chided.

"Be that as it may, Elizabeth wants me to paint a fresh miniature of her, which is what I will do. I know she is equally as slow in settling her bills, but at least she does so eventually. She

141

has already told me that she wants it for le Duc, so I shall set to work the minute the light improves. However, you will be glad to know that the merchants have, as usual, settled their accounts before the old year was out, so our coffers are full for the beginning of the new."

Alice sighed. It was an expensive business running a household and she wished Nicholas would let her run the ledgers. He never discussed details so she never knew exactly what money they had to spend so was unable to budget properly. However, he would not let her anywhere near the accounts, so she could either cause a row and insist that he talk to her about their income or remain silent like a good wife should.

A loud banging on the street door heralded a visitor so Alice withdrew. Nicholas carried the crib containing the sleeping Daniel and shut the door on his wife and son.

Returning to the main room, he found Jean De Simier warming himself at the fire.

"Bonjour, Monsieur Hillyarde. It 'ees a long time since we last saw each other? Ne c'est pas?" the Frenchman grasped Nicholas's hand and shook it firmly.

"Please, Monsieur De Simier, take a seat." Nicholas gestured to his own chair "Perhaps some mead – I hesitate to offer you wine as my cellar is nowhere as good as your own." Nicholas was genuinely pleased to see the elegant French courtier "I had heard that you had arrived at our English Court. You must find London dull in comparison to Paris?"

"Neecholas, let us dispense with formalities. Please, call me Jean."

The Frenchman settled himself into a chair by the fire and waited as his host ordered refreshments for them both.

"It is indeed a pleasure to see you again, er … Jean. To what do I owe this pleasure." Nicholas sat next to the fire, opposite his guest.

"Well, Neecholas, for one, I was reminded that le Duc and I 'ad not settled our debts with you, on account of the difficulties we were experiencing last year, so first of all, please may I settle them 'ere and now." Simier placed a small but bulging pouch on the table between them.

"Thank you, Monsieur De Simier, that is most kind. I knew I could always rely on the word of a gentleman."

"Nicholas, please, it is Jean: Et deux." Simier paused "I weesh to commission two more of your meeniature portraits."

"Delighted; to be sure;" Nicholas paused "it would be a pleasure." he paused again, waiting for his guest to say more. When he did not, Nicholas prompted him.

"Do you have anyone in mind?" Nicholas was flattered that Simier has sought him out immediately on arriving in London.

"It was le Duc's idea." De Simier reached into the inside pocket of his doublet and retrieved a small beautifully bound book, which he handed to Nicholas.

Nicholas turned it over in his hand. The treasure bindings were of the highest quality with precious and semi precious stones set in gold.

"This is beautiful." He ran his fingers over the first page and felt the surface of the vellum.

"I 'ope ze surfaces are of ze best quality for you?" De Simier appeared very keen to gain Nicholas's approval.

"Indeed" Nicholas murmured absentmindedly as he held the book up horizontally so he could better inspect the sheets, his professional eye registering that the vellum was flawless "I will have no problem painting on a surface such as this. It is perfect." Nicholas lowered the little book "The vellum alone must have cost a king's ransom."

De Simier shrugged as if the cost were of little consequence.

"And the covers" Nicholas continued "who made them?"

"I 'ave no idea" De Simier replied, with another Gallic shrug "I understand eet was an 'uguenot master 'oo fled to England just after 'e 'ad delivered them to le Duc."

It was Nicholas's turn to nod, as if disinterested. London was full of refugees fleeing from religious persecution so if the master had, indeed, fled to England, Nicholas felt certain that a man of these talents would surface at some point.

"So, who is it I am to paint?"

"Ah; one you 'ave painted many times before and the other you 'ave painted, I believe, at least once." De Simier was being his most enigmatically irritating, and it was clear that he wanted Nicholas to guess.

The first was easy. The one whom he had painted many times before had to be Elizabeth and since Nicholas had not yet painted Monsieur De Simier, it did not take much of a guess that the other was to be the Duc D'Alençon. However, Nicholas knew he had to play De Simier's game.

"Please wait there, Jean. I need to consult my workbooks as I believe I know the identity of the many, but I may need your help with the other." With that Nicholas ran up the stairs and grabbed his sketchbooks marked "France" and returned to the waiting Frenchman.

Settling himself in his chair, Nicholas scanned the pages. Faces of the French Court gazed back. Occasionally Nicholas pointed to someone who was not the Duc D'Alençon until finally he said:

"Let me see if I have this right?" Nicholas reached for a silverpoint and, on a blank page and taking the minimal number of strokes, dashed off first a likeness of Elizabeth, then sketched another image and held both up for inspection.

"Tell me, Jean, it is le Duc?"

The Frenchman clapped his hands.

"Your talent eez priceless. Yes, it eez Elizabeth and 'oo else but you could remember le Duc's visage in 'eez fingers?"

It was Nicholas's turn to make a Gallic gesture of satisfaction.

"It is a little talent." Nicholas stated, "and, Jean, I will do my best, but my best will be subject to the light at this time of year."

"Of course, of course, my dear Neecholas. 'owever, please do your best to feeneesh eet as soon as possible, as le Duc 'eez anxious to secure ze lady's 'eart."

Nicholas nodded, understanding the part he was to play in this game of diplomatic 'love'.

The Frenchman left leaving Nicholas at the door pondering his latest commission. Alice was waiting as he returned to the warmth of their main room.

"Well, that was a surprise!" Alice sat, weighing the little pouch in her hand "Do you think they have settled their account in full?"

"Alice, I have no idea, but look at this." Nicholas handed the tiny treasure bound book to his wife. The gold gleamed in the firelight and Alice's eyes widened.

"But the pages are blank!" she exclaimed as she examined the inner leaves.

"Precisely. Limners do the illumination, then the scribes do the writing!" Nicholas replied "so we shall never know what le Duc has to say to his beloved."

Alice pulled a face of disappointment then returned her attention to the pouch and emptied the contents onto the table. Forty gold coins scattered across the table.

"My God, Alice, this is much more than their outstanding account!"

The sun rose on a cold and brilliantly sunny January day, which allowed Nicholas to rise with the sun and get on with working hard on the French commission. He was determined to make the best of the short hours of daylight, whilst the weather held. His workroom was cold despite the fire blazing in the grate. Ash logs gave off a lot of heat but it was only just enough to take the chill of the room and stop the water in the water jars from freezing. To keep his hands warm he was wearing fingerless gloves.

He first studied the sketches he had made of Alençon the previous year, concluding that le Duc would not have changed that much in the few intervening months. He gave a silent prayer for his memory for features. Nicholas first practiced getting the size of the man's features in correct proportion for the page and then set to work.

The weather held and within ten days Nicholas was trudging through the snow covered streets to the Palace of Whitehall to deliver the bejewelled book before making his way to the Queen's apartments and delivering his latest miniature which Elizabeth would then present to De Simier.

Nicholas wanted to catch up on what had been happening at Court whilst he had been hard at work and knew the best place to find accurate information was in Burghley's offices. This proved to be the case as his friend, Robert Beale, was keen to relay the gossip regarding the French party.

De Simier was openly wooing the Queen on 'le Duc's' behalf. Apparently the Earl of Leicester did not seem too jealous, and in fact, was quite encouraging. Nicholas smiled to himself. If the clerks knew what he knew, they would understand why Leicester seemed complacent. The Queen had led Leicester a merry dance all these years, but Leicester now had a secret wife who hopefully would soon bear him a legitimate heir. However, it was obvious that the Queen knew nothing of this because her famous temper would have exploded had she known that her beloved Dudley had married none other than her ambitious cousin, Letitia.

Information secured, Nicholas made his way to where the Queen was seated, surrounded by her ladies and other hangers on. He could see De Simier was amusing her with some story at which they both laughed. Dudley too was laughing politely. Nicholas kept to the edges of the throng and watched as the musicians played and the jugglers juggled. It all appeared a very happy party. Finally, the Court adjourned for the midday meal and the Queen retired to her private apartments. De Simier was left to fend for himself and sat at the communal benches helping himself to roast duck and pouring himself a generous helping of red wine. Nicholas sat down beside the Frenchman.

"My, young Neecholas, I 'ad not expected to see you so soon."

"You can thank the sunny weather for my presence today." Nicholas replied, leaning forward and helping himself to a leg of roast chicken.

"Ah, it eez very cold outside despite ze sunshine. Your England 'as a cold that seeps into the bone and chills ze very marrow! I do not know 'ow you can stand it"

"I agree, Jean, the cold of Paris is much drier, but is far more deadly as it strikes straight to the heart!" Nicholas remembered the first winter he and Alice had spent in Paris and how it had hurt his chest to breathe. "England is not normally this cold, nor does it suffer from this much snow. This is a very unusual event."

The two men continued to make small talk about the weather and how Whitehall was draughty, until finally, his chicken leg finished, Nicholas wiped his hands on a piece of linen from his pocket and retrieved the leather pouch containing the treasure bound book from inside his doublet.

147

"However, the fine weather of the past week has allowed me to finish your commission."

"Thank you, Neecholas. I'm much obliged to you." De Simier put the pouch away without inspecting the contents.

"I look forward to hearing what you think of them. A bientôt." Nicholas smiled and got up, leaving the Frenchman to the rest of his meal.

Nicholas headed in the direction of the private Royal apartments and left the other packet with one of the Queen's gentlewomen, neither wishing or wanting to see the Queen on this occasion. Elizabeth had already sent Alençon one of her lace edged monogrammed handkerchiefs as a love token and if he made a big event of delivering his new portrait of her everyone would want to inspect the next gift intended for the Queen's 'beloved'.

These negotiations were obviously going to be a complicated dance of diplomacy, but Nicholas did not think that Elizabeth had any serious intention of going ahead with any marriage. He assumed that both England and France had decided that an intended alliance through marriage would be a better defence against Spain. Knowing Elizabeth as he did, Nicholas anticipated how the following months would be a dance of exquisite delicacy with the Queen appearing to be besotted with le Duc, or more probably, the charming De Simier. She had already given De Simier the nickname of her 'monkey' and he, in turn, had requested that he be added to her menagerie of beasts. This little bit of gossip made Nicholas smile. No doubt De Simier's comment about a menagerie of beasts was a side swipe at Dudley whose symbol was a ragged bear. Nicholas wondered what Elizabeth would call Alençon when she finally met him. He was no vision of loveliness being very short and having a severely pox pitted complexion. Despite his height and ugly complexion, le Duc had beautiful eyes and was extremely educated. Perhaps these features would divert Elizabeth from her suitor's lack of beauty.

There had been other rumours regarding le Duc's sexual preferences and the gossips said it was part of De Simier's duties as Master of the Wardrobe was to procure beautiful young men to provide him with 'diverting entertainments'. What substance there was to these Nicholas did not know. They had also circulated in Paris and for all he knew it might have been all be part of the French King's propaganda machine to discredit his brother. Nicholas sighed, hoping the Queen was not going to make a fool of herself. It was so undignified for her to be making eyes at a suitor so much younger than herself.

February

The thaw was sudden. Overnight, the temperature went from well below freezing to overly warm for the time of year shrouding the City in fog making it impossible for Nicholas and his apprentices to do any work. This gave Nicholas the opportunity to take stock of the various precious stones and metals he had in his strong boxes. It was mind numbingly boring, but it had to be done and it kept everyone busy.

Alice returned from seeing her sister Sarah with news.

"Father has returned from Whitehall and has heard that the thaw has been so quick that Westminster Hall is flooded and has fish flapping about inside."

Nicholas looked up from counting the pile of cut and polished rubies on his desk.

"Fish in Westminster Hall – well at least we might get some proper laws passed if that is so!" He laughed at his own joke.

"Nick, this is not good. The river is all set with ice floes and the melt water has nowhere to go."

"Alice, perhaps we should go and see this. Let's go down London Bridge and see what it's like. I could do with a break from all this counting.!"

Alice wrapped herself in her fur lined cloak and she and Nicholas made their way to the river. It was indeed all set with ice floes piled high up on the banks. They could see where the earlier tide had spilled over and caused the Hall to flood, but the time of this high tide had passed so, for now, the danger had receded.

"Alice, isn't nature amazing?" and, taking out his workbook Nicholas did a quick sketch of the chaos caused by the ice. Alice did not share Nicholas's view of this raw beauty. All she could see was the damage the ice was doing and the danger it was causing. Ships could not get to berth and deposit their cargoes so the cost of food was escalating. Many of the poor would die and she shivered to think what was happening in the countryside. She counted their blessings and was glad she had such a successful husband and that they lacked for nothing.

"Come Nick, I'm cold." Alice pulled her cloak tighter round her shoulders and they made their way home.

Easter Week

Nicholas and Alice woke early. It was Ash Wednesday and they had to attend Church. Alice leapt out of bed but before she could make it to the slop bucket, was sick.

"Alice," Nicholas jumped out of bed horrified. "What is it?"

Alice stopped retching and sat on the stool at the bottom of their bed.

"Don't worry Nick, I'm perfectly all right. It's quite normal."

"What do you mean quite normal? You're not normally sick in the morning."

Alice smiled.

"Sometimes you are so stupid, Nick. I was going to tell you soon anyway."

"Tell me what" Nicholas was perturbed. He did not want to go to Church anyway, but he would rather do that than have Alice ill.

"I'm with child."

"Oh" Nicholas sat blinking and confused. Alice had not been sick last time. "but when you fell with Daniel …."

"That was last time. Stop fretting, I'll be fine. I just need some water and a dry biscuit." Alice got up to go to the kitchen.

"No. Er, stop. I'll get them" Nicholas was already up and pulling on his breeches and shirt, "you get back to bed." He picked Alice up, placed her back in their bed and pulled the covers up around her, then dashed downstairs to their kitchen.

"Molly, I need boiled water and some dry biscuits for the mistress. Where do I find them?"

"Why, Mister 'ylliarde, don't tell me the mistress is pregnant?"

"Why does it come as no surprise to any of you women and takes us men completely unawares?"

"Because Mr 'ylliarde, she's been more than a bit peaky first thing in the morning for these last few weeks. You won't have seen it because you're always up first, whilst the mistress has been looking after young Daniel. If you'd been with her in the morning, you'd've seen she weren't 'erself."

"But she wasn't like this when she was carrying Daniel."

Molly laughed. "Mr 'ylliarde, each bairn is different. I bet this one's a girl."

Nicholas was mystified. Molly appeared to be talking with some arcane knowledge, but despite speaking in English he was

151

not sure he understood what she was saying.

"So you are telling me that girl babies make their mother's sick and boy babies don't?"

"No, Mister 'ylliarde, it don't work like that; some women are sick with boy babies and others with girl babies. Some are sick because their babies are hairy and others are just sick because they are with child."

Nicholas shook his head. "So you can't really tell if it is a boy or a girl then?"

"No, but often it works out that being sick with your second means that the second baby will be the opposite of the first, and viccy verky, which is why I think this one will be a girl."

"Er, thank you, Molly." Nicholas took the tankard of sweet mint water and the oatcakes from Molly, more confused than ever.

"I'll be up in a few minutes to make sure the mistress is all right, Mister 'ylliarde" she called up after him.

Alice was lying back against the pillow with Daniel lying in the crook of her arm looking pale but beautifully content.

Late May

"Nick, do you know if there are any early strawberries? I really, really want some strawberries." Alice pleaded.

"I shall send to Kent, but the crop may have been ruined by that snowfall at the beginning of the month. If it has, what else do you desire, my darling wife?"

"Oh, I'd forgotten about the snow. Do you think it would have ruined the crop completely?" Alice was suffering from desperate cravings and today she wanted strawberries. At the beginning of the month there had been a sudden, and very unseasonal, twelve inches of snow on London and the surrounding counties, which meant that the Kent strawberry crop was very probably ruined.

"If you are extremely lucky, the flowers might not have been out, but it is only the end of May and still early for strawberries. If I can't find any, is there anything else I can get you?" Nicholas wanted to indulge his wife as Molly assured him that these cravings were only the mistress's body telling her what it needed. However, he had found it a bit difficult to understand why Alice had been nibbling a piece of coal.

"Oranges."

Nicholas blinked. Where would he get oranges at this time of the year? Perhaps Marcus Teerlinc would be able to help. He would know if there had been any cargoes of the fruit from the Mediterranean. If not, perhaps he could raid the royal kitchens.

Unfortunately his trip to the Teerlinc warehouse was completely unsuccessful. Marcus knew of a ship due to dock within the next week or so, but none were due today and Nicholas could not find any strawberries or oranges in the markets.

The Queen was sitting reading with her ladies when he finally arrived at her apartments in Whitehall Palace.

"At last, Master Hillyarde. I do hope I haven't called you away from anything important?" Even though Elizabeth had given no set time for him to attend her, her tone implied he was late.

"I apologise for my tardiness, your Majesty, but I was trying to find strawberries for my wife."

Elizabeth raised her eyebrows, then laughed.

"Come Nicholas, tell me, do you wish for it to be a boy or a girl?"

Nicholas blushed to his roots. "I'm sorry your Majesty, but how is it that all women know immediately that my wife is with child whilst most men think I'm just spoiling her."

"Ah, ha. It's for women to know these things. I take it you were unsuccessful in your hunt?" the Queen seemed pleased

Nicholas was perplexed by the mysteries of womanhood.

"I'm afraid so. Alice said that if I couldn't get strawberries, could I find her oranges, so with your permission, I hope to raid the royal kitchens to see if they have any."

Elizabeth roared with laughter. "Of course, in fact, perhaps Mistress Hillyarde would like to share my frais du bois sent by the Duc D'Alençon."

Nicholas was speechless. The Queen was offering to share a gift of early wild French strawberries with his wife.

"Come, take these with my blessing and I hope Alice enjoys them." Elizabeth handed him one of two large boxes of ripe wood strawberries. Nicholas stammered his thanks and bowed.

"And I would like to say a special thank for the exquisite miniatures you painted of le Duc and myself in this delightful little book." Elizabeth smiled at him "Such a delightful surprise to see what le Duc actually looks like, and by someone I know who has met him."

Nicholas bowed again, wondering what she would make of his complexion should she ever meet Alençon. Elizabeth knew that his portraits of her portrayed her as beautifully divine, so he had painted Alençon in a similarly flattering way.

It was not long before he was able to return home with his precious edible gift to a delighted Alice.

"Nick, these are delicious" Alice's voice was muffled by the number of strawberries she had crammed into her mouth "if this baby is a girl, we must call her Elizabeth and ask the Queen if she would be godmother."

Alice gave birth to Elizabeth on 4th October.

November

Tucked up in bed Alice asked, in a very low whisper, if Nicholas had heard the latest news from Court.

"I gather Lord Leicester has really upset the queen this time."

"How?" Nicholas asked.

"My father was at Court the other day when Elizabeth was closeted with De Simier, and suddenly she exploded with fury."

"So?" Nicholas let her prattle on. Alice and her sisters seemed to have a network of information second only to Walsingham's. Unusually, this time the news came directly from his father-in-law. Nicholas waited for her to continue, but Alice continued to look at him saying nothing.

"Go on,?" he coaxed, from her smiles he knew Alice was dying to tell him every minute detail.

"Well, evidently, " Alice was breathy with excitement "de Simier was with Elizabeth and extolling Alençon's love for her when he leant forward and whispered privately in her ear." Alice paused again for dramatic effect and again Nichols waited for her to continue "evidently the Queen went very pale then turned to the window before bellowing that she wanted Leicester in front of her and threatening all sorts of horrors if he didn't appear immediately."

Nicholas sighed. "Go on – there must be more" he coaxed.

"Well, Elizabeth raved about Dudley's traitorous ancestors and his perfidy. How no one could trust a Dudley; that they were all a bunch of no good traitorous self-seeking bastards. She lashed out at everyone for their smallest mistake and threw missiles with horrible accuracy at anyone who came near. No one was safe and she was hurling anything she could get her hands on at everyone and everything."

Nicholas smiled at Alice's description, relieved that someone had finally broken the news of the Leicester nuptials. As anticipated, Elizabeth had exploded with rage. Her temper was famous, but the explosion on hearing the news that her

'Eyes' had married was evidently even more violent than Nicholas had anticipated. Elizabeth was a good shot and her ladies would be cursing their luck at having to attend her and he felt sorry them.

"What did your father do?" Nicholas wanted to know his father-in-law's reaction because it would give him an idea of how long to stay away from Court.

"Oh, he beat a hasty retreat. He didn't want to become associated with any bad news. Elizabeth is taking umbrage at any slight, real or imagined and he felt that it was best to stay away until she's calmed down."

Nicholas understood how betrayed Elizabeth must feel. What still bothered him was just why Dudley had decided to marry Letitia? Over the years Elizabeth had plied her favourite with all sorts of honours and position, which any fool could see would require his fidelity. Having a casual tupping with a willing wench was one thing, but marriage was different. This meant an exchange of sacred vows and promises until death.

Nicholas remembered Lady Letitia from their time in exile in Geneva. She had always been ambitious. Her father, Sir Francis Knollys, had married her off to Walter Devereux soon after they returned to England. Lady Letitia was, in his opinion, far too hoity toity.

"….. and then my step mother reminded father of the gossip about Dudley and Lady Devereux from back in the '60's."

"Sorry Alice, what was that?" Nicholas had had been so deep in his own thoughts he had missed what she had been saying.

"Well, she looked really smug and asked him if he wanted to hear all the story this time." Alice continued.

Nicholas smiled. Mistress Brandon would have reason to be smug. Robert Brandon was a stickler for discretion in very much the same way as Levina had been. Any hint of gossip being repeated in the Brandon household might mean patrons taking their custom elsewhere. For Brandon, this would be very costly indeed and Nicholas remembered how his father-in-law had threatened to beat his wife if he heard her repeating any snippet of gossip about the Court at all.

"Go on, don't keep me dangling."

Well, you know how good she is at dates and making 2 plus 2 make 4, when everyone else expects it to make 5?"

"Yes, go on Alice. Get to the point."

"In 1565 Lady Devereux was at Court and making eyes at Sir Robert."

"Yes, and …"

"well she thinks it was more than just eyes."

"Fine, Alice, where is this taking you …."

"You remember the two Devereux girls?" she asked.

"Not really. I was learning how to be a goldsmith. Your father didn't really give us much time off and we weren't exactly about to go to Court uninvited. Get on with your story."

"Well, Lady Letitia was making eyes at Dudley, so much so that Lord Devereux had to take her back to his country home. Anyhow, she would have gone any way, because she fell with child." Alice paused, seeing if Nicholas would guess at what she was about to say next.

"So – not so very surprising. They were married after all." Nicholas was getting bored with all this detail, that appeared to be leading nowhere.

"Well, remember how we decided to call Daniel, Daniel because being at the French Court was like being in the lion's den. You painted that tiny dandelion in your hat as a reminder of where you were and how it felt."

Nicholas chuckled. "Ah yes, Les Dentes de Lion."

"Quite so – but usually the first born son is called after his father" Alice paused to see if Nicholas could see where she was trying to lead him "so you would have expected Lord and Lady Devereux to call their first son, Walter, after his father."

Nicholas nodded. Alice leant up on her elbow, looked at her husband and whispered,

"But, Lady Devereux called him Robert."

Nicholas looked back at her blankly until what she was saying slowly dawned on him.

"So you think that Robert Devereux is actually Dudley's son, and not Walter Devereux's? My God Alice, what did your father say when your step-mother repeated this story?"

"Well, this time she only told this story to me and father and he went very quiet and thoughtful."

"Not surprising. So you think that perhaps Robert Dudley has finally made an honest woman of the Lady Letitia." He paused to consider the implications behind Alice's suggestion. "But I wouldn't go repeating this story to anyone."

"Don't be silly, Nick. I'm not that stupid, but it would make sense wouldn't it."

"Yes, but it's just gossip. Is there any hard evidence?"

"No, husband mine, there never is; you know how quick Dudley is to raise a woman's skirts just for a quick tumble, so I'm sure there are illegitimate Dudley's all over London."

"Yes, but I've never seen him – that is Robert Devereux. How old is he now?"

"1566 was thirteen years ago, so he's probably a page in someone's household. Certainly he's never been seen at Court, as far as I know. "

Nicholas sighed. "Well, we shall just have to wait until he turns up and then see who he looks like. If he resembles the late Lord Devereux then you will be proved wrong. I shall certainly spot any resemblance to Dudley." Then something tickled his memory. "Alice, it's just possible that she called her son Robert after her brother."

"Yes, hmm." Alice paused again. "And what about Lady Sheffield? She had Dudley's illegitimate son in August 1574, long after she was widowed. She called him Robert after his father and Dudley has publicly acknowledged him as his son." Alice paused to see if her husband was about to say something.

"He will be four or five years old now." she continued after a while. " I wonder why Edward Stafford married her? I gather she's still terribly in love with Dudley."

"Hmm." Nicholas sat deep in thought, remembering the scandal surrounding Lady Sheffield's pregnancy. Both Lady Douglas and Frances Howard had been after Dudley for years. The Queen had not been amused by their amorous pursuit of her favourite and was pleased that Lady Sheffield had finally remarried and was now occupied with being Lady Stafford. If Letitia had fallen pregnant by Dudley, her pregnancy could have been hidden because she had a husband whereas Lady Sheffield had been a widow. He wondered whether at that time Dudley's refusal to marry Lady Sheffield had been because he still harboured hopes of marrying the Queen.

"I think I shall stay away from Elizabeth until she calms down." Nicholas finally said.

"Yes, absence is probably best." Alice agreed and got up to throw another log on the fire. Daniel was asleep in his cot and baby Elizabeth sound asleep in the cradle. Alice was enjoying the undisturbed moment with her husband. November rain clattered against the windows and she made sure the shutters were secure against the rising wind. Taking two pewter tankards from the sideboard Alice filled them with some claret. Then taking the silver spice box from the shelf, she added a mixture of spices to the wine before placing the two tankards in front of the fire to heat slowly. Alice had a special poker she used for mulling wine and thrust this deep into the heart of the fire to heat it to just the right temperature. They sat in silence waiting for the poker to glow orange.

Nicholas lay back on the pillows. Alice came back to bed with the two tankards and together they sat propped against the pillows sipping the warm spiced wine. The spices were just as Nicholas liked them; not too heavy and just enough honey to take the sharpness off the wine.

"Alice," he paused " remember when I came back from France and was sent straight away up to Lord Shrewsbury's …." Nicholas paused again as Alice snuggled up to him. He could smell the camomile rinse she had used on her hair. "I came back via Wanstead"

He heard Alice's sharp intake of breath

"Oh Nick!"

"Leicester sent word to me to go to him there on my way back to London and when I got there he asked me to paint a portrait of the new Lady Leicester. You mustn't say anything to your father, your step-mother, or any of your sisters."

"I might be keen to hear the gossip, my darling husband, but it is only so I can tell you because I know how interested you are." Alice whispered then kissed him gently on his cheek.

"Alice, one thing I do know is that De Simier wouldn't have dropped this bombshell unless it were to his advantage. As far as I know there are only a handful of people who know about this so he has a good network of spies here. I also know he is due to leave for France tomorrow, so this must be his final thrust to get Elizabeth to agree to the French marriage."

"Well, there's more." Alice was even more keen to give him all the gossip. "Elizabeth has banished the Lady Letitia from Court… for ever. Dudley too!"

"Alice, she cannot survive without Dudley. He'll be back, but not too soon. However, Letitia was a different matter. By this marriage she's both insulted and made Elizabeth a laughing stock at Court and abroad."

Nicholas gave his wife his empty tankard, lay back and gazed at the painted ceiling of their bed. His face, as Mars, slept on whilst the Venus Alice gazed back at him, her long blonde hair falling around her shoulders. He had recently added Daniel's portrait as the face of the baby satyr playing with Mars's armour. *"Now I will have to add little Elizabeth's face to one of the other little satyrs."* he thought idly. Finally, he asked his wife

"If you were Lady Letitia, what would you have done if Leicester had asked you to marry him?"

"Oh. Are you asking me for a reason for Lady Devereux wanting to marry Robert Dudley?"

"Hmm. Yes. Letitia Knollys has always been ambitious, but don't you think that she has made a serious miscalculation this time?"

"Didn't you know her in Geneva?" Alice had a few questions of her own.

"Yes, but that was a long time ago and she's four years older than me. At that time, she really wanted nothing to do with a seven year old boy, nor I with her. She was always going on about how, if Mary died childless, she would be cousin to Queen Elizabeth and then would make me practice how I would have to bow every time she walked past. "

"How awful. Has she improved?"

"No; but this time I think she's seriously over-reached herself. Possibly cuckolding your husband is one thing, because no one can ever prove whether Robert Devereux is Walter Devereux's son or not. However, marrying the Queen's favourite is quite another. Elizabeth will never forgive her, and I doubt if she will forgive Dudley for a very long time, either." Nicholas paused. "I can't help but feel sorry for the man. Elizabeth has kept him at her beck and call for all these years, and whilst he's been no saint, he's had to watch her carrying on flirting with

161

possible foreign marriages for years. Mind you, I don't believe she will ever marry, she's said it often enough. Even these French negotiations are just a repeat of the political masque that gets enacted every now and again, just to keep Parliament happy."

"If Lady Letitia is so horrid, why would a man like Dudley marry her?"

"Come on Alice, Dudley is as ambitious as Letitia. It's to do with heritage."

"I don't follow you." Alice frowned.

"It's quite simple really. If the Queen dies childless, then, through Letitia – as a cousin to the queen, any male legitimate offspring of Dudley and Letitia could make a claim, albeit tenuous, to the throne when the Queen dies. Dudley's father attempted to have his son Guildford crowned king by marrying him to Lady Jane Grey, who was also a cousin. That cost both Gildford and Jane their heads – John Dudley too."

"Oh," Alice was quite taken aback "I hadn't thought of that."

"And don't forget, Dudley's first wife, Amy Robsart, died in strange circumstances, just after Elizabeth came to the throne."

"Oh, I'd quite forgotten that, too. But that was an accident."

"Yes, but Dudley's reputation was forever tainted with the mysterious death of an inconvenient wife and so, despite Elizabeth loving him deeply, they could never marry."

"Well that explains why she was shouting about never trusting a Dudley and that the whole family were a traitorous mob."

"Alice, as devious and ambitious as Dudley is, I don't believe he would have stooped to murder his then wife. She was inconvenient, but the way it was done was too obvious. I think it was murder, but not planned or ordered by Dudley. Others were at work here."

"Who?"

"Alice, you are going to have to work that one out for yourself."

"Nick, won't you give me a clue?"

"No, darling wife, and it would be dangerous for you to speculate about the why and the who, with anyone. For now you can think up a good reason why the Queen hasn't exiled Letitia to the country. "

"Oh that's easy. If I were Elizabeth, I would make sure that Dudley was removed from Court just long enough to teach him a lesson, then I would recall him and make him apologise. Then I would then keep him at my beck call everyday and give him lots of very intimate personal gifts, albeit small ones, whilst making a big public show of giving them, which might be good for you as I'm sure she will want lots of little personal tokens. As for Letitia, I would make sure she was near enough so she will have to wait everyday for her husband to come home, and that wouldn't be until I released him from Court duties which would never be until very late at night. Then I would make sure that she heard all the Court gossip about how I was making much of her husband and that obviously, despite their marriage, he was still mine at heart. That way Letitia would know exactly who was in charge of her husband and there would be nothing she could do about it."

Nicholas kissed the top of his wife's head. It was interesting how cruel women could be using emotional knives rather than physical ones. He never ceased to marvel at the way Alice could get inside Elizabeth's head, but it was curious she could not understand the logic behind State politics. To him it was obvious that, back in 1560, someone powerful had wanted to discredit Dudley and what better way than for Dudley's wife to die in suspicious circumstances so the blame reflected on Dudley, even if he had not actually done the deed. Dudley would be proved innocent, but his reputation would be so tarnished he could never become the Queen's husband.

1580

October

Elizabeth Hillyarde nestled in her mother's arms. She had just celebrated her first birthday, a second tooth and was feeling miserable as a third tried to push its way through her gums. Around her neck was a birthday gift of a string of coral beads, but young Elizabeth was far more interested in chewing the ivory and silver teething ring her grandfather had made her.

Alice was thirty weeks pregnant and her back ached. Alice idly wondered how poor women survived. She had lived all her life in a very comfortable home so had no idea of what life was like at the other end of society, neither did she want to experience it. She had always been surrounded by luxury; first in her father's household, and now her own. Alice sat considering Nicholas's success. As yet, the Queen had not given him a knighthood, or an official position at Court, neither did they own the property her father did, but she was sure that would come. She was sure that they would be able to recover financially from the stupid investment he had made in a Scottish goldmine, because everyone wanted a Hillyarde miniature and his order book for these and lockets to put them in, was full. The new baby gave a stretch and Alice rubbed her stomach where the little hand or foot was trying to push up under her ribs.

She sat listening as Nicholas told Daniel how rubies were
frozen drops of angel blood shed when the Archangel Michael
had led the heavenly host against Lucifer and all the bad angels
had been thrown out of heaven; how diamonds were the
crystallised tears cried by the good angels when little boys and
girls were naughty. Daniel's eyes grew bigger and bigger as his
father told of how sapphires were shards of heaven God had
buried deep on earth to remind us of how he had divided the
void to create heaven and earth. That pearls were drops of
melted moonbeams that had sunk to the bottom of the sea and
been swallowed by oysters.

"Nick, I hear Francis Drake has returned." Alice
announced with an certain air of authority. Little Elizabeth had
finally fallen asleep. Drake's presence at Court was the reason
Nicholas was able to sit and enjoy a rare domestic moment.

"I haven't seen him yet, but I gather he's been with the
Queen telling her all sorts of amazing stories."

"Sarah has heard that Drake landed a whole boatload of
Spanish gold and Burghley wants to send it back."

Nicholas laughed. As ever, Alice's sister was well informed.

"Somehow, I don't think that'll happen. Dudley,
Walsingham, Hatton and, I believe, the Queen, put their own
money into that voyage so they won't be giving up their profit for
the King of Spain. Elizabeth's still smarting from Philip's
attempt to invade Ireland so Drake giving him a bloody nose and
relieving him of some of his plunder is some recompense.
Burghley might want to avoid upsetting the Spanish, but these
members of the Privy Council have too much of a vested interest
to allow the return of that treasure."

Daniel climbed off his father's knee, toddled over to his
mother. He was feeling sleepy and his mother seemed a more
comfortable option than his father, despite her large bump.

Besides, he could not have his sister having taking all their mother's attention.

"Good. Philip is far too interested in returning England to Catholic ways. He would have us all burnt at the stake if he could. It's too horrible to think that he was once King of England."

There was a knock on the door and a dark moustachioed man entered, walking with a rolling gait.

"Mr Nicholas, Captain Francis Drake." Molly announced from behind the stranger.

The illustrious sea captain bowed. Nicholas stood up and returned the captain's bow.

"Forgive me for bursting into your domestic bliss, Mr Hillyarde. There isn't too much ceremony at sea, so I forget sometimes. " Drake blustered, suddenly embarrassed at interrupting what was clearly a family moment.

"Mistress Alice, my wife" Nicholas introduced Alice, who inclined her head and smiled at the new comer. Daniel regarded the stranger from behind his thumb and nestled closer to his mother for protection, whilst Elizabeth stirred slightly then fell back asleep, still sucking on the teething ring.

"Mistress Hillyarde, you have a fine family." Drake bent and tickled Daniel under the chin, then continued "To cut to the chase, Mr Hillyarde, the Queen told me you were just the man to set fine gems so I decided to come immediately to you."

"The Queen does me much honour with her recommendation." Nicholas smiled and gestured for Drake to take a seat at their table.

Molly reappeared with a tray of refreshments and poured her master and Captain Drake tankards of ale. The sea captain thanked her and took a deep swig. Nicholas sipped his politely, waiting for Drake to continue.

"Mistress Hillyarde, this is a fine ale, and after the 'interesting' drink we get at sea, 'tis a pleasure to taste som'at so pure." Drake wiped his moustaches on the back of his hand. Alice murmured her thanks at his compliment.

"Captain Drake, I gather from the Court that you were with the Queen for some hours yesterday." Nicholas smiled at his new patron.

"Indeed I was. She wanted to hear all the details of my voyaging. However, I would like you to have a look at some settings as I don't altogether trust some'at that isn't English made." Drake continued "'Tis a gift for 'er Majesty, but some of the stones be a little loose so, before I present it to her, I'd like these secured. My Lord Leicester also suggested I come to you, being as we are both Devon men."

"Indeed we are," Nicholas agreed. "The Queen seems fond of men from our part of the world."

"'Tis so; Hawkins made the same observation, but then Exeter was loyal to the Protestant cause when her sister was on the throne, so perhaps Queen Bess feels she can trust us Devonians."

Whilst it was interesting to muse on just why the Queen liked men from the West Country, Nicholas wanted to know what it was that Drake wanted him to look at. His fingers itched to see the quality of the stones and the gold and the workmanship. Would it be Spanish or was it something from the New World?

Drake opened the satchel he had carried in with him, brought out a bundle of red flannel and handed it to Nicholas, who unwrapped the soft folds of fabric to reveal a diadem of bright yellow gold set with diamonds and three giant emeralds. Nicholas examined the stones. Some were a little loose in their settings, but it would be an easy job for these to be made secure.

The circle was also slightly bent on one side as if the piece had been dropped.

The emeralds were enormous rectangles of pure green. The centre stone was the length of his little finger whilst the two either side of it were only slightly smaller. Emeralds were notoriously difficult to work and usually full of flaws, but these three were almost perfect. The crown was heavy; heavy enough to sit on a head without slipping, and Nicholas wondered whether it would give the wearer a headache.

"Captain Drake, this won't be difficult. I suggest that we polish the gold as it is slightly scratched here and there" he pointed out the scratched surfaces "and then clean the settings of dust and other dirt and ensure the stones are solidly secure. This is a very sound piece." Nicholas said admiringly, gently stroking the rim and then holding the crown up to the light and turning it slowly so the emeralds glowed pure green in the light of the fire.

Alice watched. *"It is as if he is caressing a lover"* she mused, remembering how shy they had both been when they had first bedded on their wedding night. Nicholas had been as tender with her that night as he was handling this absolutely exquisite gold crown that had come thousands of miles around the world. Alice hoped she would be able to try it on just once.

"'Found it at the bottom of a Spanish captain's treasure chest on a galleon we captured off the coast of Peru, so I presume he'd taken it off the Incas." Drake explained.

Nicholas continued to examine the inside of the crown. "Yes, it's not a European way of working, but very skilled nevertheless. When do you want it by?" Knowing that Drake's pockets were stuffed with Spanish gold was comforting because it meant that his new customer would be able to pay promptly.

"As soon as possible. I'm to see the Queen again on Thursday and would very much like to present her with it then."

Nicholas sighed. Anything was possible and his fingers itched to work on such a piece.

"And I have a diamond cross that needs checking over, too, but that is not so urgent." Drake continued producing a thick gold chain set with diamonds from which dangled a gold crucifix also set with diamonds. He dumped it unceremoniously on the table.

"Do you think it fit for the Queen?" Drake enquired.

Nicholas looked at the gold and diamonds piled on the table. He lifted the chain checking to see if the gold links were sound and again to see if any of the stones wiggled in their settings. There were a couple, but again, nothing that could not be easily fixed. The crucifix was nearly four inches in length. A large square cut diamond sat where the two arms met and that setting was quite loose with two of the claws showing considerable wear. The other stones were also square cut and would glitter very pleasingly when cleaned. The worn claws suggested it had been handled often, which caused Nicholas to wonder who it was who had originally owned it. As if reading his mind Drake continued.

"We were just off the coast of the New World when we sighted a Spanish galleon. She was lying low in the water so we presumed she was loaded with treasure."

Nicholas nodded; just the thought of being at sea made him nauseous.

"She was just too much of a wallowing duck to ignore, so we had to pluck it of it's cargo to help it float." He explained with a certain swagger, as if he liked nothing better than to tweak the nose of the King of Spain.

"Was she on her way back to Spain?" Alice enquired.

"Never asked. Our lightening her load just means there're fewer Spaniards to plague good English merchantmen. However, this one also had a big fat Churchman on board who was mighty reluctant to hand over anything, but my boys persuaded him. Shame he found it difficult to swim in those long robes of his!"

Drake's casual reference to the priest's watery fate made Nicholas shudder.

"So this is a piece of Catholic plunder." Nicholas stated.

"Aye, that it is, 'n I thought it would be so much better round the neck of our own dear Queen than that of a fat Catholic priest."

Nicholas nodded. Since both the crown and the crucifix were destined for the Queen he decided he would perform this simple job himself despite it being something a novice could easily do.

"We Devon men must stick together, Nicholas. But now I must attend the Lords Leicester, Walsingham and Hatton to tell of my adventures. When shall I return?"

"Today is Monday, so to do a proper job I can have the crown ready for you by Wednesday." Nicholas offered. It would only take a matter of a couple of hours to repair the settings and clean and polish the crown, but Nicholas wanted time to examine the pieces more closely. "Perhaps you would like to come and share our evening meal as we too would much appreciate hearing more of your adventures."

"My, this would be very welcome. I find Court fare somewhat better than our sea rations, but it is a very big place and my lodgings are quite lonely. Thank you, I would very much enjoy a hot meal in the bosom of the Hillyarde family."

Alice smiled. *"Cheeky man,"* she thought *"you must have no end of invitations being as you are the most celebrated man in London at the moment! However, whatever your motive, at least I will be able to tell my sister that I'm entertaining the famous Captain Drake!"*

Drake and Nicholas shook hands to seal the deal and Nicholas showed the sea captain to the door, leaving Alice gazing at the abandoned pieces and musing on the cavalier attitude her husband had towards these incredibly valuable items. She knew enough to know that the crown was of very pure gold and wondered how it was that the savages from the New World were able to produce something so sophisticated. Perhaps she would be able to ask the famous sea captain when he came to dinner.

"Well Alice" Nicholas's return interrupted his wife's thoughts "I think this would look very fine on your head." Nicholas picked up the crown and set it on his wife's head.

"Oh Nick, it's not nearly as heavy as I thought it'd be!" Alice was surprised at the way it sat on her head quite comfortably. "If I didn't know better I might think you'd made it for me."

"Well," Nicholas smiled as he admired his wife wearing the emerald diadem "you've answered one question for me. It won't give our Queen a headache!"

"And what about the crucifix, Nick?"

Daniel got down and toddled over to his father, taking the cross dangling from his father's hand. He walked back across the room and handed it to his mother "Da, Mama." Alice reached down and kissed her son's head.

"Thank you, Daniel. It's beautiful, but I think your father needs it."

Nicholas duly reset the loose stones and the two pieces were polished and waiting for collection on the Wednesday evening. Alice made sure that supper was especially fine and, late in the afternoon, Drake called at the Maydenhead.

Molly rang the dinner gong summoning to the dinner table.

"Mr Hillyarde, this crown looks fair wonderful now you've cleaned it up a bit, and the crucifix too. What's your fee?"

"Captain Drake we would all like to hear of your adventures. The Court is agog with your tales of what you've seen and done and I'm sure my household would very much appreciate hearing these from your own lips."

Alice sighed in frustration. Making the various pieces of jewellery sound had not taken long, but had still taken time and here was her husband asking only a sailor's tale in return. Tales did not pay bills, however entertaining they might be.

"Thank you, Mr Hillyarde." Drake seated himself at the table as Molly supervised the dishes being brought from the kitchen. Everyone was eager to hear Drake's stories and sat waiting expectantly.

"Shall I tell you all about the time we caught the Cacafuego?"

"If my Spanish serves me right, this is about a ship called the Fire Shitter! Surely that can't be her real name?" Nicholas laughed.

"Indeed, it isn't. The ¡Nuestro Senora De la Concepcion; was a galleon with a great amount of guns."

"Don't you think there's something irreverent about calling a ship named after the Virgin Mary, a fire shitter?"

"That might be so if you are a Catholic, but she was a mightily gunned ship, so justly deserved her name as she could spew forth cannon fire like …." Alice coughed a warning about his language and Drake left the rest of his description to his audience's imagination.

"It was on the 1st of March, just as we were coming up to a set of islands called the Esmeraldas." Drake continued. "Days before, we'd slunk through the Magellan straits into the Pacific and I tell you that can be fearsome. In that part of the world there can be winds that would blow away St Paul's and the waves be as big as mountains that will smash you to smithereens against rocks that look like dragons teeth, but the day we slipped through it was as calm as a mill pond. The Spanish had no idea we had rounded the Horn so we made our way up the coast and attacked the town of El Callao."

His audience sat spellbound.

"We came up on the town and opened fire with a great fusillade of shot and cannon and soon them Spaniards were flying a white flag. What amazes me is how the Spanish get everywhere. They've little ports all the way up the Pacific coast right up through Mexico and up into the land of the red Indian."

"But what about the Cacafuego?" Cook prompted.

"I was just coming to that. The mayor of El Callao told me that the 'fuego had sailed only a day before, ladened with treasure from the interior."

"How come he just told you?" It was a fair question.

"Well, he wasn't that keen first of all, and took some persuading. We found various documents in the mayor's office that suggested one of the Spanish treasure ships had been in port."

"So did you pull out his finger nails to get him to speak?"

"Cook, that's enough, that sort of question will give Daniel nightmares."

"Sorry Mistress Alice. I only wanted to know if the Spanish were cowards."

"Go on, Francis," Nicholas coaxed.

"Trust me, they squeal like a stuck pig when given a little coaxing, shall we say. Anyhow, the 'fuego was only a day ahead of us and we are a fast ship. We had a man in the crow's nest searching for any sign of her on the horizon and soon there she was, wallowing like a pig in mud without a care in the world. However, we threw out some sea anchors, disguised the 'Hind to look like a Spanish merchantman and took the 'fuego by surprise, raking her with cannon shot and downing her mizzen mast ..." Alice threw him a look warning him not to be too violently descriptive "... and before you knew it Cap'n Juan De Anton had surrendered."

"So how laden was she?" Peter asked.

"Enough to make King Philip very angry!" Francis laughed "So much so, I don't think I'm too popular in Spain."

Everyone laughed.

"Since the Spanish captain had given in so quietly, we had dinner with them, then put 'em ashore in Panama. It seemed fair enough since the Caribbean is only some forty or so miles away at the narrowest point so Cap'n Anton and his crew could walk it in a matter of days."

"And by letting them free, Philip would eventually know exactly who had captured his treasure ship." Nicholas observed.

"Quite so, Mr Hillyarde. We wouldn't want him thinking that it had just foundered in the Straits would we?"

"Captain Drake," this time it was Alice who spoke. "I'm intrigued as to how you were able to capture such a powerful ship? I understand that she is very large and I believe our, or rather, your ship is considerably smaller. You clearly had God on your side."

Nicholas threw his wife a warning glance. She was virtually accusing Drake of unbelievable embellishment.

"You might well ask, Mistress Hillyarde, and in your place I too would be sceptical. However, we have John Hawkins to thank for our success." Drake took a deep swing from his tankard to whet his throat.

"For some time now, Hawkins has been concerned with re-designing our navy. The Spanish might be large and carry many guns, but they lack the agility of our ships and weaponry."

"How are they different?" Nicholas was now as curious as Alice to find out how the privateers were so successful against the mighty Spanish galleons.

"The Spanish rely on fire power - they have larger cannon and therefore a longer range. However, these guns are fixed to their gun deck so reloading is difficult and dangerous." Drake's audience looked at him blankly, not understanding the implications of what he was telling them. Alice was the first to understand how this might benefit the English.

""So once the Spaniard has discharged its cannons you are able to dart in and rake their sides with cannon fire whilst the Spanish are busy are trying to reload their guns."

"Precisely so, Mistress Hillyarde. You would have thought that by now the Spanish would have learnt something about our methods and done some'at about the design of their ships, but no!"

Nicholas was astounded by his wife's perception and knowledge of sea warfare and thought Drake had a good point. If he was in charge of the Spanish navy he would be studying why the English were so good at capturing the big Spanish ships and then start copying their designs.

"So, from what you are saying, are we to understand that the Spanish reload their cannon by climbing down the outside of their ships? That doesn't seem sensible, in fact, why would you design something so difficult and dangerous?"

"Nicholas, I've not taken the time to study how they reload, nor do I care, just as long as I can get in there, relieve Philip of his treasure and bring it home. If he's silly enough to continue using fixed guns, then it's all the better for us."

"Oh, I agree. Just out of interest, Francis, what do our ships carry?"

"Hawkins has re-designed our vessels so they're faster in the water. Not only can we manoeuvre better, our weaponry is mounted on wheels and recoils back into the gun deck for re-loading. We can load and re-load faster than you can say King Philip of Spain."

Drake became a frequent visitor to the Hillyarde household and, on these visits, regaled the whole household with more extravagant tales of his adventures against the Spaniards; descriptions of luxuriant dense jungles full of exotic birds and animals, of the natives of the Caribbean and the islands of the Pacific. How the Pacific was so wide that, had they not known it was navigable, they would have thought they were about to sail off the edge of the world. Tales of the North American Indians who lived a wandering life following the herds of buffalo they hunted for meat and hides. How these herds were so vast that it was told that, if you stood on a hill and they passed below, the herd might take days to pass in front of you. How the Indian warriors wore eagle feathers in their hair, how they had no cities or houses, but wandered the plains following the buffalo and living in tents and that they had no need for money and worshipped sky gods.

Alice used the excuse that his tales of sea fights with the Spanish and making prisoners walk the plank, gave the children nightmares, but she was the one who hated the gory stories as she thought it might affect her unborn baby.

Alice gave birth to their second son on Christmas Eve and Nicholas asked Drake to be godfather, naming their new son Francis in his honour.

1581

"My wife has written and told me I've been away so long, she's almost forgotten what I look like, so our gracious Majesty suggested you could do one of 'em portraits of me for my wife to remember me by." It was a bashful Drake who asked the favour.

Nicholas smiled, wondering why Drake needed to explain himself.

"Would you like me to design a locket too?"

"Like the ones you've done for those at Court?" Drake brightened at this suggestion. "Absolutely. I wouldn't want my wife to think she's going to get anything inferior just because she lives in the country. I've got some broken bits of gold King Philip doesn't want and you might be able to melt down and use." Drake lifted his bag and tipped the contents on to a table. Gold, diamonds, emeralds, silver coins all spilled out into a pile. Nicholas spread them about. There were rings, broken cloak clasps, a crushed piece of a gold sword hilt; various precious stones lying loose looked like pieces of coloured glass.

"Interesting. Are they all Spanish?" Nicholas picked up a square cut diamond and held it to the light. If Drake had not known better he thought that out of its setting, this diamond, which was the size of his little fingernail, looked like nothing better than a shard of glass.

"No, a mixture. Some are Spanish and some probably Portuguese. The emeralds are all from the New World."

Nicholas examined the various broken bits of gold.

"These native pieces are very pure. The gold is a very bright yellow and very soft, whereas this sword hilt is paler, which suggests it's mixed with another metal to make it a bit more robust. However, I can't see that this hilt was made for anything other than a dress sword?"

Drake nodded in agreement.

"It's a shame it's so smashed." Nicholas continued "Do you have the original blade?" he paused before suggesting "Perhaps we could remodel it?"

Drake shook his head and laughed. "Unfortunately no, and you are right. The man wielding it couldn't fight to kill a fly. I don't think he'd ever seen action and after a pass or two, he was easily disarmed. Had all the grace of a dancer, but was useless in a deck fight. That blade somehow got stuck in the deck and broke in two in the mêlée. I saved the hilt purely because I liked it at the time. Unfortunately it got broken - I don't know how, so melt it down and make something less Spanish out of it."

"I'll make a list of what you have so you'll know what I use." Nicholas scooped the pile of gold and stones back into the pouch. He was pleased the fire was lit but, even so, the room was still chilly. The February day was sunny and since the room faced North, the light was muted.

Drake sat on a stool near the window whilst Nicholas went through a pile of prepared vellums looking for right one to begin Drake's portrait. Despite being in London since the previous October, Drake's skin was still tanned from his time at sea so none of the prepared vellums were any good. Nicholas took a

179

completely virgin piece from his shelf, picked up his brush and, with deft flickers, captured Drake's features in the centre of the skin.

"I'll try and get as much done whilst the light is good."

Drake nodded and made himself comfortable.

"It's much like being in a crow's nest up here, Nicholas, except instead of nothing but sea, you have a good view of your neighbour's roof and the fields beyond."

Nicholas smiled. This was not the first time the view from these windows had been commented on, but it was the first time it had been likened to a ship's crow's nest.

"It's not often I'm able to paint in winter. The light usually isn't good enough and more often than not, the smoke and smuts make it worse; we're lucky today as the wind is blowing the smog all south so Kent will be getting the benefit of the stink of the City."

"At least that's one benefit of being at sea. All the muck and shit goes overboard. If the cargo's human, then the boat stinks because you can't let 'em above decks in case they try 'n jump o'er board. You ever seen a black man, Nicholas?"

Nicholas shook his head. He had heard how fortunes were being made shipping black people as slaves from Africa to the New World.

"You being an artist an' that, you'd find the colour of their skin fascinating. We call 'em black, but their skin is all colours from dark, nearly blue black, through to a lighter brown, depending on where the traders 'ave caught 'em. You can tell those with Arab blood as they have fine features and almond shaped eyes and the women are quite beautiful."

Nicholas smiled as he continued to capture Drake's features on the small vellum.

"Bit difficult for me to comment, Captain, never having seen a black man."

"Quite so, Nicholas. However, if you ever get the chance to examine one of 'em, you take it. They are fascinating. However, on a different subject. I'm giving a banquet for her Majesty, at Deptford on my ship the Hind, in April for those who invested in my last voyage. What do you think would please the queen by way of a gift?"

Nicholas thought a minute. "Do you wish to make a statement?"

Drake smiled. "Nicholas, I would. Something that would please the queen mightily."

"Perhaps you might like to add to her menagerie?"

Drake paused. He may have been out of the country for some years, but he had quickly picked up the politics at Court.

"I'll leave it to you, but do you have som'at in mind?"

"Francis, what about a gold frog. I can use the sword hilt perhaps, and the various loose diamonds can then be set within the frog's back."

"Nick, that sounds perfect. Spanish plunder made up as a French Frog that will hop to the Queen's command." Drake threw back his head and roared with laughter at his own joke, "Nicholas, I like it. But I need it for the banquet."

"No matter, Francis. It will be done."

"And what else? I can't just give her a frog!"

"Perhaps a map of your travels."

"Now that I can do, and perhaps a Spanish silver coffer for her to keep 'em in, too." Drake paused. "Now what do you think of my idea for this banquet? Don't you think it'll give us a chance to show those foreign ambassadors just how they should enjoy themselves. Perhaps Philip might like to come 'n see just 'ow I'm spending some of his gold!"

Nicholas chuckled at Drake's political pokes at the various European Courts, particularly Philip II's. By all accounts, the Spanish court was not a jolly place.

Nicholas continued working on Drake's portrait until the light began to fade, keeping up a light banter about the proposed banquet and occasionally making a suggestion for the entertainment Drake was planning. A tinkle of bells, a pause and a soft knock followed by an immediate opening of the door indicated that the knock was a cursory warning, rather than a request.

"You two men have been up here all day and now it's time for a meal. Perhaps you would like to come and join us now the light has gone?" This was a statement of what Alice expected them to do, as opposed to an invitation. The two men followed her meekly downstairs. By now Drake knew the household routine and took his accustomed place at the table.

"Mistress Hillyarde, as ever, your table does you proud 'n I would like to 'ave the opportunity to repay some of your benevolent 'ospitality."

Alice smiled at her guest, but the smile did not quite reach her eyes. "Thank you Captain Drake. It is always a pleasure to have you here and to listen to the stories of your adventures."

Nicholas threw his wife a warning glance. He knew her statement was in direct contrast to what she thought. At first she had been flattered by Drake's presence but now it irritated her because he disrupted the whole household. She was always complaining that his outlandish tales about savage Indians and gruesome fights with the Spanish gave the children nightmares, but she also thought that his stories were probably the result of too many days at sea, with only his crew for company, because they sounded so implausible. However, for now she kept these thoughts to herself.

During a pause in the conversation Drake addressed Alice directly.

"Mistress Hillyarde, I would deem it a great honour if you would grace the banquet I am giving for the Queen, on board my ship the Golden Hind at Deptford on the fourth of April?"

"Oh, Captain Drake ...." She stammered. The unexpected invitation rendered her speechless. Alice blushed, remembering all her acid comments about Drake's adventures. This invitation would more than repay the hospitality he had enjoyed in her house and go a long way to repairing her opinion of Drake's character.

"Francis," Nicholas was amused by his wife's embarrassment "I think you have rendered my wife unusually mute, so I shall thank you, on her behalf, and say how we very much look forward to attending."

April

Just after Drake had announced his banquet, Elizabeth had summoned Nicholas for a private audience and since then he had been hard at work on a very special, very secret commission. His brief was to symbolise the thankfulness of a grateful nation. He had come across some carved cameos and one, in particular, had caught his eye.

The Drake jewel, as he called it, now sat on his work top next to the very realistic diamond encrusted solid gold frog made out of Spanish gold that Drake intended to present to Elizabeth.

Nicholas took a square velvet lined box from a shelf. The velvet was a particularly fine dark green and it was as if the frog sat in a mossy hollow. The diamonds were perfectly matched and two emeralds stared back as eyes. Black enamelling mimicked the natural markings on the frog's back and, despite the encrustation of gems, the piece was very lifelike.

His workshop had made a special silk and velvet lined case for the Drake jewel. The colour of the fabric was deliberately chosen to represent the sea and Nicholas laid the exquisite jewel on the dark blue velvet.

He chuckled as he looked at these two exquisite pieces of his design. He had thoroughly enjoyed the conspiracy surrounding the whole saga of these commissions. After giving them each a final polish, he slipped the box with the Drake jewel inside his doublet for safety and left to deliver it to the Palace.

Later that day, Nicholas and Alice presented themselves early at Deptford and were now standing in line, waiting to board the Golden Hind.

"Nick, it's so small. How on earth did Francis manage all that adventuring in something the size of an oversized bucket?"

"It may be small, but if you remember all the tales, it is sufficiently efficient to do much damage to Philip's ships. Perhaps small means faster or, maybe, easier to handle."

They made their way to where Drake was waiting to receive his guests.

"My, Mistress Hillyarde, you look most beautiful tonight. You do your husband proud."

Alice blushed at Drake's compliment. She had managed to persuade Nicholas she needed a new gown for this occasion because, she had argued, she deserved something new for presenting him with a second son. Her diamond earrings matched the glorious new ring that glittered on her finger.

"And Nicholas, I trust you 'ave hopped aboard with my surprise?"

"Indeed, Francis," Nicholas bowed slightly and presented the square box from with an open lid. The gold frog gazed up at the three of them.

"Mistress Alice, your husband is a truly gifted man." Drake turned to Nicholas. "Is this made from that sword hilt perhaps?"

"Indeed it is. I thought you would like the irony of a Spanish sword hilt becoming a French Frog!"

Drake chuckled. "That is something that won't be lost on Mendoza either! Perhaps we should let it be known that the gold came from the capture of their "Cacafuego"?"

"Wasn't that the ship you captured in the Pacific." Alice asked.

"Mistress Alice, indeed it was. Nothing would give me more pleasure than for the King of Spain to know of the good use to which we have put his treasure. Now forgive me, I must put this somewhere safe until later." Drake left them standing on deck watching the various guests make their way towards the ship.

"Alice, do you get the feeling that Drake has a personal vendetta against Philip."

"And I thought his stories were all just eyewash!"

"Oh no. Walsingham has told me Philip has put a price of some 4,000 gold doubloons on Drake's head."

"No!" Alice's voice was shocked "that's a fortune."

"Large enough to encourage betrayal. However, Drake knows that he's quite safe from his crew. If any of his men went to claim the reward, Philip would deem them equally guilty and either imprison them, or more likely string 'em up as a deterrent, and they know that."

A flourish of trumpets announced the arrival of Sir Christopher Hatton.

"Sir Christopher, welcome aboard the Golden Hind." Drake bowed as Hatton came on deck.

"Francis, if King Philip could see the size of the Hind he would know you had God on your side. I had no idea she was as small as this!"

"Sir Christopher, she may be small, but then so are fleas and we all know how irritating they are." Drake was full of bonhomie and thoroughly enjoying welcoming his guests aboard his famous ship.

Alice tugged at her husband's sleeve to get his attention. "Nick, that gold frog - I had no idea you were so you were busy goldsmithing behind your locked doors."

"What did you think I was doing?"

Alice blushed, "I thought you might be painting yet another portrait of Elizabeth."

"Oh yes, that too." Nicholas grinned at her "but you'll have to wait and see. Come, let's find our places."

"Nick" Alice hooked her arm through her husband's. "I thought Drake went to see in a ship called The Pelican."

"He did, but renamed it the Golden Hind in honour of Hatton."

"Why?"

"Probably something to do with Hatton's investment in the voyage. Look Alice, there're the French and Spanish Ambassadors." Nick pointed to where the French Ambassador and the Spaniard, Bernardino De Mendoza, were pointedly ignoring each other as they made their way towards the gangplank. "And, I think that's Elizabeth in the distance."

Another flourish of trumpets heralded the Queen's imminent arrival, even though her entourage was still a good few hundred yards away. The crowd at the foot of the gangplank bustled forward in their haste to get aboard.

Drake had taken great pains in the planning of this banquet. The tables groaned under the weight of the elaborate plate and fantastic dishes set before them. Musicians entertained them all throughout the meal with new and favourite melodies. Drake had evidently abandoned some of the more exotic entertainments he and Nicholas had discussed, but there were jugglers, fire eaters, sword swallowers, and, as a finale, his crew dressed up as red Indians and danced what were described as dances performed by the Red Indians of the New World. Drake then regaled everyone with a long account of his adventures, most of which Nicholas and Alice had heard before.

Diplomatically, Drake refrained from telling the assembled

company how he had captured the galleon, La Nuestro Senora De la Concepcion, but instead told a tale about a ship he called the Cacafuego, which was so thinly disguised that no-one could fail to recognise it as the famous treasure ship. Alice and Nicholas found it highly amusing that the Spaniard was clearly failing to find anything even vaguely amusing in Drake's graphic description of the capture of this particular galleon.

After four hours of story telling, Drake presented Elizabeth with a map showing his travels around the world, paintings of all the exotic fish and animals he had seen and a silver coffer to keep them in. Finally he presented the queen with a wooden box carved all over with water lilies and leaves, which he opened to reveal the golden frog sitting squatting on green velvet. The Queen clapped her hands with delight.

"Nick" Alice pulled her husband's sleeve to get his attention. "Who's that over there, sitting next to the French Ambassador?"

Nicholas looked towards where Alice was pointing. A very good looking man with curled mustachios and a well trimmed pointed beard was talking animatedly with his neighbour.

"Is he a new member of the French embassy?" Alice asked.

"Not that I know of. There have been no new arrivals there to my knowledge. Besides, this is Drake's celebration so more likely to be someone he knows." A fanfare of trumpets interrupted anything further Nicholas might have said to his wife.

"My Lords Ladies and Gentlemen. The Queen."

Everyone stood as the Queen stood, and then sat and listened as she replied to Drake's loquacious speech. Unfortunately Nicholas and Alice could not hear clearly what she was saying, but they watched as she beckoned a page to come forward but they were too far away to hear what she asked him to do.

"Nick, what do you suppose she's going to do now?"

Drake and Elizabeth moved to the empty space where all could see them and then the French Ambassador joined them. Drake was looking very flushed as he knelt.

"Well," Nicholas smiled "Who'd've thought it. Sir Francis Drake. Either that or she's going to cut his head off!"

Alice giggled. "That would please Philip!"

The Queen unsheathed the gilded ceremonial sword, but instead of dubbing Drake's shoulder herself, invited the Frenchman to do so.

Nicholas chuckled. "Alice, she's a marvel."

"What do you mean?"

"Actions speak louder than words and that will really irritate Philip?"

Alice frowned, thinking hard "Oh, now that's really clever! His sworn enemy Drake being dubbed a knight of the English realm by the French ambassador. She's telling the world there is an English alliance with France."

"Look at Mendoza."

Alice looked across at the Spaniard whose furious scowl suggested a man who was more than irritated.

Drake remained kneeling and another page approached, this time with a velvet cushion. The Queen lifted and presented Nicholas's jewel as a token of her personal appreciation of his services to England.

"Oh, Nick. Did you make this?" Nicholas nodded, watching Drake's face as he opened the locket.

"I'll show you the drawings when we get home, but no doubt Francis will show you the real thing at some point."

"I'm so proud of you." He could feel his wife quivering with excitement.

"Alice," Nicholas paused for a moment "the whole of London will talk of this evening for a long time. Elizabeth made a very public statement tonight by knighting our friend. I think we could do our part to ensure that Mendoza learns that the frog is made of Spanish gold, don't you." Nicholas looked meaningfully at his wife. Alice blushed. Her forte was rooting out snippets of information, not planting them.

"Alice." His wife was nowhere to be found.

"Oh Mr Hillyarde, the mistress said to tell yer that she's gone to visit her sister and she'll be back later."

"Thank you Molly. Did she say how much later?"

"Well she's been gone an hour, so I don't suppose she'll be much longer."

"Thank you – where are the children? The house is incredibly quiet."

"Oh, they're with Cook who's making special fruitbread for them."

"Molly, what would we do without you and Cook."

Molly bobbed a curtsey and disappeared back to the kitchen and he retreated to his workshop to await his wife's return.

It was a further hour before Alice appeared, flushed from hurrying.

"Nick, do you remember that good looking stranger on The Hind?"

"You mean Walter Raleigh?"

"Bother – I thought I'd found out sooner than you!"

"It seems we have both been wondering who he was. What is more, he wants me to paint his portrait."

"Will he be coming here?"

"Alice, as much as you might want to meet Raleigh, trust me, I hear he's no angel. He might be very good looking, but he's quite arrogant; and no, he won't be coming here. I'm going

189

to paint him at the Palace. Evidently Elizabeth is very taken with him and he can't spare the time to visit here."

"If you ask me, all you handsome men are just the same! Here's something you might not know about Capt Raleigh, my dear husband, because it's not the sort of thing that interests you." Alice paused for dramatic effect. "Raleigh is related to Kat Ashley, so perhaps that's why the Queen wants him near her."

"Sorry, Alice, I don't follow your thinking."

"Kat Ashley – the one Elizabeth appointed her First Lady of the Bedchamber immediately she came to the throne? Kat Ashley who had been with her since childhood? You know how sentimental Elizabeth is about those who are loyal to her ..." Nicholas sat there looking at her blankly wondering what his wife was driving at.

Alice raised her eyes to heaven. "Oh, for heavens sake, Nick, he's a connection with someone whom she loved dearly!"

"Ah ... so you think it's more than just his looks that are so attractive to her?"

"You really don't understand women do you, husband mine?" Alice sighed. "I'll leave you to whatever it is you're doing. I've got work to do."

"Well, now that the French have gone, no doubt Elizabeth will be more her normal self, which means life can return to normal and with another mouth soon to feed, I hope those accounts for all the expensive tokens I made for her get settled!"

"Sometimes, Nick, you are just too soft."

"I know, Alice, but at least she does settle her bills even if she takes an age so to do."

"You know too well it's nothing to do with Elizabeth. You just don't shout loud enough at the right people!"

Nicholas swallowed his response. He should never have said anything about money. A row was brewing and he knew Alice was right, except she just did not seem to understand that it was not always easy to be book-keeper, designer, courtier and husband. Money just did not interest him in the same way it did her. It was the designing and the painting that gave him the reason to live. The thought that perhaps he should ask his wife to look after the ledgers after this baby was born was an idea which bore closer thought, but he had at least until March to think it over.

"Robert, this is far too serious to be handled within these walls. We'll have to inform her Majesty." It was not like Walsingham to raise his voice and since it clearly audible through the door, Nicholas wondered what it was that was causing all the rumpus.

"Elizabeth might not like the effect it has on our relationship with Spain, but the evidence is all too clear ......" Burghley's voice faded and Nicholas realised that he must have retreated further into the warren of rooms that made up his office. He counted slowly to 50 before opening the door; if he entered immediately those inside might realise he had been listening behind the door.

Robert Beale was Clerk to the Privy Council and weighty affairs of state were an everyday event for him, but he was holding his head in his hands and looked worried and exasperated. Hearing the door open, he looked up.

"Ah Mr Hillyarde. You are a welcome sight. Come, sit down and tell me something jolly." Beale sighed wearily, but appeared genuinely pleased at Nicholas's entry.

"I had hoped to have a few moments with Sir Francis" Nicholas asked. From the atmosphere in the room and the overhead conversation he had realised that this was probably out of the question, but there was no harm in asking. Besides it made it look as if he had no knowledge of Burghley's outburst.

191

"Today might not be the best." Beale explained. Nicholas raised his eyebrow, inviting Beale to continue his explanation. "I can tell you Mr Hillyarde as I know you're like a crab. It's not been an easy time of late."

"I assume you mean the rumours regarding yet another Catholic plot to kill the Queen?"

"Ah, is this why you wish to see Sir Francis?"

Nicholas nodded. "It is indeed."

The door to the inner sanctum opened and Lord Burghley turned and addressed the Secretary of State.

"Francis, Norton takes too much delight in his work. How can you tell me that the information he extracts is reliable." Nicholas recognised the name as that of the resident executioner and questioner at the Tower. Burghley was clearly unhappy about the man's methods of questioning.

"Ah Nicholas, I hope you have something with which to cheer us today?"

"Er, mayhap Lord Burghley. It concerns James Bell."

"Indeed. Perhaps you would like to come into my office, Nicholas." Sir Francis invited.

Burghley looked at both Robert Beale and Nicholas. "Sometimes," he sighed "God alone knows what I would give to be able to go and attend my roses! However, since He isn't communicating with any of us, I shall go and talk to the Queen."

The great man left and Nicholas followed Sir Francis into his office leaving Beale at his desk. Nicholas waited whilst the spymaster made himself comfortable.

"Sir Francis, James Bell is around and about in London. It may not be anything, but I saw him talking to one of Ambassador Castelnau's household just last night."

Sir Francis smiled and made a note of what Nicholas had told him, then waited for him to continue.

"I was on my way back from the Teerlinc warehouses when I saw him enter one of the ale houses. I followed him and saw him meet there with a Giordano Bruno, who is as you probably already know, one of the French Ambassador's household. They were talking Italian and Bell was telling Bruno that he had a message from France and that the Duc was expected to hear any day that their cause was to be blessed by heaven."

Sir Francis noted this down beside the previous note. "Go on."

"He told Bruno that he had recently returned from France, by way of Jersey and asked him to pass a letter to the Ambassador. At this point Bruno explained that he was just a house guest, but thought he might be able to give it to the Ambassador some how."

"Nicholas, did Bell seem to know Bruno well?"

"No, I don't think so. When he came into the inn he asked the landlord if anyone had been asking for him."

"Was Bruno already there?"

"No, he came in just a few minutes later, but he recognised Bell immediately."

"Hmmm." Sir Francis wrote all this down.

"And I have to say, Sir Francis, I've heard some scurrilous things about the French Ambassador."

"Go on."

"I had a lady come to have her portrait painted and she was fair fit to burst with gossip she had heard about the Ambassador."

Sir Francis smiled again. "Nicholas, I too have heard similar rumours. In fact I've received a letter from the good Ambassador who is fairly spluttering with indignation. I've no idea where these rumours started, but perhaps you would like to hear what he has to say?"

"The Ambassador is such a genial man that I find it difficult to believe such things of him, but sometimes appearances are deceptive." Nicholas had painted the man only a few months before. "However, he has kind eyes, which makes me think that this has to be some meddling mischief. Thank you, I would very much appreciate hearing what he has to say."

Sir Francis picked a letter off the top of a pile on his desk and handed it across the desk. Nicholas read the Ambassador's indignant outpourings:

"... *several in your court and throughout the kingdom who would like, in attacking my honour, to charge the French in general; have incited a good-for-nothing hussy of a woman to make wicked statements about me and of my actions, which are highly honourable and God-fearing.*

I have had her forbidden my house, not wishing to hear the thousand slanderous lies which she told everyone and in recompense, they take pleasure at your court and elsewhere in using her as a trumpeter to accuse all France under my name.

It seems to me that the least that can be done is to put a stop to these rumours and give the hussy the whip and pierce her tongue with a hot iron: first making her declare who had incited her and taken pleasure in making her utter such slanders, as she would not otherwise have done for the sake of the alms she has received at my house."

"The lady who told me all about the Ambassador says she has never been to his house, so she was clearly just repeating gossip. Interesting how the Ambassador is so indignant about what could just be idle tittle tattle."

"Indeed, Nicholas, I too thought as much."

Nicholas was flattered that Sir Francis had given him the letter to read.

"If I happen to come across Mr Bell, do you still want me to let you know?"

"Indeed so. This young man seems to pop up in interesting places. It may be nothing, but then again ….. " Sir Francis smiled at his visitor, leaving the sentence unfinished. He rose and accompanied Nicholas to the door. "These are trying times, Nicholas. If I'm not about at Whitehall, you can always come to Seething Lane."

Nicholas left feeling, as ever, slightly uncomfortable.

Walsingham sat reviewing the evidence so far. How long would it take his man Bruno to report his meeting with Mr Bell. Then there were the letters, intercepted by his Scottish spy, that the French Ambassador was sending to Scotland. The letters, addressed to Francois De Roncherolles, Seigneur De Mainville had been intercepted, read, noted and returned. De Mainville had accepted the apology for the delay in delivery only because the seals had appeared unbroken. Yet again Walsingham was grateful for the skill of Arthur Gregory, who could prise apart a seal and open a document, record the contents and return the document to its original state. These letters had yielded interesting information, and by delivering them to their intended recipient, Walsingham was waiting to see what happened next.

There was some evidence pointing to the French Embassy being the centre of a plot concerning Mary Stuart, but Walsingham was convinced that Spain was also involved. In order to implicate the Scottish Queen and the Spanish Ambassador he would need specific evidence.

A knock disturbed the spymaster's thoughts and a page entered and delivered a sealed wafer. Walsingham waited until the door closed before slipping a thin, sharp blade under the wax. The seal remained unbroken, but the surface of the paper showed where the wax had stuck. It was a small vanity to try and see if he could do it as well as Gregory, but so far, he had never managed to reseal anything to its original condition.

As he unfolded the paper he recognised the astrological sign for Jupiter which confirmed this note was from his spy,

Bruno. The note was written in French and Bruno was reporting that the ambassador had received a letter from the Duc De Guise encouraging him to continue his endeavours on behalf of Mary Stuart and that the Ambassador had recently sent the Scottish Queen 1500 écus sol. More interestingly, the spy told that Francis Throgmorton had dined at the Ambassador's house the previous night.

Walsingham leaned back and sighed. At last, here was something concrete. This must be the letter Bell had carried from France. Walsingham was glad his old friend Nicholas Throgmorton was not alive to see his nephew prepared to commit treason.

November

"'Morning Mr Beale. I hear it rumoured arrests are imminent."

"It's more than rumours, Nicholas." Robert Beale stated. "Francis Throgmorton has been arrested and is now being questioned in the Tower."

Nicholas swallowed in fear, his imagination producing images of various instruments being wielded to extract information from the luckless man. Thomas Norton was the queen's questioner and his reputation was so frightening that Alice used his name as a threat to keep the children well behaved. Nicholas hoped Throgmorton would be sensible and tell the man whatever it was Walsingham wanted to know before the questioner became too involved in his work.

"You would have hoped that England would have had enough of religious persecution. It's not as if Elizabeth is so religiously radical, more's the pity!" Beale continued. "Why is it that Spain and France always want to return us to Rome? Perhaps if we caught and executed a few more priests, it'd discourage others to dabble in Catholicism. Elizabeth is far too liberal in turning a blind eye to what these recusants are up to."

"I totally agree with you and I hope this ends soon. The rumours are endless and I hear nothing but suggestions of who might be turning back to the old religion."

Beale sighed, leant back and looked at the ceiling. "I believe we will hear that young Throgmorton is involved in a plot to return England to Catholicism, but that won't be all." He sighed "We can't prove it yet, but we think the King of Spain is using Mendoza to channel money through to the Scottish Queen."

Nicholas was aghast.

"You got all this by tort..., sorry, I mean questioning?"

"It appears you've read my paper against the use of torture. I think it's no way to find out information. However, Walsingham has insisted that the boy be put to the questioner, despite finding letters and papers in Throgmorton's rooms showing plans and harbours, and lists of Catholic noblemen who can be relied upon in the event of an invasion. And , what is more, we netted Lord Henry Howard as a co-conspirator at the same time."

Nicholas sat down, horrified. He had painted Henry Howard's portrait only a few months earlier. Before he could fully digest Beale's story, the door flew open and a messenger burst in running and breathless.

"Sirs, I've an urgent message for Sir Francis from Mr Norton."

Beale shot Nicholas a knowing glance.

"Thank you lad. I'll give it to Sir Francis."

"I'm sorry Mr Beale, but Mr Norton was very specific. This is for Sir Francis's eyes only." The man was not going to hand over the envelope. Beale nodded.

"Hold here." Beale got up, knocked on the inner door and disappeared inside. Hillyarde remained seated.

The inner door re-opened and Sir Francis appeared, just ahead of Lord Burghley.

The messenger recognised the spymaster immediately and handed him the envelope. Sir Francis tore open the seal and scanned the contents. A look of sheer delight shone from his face as he handed the parchment to Lord Burghley.

"You may not agree with these methods, Mr Beale, but I've seen as resolute men as Throgmorton stoop, notwithstanding the great show he has made of Roman resolution. On the second racking he has told us all."

"So much for dying a thousand deaths rather than accuse anyone." Burghley commented scathingly.

Sir Francis dismissed the messenger with thanks and some coin and turned to Nicholas.

"Nicholas, I think you should know that we believe your Mr Bell has links with the Duc of Guise. We have not picked him up as he is only a small fish and may yet prove useful."

"So I wasn't just imagining his duplicity?"

"No, but as yet we have no hard evidence to be able to arrest him so if you do see him, let me know." The spymaster smiled. Whilst the information Nicholas passed on was often simple gossip, in this instance it had proved important.

"Throgmorton has confessed that in a letter it was told that the Duc De Guise was to lead an invasion landing at Arundel, they would then link up with various faithful families and progress north to liberate Mary Stuart, kill Elizabeth and place a Catholic queen on the throne and so England would be returned to Rome. This plot should have been well underway by now, but evidently the Pope and Philip have not yet furnished funds."

"So, how do you believe Bell is connected with Throgmorton?"

"Nicholas" It was Lord Burghley's turn to speak. "It's quite likely Bell is a courier. We would, however, like you to continue watching for him. At the moment he's disappeared, but we are sure he'll appear again. People like him always do."

"Certainly Lord Burghley. However, how do you deal with someone like an Ambassador?"

"Ah. That will happen in due course. First we have to make sure justice is done and deter others from similar thoughts." Walsingham was the one to reply. His words carried a menace that chilled Nicholas to the bone. The deterrents Walsingham might consider suitable were not ones he wanted to think about too closely.

1584

January

"Mr Hillyarde, so good to see you. It's been a rather exhausting week, what with the Privy Council meeting and everything." Robert Beale was delighted to have a visitor and even more pleased to find it was his friend.

"So I understand, Robert. I've heard the Spanish Ambassador has decided to return to Madrid."

"Indeed, but I have to tell you, it was not of his choosing."

Nicholas raised his eyebrows in surprise. "The rumours are that Mendoza is sick of the English weather and suffering from such aches and pains that he has decided to return to Spain for some much needed warmth."

"Oh no, nothing of the kind. That sounds like Spanish propaganda. It was so dramatic I think you should hear it just as it happened." Nicholas settled himself comfortably in the chair opposite Beale. "Just two days ago, the Privy Council assembled at the London home of Sir Thomas Bromley. Sir Francis sat waiting quietly, holding what appeared to be a single piece of paper. You could tell he was looking forward to the events of the afternoon because he wore that smile we only ever see when he has a trap about to snap shut on some unsuspecting victim. His fellow Privy Councillors obviously had no idea what was about to happen and sat in silence all looking very grim. Walsingham had told them that he wanted this special meeting of the Council in order for the Spanish Ambassador to answer some serious allegations. Anyway, Mendoza was late. Eventually we heard a commotion in the hall and he was shown into the room with much Spanish huffing and puffing about how he was being treated. No chair was offered and Mendoza had to stand there like a naughty boy."

Nicholas laughed. He could imagine the arrogant Spaniard standing, hands on hip, getting more and more irritated as he waited to be offered the usual courtesies.

"So what happened?" His friend was clearly enjoying relating Mendoza's discomfiture.

"Walsingham stood up, picked up the piece of paper in front of him, turned it over and read it to the Spaniard"

"Well, don't keep me in suspense. What had Mendoza done?"

"Walsingham looked at Mendoza and accused him, straight out, of plotting against the Queen."

Nicholas was stunned. "That was a tall accusation and he must have had some solid evidence for this, so what did Sir Francis actually say?"

"Don Bernardino" Beale put on his most theatrical look as he pretended to be Sir Francis "you have had secret intelligence with the Scots Queen. You have conspired with certain of her majesty's subjects for her delivery. Further, you have sought the Catholics in this realm to join with foreign forces if the Catholic Princes should send any. You have put them in comfort that the King of Spain would assist them and contribute half the charges."

"So I take it Sir Francis accused Mendoza of being the hub of the plot and of promising Spanish money?" Nicholas was amazed.

" Yes, and there's more. He went on – 'You were aware of the coming into this realm of one Charles Paget, a known fugitive and servant of the Scots Queen, who was sent to discover loyal Catholics and to list ports and landing places.' At which point Mendoza spluttered incomprehensibly and his face turned purple with rage."

"I've never seen the man lose his temper, but I can imagine he would be nasty when roused. If it were me, I would be furious to be accused like that in front of others. But so far this is just speculation."

"Too true. " Beale agreed "He spluttered about how this was outrageous and how dare Sir Francis accuse him without evidence, demanding that the Secretary of State prove his implication in the plot or withdraw these groundless accusations."

"I can imagine Walsingham wouldn't have accused him without solid evidence. So how did he close the net."

"Quite so. Walsingham paused and when Mendoza had ceased spluttering he continued. 'And further,' – pausing a moment more, making the Spaniard even more uncomfortable 'you have received a green velvet casket containing the plans and papers of these conspiracies.…" Beale paused for his own dramatic dénouement "sent to you by Francis Throgmorton."

Nicholas raised his eyebrow. "That was quite an accusation."

"Exactly. The look Mendoza gave the Secretary of State was one of pure hatred. He knew he was caught. If Walsingham knew of the casket then he knew of the plot, so why deny it. He turned and declared ' I, Don Bernardino De Mendoza, was born not to disturb kings, but to conquer them."

"I suppose, being an ambassador, Sir Francis can't put him in the Tower, as much as he might like to. So, Robert, did Walsingham tell him to get out of England?"

"Exactly that. He said 'In which case, Senor Mendoza, the queen, preferring your room to your company, graciously gives you fifteen days to depart this realm.', which is the real reason why Mendoza is packing up and going back to Madrid."

"So what's going to happen to the others?"

" Throgmorton will hang at some point, if only to be a lesson to others who might be plotting against the Queen. But, with Mendoza gone and Throgmorton and Howard in the Tower, all the small fish will have swum to deeper water to hide."

"Well Robert, if I see Mr Bell I'll be telling Sir Francis. He may only be a courier, but who knows what he's carrying."

"You are just as much a part of Sir Francis's information service as his other spies. Only by putting little bits of information together can we have a hope of protecting the Queen."

Nicholas was very pleased that his information had been instrumental in exposing this plot and returned home, glad the Queen was safe.

May

The sun danced on the wavelets of the rising river Thames and Nicholas stood reflecting on how he might paint the continuous rippling shadow and sparkle of the water. The flickering of the constantly moving water teased and challenged; it would be a great artistic feat to capture that ephemeral interplay of light and dark. However, mastering this would be pointless because there was no-one who would appreciate the technical difficulty of capturing this glittering effect. The English did not appreciate portrayals of classical legends nor did they appear to want paintings showing London or the countryside; they only wanted their own portraits telling the world how wealthy and successful they were. He almost yearned for the French palaces all decorated with their great paintings of classical myths. These paintings showed people having fun. Satyrs, centaurs, cherubs and naked people danced across walls and ceilings encouraging the audience to join them in their revels. These were great celebrations of life.

The religious paintings were not to his taste, but they would brighten up the inside of many of the English churches, now all painted white with lime wash. If the walls of the Church of St Vedast were decorated it might stop him day dreaming during the Sunday service and would certainly keep his young rabble occupied whilst the minister droned his interminable sermons.

Nicholas sighed. All his patrons ever wanted were portraits of themselves, their lovers, their brothers, sisters, spouses or of her Glorious Majesty. Her likeness was so much in demand he could now paint it without ever having to refer to his sketchbooks. The Court gossips told anyone who would listen, how he could portray her likeness in four lines, which was not strictly true, but added to the glamour surrounding his talent. This sort of myth was good for business since everyone wanted to be able to boast to their friends that they owned a Hillyarde miniature. There were other painters who were almost as good, but none were allowed near the Queen. Nicholas sighed, if only Elizabeth would sign the patent giving him the sole right to portray her image 'in little' He knew his large paintings were not as good as George Gower's, but then George did not paint miniatures and it was these the Queen liked best.

Nicholas stood thinking about his first tiny portrait of her and then how she had demanded two larger portraits. Levina had explained how Elizabeth, as a divinely appointed queen, was like the phoenix in having a singular existence. Elizabeth had worn such a wistful expression during their sittings for both these paintings it set him wondering, not for the first time, if she regretted her decision of never marrying and having children. It was a bit late now, because, no matter what the doctors said, at fifty one, the Queen was way past childbearing age so it was very unlikely she would ever marry the D'Alençon, despite her protestations of doing so.

Nicholas shuddered. If the late Queen Mary had given birth to a child, England would now be part of the Hapsburg Empire and presumably a vassal state of Spain. Would this child have become King or Queen of England and of all the Spanish territories? Or would he or she been a puppet monarch raising taxes from the English people to pay tribute to Spain? These were very depressing thoughts so Nicholas returned to his contemplation of Elizabeth.

Nicholas was glad he had been able to paint the Queen when she was still in her in her prime, but now her looks were fading. The Royal Jewels were as famous as Elizabeth's red hair and virginity, and it was these that had provided his inspiration for his latest portraits. He often consulted Levina's little manual and, using her section on how to portray precious stones, had devised a way to paint Elizabeth's jewels and pearls in such a way they appeared real. He painted dots of coloured resin over burnished dots of silver leaf and, because they were ever so slightly raised, they glittered as they caught the light. Sometimes he painted her with flowing red hair as a symbol of her virginity, or as Cynthia, virgin goddess of the moon with a crescent moon jewel in her hair. Her portraits now appeared ageless and Gower and all the other artists were following his lead.

Nicholas had made and designed a great many of her jewels, but Richard Brandon's workshop had made even more and, as a tribute to his father-in-law, it was always these he portrayed in his portraits of the queen. Thoughts of his father-in-law saddened him. There had been a huge row over money only a few days before, and Brandon had threatened to change his Will. Nicholas did not believe his father-in-law would disinherit his daughter and he hoped that he could mend this rift.

However, Brandon was a man who did not make threats lightly. It distressed him that things had become so strained between them. His father-in-law did not seem to understand how difficult it was to keep up appearances, especially with Alice's expensive tastes and a large family all wanting clothes, food and attention.

Nicholas pondered his various ill advised investments that had lost a lot of money, and worse, there was the list of bad debts that never seemed to get any shorter. It was difficult to refuse members of the Court. Many of them he looked on as friends and he found it difficult to tell a friend 'no' and ask that they settle their debts first before running up new ones.

On the positive side, this year was proving especially good for commissions. Elizabeth had asked him to devise a new Great Seal. It was a great honour, but it would involve some considerable personal investment until the design was finally approved, engraved and finished. His work would be the final stamp on all important state papers and treaties. It was a tremendous honour, but why was it that these great commissions meant he had to fund the whole enterprise until it was finished. It would be so much easier if he was given a budget or some idea of when he would be paid. A monthly budget would make life so much easier, but he knew this would never happen.

Levina had designed the last Great Seal but she had been retained by Elizabeth and paid an annuity of £40 a year. The design of Elizabeth's first Great Seal had been part of her duties. It was a privilege to be given such a commission but he knew it would take months before he saw any money. Surely, Brandon of all people, should understand the financial problems associated with these royal commissions. At least Sir Walter Mildmay had been pleased with the illuminated E on the charter founding the new Emmanuel College at Cambridge.

Lost deep in musing on light, money, family relationships and how the Queen always seemed to want him to subsidise her

State image, Nicholas did not see the young man walking purposefully towards him.

"Mr Hillyarde. A moment if you please." Hearing his name, Nicholas turned, waited until the stranger reached him then nodded his head in acknowledgement.

"I beg your pardon for interrupting your walk, but your wife said I would find you here." the stranger continued. Nicholas smiled. Alice knew how he would walk by the Thames when he had something to think over. The bustle of the river and the keening of the seagulls seemed to sooth any troubled thoughts.

"Indeed. What can I do for you?" Nicholas asked.

The young man was quite tall, with sandy hair and beard, oval face and wide hazel eyes. His hair curled round his ears, but was neatly trimmed. The eyes were quite innocent, without lines of worry, or even laughter. Nicholas thought he must be about twenty two or three years old, old enough to grow a beard, but with a face not yet marked by life's joys, trials and tribulations. His clothes were expensively cut and his cloak lined with fur.

"Forgive me for seeking you out like this, but I'm in a hurry and cannot afford the time to come back another day."

Nicholas smiled. This busy young man was not prepared to wait half an hour until he returned home.

"And also, talking to you out in the open is so much better than behind doors, where walls may have ears."

"If secrecy is your priority sir, then the open air is not as good a place as one might think, because anyone may see you talking to me." Nicholas responded.

"I don't mind who sees us together, but I do not wish them to hear our conversation," the stranger explained.

Nicholas was intrigued. Was this a man with a dangerous secret, or perhaps it was something he felt guilty about. Nicholas was the keeper of so many secrets that another would not make any difference.

"I would like you to paint my likeness in little."

Nicholas raised his eyebrows slightly. This was, after all, what he was famous for, but so far it did not explain either the subterfuge or why the man had sought him out with such an emphasis on speed.

"You say you are in a hurry?" Nicholas pushed.

"Yes, I am to go abroad within a week and I would like it to be finished before I go. Is this possible?"

"It is, but I have much work at present." Nicholas did not want to appear too eager. If the man were in that much of a hurry, he felt he could raise his usual price and cover some of his more pressing domestic requirements.

"I am aware that this is short notice, but I would be willing to pay more than your usual fee. I would have come to you earlier except my journey has arisen unexpectedly and it may be many years before I return."

There was something vaguely familiar about the man, but Nicholas could not put his finger on what it was.

"Come, sir. It appears we have no time to lose. If we return to my house, we can catch the best of the daylight and perhaps I can capture the first likeness. However, it is unfair that you know my name, but I know not yours."

"Arthur Southron at your service, Mr Hillyarde." Arthur Southron bowed and Nicholas bowed slightly at the waist in return, none the wiser as to why this man's features seemed familiar.

They walked back to The Maydenhead where Nicholas first inspected the setting of cabochon garnets into a gold ring. The russet red stones rested in their settings like drops of blood.

Nicholas led his guest through the ground floor workshop and up the steep winding stairs. As they stepped on to the top landing, bells tinkled softly behind the workroom door.

"As you can hear, Mr Southron, I like my sitters to feel relaxed whilst I paint them. No one can come up here without coming through either the shop or the house. The bells are connected to thin wires on the bottom of the boards. When anyone steps on them, the bells ring and I know someone is three steps from the top. Come, sit down and make yourself comfortable."

Mr Southron divested himself of his cloak and examined the views over the City and the countryside beyond; these were interrupted by several rows of chimneys whose smoke was being blown towards the river. A bench in front of this window was neatly filled with rows of pots of clean brushes, racks of glass phials containing powdered pigments and small stacks of vellum rectangles approximately three inches square. A large flat scallop shell served as a palette and there were a row of mussel shells containing different colours. Pots of dirty and clean water sat at the right hand side of a small desk easel and there was a tall stool for Nicholas to sit on. A fire was laid in the grate just waiting for a spark to catch the kindling.

"Mr Hillyarde, this may be a strange request, but I would like you to paint me holding a lady's hand issuing from a cloud."

"The most important part is, of course, the face but much can also be conveyed by gesture, symbol or motto. I will need to do some sketches to get the gesture correct."

The young man nodded.

"Mr Southron, would you like some refreshment? Some honey cakes and mead, perhaps?" Nicholas raised his eyebrows in enquiry as he asked his guest about refreshments.

"That would be most kind, thank you." Arthur got up and placed a cushion on the wooden seat to relieve the hardness. He had been warned that sitting for his portrait would take some time and was determined to make himself as comfortable as possible. Nicholas reached for a handle near the door and pulled hard. In the distance another bell could be heard, followed shortly by someone running up the stairs. The bells tinkled, then there was a brief pause before the person knocked on the door.

"Come."

Panting after her exertion of running up the four flights of stairs, Molly entered and stood awaiting instructions.

"Honey cakes, mead and some of my usual, Molly." Nicholas turned back to Arthur. Molly nodded, sighed and mumbled, 'yes sir'.

"I wish I could have some sort of device so I could talk directly to the kitchen. The poor girl has better things to do than run up and down stairs for me." Nicholas said by way of making light conversation.

He chose a vellum from the stack on his work bench. This pre-preparation cut down the time for painting and, as time was of the essence in this instance, he was going to need as much time as possible to devote to the finer details. Androgynous outlines of shoulders and body waited to be filled with detail. He had chosen this vellum because the pale pink void was very close in colour to his sitter's pale complexion.

Nicholas made several sketches of the man's face in his workbook and practised getting a consistent likeness before committing anything to the vellum surface. He worked away sketching from different angles, then took the plunge and started on the final image.

He waited for his guest to talk. They always did. There was no point in pressing anyone to make conversation. It simply put people on their guard and looked as if he were fishing for information. Experience had taught him that silence was a large hole that people needed to fill. Personally, he preferred it because he could concentrate and get on with the job in hand. This had been born out when he had painted the indomitable

Lady Shrewsbury who had said virtually nothing, and so his painting time had taken a third of the usual time. His clients sometimes filled the well of silence by confiding some guilty secret, which, more often than not, was that they were having an illicit love affair and this portrait was to be a secret love token.

Nicholas sat behind a little desk about six feet in front of his guest. A large expensive Venetian glass mirror hung on the back wall reflecting natural light back into the room and the walls were painted white, reflecting more light and creating a light and airy space. The sky was hazy enough to take the sharpness out of the May sunlight and was perfect to work by. Shelves filled one wall, with books and stacks of paper loosely bound together with interesting objects weighting them down or resting next to them. The books were Nicholas's early sketch books and those he had inherited from Levina. Amongst the objects was a small armillary sphere, some unusually shaped stones, three exotic sea shells and a small framed miniature of a man wearing a hat and a fur trimmed coat. He had a curly, greying beard.

A stack of dry logs was piled neatly against the wall under the shelves and a leather bucket was filled with coal. A low footstool sat to one side of the fireplace next to a chair.

Mr Southron liked the room. He felt privileged that he had been allowed into the private recesses of the great Hillyarde and began to relax. The bells tinkled again. Neither man had heard Molly's soft footsteps as she climbed the stairs, providing a first hand demonstration of Nicholas's alarm system. Mr Southron thought it very fine as he realised it gave the occupants of the room just enough time to change their conversation or, he thought mischievously, perhaps adjust their clothing. He dismissed this thought virtually as soon as it popped into his head since Hillyarde's reputation was one of absolute discretion.

The door opened and Molly entered carrying a wooden tray holding a silver ewer, two silver tankards and a painted clay jug and earthenware plate with warm honey cakes tucked into the fold of a linen napkin. She poured the mead into one of the tankards and brought it across to the young man. He accepted a honey cake from the proffered plate. Both were excellent. After pouring Nicholas his mint infusion and leaving it on the desk, Molly slipped out of the door. She knew better than to try and stay if Nicholas were painting, but sometimes he would show her a design for a piece of jewellery. She liked it when he did this because it made her feel privileged.

Nicholas sipped his mint infusion as he worked, waiting for his sitter to make some conversation; at last Mr Southron relaxed enough to speak.

"Mr Hillyarde, I am grateful you are able to accommodate my request so soon."

"Mr Southron, you appeared anxious to have this done as soon as possible and you have an interesting face."

The man looked out of the window and Nicholas waited for his response, continuing to block out the details of Arthur's face on to the vellum. He sensed the young man was weighing up what to say to him.

"I'm off to Europe, as I think I told you."

Nicholas waited for the young man to continue, but the silence grew.

"I spent some time in Europe when I was a boy," Nicholas responded at length.

"Oh, where?"

"Geneva mainly. It was very mountainous and very cold in winter. Then later I spent two years in Paris, painting members of the French Court."

The man smiled. "At least the mountains and snow would be beautiful to look at, but I'm going to the Low Countries which will probably be grey with rain and fog and so very dismal."

212

"Ah well then, you won't feel as if you are too far from home!" Nicholas grinned.

Both men laughed.

Nicholas stopped blocking out the details of the face on the vellum and, on a new sheet in his sketch book, started making notes of the colour of Arthur's eyes, hair and clothes. He knew the best way of fulfilling his sitter's request was to get him to relax and to do this, he must concentrate on the matter in hand and not pry.

"Please can you raise your right arm, as if holding a hand from above."

Arthur complied and Nicholas sketched for some minutes, trying hard to make the pose work.

"Somehow this pose just doesn't look natural.. Would you mind if I asked my wife to join us and she can be your hand from the sky. Once we get the pose then we can deal with the hands, but just at the moment…." Nicholas let the sentence drift into silence.

"What do you mean?" the young man frowned, lowering his arm.

"Come and have a look" Nicholas invited and his sitter stood up. Arthur's knees clicked; the result of sitting still for a long time. Nicholas's sketches were scattered across the desk.

"So you think it would help if I held your wife's hand?" he suggested as he stood looking at the various sketches Nicholas had drawn. The way the two hands interlinked was interesting, but did not seem to be very realistic.

"Exactly. She won't mind. I just hope she isn't busy, otherwise she'll be bad tempered." Nicholas confided.

"Well, if you think it would be of help, and you don't mind me holding your wife's hand, then why not?"

Nicholas was drawn to this young man. There was something about him which was attractive, but he had no idea

213

what it was or why he found it so. He leant across and pulled on the bell handle once again. A few minutes later Molly again puffed her way up the final flight of stairs and was asked to tell Mistress Hillyarde that she was required in the studio.

"Mister 'illyard, Mistress Alice is out." Molly puffed.

"Well Molly, can you spare an hour? I need someone to stand and hold Mr Southron's hand, whilst I draw it."

"Oh my!" Molly gasped, blushing to her roots, rushed out of the room and down the stairs as if the devil were after her.

Nicholas shook his head. "Sometimes I think this is a mad house. I've never asked Molly to do anything before. I didn't think she would react like this – I'm sorry."

"The price of fame, Mr Hillyarde or may I call you Nicholas? Please call me Arthur. A girl like Molly will be forever immortalised by having her hand used in one of your little paintings."

"Now that is something I hadn't thought of. Thank you, Arthur." The use of first names made their relationship more relaxed. From experience Nicholas knew this would show in his work. He also made a note in his sketchbook to thank Molly for posing.

The two men stood and Arthur stretched, finding some relief from the position he had maintained for the last couple of hours. Nicholas thought the composition needed something else, but he was not sure what it was. Arthur had placed his hat and cape on a stool and the cocky white feather trim stuck in the hat band caught Nicholas's eye.

"Why not wear your hat?" he suggested to Arthur. "It is the latest fashion and the grey compliments your eyes."

Arthur liked that idea. He had spent a great deal of money on his wardrobe and this hat was his favourite.

A few minutes later a very red faced and puffed out Molly re-appeared.

"Sorry Mr Hillyarde, oi just 'ad to make sure that the kitchen were all right to leave, 'n that cook didn't need me. I told 'er you needed me and she said you could 'ave me for one hour, but after that you 'ad to explain it to't mistress."

Nicholas smiled. Cook was the lynchpin of the household and key to the house running smoothly.

"I'll do my best to get finished in the hour, Molly, but if it takes longer, then it takes longer."

Later that night as the house was settling down for the night, the timbers creaked and the occasional snore could be heard coming from the apprentices. Nicholas and Alice lay in their big four poster bed with the curtains drawn tightly around them. Alice ensured that the pillows were always beautifully fluffy and had soft linen covers on them. The feather mattress was shaken regularly and so was very comfortable. Sheets of fine linen under thick blankets of good English wool kept them warm and when it was really cold, a throw of rabbit skins kept them as warm as toast. Alice snuggled into Nicholas's shoulder and he held her close. He wound a strand of her blonde hair through his fingers.

"Did you see my client at all, Alice?" he asked.

"Don't be silly. I was busy all day, especially since you pinched Molly for your 'hand from the sky' portrait." Alice poked him playfully. "Sometimes, husband mine, you don't seem to understand that this house doesn't run itself. If you want me to meet this mystery man, why not ask him to stay for dinner, or would that be too familiar?"

Nicholas lay winding Alice's hair through his fingers. He loved the silken feel of it and how it always smelled of rosemary or camomile. After some time he replied.

"Yes," he paused, "that would be good. In fact, that would be splendid. He seems quite a lonely man to me."

Arthur presented himself very early the next day. Alice had ensured there were pitchers of Nicholas's mint infusion and mead, some more honey cakes as well as some oatcakes, Devon cheese and some very early fresh strawberries for their refreshment during the day so the two men would be completely undisturbed.

After a while Nicholas broke the silence.

"Would you like to stay for today's meal, Arthur? I want to take advantage of the light while it lasts, which means today is going to be a very long one."

"Thank you that would be most welcome." came Arthur's reply.

Nicholas pulled the cord, Molly appeared and was told of the extra guest.

"Yes Mr 'illyarde, Mistress Alice said that you'd be asking Mr Southron to stay for dinner and also to tell you that she is up to her elbows in flour at the moment."

Molly strained to see how the little image was coming on. She liked Arthur because he had soft hands. Nicholas shoed her away and turned to his sitter.

"Arthur, it sounds as if you are in for a treat. If Alice is making pastry, it means she's probably making my favourite - beef pie, with a good thick gravy." Molly was still trying to get a look at the little image. Nicholas turned to his servant girl. "Molly, are we?"

"Absolutely. We have leeks and turnips and parsnips, and the meat is already simmering in a good, dark ale. I even managed to get some field mushrooms this morning." Molly was clearly looking forward to tonight's supper. "Cook has also made some fine white bread and Mistress has got some of that claret out of the cellar that you like."

Arthur smiled in genuine admiration.

"This sounds wonderful, Molly. Tell your mistress I look forward to this feast."

Nicholas dipped his brush into the grey paint on his mother of pearl palette and, in tiny strokes, filled in part of the detail of Arthur's dark grey doublet.

"Thank you Molly. We shall be down when the light fails."

The young girl left the room reluctantly, the bells tinkling softly as she trotted down the stairs. The kitchen would be in chaos. There were some things only Alice cooked so when she invaded the kitchen, Cook had to bite her tongue and put up with the mistress taking over and, according to Cook, "'turnin the 'ole 'ouse upsoid durn'".

"Nicholas, thank you for inviting me to dine with your family. You are most kind. I was told you were a kind man, as well as talented" Arthur paused "and that I could trust you."

Nicholas smiled and continued with his work.

"May I ask who?"

"Sir Dru Drury."

Nicholas frowned in thought. No face sprang to mind, but that only meant he had not painted the knight's portrait so he wondered why he had made the recommendation.

"He's a friend of Sir John Ashley." Arthur volunteered.

"Ah." Nicholas responded. He knew Sir John through the Court, but he had never painted him either. What intrigued him was how Arthur was associated with Ashley, whose late wife, Kat, as First Lady of the Bedchamber had been as close to the Queen as anyone could be.

"Do you come far?" he asked. Arthur's reply might reveal a bit more of this relationship.

"No, at the moment I'm staying just to the north of here, with Sir John, but I was brought up on the Queen's manor at Enfield." Arthur's reply added fuel to Nicholas's curiosity. His sitter, from his clothes, demeanour and manner was clearly a man of some refinement, but it did not explain why Ashley as [*was ?*] involved.

"Have you thought whether you might like to add a motto to your portrait, Arthur?"

Nicholas was interested to see if this young man would want a complex motto that would hint at the identity of the woman behind the anonymous hand; perhaps Arthur already had one in mind, or better still, he would ask Nicholas to think one up. Creating mottoes was the interesting part of any commission. This was often when clients revealed their close personal secrets.

"No, I hadn't, but indeed, it's a good idea." Arthur replied and paused deep in thought this time. "At the moment, all I can think of is something from Cicero, but it is entirely inappropriate."

"Arthur, that might be so, but it might give us something of a starting point." Nicholas waited for Arthur to continue.

"Well, what sprang to mind was 'Inter arma, leges tacent – laws are silent in war."

Nicholas was impressed. A Latin motto and a quote he recognised came from Cicero's 'Pro Milone', but he had to agree, hardly appropriate if the hand from the cloud were that of a secret lover.

Nicholas picked up another fine brush and applied a dribble of white paint to Arthur's collar. The paint was thick and cast tiny shadows making the lace appear real.

"You speak Latin?" Nicholas observed.

"All part of my education, including ancient Greek, French, Italian, rhetoric, dancing, swordsmanship and all the other equipment for a life as a gentleman."

"Your parents must be very proud of your achievements." Nicholas suggested. He was not learning very much other than confirming that Arthur was educated, probably of gentle birth and just a bit arrogant.

"Sir John paid for my education." Arthur offered.

That really puzzled Nicholas. Why had John Ashley paid for the education of someone called Southron.

Nicholas worked on through the afternoon whilst they discussed the Spanish Netherland problem and the plight of the French Protestants. Arthur seemed very well informed about events in Europe. Nicholas knew something about the true nature of these affairs from his visits to Court. Arthur repeated the gossip that de Guise was trying to get the Queen to back the French Protestants. Nicholas listened as Arthur told him much more that he knew was merely gossip. Lately he had begun to wonder just how much of this tittle tattle came from Walsingham's office was part of the spymaster's game of mis-information. Nicholas was grateful that he was no longer directly part of that shady world. Delivering a letter surreptitiously to Mary Stuart was enough to prove to him that it could be all very dangerous. It was a young man's game and the thought crossed his mind that perhaps Arthur was one of Burghley or Walsingham's spies. Finally, just as the light was fading, Nicholas stepped back to consider his work. The portrait was, to all intent and purpose, finished.

"May I see?" Arthur enquired. Nicholas moved to one side so Arthur could stand next to him in front of the little easel.

"I shall let this dry overnight and then tomorrow, add any motto you might want, then trim it."

"If you could give me a pen, Nicholas, I think I have thought of something suitable." Nicholas handed Arthur a pen, paper and ink. Arthur wrote something carefully the folded the paper in half and left it on the desk. A gong clanged, making both men jump.

"That will be our call for dinner. Come, Arthur. Alice will be extremely cross if we dally."

With the curtains drawn tightly around their four poster bed, Alice and Nicholas were lying snuggled under the covers. It had been raining since dusk and the night had grown cold.

Alice had produced a delicious supper with early Kent strawberries and fresh cream to follow. Nicholas had eaten and drunk too much. The pie had been delicious and he had eaten some of the vegetables just to please Alice, but he knew he would pay the price for drinking the claret. He could not understand why Alice was so fond of vegetables and, as for fresh strawberries, well he could take them or leave them. He had also noticed that, sometimes after he had eaten them, his left big toe was extremely painful and he wondered if there were a connection between this pain and eating strawberries. The doctor had told him that there was absolutely no connection with what he ate or drank and had diagnosed a build up of humours. Nicholas had then been bled, which had made him feel faint and then been charged a fortune for the consultation and the bleeding, which had made him feel even worse. It was not something he relished trying again. Furthermore he remained unconvinced by the doctor's diagnosis. It made more sense that it was something he ate as these attacks were more frequent in the strawberry season than at other times of the year. However, he had occasionally had an attack at other times so perhaps the doctor was right and the strawberry connection was just a fanciful notion on his part otherwise he would only have these attacks during the strawberry season.

Nicholas was conscious that his left toe was becoming more sore so he moved his leg to relieve the pressure of the bedcovers. If he mentioned it to Alice, she would make him drink cabbage water. It tasted foul and he hated it. Perhaps the attack would pass; sometimes they did. He had to admit the cabbage water did seem to do the trick, but it was so revolting he would rather put up with the pain for now, just in case his sore toe was nothing to do with supper.

"Nick," breathed Alice, as she lay with her head on his chest. "Didn't Mr Southron remind you of anyone?"

"His face is familiar somehow, but I can't put my finger as to why."

"Well, darling husband," Alice whispered, "perhaps you see too many faces, which is why you cannot see the wood for the trees."

"What do you mean? And why are you whispering?" Nicholas whispered back, absentmindedly kissing the top of her head.

"Because he reminds me of the Queen," she whispered softly "and the Earl of Leicester."

Nicholas was stunned. "Never, ever, repeat what you have just said," he hissed "unless you wish to spend the rest of your days in the Tower."

"If you didn't want to know the answer, why ask the question?" She said grumpily and turned over, closing the conversation.

Nicholas lay for some time with his hands behind his head, bed gazing up at his copy of a painting they had seen in Paris. It was called The Seduction of Mars and he had painted it as a surprise for Alice when he had ordered their new bed. He gazed up at the blonde goddess Venus and her sleeping lover, Mars, thankful that he did not have to produce these large paintings for a living. The painting had been a challenge, but not as much as the first time he had painted the Queen.

The Queen's face, which he knew so well, floated at the forefront of his memory. Dudley's features superimposed themselves over Elizabeth's as if in some bizarre embrace.

"My God!" he breathed. "My God, Alice, you're right!"

"I thought you said I wasn't to repeat what I said." came her muffled response.

"I still mean it, but you're right."

Nicholas jumped out of bed and started dressing.

"What are you doing, Nick? It's late and it's cold. Where are you going?"

"I'll never sleep, I'm going upstairs. Go to sleep and forget all about it." Nicholas kissed her forehead and pulled the covers up around her. "I need to look for something."

Alice reached up and put her arms around his neck trying to entice him back to bed, but he was not to be lured. Disentangling himself from her arms, he crept upstairs to his workroom, the jangling of the little bells of his alarm all the more noticeable now that the household was asleep.

The rain clouds were breaking up and the moonlight filtered in through the window giving just sufficient light for him to find his way to light the candles. He needed to sort through Levina's notebooks. If anyone had known if the Queen had a secret, she would. His mind was racing; all sorts of things were beginning to make sense.

London was asleep and Nicholas felt as if he were the only person alive. Placing a pile of Levina's notebooks on his desk he took the top book, placed it in front of him and turned the pages. Levina had sketched many members of the Court. He recognised the late Duke of Norfolk who looked back at him, a broken and haggard man. The Duke had been executed in June '72 and this portrait had been done when he was in the Tower. This year was far too late for anything that might have evidence of an event of the sort he was looking for. Nicholas wondered what had prompted Levina to visit the Duke in the Tower.

Nicholas leafed through the rest of the pile until he found a sketchbook dated the first year of Elizabeth's reign. There were all sorts of sketches of Elizabeth and Nicholas recognised them as Levina's templates for the images shown in the P that appeared on each Roll recording the proceedings of the Queen's

Bench. This book contained detailed sketches of Elizabeth in her coronation robes, with notes about colour written both in Flemish and English.

There were quite a few sketches of Robert Dudley and then turning a page, he laughed; there were three young boys one of whom he recognised as himself, and the other two as Thomas Bodley and Levina's own son, Marcus. The page was dated '1st Accession Day'. Levina had noted, in English, that she hoped that Masters Nicholas and Thomas would not be too bruised after their battles. She must have drawn those portraits immediately Tom and he had left her house that day so long ago. Nicholas smiled at the discovery.

There were separate books containing the portraits of Henry, Katharine Parr, Edward, Mary and Elizabeth each in their own separate books, dating back to 1547. It appeared Levina had used her sketchbooks as an ad hoc diary so Nicholas sorted them into date order before continuing his search.

All these sketched portraits were not unlike the Holbein sketches she had made him study and Nicholas sat back and wondered why, when she was teaching him how to observe and record people's features, she had not shown him her own work. It was some time before it dawned on him that perhaps she was shy. By looking at the late master's work she would not have to open herself up to criticism. Holbein was, after all, still an artistic giant even though he had been dead for over forty years. Also, since the majority of Holbein's sitters were also dead, there had been no danger of any indiscretions being made by a naive young artist.

Nicholas gazed sightlessly out of the window musing on Arthur's age. Flicking through the pages of a book dated 1560-61, there were sketches of various nobles, the Queen and a little landscape sketch of St Paul's being hit by lightning dated 4th June, 1561. Nicholas was surprised at this. It seemed she had recorded the event because the lightening strike was significant.

Further examination yielded nothing, but Nicholas was convinced that if anyone knew of a secret of this magnitude, it would have been Levina. He knew it would be unlikely he would find anything written down, but was sure there had to be evidence in some form or other.

Nicholas looked at the nearly completed portrait, cradling it in his hand to catch the candlelight. Alice was so right. This young man's face could be a combination of the Queen's and Dudley's. But surely Elizabeth would have named any son after her own father? Nicholas examined that possibility and concluded that any child named Henry, just as much a child called Edward, especially if that child had red hair and was being brought up on a royal estate, might cause gossip.

The existence of a secret son could explain why the queen was so dedicated to the Arthurian legend. Arthur, the legendary king who had saved England in its darkest hour. Arthur who was buried in Avalon, a place of legend somewhere in the Western Isles. That same legend foretold that Arthur would come again in England's hour of need which was why he was also known as "Rex Quondam, Rex Futuris" – The Once and Future King.

Nicholas chuckled, realising how typical it would be for Elizabeth to name her son after a great legendary kin in order for him to fulfil the prophesy that Arthur would appear in the hour of England's greatest need, that is to say when there was no clear line of succession to the English throne.

Nicholas sat back and wondered if there were any other aspects of the legend that might be similar to the Arthurian legend. King Arthur's conception and birth had a vague parallel in that Uther Pendragon had not been married to Ygraine when she had conceived. When the baby had been born, Merlin had whisked him away to be brought up in secret. Arthur Southron had told of how he had been brought up by a foster father.

And what had happened to Ygraine? Nicholas could not remember if there had been more children after Uther had married her, but if there had been no brothers or sisters, then Ygraine might have appeared virginal.

Elizabeth had stated from the outset that she was the Virgin Queen and he realised this was possibly another example of Elizabeth's clever doublespeak. It was not because she was actually a virgin, which up to this very evening he had believed, but because she was unmarried it made sense to create the myth that she was a virgin.

Marcus said he could tell if two people were lovers from the way they were when they were together. Nicholas always knew when someone was hiding something from him. There was always something about the eyes and the way the muscles around the mouth worked, but he was always far too interested in the way a person's face was put together than to spend time analysing their body language. Evidently it was the little gestures that gave people away. A woman would never touch another man, unless she was intimate with him. Nicholas did not think this was true because brothers and sisters touched each other, but Marcus had pointed out that the way they touched was not the same. Brothers and sisters would be bold with an arm flung round a shoulder or a bold peck on the cheek. Lovers were coy. Lovers would brush fingers hoping no one saw, or fling a quick sideways glance hoping to catch their beloved's eye and then quickly look away; their gestures were covert. Nicholas had never thought about analysing how the Queen and Dudley behaved together.

Certainly, Dudley took liberties with Elizabeth that no other man did, but was that because he was her lover, or because they had known each other for a long time? However, Dudley always rested his hand on Elizabeth's waist just that fraction longer than was acceptable. The very first time he had met the Queen, Dudley had used the excuse of comparing his portrait of

Levina to the lady herself, to do just this.

Nicholas shook his head to try and look objectively for counter arguments.

Elizabeth's birthday was in September, so was born under the astrological sign of Virgo, which provided a very obvious explanation as to why she might call herself the Virgin Queen. Doctor Dee might have the answer to this astrological question, but that would mean involving someone else, and, besides, there did not have to be just one reason.

Elizabeth was not the first English Queen regnant. That had been her sister. Mary had been unmarried, a devout Catholic and probably very much a virgin when she had inherited the throne. In contrast to Elizabeth, she had been very quick to marry so she could provide an heir to her throne as a dutiful queen should. But her marriage had been to her cousin, and, not only that, her over-riding desire was to bring England back into the Church of Rome and to continue that unification through the fruit of her body. By marrying Philip, England became united with Spain! No wonder his father had sent him off with the Bodleys.

He thought for a minute, pondering why it was only him. As the eldest son it must have been because his father wanted his heir to be safe from any Catholic persecution. He scribbled a note in his sketchbook to ask his father about this the next time he saw him and returned to his contemplation of Henry VIII's daughters.

Was there anything in their names? Henry had obviously called his two daughters after the two most important women in Christianity, but why? As his first born child, who might one day, be Queen, Mary had been named in honour of the Virgin. Henry was clearly stating the succession was by divine right.

Henry then named his second daughter, Elizabeth. Her grandfather had united the two houses of Lancaster and York when he had married her grandmother, Elizabeth of York, which was an obvious link with the queen. However, and he thought this a very obscure connection, was there a connection with the biblical Elizabeth, the mother of John the Baptist who had conceived after years of barrenness. Catherine's miscarriages were a form of barrenness and Henry had already proved he was potent and could father sons because his mistress, Elizabeth Blount, had given him Henry Fitzroy.

It was also rumoured that Henry had also made Mary Boleyn pregnant, (who had been quickly married off to William Carey) and she had produced a girl, which might have further underscored Henry's potency. Nicholas's line of thought was leading him down some dark paths. He tried to see why Henry might have given his second daughter a name with a double intent. Perhaps it was when Anne Boleyn presented him with a daughter instead of a son, he called her Elizabeth to honour his mother and continue to link the Tudors with the Holy Family. Having two daughters named after two of the most important women in Christianity would underline Henry's title as Defender of the Faith despite his break from Rome and the Tudor's divine right to rule.

It was a convoluted thought, but everything appeared layered with meaning. If you were involved with the Court in any way whatsoever, you knew you could never take anything at face value.

Nicholas sighed; and what about Edward? If he continued with the same line of argument about the Holy family, surely Henry's heir should have been named James or John. So why had Henry's legitimate son been called Edward? The most likely answer was that the boy had been called after The Confessor. Nicholas leaned his chin on his hands and looked out of the window. He had been making notes and these seem to be forming a pattern. If Elizabeth had called Arthur after the great warrior king of England then perhaps she was following her father's logic of calling her brother Edward after the last Anglo Saxon King of England. After all, her grandfather had called her uncle Arthur for these very same reasons.

But that logic did not make sense where Fitzroy was concerned. Why had Henry named his illegitimate son after himself? Perhaps, by naming Henry Fitzroy after himself, it appeared that Henry was declaring that if his mistress could bear him a son, so could the queen, which would be a very public royal slap in the queen's face! Nicholas remembered a Holbein miniature of Fitzroy in a book of miniatures in the royal library. The boy looked really ill and had died shortly after it was painted, but despite his illness he resembled his grandfather and father. They all had quite pointed faces and small mouths, but Fitzroy did not have the calculating eyes of his father or grandfather. If the King had died and Fitzroy had survived, then even as a bastard, Fitzroy might have become king.

All this speculation did not answer his question and there was the greater question of how, if Elizabeth had borne a child, had she concealed both her pregnancy and the birth?

Arthur was probably about twenty three years of age so the most likely date for Arthur's birth was 1561. From everthing he knew about the queen he knew Elizabeth had been constantly urged to marry right from the beginning of her reign, but equally she was resisting their supplication and telling Parliament she would never do so.

Perhaps, and he hesitated to even think it, just perhaps Elizabeth had decided that she could marry no one but Dudley, but because he was already married Elizabeth had decided she would marry no-one. Was Elizabeth that romantic? Where Dudley was concerned she might have been, but knowing her strong sense of duty it seemed unlikely she would put her heart ahead of her duty.

Then there was Dudley himself. His marriage to Amy Robsart had saved his head when Mary had come to the throne, but when Elizabeth succeeds suddenly she becomes inconvenient. Was her death a fortuitous event, or planned? To a casual outsider it would appear that Lady Dudley's death would have enabled him to be permanently at the Queen's side. However, her death cast the odious taint of unproven wife killer over Dudley ensuring that he would never be able marry the Queen. The most he could ever hope to be was a close 'friend'.

Since rumour had it that Lady Dudley had been in good health, her death seemed just too convenient and obvious. Nicholas knew Dudley was extremely ambitious, but also that he was subtle. He would never had plotted a murder that could immediately be laid at his door and so endanger not only his ambitions, but also his life. This plot, if plot there were, had been concocted by someone even more subtle than Robert Dudley and there was only one mind that could be that devious and who also had the power and the means.

The full moon gave Nicholas a clear light to examine the little sketchbook in front of him. There were no sketches of babies for the year 1561, but there were many he recognised of being of Marcus and himself. These reminded him that he had not seen his friend for some time. He shook his head as if to shake these memories out of his brain and return to his contemplation.

On a more practical level, if Elizabeth had fallen pregnant, how had she disguised the fact? It was extremely unlikely anyone would have left a written document saying "Today is the whatever of the month of whenever, and the Queen gave birth to a healthy baby boy." The only evidence he had for a date was Levina's sketch of lightning striking St Paul's. She had even noted that the date of 4th June, 1561. Was Levina making a statement that the very essence of England was threatened by this lightning bolt from the heavens, that is to say, Arthur's birth? If so, Arthur had been born under the zodiac sign of Gemini, the twins.

Counting back nine months from June 1561 brought Nicholas to September 1560. What if Elizabeth had not known she was carrying Dudley's child, so her falling with child and Lady Dudley's death had become a tragic series of events? Lord Burghley was her most trusted servant, and had no liking for Dudley. Had he ordered Lady Dudley's murder? He made note to find out what date Lady Dudley had died.

If his theory was correct, this put a completely different reading to Elizabeth's personal symbols.

First there was the Phoenix? The myth was that only one phoenix could exist at any one time and when the time came for it to die it threw itself into the sacred fire and another would rise from the flames to take its place. How symbolic would that be if Elizabeth had an heir hidden away who would rise from the ashes of the reign of The Virgin Queen? This had been the first large portrait he had been commissioned to paint.

Then there was the Pelican? The Pelican mother pecking her breast and sacrificing her own lifeblood for the sake of her children. It had taken him a month to paint that portrait and, up until now, he had thought it signified Elizabeth's sacrifice of foregoing the pleasures of marriage and motherhood for the sake of her people.

However, if Arthur were Elizabeth's son, this portrait could be read as a statement of her maternal sacrifice in order to protect her child and instead of feeding her chick, the blood from her breast signified her bleeding heart caused by separation.

Nicholas pondered what might have happened if it had become widely known there was such a child. Every plotter who wanted Elizabeth off the throne would have either wanted to kill her and her son, or, depending on who discovered this secret, have the child brought up in whichever was the religion of a regency. But was there any precedent for a child to be taken from a royal mother and brought up in a religion different from the parents, far away from the Court and the influence of the parents. Right on England's doorstep, James VI of Scotland been taken from Mary Stuart virtually the day he was born, and brought up a by his grandmother. But Mary Stuart had been married which made her son the legitimate heir to the Scottish throne.

The unmarried Elizabeth would have been so disgraced, not even Burghley would have been able to save her. At best she would have become at best a laughing stock, at worst, her life, the baby's and probably Dudley's too, would have been forfeit and England would have been thrown into civil war.

If he accepted that Arthur were the queen's son, the various conversations he had had with the Queen began to make a very different sense. When Elizabeth had questioned him about his exile, he had assumed she wanted to compare his experiences with her own. He remembered her sad expression when he had told her how he did not really remember his real mother because he had left home aged seven and never returned to live with his family in Exeter. He had assumed she was comparing his experience with her permanent separation from her own mother when she was only three.

But what if his experiences were the closest Elizabeth could get to understanding those of her own son's? Perhaps her questions were the closest she could come to knowing what her son might have experienced during his boyhood. This reminded him of how kind Mrs Bodley and Levina had been to him, how he looked on both of them as his mothers and had said as much to the Queen. She had been sympathetic and had mentioned Kat Ashley whom she had known since childhood. If Arthur were her son, his confirmation of how he had felt about the women who had been so influential in his own life, must have hurt her.

Elizabeth had looked wistful and sad, but other than that, had given nothing away. However, there was a link. The late Kat Ashley had been married to Sir John Ashley, who was Arthur's guardian.

The more he thought about it, the more Nicholas was convinced that Arthur might be Elizabeth's phoenix.

Only those who could be completely trusted by both Elizabeth and Dudley would be party to their secret. First of all there was Kat Ashley, loyal to Elizabeth since childhood. Her husband, Sir John, was still a very active member of Elizabeth's household. Arthur himself had told how Ashley had paid for his education. Levina said how Lord Burghley was trusted implicitly by Elizabeth, therefore, so it stood to reason that he was probably the only one trusted enough to organise any illegitimate infant being spirited away and brought up in secret? What if the faithful Levina had been party to Elizabeth's secret and, if so, she must have left some evidence somewhere?

The virgin epithet, Elizabeth's symbols, how her questions were multi-layered, all pointed to a very well kept royal secret. What other evidence might there be and, moreover, where would he find it.

The moon disappeared behind more clouds and raindrops pattered against the window. The candle burned lower and tiredness tugged at his eyelids. The bells softly tinkled their warning before the door opened. Alice had wrapped a shawl tightly round her shoulders to keep out the night chill.

"Nick, come to bed." She wound her arms round her husband's neck and kissed his ear. This time Nicholas decided to give in and returned to the warmth of his bed and the arms of his wife.

Arthur was due to collect the finished miniature sometime near noon and Nicholas had slept late, exhausted by his nocturnal ponderings. The overnight rain had passed and the late May sun was drying the remaining puddles. Nicholas was again in his eyrie and he could hear the cries of the costermongers in the street below mixing with the general hubbub of the City.

All he had to do was to write Arthur's motto, *Attici Amoris Ergo*, in gold ink in the space between the linked hands and Arthur's head.

"*Attici Amoris Ergo*" appeared to be gibberish.

Nicholas sat with the Latin words rolling round in his head like dice, waiting for them to fall and reveal their meaning.

Therefore by the love of Atticus,
Therefore with the love of Atticus,
Therefore from the love Atticus.
Or was it
Therefore of, or even *through, the love of Atticus.*

It did not make any sense at all, no matter which way it was translated. Arthur had been very specific as to where he wanted the words put.

"*Now why would Arthur be so insistent to put these here, unless he means to say something important? He seems to be trying to link the hidden woman with himself and Atticus, so what is that link between a long dead Roman and Arthur Southron?*" but it was no use asking himself questions he knew would not be answered today and that could never be asked of his client.

He had decided to replace the original card backing because a court card might take on more significance than intended, so he had prised off the original Knave of Diamonds and after removing all the court cards and Aces from the new pack of playing cards, had drawn a card at random and re-pasted the little image onto it. Nicholas did not even look at which card he had drawn. Nicholas finished the final 'o' and put down his pen.

The warning bells tinkled, not sounding as loud as they had in the depths of the previous night. Nicholas turned as Alice showed Arthur into the room. Nicholas smiled a greeting and held out his hand. He had a genuine sympathy for this young man who, if he really were Elizabeth's son, carried a heavy burden. There would be many who would want to see him dead.

"Thank you so very much for accommodating my request so fast, Nicholas;" Arthur said as he shook Nicholas's hand and, turning to Alice, "and thank you, Mistress Hillyarde, for such a fine dinner last night." Arthur smiled his thanks.

"I hope you will be pleased with this," Nicholas lifted the finished image from the small desk easel and laid the limning on the palm of Arthur's hand. "Be careful, the gold ink around the edge is only just dry."

Arthur held his portrait by the edges and smiled. It was a good likeness.

"Your fame is well deserved, Nicholas, but I won't take it with me. Instead, please will you send it to Sir John Ashley." Arthur smiled a sad smile as he dropped the small oval into the limewood box Nicholas held open.

"Why, certainly. I will deliver it myself to ensure its safety." Nicholas confirmed. Alice sat quietly by the fireplace, the two men had forgotten her existence. She sat and pondered Arthur's very specific delivery request. To keep a secret child from prying eyes and ears it would need the loyalty of people like the Ashley's. Alice hoped Nicholas would share some of his thoughts of his sleepless night. She did not want him getting himself into a state. Her midwife was convinced that stress and worry caused the body all sorts of problems. She had enough problems keeping Nicholas's gout at bay, which seemed to happen in May and June and in times of stress. Strawberries might be a possible cause because of the timings, and stress and worry might also contribute to his affliction.

"My thanks, Nicholas." Arthur leant across and placed a small leather pouch on the workbench, to which neither man made reference. Gentlemen did not discuss money, but Alice gauged from the way it bulged there was more than sufficient to cover Nicholas's fee.

"Good luck, Arthur. Your travels take you into difficult territory. I wish you Godspeed." Nicholas smiled at the young man. The commission completed Arthur picked up his cape and left. Nicholas and Alice watched Arthur walk away towards St Paul's.

"Well Alice, what do you make of that?" Nicholas asked his wife, not expecting an immediate response.

"I have things to do like produce a mid-day meal for you and your workshop, dear husband, so idle gossip will have to wait."

Later, Nicholas retreated upstairs ostensibly to work, but in reality he needed somewhere quiet to think and where he would not be disturbed. Much later, Alice climbed the stairs with a tray laden with cold pie, apples and a pile of strawberries as a supper for them both. The children were all settled in bed and the other members of the household would soon follow. The plain oval lime wood box lay on the workbench as well as Arthur's payment. Alice poured the money onto the worktop. The bag contained eight pounds – more than double the usual fee. It was raining again so Nicholas lit the fire and they sat in front of it watching the flames. Alice sat at his feet on a little stool, leaning against his knees.

"Nick, you aren't going to go digging around looking for clues to Arthur's parentage, are you?" she asked. Alice understood her husband well and knew he would not let this conundrum lie. He was far too curious. Her father had warned her about this side of Nicholas's nature. It went hand in hand with the speculative side of Nicholas's character, which Brandon distrusted. Alice sighed, she had hoped Nicholas had learnt his lesson when the Scottish adventure had gone wrong. He had lost a lot of money. They needed the continuing patronage of the Court and especially people like Leicester and the queen.

Nicholas stroked her hair absentmindedly as he stared into the fire. The flames danced, forming exotic yellow and orange shapes and throwing long purple shadows across the room. Alice looked up at the ceiling. The shadows danced there too, but was it a gavotte of love and romance with dark secrets?

"Could you let this puzzle be, my dear husband?" Alice asked. The silence grew longer until she pinched the inside of his thigh to get his attention. Nicholas stretched his leg, as if only just registering the discomfiture.

"Sorry, Alice. I was miles away," he murmured.

Alice sighed. She recognised all the signs. Arthur was becoming an obsession and she knew Nicholas would not rest until he had found a satisfactory answer. However, she had some news which might focus Nicholas's attention away from Arthur's parentage for a while.

"Nicholas, what would you say if I were to tell you that Daniel, Elizabeth, Francis and Laurence were to have a baby brother or sister?"

Nicholas let the news sink in slowly. That would explain why Alice ate so many strawberries last night and again tonight. She was pregnant – again. Nicholas said nothing. What was there to say. Another mouth to feed, clothe and worry about. Alice let the silence grow.

"Alice," Nicholas's tone was distracted and Alice despaired at what might come next. It was as if he had not heard her announcement. "how would you feel if you had to give Daniel away, for his own safety's sake."

His question confirmed Alice's worst fears. Nicholas was determined to explore the mystery of Arthur Southron until he had solved it.

"I couldn't. Come on Nick, it's time for bed."

June

Nicholas approached the tanneries with his nose buried deep in a nosegay of heavily scented roses and herbs in an attempt to assuage the stench. He had come to collect some sheets of vellum and to ensure they were flawless before he took delivery. The tanning process was corrosive and stank, but the resulting parchments and vellums were far more durable than paper.

"'morning Mr 'illyarde" the chief tanner greeted him. "'tis good to see yer."

"Indeed Mr Tanner."

"As requested, Mr 'illyarde, I've kept only the best calfskin for yer. A couple are from calves born dead and knowing this, I cured 'em specially for yer." Mr Tanner picked two small hides off a shelf and handed them over. Nicholas ran his hand over the surface. The man had done a superb job.

"This is indeed very fine. How come you have the hide of a stillborn?"

"Well, Mr 'illyarde, you being a limner and all that, I'd thought you'd know that the finest surface for your line o' work be the skin of an animal that 'adn't breathed. That way there be no damage from fly strike or anything else, provided we get the carcase before it goes bad."

Nicholas turned the piece over and the other side was as smooth as the first. "And you have two of these hides."

"Yep. Not easy to get, but knowing you were to come to inspect hides for your delivery I thought you might appreciate the finer surface."

"Indeed Mr Tanner. I'll take them and my usual order."

"Mr 'illyarde that be good of you. And if I should be able to do more of the same, I take it you'd be interested."

"Indeed. The surface is the best I've seen. I look forward to painting on these. Thank you for your thought."

"I aim ter please and I wouldn't want yer going elsewhere for your vellums, so I've got to provide the best for yer, especially since many of the gentry have their faces painted on my 'ides!"

Nicholas laughed. "That's a very good reason Mr Tanner. However, some of those who have their portraits painted have no idea they might be decorating a cow's arse!"

The master tanner howled with laughter at this thought. "Now there's a thing. Some of 'em women who think they are so better than most, decoratin' a cow's arse. You've made my day." The man wiped tears of mirth from his cheeks.

Leaving the man chuckling Nicholas walked to the Teerlinc warehouses to catch up on any news. Marcus was in his office.

"Have you heard the news from France, Nicholas?"

"Don't tell me the date is set and the queen is finally going to marry Alençon? I'll eat my hat if that's so"

"No, Nick. In fact, exactly the opposite. He's dead."

"What?" Nicholas was shocked "When – er how?"

"No details, just that he's dead. It was a merchant in from Calais that gave me the news."

"Now that's sad. I wonder how the Queen will react?" Nicholas mused. "I was never sure she was serious about marrying him, but this will be a serious blow. Despite the fact he was so much younger than her, I think she was quite fond of him, in a sisterly sort of way." Nicholas paused remembering the first time he had seen Alençon. "He was interesting. Terrible skin, but nice eyes. None of the French royals are ones you want to get to know well. They scheme against each other all the time."

"So do you think it was murder?"

"Marcus, I wouldn't like to speculate until we hear a little more and to that end, I think we should see what our local landlord has to tell us."

"What a splendid thought. Roast Beef and a jug of wine?"

The two men adjourned for their meal and to see if they could hear any gossip. Evidently Alençon had died from anything from natural causes to being struck by lightning. The devil himself had come and taken his soul away, according to some.

Alice returned from her sister's house and wanted to know how the queen was faring having heard the news about Alençon's death.

"Actually Alice, I don't know. I was with Marcus all afternoon. I'll know more tomorrow, but I never was convinced that Elizabeth was serous about marrying him."

"Nick, if Arthur is who we think he is, she won't marry anyone. Despite everything, she's still dedicated to Dudley and perhaps they have Arthur to bind them completely. Besides, she will be fifty one years old in September and, even if she is a queen, no one will want to marry a woman who is no longer able to bear children."

"How sad. Alice, I never see her as getting old."

"I think you are more than a little bit in love with her yourself!" Alice teased.

"That may be so, my darling wife, but it is a completely different love from the one I have for you." Nicholas wrapped his arms around his wife's waist.

"How so different?"

"I think of her as a sort of sister."

"How so?"

"We have much in common such as we were both separated from our parents, but more because she cares that I'm happy and that you and the children are happy. She always wants to know how they and you are faring. Why do you think she sent you those strawberries when you were pregnant."

"O, I'd forgotten those … we named Elizabeth after her because of it."

"Those strawberries had been sent to her by Alençon."

"Oh, Nick. She'd shared a lover's gift with me and I never knew."

"She was just pleased to be able to do something to quell your strawberry craving and maybe, and I might be completely wrong in thinking this, but maybe it was because she sympathised."

"Are you thinking she knows what it's like to have that sort of craving?"

"hmmm… not sure, but we will never know."

July

"Nicholas" Alice called up to him. "Nick" her call was louder as she clambered the stairs. Hillyarde resented his wife's interruption. He was playing with various designs for the new Great Seal. The bells tinkled as she reached the top steps and, from habit, he turned his sketchbook over.

"Nick, have you heard?"

"What!" his response was terse, then he realised that Alice was anxious. She did not normally disturb him when he was at work. "I'm sorry, Alice. I shouldn't have snapped at you."

"Nick, Sarah's downstairs and she's just come from father's." Alice's face was pink from the exertion of getting up the stairs and her eyes were wide with fright.

"Alice, what's got you so upset."

"William of Orange has been assassinated."

"What?"

"You heard. William of Orange has been shot through the chest and murdered."

"This is dreadful. First Alençon and now this. Was it the Spanish?"

"I've not got the details, but Sarah was there when one of father's merchant friends came to tell him what had happened in Middleburg. Evidently someone approached the Prince and shot him straight in the chest, killing him instantly."

"When you say approached - how close was he?"

"I heard this merchant say it was at point blank range"

"This will panic the Queen. William must have been killed because he was Protestant." Nicholas stated. "Throgmorton's rotting in the Tower, and I did think that he might continue to rot, but Orange's assassination will seal his fate."

"That's the other thing. Cook's just come back from the market and she tells me she's heard Throgmorton's to be executed at Tyburn tomorrow."

Alice sat down on the stool and looked at her husband. She glanced over to the door to make sure she had shut it behind her.

"Nick, do you think Arthur is all right? Didn't he say he was going to the Low Countries?" Her whispered question caught him unawares.

"I don't know. We don't know where he is, but I'm sure he's safe."

"I hope so." Alice rubbed her expanding waistline. She was at the stage where she just looked plump. Despite her worried look and larger girth, she was beautiful.

"Europe's not a safe place to be, Alice, especially for anyone Protestant. France is as divided as ever, and now the Protestants in the Low Countries have no leader."

"So what do you think will happen?"

"Since the majority of the French are Catholic, France is focussing inwards. Now that Orange is dead, Parma will take advantage of the Protestant demoralisation and grab as much territory as he can, which leaves the United Provinces isolated unless Elizabeth is prepared to support them. If Arthur is in Flanders or the United Provinces, he could be in a great deal of danger."

"Perhaps he'll pretend to be a Catholic, like we did in Paris?"

Nicholas smiled hopefully. "Perhaps, Alice. If he's got any sense he will!"

November

The summer had been a busy one and Nicholas still had to deliver Arthur's portrait to Sir John Ashley. For the time being, Arthur was safely in his little box locked away in Nicholas's studio. The motto "*Attici Amoris Ergo*" tickled away at the back of Nicholas's mind day and night and it still did not make sense. Nicholas had waited patiently all summer before undertaking any further investigations. The long daylight hours of summer was a good time for painting and meant his candle bill was much reduced.

Alice's pregnancy developed as all her pregnancies did. She bloomed and looked lovelier than ever. Luckily her passion for strawberries had not lasted long. With another mouth to feed, Nicholas was glad that his order book was full and not just for portraits, he was creating some beautiful jewellery.

He had given much thought of where he might look for any evidence of an illegitimate royal birth. He had discovered that Lord Burghley had been appointed as Chancellor of the Court of Wards in January 1561. Any child who was made a Ward of Court came under this Court's 'protection'. Since Lord Burghley had been made chancellor at the same time the gossips were talking of nothing else except Elizabeth and Dudley and their scandalous behaviour, there may well have been a reason for Burghley being given this appointment other than a reward for his previous service; was the timing merely coincidence or was it date evidence to bolster his theory. Nicholas wondered if it was worth delving to find if there was anything in the records regarding a child called Arthur Southron. Equally, he wondered whether he seeing conspiracies where there were really only coincidences.

He remained convinced Levina must have known of this secret despite not finding anything other than the lightning strike of St Paul's dated 4th June and he had managed to find out that this had actually happened. Elizabeth often talked about her when he was sketching at Court. Her reminiscences made him think that perhaps her fondness was a result of some great favour?

Perhaps Levina had been the conduit for news of Arthur's development. Nicholas remembered how she had often travelled with George to Hatfield, ostensibly because George had a number of business dealings with Lord Burghley. St Albans was very near Enfield so, in theory, it would not have been difficult for them to divert to Enfield either on their way to or from seeing Lord Burghley.

As an artist, Levina would have been the ideal person to record Arthur's development passing this information on to the Queen in what appeared to be idle conversation. After all, a picture was worth a thousand words and he, himself, had turned the hidden visual message into an art form. The Queen would have these but, if there were a picture, the risk of discovery had to be minimal otherwise the Queen's secret would be revealed too soon.

Possible hiding places of evidence continued to baffle him until one day the stack of Levina's work books on his bookshelf toppled over onto the floor and a loose sheet of paper with a sketch of a capital 'P' flew out. It was an outline sketch of the monarch filling the oval of the P. Nicholas looked at the letter for a long time. He wondered whether this was another coincidence? Surely not? He was beginning to believe there were no such things as coincidences. So, if it were not a coincidence, what was the significance of the illuminated P.

Nicholas sat and thought. What was significant about an illuminated P? Who used it, and where was it used? With blinding realisation he realised that there was great significance in the P; in fact, it was the perfect hiding place. The front sheet of the Plea Rolls was a centuries old formal format where the illuminated first letter of the first word on the front sheet of each of the Rolls depicted the monarch as the representative of God's mercy and justice. These were important records but, as far as Nicholas was aware, consulted only by lawyers or their clerks and for them the important part of the roll was the written content, not the fancy fronts. Who would look at picture in the P on the front sheet when all the important information was contained in the written words.

If anyone wanted to make a statement about a monarch the P's were the perfect place. These records were rarely looked at so no official eyebrows would be raised. Illuminating the 'P' had been one of the regular jobs Levina had supervised as limner to the monarch. Nicholas had watched her often enough when she was teaching him and he had even been allowed to paint one or two when he had become vaguely competent with a paintbrush precisely because no one ever looked at these covers. The inside of the 'P' was virtually the same size as one of his miniatures. He might have taken over Levina's position as miniature portrait painter, but he did not usually get involved with initial illuminations on legal documents, at least not since he had been allowed to do some as a student. Recently he had been asked to design the letter E at the beginning of the founding charter for Emmanuel College, Cambridge, but that had been the exception.

Picking up the scattered sketch books Nicholas sorted them into date order. This time starting with the very early ones and paying more attention to poses that might appear in the P's. In addition to the elderly bearded Henry and his Queen, Katharine Parr, there were sketches of Prince Edward and both the princesses. Nicholas chuckled. Mary always looked bad tempered. Philip must have found it difficult to get excited about bedding his wife and Nicholas found he was feeling a certain sympathy for Philip, despite the fact he was a Catholic zealot.

It caused him to muse on his own marriage. Alice was a beautiful woman and they loved each other. He did not envy kings who had to marry for a whole raft of reasons other than love. Neither did he envy them the women who threw themselves at rich and powerful men just because they were rich and powerful. Kings were always able to go and find fun elsewhere with prettier and more exciting partners, but that could lead to all sorts of problems. Was it not the result of just such a possible inappropriate royal liaison exactly what he was investigating? But this was a Queen, not a King. Elizabeth was still infatuated by Dudley, despite his marriage to Lady Devereux, Nicholas was still unable to think of her as Lady Leicester. Dudley, on the other hand, had a reputation as a womaniser extraordinaire. He had been rakishly attractive when he was young and his good looks, together with his position at Court, meant that women had thrown themselves at him for whatever reason they could find, but Dudley was now a portly elderly courtier, whom, the Queen had recently suggested, should dine on the leg of a wren in order to reduce his weight.

Nicholas returned to his examination of the sketch books. A sketch labelled 'Edward, First Year Easter Term', showed a very young Edward looking incredibly lost on a vast throne dressed in coronation robes. It was a pen and ink full page sketch with a note next to it written in Flemish. Nicholas had no idea what it said and assumed that Levina had sketched this at a rehearsal for the Coronation. In the books for 1547 and 8 there were studies of various men and women, some of them he recognised as being of a young Princess Elizabeth and Robert Dudley and others he thought might be Jane Grey, Ambrose and Guildford Dudley.

There were no sketchbooks from late 1549 until mid 1551 and Nicholas remembered that Levina and George had returned to Bruges to visit her father. They had only planned to stay for six months, but she had fallen pregnant. Because she had been ill at the beginning of the pregnancy and confined to bed this had delayed their departure and, not wishing to risk a winter crossing, they had stayed in Bruges until the spring of 1551. That spring the weather had been bad and the March gales had been more violent than usual. Whilst they had waited in Calais for a break in the weather, Levina had given birth to Marcus. Sadly, because she had been so ill during her pregnancy, they had decided not to risk having any more children. Nicholas sighed. He had a brood and now another on the way. There was never any problem with Alice's pregnancies; she produced babies as if she were shelling peas.

Nicholas turned to the books dated 1553 and wondered if Levina's use of visual rhetoric would be different for a Catholic monarch. The accession of Mary was indeed completely different. These sketchbooks showed images of a young queen with flowing hair. There were many sketches and many notes, again in Flemish. Sketches of angels carrying blank banners and groups of men riding horses leading bands of infantry suggesting Levina was contemplating a complicated narrative of how Mary came to the throne. Perhaps there had been much discussion as to how the Queen would be portrayed. There was no final sketch so Nicholas had no idea what the eventual illustration was about, or what it looked like. The use of narrative made him wonder whether earlier 'P's' might hold other political statements about Henry or Edward.

Turning the pages he found there were no further sketches for the Marian 'Ps'. There were all sorts of sketches for other narratives. Mary kneeling at prayer, Mary touching the neck of a young boy with a priest standing behind her, complicated masks and grotesques, baskets of fruit and two figures standing on plinths. Mary was always recognisable by her distinctive head-dress, even if her features were not filled in. These sketches were all under the heading of "Crampe Ring Service".

However, these sketches only confirmed what he already knew, which was that Levina had worked on the Accession 'P's for both Edward and Mary. The narrative sketches suggested Levina had been engaged in producing something else at this time. He would have to examine the final images on the Plea Rolls. Nicholas had no idea how much it might cost him, not only in money, but also in time which was why he had left his investigation until the shorter winter days when the light was bad and he could use the excuse of the poor light as justification for not painting or designing jewellery.

He had decided that The Feast of All Hallows was the date he could start searching for clues and 1st November dawned a typical English dull grey November day. The wind was increasing and was tearing the last remaining leaves from the trees. It was a south-westerly and he thought of the various merchantmen he knew, Drake in particular. Drake, Hawkins and Raleigh, were kings of the sea. Elizabeth seemed fond of Devon men and he wondered if it was because of her relationship with him that she favoured his fellow Devonians. This was pure vanity on his part and it was more likely it was because they were skilled seamen who captured much needed Spanish gold for England. "English Privateers" was a polite English name for the likes of Drake and the others. Philip of Spain called them pirates, but Nicholas supposed that what you were called depended from which viewpoint you were seen. Nicholas wished them all a safe journey home before the winter gales set in properly. He would soon know when any of them were back because they would most certainly come and present themselves at Court. Elizabeth would be diverted and the whole Court entertained with their tales.

As he entered the gates to the King's Bench Court archives, Nicholas's thoughts turned from the conditions at sea to his own personal puzzle.

A clerk sat at a desk writing by the light of a flickering candle. His robe was a thick wool and he wore mittens to keep his hands warm. Nicholas wondered what he was working on and coughed to attract his attention.

"Good morning."

The clerk first raised his head and then his eyebrows at seeing the famous Mr Hillyarde.

"Mr Hillyarde, how can I help?" the clerk enquired. Nicholas was now used to being recognised and rather enjoyed the status. He had never before visited the archives and realised he would be a figure of curiosity. It was a bit odd that an artist would want to look through Court records so his reason had to be believable.

"Thank you, I'm wanting to look at the Plea rolls." Nicholas explained. Sometimes it was easier to tell the truth. After all were not the best deceits made on a foundation of truth?

"Now that's a curious thing." The clerk tried to draw him out to find out why. "Normally, it's the inside of the Rolls which be the most interesting for visitors to these archives, but I assume you wish to see the illuminated fronts?"

Nicholas now wished he had not offered any explanation.

"I'm looking for some inspiration for a present for her Majesty. She loves novelty and another piece of jewellery may well bore her. I thought perhaps a painting telling a story and I believe something about her father might lie within the 'Ps'. " Nicholas knew that if he said it was for the Queen, which was a credible explanation considering his position, it might deflect another query.

"Hmm." The clerk accepted this story. "Normally we make a charge for getting out the necessary Roll and then for copying anything in it. How many do you want to look at?" Nicholas's request presented a problem because if this examination was not for a law case, the clerk was at a loss as to whether to charge the normal fee.

"I'm willing to pay a fee for the privilege of looking at the documents." Nicholas offered. "However, it is only the front cover I wish to peruse and as to the number, well, I would like access to many. I assume they are stored in date order?"

The clerk was thankful that there was not going to be any need for copying information, which meant none of the scribes would be required and if it were only the pictures Mr Hillyarde wanted to look at then presumably he would be doing his own copying. The clerk liked the idea of being able to help, but he would still need to make a nominal charge, after all he had to make sure that the room was unlocked and locked at the end of the day. There were few other clerks in the building as most of them were in working Court so there was no-one he could assign to lifting down the various documents for the famous artist just to look at the fronts.

"How long do you think you will need?" he enquired.

"Mr Clerk, I cannot say. A day, or perhaps two, maybe more," Nicholas replied "what about tuppence for each day I'm here and, if you show me where the reign of Henry begins, then I can get each Roll out by myself."

The clerk sat back and appeared to consider this, but had he already decided he could not risk upsetting Mr Hillyarde.

"Agreed. Come with me and I will explain our system. But remember, you are only allowed one Roll at a time and they must be replaced exactly as you found them."

The clerk got down from his stool and led the way to the storage rooms at the back of the building far away from the Court offices. The further they went from the front of the building, the more gloomy the corridors became. The clerk's long black robes swept a clear path in the dust, which showed how few people came down here. Stopping at the end of a long corridor he turned the handle on a stout oak door that opened on to a room with walls lined with shelves with the rest of the space filled with freestanding book shelves, all filled with stacks of documents. The shelves were labelled sequentially, the earliest being the furthest from the door. The room smelt of old parchment and it was obvious from the deep layer of dust on the desk that no-one had been in here for a very long time.

"This room contains all the Rolls from Henry VII right through until the law terms of 1584," The clerk explained. "The shelves are all marked with the reigns of the various monarchs and the particular law terms. Only take one down at a time and replace it before getting another one. We wouldn't want them getting out of order, would we. There is a pair of steps in the corner so you can get to those on the top shelves."

Nicholas nodded as he followed the man's gesture and espied a set of carved wooden steps. There was a wide oak stool placed in front of the desk in case he wanted to sit and study. He was glad he had a cloth with him so he could wipe away the dust.

"Mr Hillyarde, the Court buildings will close at dusk, but I will come and get you before that, so you don't get locked in." the clerk advised.

"Thank you," Nicholas responded "you are very kind."
The man smiled then left him alone.

Nicholas was glad the room was deserted. He had no idea what he was looking for and just hoped he would recognise it when he found it.

Taking a Roll at random from a shelf marked Henricus VIII, Nicholas folded back the blank top sheet of parchment. There was the illuminated 'P' with a profile pen and ink portrait of the King facing left, surrounded with fluttering cherubs shooting arrows into hearts. The artist was very competent and Nicholas worked out that the Roll came from the seventeenth year of Henry's reign, so the was year 1526. He smiled. This Roll dated from the beginning of Henry VIII's infatuation for Anne Boleyn. The cheeky cherubs with their quivers and bows were clearly the artist's own comment on the King's obsession for the Mistress Boleyn and had to be by Lucas Horenbout.

Nicholas could not believe his luck. At his very first search he had chanced on an image that proved his theory that the 'P's' had been used to make a comment on the sovereign long before Levina came to England and the image was by none other than Levina's cousin.

Nicholas took down another Roll, this time from 1545, but this had a crude image of the King sitting on his throne. There was no subtlety either in execution or allegory. It was merely an image of the sovereign as he was on his coronation day years before, when he had taken the oath to be the purveyor of God's justice and mercy. It was a shame that this was such a crude painting and Nicholas replaced the Roll where he had found it.

Moving down the row he came to the beginning of Edward's reign. Reaching up he pulled out the first long bundle of parchments and placed it on the desk. He lifted the front protective sheet and there was an ink sketch of the young Edward sitting on his throne. This was virtually identical to the sketch of the apprehensive Edward in Levina's workbook for 1547.

Nicholas thought about how the very young Edward must have felt and decided Levina had managed to capture a feeling of awe touched with fear as well as arrogance in the expression of the young prince. The portrait was tiny and Edward appeared swamped by his robes as he sat on the large throne. The sceptre and orb seemed overly large and the top of the P was dominated by an enormous imperial crown. Everything seemed large, except Edward. The whole sheet was monochrome and there was no ornamentation at all. The subtle use of making everything appear over-sized was stating this was a boy king. There was nothing colourful to celebrate Edward's accession.

He replaced the Edward Roll in its place and moved on to the shelf labelled Mary. Mary had been a mature woman when she had succeeded her brother and Nicholas hoped there would be something elaborate. He was not disappointed.

The page was a glittering design with the formal lettering in gold leaf and the whole page dominated by the large illuminated 'P' decorated with burnished silver leaf. The centre of the 'P' was a glorious colour narrative sketch telling the story of just how Mary came to the throne. Two angels carrying blank banners, (similar to the ones in Levina's workbook for 1553), were either side of the seated Mary. In the background to the left, she was being led to the throne by two more angels, recognisable by her head-dress. On the other side of the throne there were mounted figures. A pile of weapons lay on the ground beside the mounted knights and an army could be seen in the distance. This little vignette was telling how the rebels had surrendered to the Queen's forces after their attempt to put Lady Jane Grey on the throne. It was a shame the little picture was unfinished and the banners were not filled in. Unsurprisingly, Mary looked solemn. She was seated on a throne covered by a Cloth of Estate and wearing the traditional ceremonial robes worn by every anointed monarch during the coronation ceremony. The crown sat easily on her head and her hair flowed down around her shoulders. The Holy Spirit in the form of a silver dove hovering above her head proclaimed her divine right to rule as an anointed queen.

The pretty illuminated 'P' was a celebration of the accession of England's first Queen regnant. It was a shame it was unfinished, but there was enough to show that Nicholas was on the right track. He decided to see what Elizabeth's Accession Roll showed. Mary had died on 17th November which was very nearly the end of the Michelmas Term of the sixth year of Mary's reign, in other words in November 1558. If Levina had been the artist given the task of illuminating the accession P for Elizabeth, then Nicholas was sure this one would be very special.

Leaving the Mary Accession Roll on the desk Nicholas went and retrieved the Michelmas Term of 1558. It was as dusty as the others and clearly never been examined since the day it had been placed on the shelves. Folding back the outer sheet there was indeed an illuminated 'P', but not quite what Nicholas had anticipated. He had hoped it would resemble the very first little miniature he had ever seen of Elizabeth in her golden coronation robes.

A painted figure holding the orb and the sword, was seated on a throne with a crown floating above her head and he recognised Levina's hand wielding the brush. The monarch wore Mary's typical head-dress and gown, but her face had lost the scowl. This P was nothing like the joyous 'P' of Mary's Accession.

Nicholas sat on the stool comparing the two fronts. The crown surmounting the Elizabeth Accession 'P' was gilded and beautiful, and the elaborate strapwork had gone, replaced by elaborate Italianate design. The rest of the word was gilded, even though it was shortened because the belly of the 'P' was so fat.

It did not make sense. Why would Mary's Accession 'P' be so elaborate and Elizabeth's not. Nicholas sat staring at the two

Rolls and the two Queens stared sightlessly back.

By November 1558 King Philip had long since returned to Spain, which was probably why Levina had painted Mary seated on her own. Because Mary had been seriously ill Levina might have decided to paint the queen without a face or a crown. If Mary died then Levina could paint in a suspended crown and no-one would be any the wiser. Nicholas read the words and there it was, the statement that during that law term Mary had reigned as Queen of England with her husband Philip and then Elizabeth had succeeded and was now Queen. Since the words told that Mary had died during this law term, it made sense that this image had been painted before the words, which would explain why the Queen was dressed like the Mary in the previous Ps. Levina had probably left the monarch's features blank until after the end of the Michelmas term or Mary's death, depending on which happened first. It was unprecedented to have a rightful heir to be a woman, let alone be succeeded by another, so yet again Levina had come up with a way of portraying this second female accession.

The sound of footsteps on the worn flagstones in the corridor brought Nicholas back from his thoughts. Quickly folding the top sheet over the Mary Accession Roll, he pushed it back into its place on the shelf. He did not want to be banned for not obeying the rule of only one Roll out at a time. The footsteps passed and receded into the distance leaving Nicholas still pondering this 'P'. If this Michelmas Term Roll image had been changed to show Elizabeth's Accession then what was her Coronation 'P' like?

Nicholas pulled the next roll of from the shelf. Sure enough, there was the crowned monarch with 'Vivat Regina' declared above her head. But it was just a simple sketched image, no flamboyance at all, no colour, minimal gilding and a return to the traditional strapwork decoration up the stem of the P.

Elizabeth was seated on the throne, but her face was in profile. Nicholas smiled. An allusion to classical Rome thus stating that, with this monarch, a new classical order was established. The thought that this sheet would also have been quick and cheap to produce flitted across his mind.

Elizabeth's Coronation 'P' did not have any elaborate narrative, but instead she was shown with her face in profile like a Roman Caesar, wearing the traditional robes and like her sister, her hair flowing down her back. The concept of Elizabeth, The Virgin Queen was established in the Coronation P of the first full term of Elizabeth Tudor.

His searches confirmed his theory that the 'P' was sometimes used as a place to make visual comments. Levina had not painted or sketched all the P's, but she had depicted the accessions of all three monarchs. His stomach growled and he sat and munched on some bread, cheese and apples. Alice had included a bottle of his mint infusion sweetened with honey.

In 1558 Geneva the news of the burnings of Protestant martyrs had frightened him. He remembered overhearing Mr Bodley talking to the preacher, Mr Knox, saying that it was a bad time for those left at home and both men had been wondering how the Hillyardes were faring in Exeter. Nicholas remembered how his stomach had knotted as he had pondered the possibility of his mother or father being burnt at the stake. Surely Exeter was far enough away from London for his family to be safe, but the lack of news had been worrying and he had lain awake many a night wondering about his mother and father.

Nicholas decided to go home and come back tomorrow after he had given himself time to reflect on today's investigations. He left the room with his notes carefully stowed away in his pocket. He had jotted down the dates and the details of the 'P's' done by Levina, but these notes would not be incriminating should anyone see them, or worse still, if he lost them. There were some sketches of cherubs, but nothing else. Back in his studio he would be able to look at Levina's various sketchbooks and perhaps see where she was involved in these illuminations and where she was not.

The clerk was still scratching away at his work, the goose quill pen scraping across the surface of the parchment The man looked up as Nicholas approached.

"All finished?" the clerk enquired.

"For today," Nicholas replied, placing two pennies on the desk. "What time will you be here tomorrow?"

"Two hours before noon is when I can open the archive for you."

Nicholas nodded, tomorrow he would be able to work until the archive closed.

The following morning Nicholas took two candles from the cupboard together with an earthenware candle holder and put them in his bag. It would be very difficult to see the fine detail of the 'P's' in the archives unless he had extra light. The sky was a leaden grey and threatened rain.

"Don't be late, Nicholas," Alice murmured as Nicholas kissed her on the cheek. He had that far away look which meant he was not listening, even though he murmured "Yes dear" in reply and kissed her again, this time on her forehead. Alice rubbed her back. She was heavily pregnant and the baby seemed to spend all day and night kicking. Unfortunately she was also suffering continual indigestion and this was not relieved by anything. It would be a Christmas baby and she hoped it would come before the festivities. It would be nice to be able to enjoy the Christmas treats without suffering the agony of indigestion. She watched Nicholas weaving his way between the City crowds before she shut the door. Cook was pickling onions and Alice needed to the silver spice box for the various spices to make them special.

Nicholas's work-room was neat and tidy as ever and a portrait sat propped on the small desk easel. Alice walked over and saw that it was another version of Arthur. She sighed and wondered why he had painted this one. It was complete with the motto, but Arthur's face did not have the same feel as the original portrait.

As Nicholas made his way to the archives, he wondered which Rolls he should look at and decided that Mary's reign would be the one that might contain interesting images. Why there were no sketches for any 'P's' at this time in Levina's books puzzled him. She had certainly been at Court because she had told him how the ladies of the Court had spent a huge amount of time on their knees praying for Mary to conceive. Not for the first time did Nicholas wish he had spent more time listening and learning what Levina had been telling him about her life at Court.

The clerk was as good as his word and when Nicholas arrived at 10 o'clock the doors were already unlocked and open with the clerk waiting for him.

"Good morning Mr Hillyarde. The weather seems to have changed for the worst." The man had the soft features of a man who had spent most of his life hunched over a desk and his blue eyes squinted as he looked up at Nicholas.

"Mr Hillyarde, I've taken the liberty of setting a candle in the room for you. 'tis a dark day and it can't be easy for you looking at the Rolls."

"Thank you, that's very kind," he responded. The clerk continued: "And the fire has been lit too. When the weather is like this, it sometimes makes the room damp and, over time, this affects the parchment, turning it black. If there is anything else we can do for you, then please let me know."

They reached the oak door and Nicholas entered. The room did not smell quite as musty as it had the day before and a new candle sat in a holder on the desk at the window. Next to it had been placed a jug, a pewter beaker and some bread and cheese under a linen napkin. It was a very kind gesture and he appreciated it. He was glad that a fire crackled away in the small fireplace, dispelling the musty dankness. He wondered whether someone would come to tend it later. Judging by the dust in the corridor and on the Rolls themselves, not often.

Nicholas took off his cloak and folded it, placing it on the bench to use as a cushion. Opening his bag, he took out his notebook and pens and set them on one side.

He took down the Rolls from the first four months of Mary's reign. Mary's Justices had been kept very busy and the Rolls were thick and heavy. Up until her marriage to Philip, the P's showed her as the monarch, in her traditional coronation robes, holding the various symbols of office. It was not Levina's work and there had been absolutely no attempt to paint the face of the Queen as a realistic likeness. The Trinity P celebrated Mary's marriage to Philip in the summer of 1554.

The construction of these images was very simple and Nicholas wondered who had drawn them. He put the Rolls back in their place and took down the Hilary Term for 1555. A simple pen and ink drawing of Mary and Philip sitting on their thrones side by side. Mary was shown wearing her distinctive head-dress and looking more like the grumpy Mary as painted in the large portraits of her.

Similarly, the next ones. Nothing too remarkable except that the perspective was poor and not any significant visual comment right up until November of 1558 and Elizabeth's accession. No-one had made any specific visual comments except Levina who had illuminated the Accession P showing the events leading up to Mary's coronation. He made detailed notes and sketches regarding the image for the queen in each P and decided it was time for lunch.

He sat and thought as he ate. The rain trickled down the window panes. The trees were all bare and the scene was quite depressing so Nicholas moved to sit by the fire. There was a stack of logs and he placed a couple on the glowing embers. The logs were seasoned ash and caught quickly. He munched on the lunch the clerk had left him. It had been a nice gesture and Nicholas doodled a portrait of the clerk on a spare sheet of paper. The man's nose hooked slightly and his forehead had become crinkled with years of straining to see in poor candlelight. Nicholas added the laughter lines at the corner of the man's eyes and sat back pleased with the finished sketch.

If the Elizabeth 'P's' were all like Mary's there appeared to be nothing significant drawn by anyone. He wondered whether it was because Mary and Elizabeth were queens and not kings?

The early days of Elizabeth's reign were simple pen and ink images of the monarch in coronation robes and he recognised Levina's hand in the majority of the sketches from those he had seen in her sketchbooks. He also noted that the stem of the 'P' had reverted from Italianate Renaissance design to being decorated with elaborate ink strapwork, which was relatively quick, extremely decorative and cheap. Occasionally a letter would be gilded but there was no flashy use of colour. Sometimes Elizabeth look amused, but there she sat, The Virgin Queen, her flowing hair a testimony to her declared vow that she would not marry and therefore remain a virgin all her life. Had she not, on one occasion, waved her hand on which she wore the Coronation ring, asking how could she marry when she was already married to the nation?

Nicholas took down the Rolls for 1561 because he had promised himself that he would look at all of them up until 1565. All were simple pen and ink drawings. From the Hilary term onwards a simple pen and ink drawing showed Elizabeth looking very superior and aloof, even smug, but the only difference was her hair was no longer loose. Nicholas did a quick copy of the image, then sat and looked at his notes of the Marian 'Ps'. He lifted the Marian Roll of 1555 down again and placed it side by side to this one of 1561.

Had their images changed because both Queen's had been on the throne the same length of time? Nicholas counted the number of law terms for both queens. By early 1555 Mary had been on the throne for five Law terms, but by 1561 Elizabeth had been on the throne for nine, so this was clearly not the case.

This seemed to be evidence of something, but he was unable to comprehend its significance. It had been worth copying the Marian image so he could ponder it at home and he wondered if there was anything in Levina's books he had missed.

Further questing through the next few years produced nothing more except for an exquisite image in 1565 of Elizabeth looking incredibly sad and lost deep in thought. It was very like the coronation miniature Levina had painted for Dudley, but sadness flowed off the page. Nicholas smiled at the subtlety of emotion Levina had captured in this portrait and wondered why Elizabeth had been so sad.

There was nothing more for him here and Nicholas packed up his things. He was pleased with his day's work. At least it had stopped raining so he would not get wet on the way home. He had definitely found out something, but had no idea what. Perhaps Alice would be able to cast some light on his discoveries.

The clerk looked up as Nicholas approached.

"Thank you for your kindness, Mr Clerk. The lunch was very welcome and the fire too."

"Will you be back tomorrow Mr Hillyarde?" the clerk replied.

"No, I've gleaned as much as I can. The ones at the time the Queen's father was courting her mother are quite lyrical with little cherubs and the hearts." The man would remember this statement and conclude that Nicholas was planning something to celebrate her parentage. Nicholas placed a silver sixpence and the small pencil portrait of the clerk on the man's desk.

"Oh Mr Hillyarde, thank you. You are most kind."

Nicholas walked through the door leaving the clerk well pleased with his remuneration. Little gestures such as the gift of the sketch were Nicholas's way of thanking the man for his thoughtfulness. The man's status would be raised considerably if he could show his friends his portrait sketch by none other than the famous Mr Hillyarde. He would no doubt expand Nicholas's story that he had come here for inspiration and tell of the cherubs fluttering around Henry VIII.

Later, long after the household had settled down for the night, Nicholas and Alice were tucked up in their four-poster bed whilst the wind hurled the rain against the mullions and howled down the chimney. Alice lay on her side whilst Nicholas rubbed her aching back and whispered his discoveries to her.

"So what do you think the two artists are trying to tell me, Alice? There seems no reason for Mary and Elizabeth's images to change when they do. Surely, if it were to change, they would both change after the same length of time."

"So, tell me again, what was the date that Mary's image changes?" Alice asked.

"Hilary Term, 1555." Nicholas replied.

"Which was how long after she had married Philip?" came her next question.

"Six months. But what are you getting at?" Nicholas was trying to follow Alice's logic, but, as usual, it eluded him.

"Never mind, Nick. Tell me again the dates of Elizabeth's change."

"Easter Term, 1561, which was nine terms after she had come to the throne."

"Did you do a copy of these?" Alice sat up and looked at her husband.

"Of course!"

"Well, let me have a look because you are asking me to keep a lot in my head and this baby is trying very hard to kick all these facts out again." Alice rubbed her distended stomach to enforce her statement.

"Oh, yes." Nicholas reluctantly left the warmth of their bed and retrieved his note books. Alice had plumped the pillows and sat up waiting for him to show her his discoveries. Mary was a grumpy looking woman, looking nothing like a queen. She looked more like a carved wooden creature and Alice wondered if the artist had done that deliberately, or perhaps had been chosen because he did not, or could not, do portraits. Philip's distinctive jaw made Alice shudder as she remembered just how close England had come to becoming a vassal state of Spain.

Nicholas waited as his wife looked at his researches. Occasionally she looked up and counted on her fingers. He knew she was counting the number of terms between the changes of images, just has he had done, but Alice said nothing. Her lack of verbal reasoning irritated him, but he also knew that she would stop if he tried to talk to her, so he could only wait.

Finally, Alice stopped examining his notes and drawings.

"And that is over two and a half years after Elizabeth acceded to the throne?" Alice's question was more of a confirmation of her calculations. Nicholas nodded. This had been one of those things he had been trying to solve. It made better sense if the Queen's had some reason for this image change and logic suggested that it would be the same number of months into their reign.

"It's simple." she whispered.

"It is?" Nicholas could not agree. It was far from simple to him so he waited for her to expand her statement. Alice put his sketches of Mary on the coverlet side by side. "See how Mary is shown in the Michelmas Term of 1554 where she has long with flowing hair. Here is the image of Mary for the Hilary Term of 1555 showing her with her usual head-dress and veil."

Nicholas nodded and wondered why his wife was concentrating on royal fashion.

Alice sighed. She was going to have to lead Nicholas by the hand.

"By painting the individual Queen's with their hair up, these artists are recording evidence that they are no longer virgins." Alice paused, enjoying her superior knowledge.

"Go on," Nicholas prompted.

"Come on Nick, you must have guessed by now?"

"Alice, stop being irritating and tell me what you are thinking."

"Sometimes husband, you can be really stupid." Alice looked at her husband and smiled a superior smile. The baby had stopped kicking as if he too was waiting for her to reveal her thoughts.

Nicholas was baffled. As far as he knew there was no recognised symbolism that limners used for marriage because until Mary, there had never been a Queen that had ruled in her own right. Levina's sketch books had revealed nothing.

"Nick, there is only one solid evidence for a woman not being a Virgin." Alice paused. She was relieved that the baby was no longer trying to kick her ribs through her chest.

"Go, on." Nicholas prompted. He was still trying to think of anything Levina might have told him about symbolism.

"The artists were recording the fact that the Queen's were pregnant." she finished.

Nicholas lay back and gazed up at the Alice Venus and Nicholas Mars

"Alice, am I being really stupid, but I can't see how."

"Nick, what is it that the artists and limners all use as a visual symbol of the Virgin's virginity?" Alice paused, waiting to see if her husband would grasp what she was telling him.

"Oh, my God!" Nicholas finally saw what his wife was trying to make him realise. "Of course, The Virgin Mary has flowing hair. Only the Virgin remained a virgin after she gave birth to Christ, which is why she is always portrayed with her hair down. Alice, you are a genius. To think that the way a woman dresses her hair could be the answer. It is such a simple image." Nicholas kissed her and the baby gave her a hefty kick to remind her that he was now awake.

"Probably only lawyers would ever look at these and they wouldn't be interested in the decoration of a P, would they?" she replied. "Don't these follow a traditional format, so it would be very unlikely anyone else would be interested or want to, look at them?"

"Of course," Nicholas was so excited "the best way to show a marriage has been consummated is to provide some visual evidence that the Queen is pregnant. So when Mary declared she was pregnant the limner may have decided that the best way of showing this was in the 'P's'. This might have just been a personal statement by the limner rather than a specific instruction from a judge. Do we know when Mary declared she was pregnant?"

Alice thought for a bit. "I believe it was some time towards the end of November 1554, but I will check. I'm sure Sarah will know."

Nicholas was bursting with excitement. "Well if that's the case, then it makes sense that the P for the law term following, being the Hilary Term for 1555, would show the different image of the queen. So when Elizabeth fell pregnant in 1561, Levina used the same method to record her pregnancy. The image is only a pen and ink sketch like most of the others at this date, and who looks at the front sheet anyway? Alice, it's so subtle it's genius."

"Wait, Nicholas, surely there must have been royal pregnancies before, so how was it recorded that the Queen was pregnant in Henry's time? Were any of them portrayed here?" Alice's question was valid. "And why wouldn't it be in the law term Mary declared she was carrying?"

"I'll answer the last question first because it's easier. The P's are the first thing to be done on the front sheets, then the declaration of which term and which sovereign, then the various cases are attached, so the P would have been done long before the end of November 1554. The only exception is in 1588 when Mary was dying."

As to whether there are other queens shown pregnant, I have no idea, dear wife, I didn't look, but I don't think so. Most of the Henry 'P's' are of him, except a couple in the 1520's when he was infatuated by Anne Boleyn and have cupid's fluttering around Henry's head. What is important is that Mary was the first Queen of England in her own right, and Elizabeth the second, which means that they are on the throne by God's divine will and therefore will be the sovereign portrayed in the 'P'. By tradition, the 'P's' only show the sovereign, but sometimes the artist shows something else, but it always references the monarch. Having an heir on the way would be so important, I knew someone would find some way of showing the Queen was with child."

"Shhhhh. You'll wake the whole house" Alice chided.

"Alice, you are a genius. But if Elizabeth had been pregnant then it would not have been a case of rejoicing. She would have been in mortal danger, but with a royal pregnancy being so important, someone decided it was necessary to record the fact she was with child somewhere, so why not put it in a tiny image where the sovereign's divine right to rule is shown time and time again?" Nicholas continued reasoning aloud. "But in Elizabeth's case, the image would have to be subtle and this is so subtle because it is just a pen and ink sketch, just like all the others of this time." Nicholas paused "This might be a visual clue, but there has to be evidence other than a P, surely?"

Alice lay back and thought for a few minutes.

"Nick, we've all heard the gossip about Elizabeth in the early days, but if I remember rightly, in 1561 Burghley had been out of favour because he was so against Elizabeth's relationship with Dudley. However, if she was pregnant, she would have needed those whom she trusted around her more than ever." Alice gasped and put her hand to her stomach. Her excitement interrupted as the baby gave her another hefty kick under the ribs. This baby was a lively one and very good at making his presence felt. "Ow!" she rubbed her belly where a little foot was trying to curl its toes between her ribs.

"Alice, you are so right. Levina always said that Burghley was the only one the queen trusted and now this all makes so much sense. When did Dudley's wife die?" Nicholas's mind was speeding through so many channels.

"September 1560, so I believe" Alice replied, through gritted teeth, breathing deeply as the baby kicked again, resenting the solid obstruction of its mother's ribs and trying hard to push them out of the way.

"Of course, ……. And what year was it the Queen had small pox?"

"1562 – October. Why?" Alice could not see the relevance of Nicholas's question.

"No reason, but there's another image all beautifully painted and the Queen is looking so sad and despairing, I thought

266

perhaps it was when she had small pox."

"Perhaps is was painted when Arthur was sent to a foster home? Maybe…" Alice paused. The kicking stopped allowing her to collect her thoughts ".. was it Levina who did this one?"

"Yes, yes, and I feel she's leaving me clues all over the place, if only I have the wit to work them out." Nicholas lay back and put his arm around Alice's shoulders.

"Well, maybe darling husband, Elizabeth is looking so sad because she knows she cannot go and see the boy because someone might put two and two together. Arthur does have very distinctive coloured hair and I should think when he was a child, it would have been very red. If you had seen Elizabeth and a red haired boy together, what would you have thought? The gossips would have had a field day."

Alice sighed and shook her head. It amazed her that her husband needed so much coaxing to put two and two together. Men really were not very intelligent when it came to these things. Even someone as sensitive as her husband had difficulty in understanding the subtle ways of women. Most were only interested in commerce or hunting and warring, or worse, wenching and gambling! Very few understood the nuance and subtlety of their womenfolk and, she thought to herself, those were the ones who truly loved their wives. It was such a shame that more men did not listen to the women in their families; it would save so many problems.

"Also, the Queen has made it very clear to Parliament that she would never marry even though she knew they would continue to arrange suitable suitors for her so she could provide an heir. This second P - is it painted in the same year that, her cousin, Lady Devereux gave birth to her son Robert?" Alice was throwing various suggestions up in the air. "If so, perhaps Levina was showing how Elizabeth had come to terms with the realisation that she would never be able to marry Dudley and how

267

doubly saddened she was at his flirting outrageously with Lady Devereux, who might well be carrying Dudley's natural son."

"Alice, do you think she knows Robert Devereux is possibly Dudley's son?"

"Possibly. Ouch ..." Alice rubbed the spot where the next Hillyarde was still kicking enthusiastically against her ribs. "Poor woman .... never being able to acknowledge her own son, she has to watch whilst her beloved courts another woman, and right under her nose. Not only that, he then places his cuckoo in another man's nest. It would be enough to make anyone sad."

"Alice," Nicholas paused as he searched his memory "I think 1565 was when Levina and George started going up to Hatfield regularly, so perhaps they weren't actually going to Hatfield, but to where Arthur was being brought up at Enfield, then reporting back to the Queen on the child's progress. Alice, you are a genius, which is why I married you."

"And if you don't get any sleep Nick, you won't be able to think straight," came her reply.

"All right, I hear you, but why the strange motto, darling wife?" Nicholas asked, but Alice was apparently asleep.

"My dear Nicholas, come in, come in." Thomas Bodley clasped his childhood friend by the hands and shook them hard. "How long is it since I last saw you?"

Nicholas returned the greeting and smiled, quietly observing Thomas had less hair and was chubbier than the last time they had met.

"I think it must be at least two years. Life is obviously treating you well and I hear you are becoming quite the celebrated academic."

Thomas laughed.

"You mean my book collection? One of the perks of travel. I get to some of the great publishing centres of Europe.

Venice, in particular, has a great number of booksellers and I have added various rare editions to my library. I may even have to move house. Come, let me show you."

Thomas led Nicholas to a large room where one wall was filled with two windows overlooking a garden. Outside, the trees were bare, their stark branches reaching up into the cold bright blue of the early December sky. Neatly clipped knee high box hedges defined the flower beds of a fashionable knot garden and the raked gravel paths between the beds glistened with frost in the cold winter sun.

Shelves, groaning under the weight of Thomas's books, lined two walls from floor to ceiling. The chimney breast was flanked by two more sets of oak shelves carrying more books whilst a fire crackled in the grate. One shelf was not quite full, but Nicholas did not think that it would be long until these spaces would be filled.

"This is quite a collection, Tom. It must have taken you years to put this together." Nicholas was truly amazed. Here were the complete works of Petrarch, Dante and Boccaccio. Durer's writings on art he knew and recognised a first edition of 1521. The preacher John Knox's various publications were here too, as well as the works of Zwingli, Calvin, Erasmus and Luther. Nicholas and Thomas had sat through many a sermon from both Knox and Calvin when they were living in Geneva. Knox's views had been widely known in England and when Elizabeth came to the throne it had taken some time for him to get a permission to pass through England to return home to Scotland. The vitriolic preacher had since sat in Scotland continuing to preach fire and brimstone to the Scots, who had been quite receptive to his philosophy.

"One of the privileges of being in the corps diplomatique, Nick. People learn of my interest and search out rare editions for me. Come, tell me about yourself, Nick. What are you doing? I hear the Queen is very pleased with the new Seal, and your miniatures are the talk of the Court. How are Alice and the children?" Thomas sat down on one chair next to the fire and Nicholas did the same on the other. "I gather you are about to have another?"

"Tom, you are very well informed. Yes, the next one is due at Christmas. We have quite a brood. Alice is such an admirable mother and wife and the children are all thriving. I am truly blessed to have her. Yes, the design for the second Great Seal is now finished and I hope being cast as we speak. What is more, I believe the Queen will sign the warrant giving me exclusive rights over her image 'in little' any day now. George Gower is to be Sergeant Painter, and no doubt will love creating all the large portraits. I wish him well because he will also have to create all those damn machinery pieces for the masques and balls Elizabeth loves so much. Between you and me, I've had enough of Arthur's Court to last a lifetime! However, the Queen is still obsessed with Camelot so it will be Gower's job to create all the Arthurian surprises when required, so good luck to him."

"That is good, very good. Have you heard from Marcus?"

Nicholas nodded and brought Thomas up to date with all Marcus's news. They continued to exchange news until Nicholas felt it polite to address the real reason why he had sought his old friend out.

The ash logs were burning well and giving out a terrific heat. The two men sat sipping mulled wine and enjoying the warmth at their feet and in their stomachs.

"I was hoping, Tom, you could give me some insight into Atticus." Nicholas asked.

"Oh, why him?" Bodley was puzzled. They had both struggled over their Latin lessons.

"I was asked to add a motto to a miniature referring to Atticus and I wondered why." Nicholas had decided to stick with the basic truth, but to reveal nothing about Arthur. "The fact the legend makes reference to Atticus made me wonder who he actually was. Of course, I don't want to ask my client as it's probably refers to something deeply personal. "

"I see." Thomas leaned back into the big feather cushions covered in wool-work, his elbows resting on the arm of the chair and his hands cradling the silver wine cup. "Was there no other clue?"

"Nothing." Nicholas replied.

"Tell me the motto?" Thomas asked. There was no way round this direct enquiry.

"Attici Amoris Ergo."

"But that makes no sense at all." Thomas commented. "why would someone want a statement that said, Therefore, by, with, from, or of the love of Atticus?"

"That's why I came to you, because you were so much better at deciphering the subtle nuances of Cicero." The hardness of the school room chairs stood out in Nicholas's memory far more than vestiges of the content of their Latin lessons.

Thomas leaned back and gazed at the ceiling. "Another interpretation could be, through the love of Atticus. But even so, your motto appears to be gibberish." Thomas frowned and shook his head as if to flick the words from his head.

"That's what I think, but who was Atticus, apart from being the best friend of Cicero? That much I do remember!" Nicholas waited for his friend to compose his thoughts. Thomas poured them both more wine.

"Cicero and Titus Pomponius Atticus were childhood friends and Atticus's sister married Cicero's brother Quintus, so they were related through marriage. His father was fairly wealthy, so Atticus would have been well educated. He was then adopted by an even richer uncle, who didn't have an heir." Thomas warmed to his subject "Cicero wrote his De Amicitatis as a commentary on friendship, based on their relationship. However, unlike his friend Cicero, Atticus preferred not to stand for the Senate." Thomas paused and sipped his wine to lubricate his throat. Nicholas waited for his friend to continue.

"Atticus was very wealthy and realised politics could be expensive both financially and in terms of status, so he was much keener on looking after his estates and kept well away from the corruption that was Rome. He died in Athens you know." Thomas was enjoying his role of Latin history teacher.

"Why did he go to Greece?" Nicholas wondered whether this was relevant to his quest.

"He moved to Athens quite early on. Life in Greece was probably far more appealing to him, if you know what I mean." Thomas pursed his lips and raised his eyebrows. Nicholas looked at his friend for a minute trying to understand what Thomas was trying to tell him. Thomas continued to look at him quizzically, waiting for Nicholas to realise what it was he was saying.

"Oh!" suddenly it dawned "you mean that Atticus preferred men?"

"Now that would be impossible to prove because Atticus did marry, albeit late in life and from that union, had a daughter. Through marriage he was related to Crassus. You remember, he was the Roman general who was killed by the Parthians who then cut off his head and filled his mouth with gold to satisfy his greed for that metal." Thomas was, so far, proving a mine of completely useless information. " Atticus committed suicide at the age of 78 by starving himself to death because he was suffering from an incurable disease. Don't ask me what it was."

"So what else was he, apart from living in self-imposed exile, a wealthy banker, a philosopher and a childhood friend of one of the greatest Roman orators." Nicholas was beginning to think that Arthur's motto was what it appeared to be - complete gibberish and a bad attempt at scholarship.

"Well, Atticus was of Roman nobility." Thomas continued. "In particular, he was a knight of equestrian rank. We would call him Master of Horse, which is …."

Nicholas did not hear the rest of Thomas's explanation. Clearly, the motto was not gibberish, but designed to appear so unless you knew something about Roman aristocracy. Nicholas needed to think about everything Thomas had told him and to talk it over privately with Alice.

"…. So is this information of any use?" Thomas's question required an answer.

"Well, no." Nicholas lied. "I think my sitter is just trying to appear better educated than he really is."

"Oh dear. That is a shame. I thought my knowledge would enable you to solve some cryptic puzzle." Thomas was disappointed that his scholarly insight had apparently proved useless.

Alice was seated telling the children Aesop's fable of the fox, the crow and the piece of cheese. Young Daniel was sitting cross legged on the floor, a very grown up six and a half year old who had his father's dark, curly hair and dark brown eyes. It seemed such a short time since Alice and he were in France, avoiding the intrigues of the French Court and completely free from the responsibilities of a family. Young Elizabeth, her blonde curls escaping her night cap, had just celebrated her fifth birthday and was the spitting image of her mother. Francis was going to be four years old in two weeks time and he had Nicholas's dark hair, but his mother's blue eyes. Laurence was two and a half. He sat on one side of Alice, with her arm around him and Little Lettice was curled in the crook of Alice's other arm, stroking 'The Bump'. Lettice was sucking her thumb and very nearly asleep.

273

At his entrance the older children jumped up shouting 'Daddy, Daddy' and ran to their father who swept them into his arms. Lettice wailed horribly, frightened by the noise that had woken her. Alice held her close and stroked her hair, comforting her.

Seeing his family all together sitting safely in this lovely warm room was the embodiment of one of his ambitions. He was proud to be an Englishman and living in London. Not for his family, the sad exile from family and friends. His children would have everything he had missed as a child and most of all, this meant being with their parents. Momentarily he wondered what Arthur was doing.

Later that evening, when household was safely asleep, Nicholas told Alice everything Thomas had told him about Cicero, Atticus and Roman society. Alice lay curled in a ball whilst Nicholas rubbed her aching back.

"Nick, do you think Arthur's safe?"

"Alice, I hope so."

Rex Quondam Rex Futuris?

Nicholas stood with his back to the fire in Lord Burghley's office. Sir Francis Walsingham and Lord Burghley sat on large chairs either side of the fire. He had gone to sign the Bond of Association and was now bound to 'withstand, pursue and offend... by force of arms, as by all other means of revenge, all manner of persons... and their abettors that shall attempt any act, or counsel or consent to any thing that shall tend to the harm of her majesty's royal person and will never desist from all manner of forcible pursuit against such persons, to the utter extermination of them, their counsellors, aiders and abettors"..

He had decided to tell Lord Burghley how he had been approached and asked to paint a miniature portrait of a young man calling himself Arthur Southron. So far he had not shown

274

them the contents of the little lime box he had safely in his pocket.

"So why do you think I would be interested in this young man?" Burghley asked. He was wrapped against the early December cold despite the fact his office was heated by a blazing log fire. The old man leaned over the table and picked up a glass decanter, poured some red wine into three small pewter tankards, reached to pick up the mulling poke which had been heating in the middle of the blaze, and plunged the poker into the first tankard. The liquid spluttered against the hot metal and the scent of hot wine and spices filled the room. Burghley did this twice more, handing the first tankard to Walsingham and the second to Nicholas .

Nicholas reached into his pocket and handed him the lime box. Lord Burghley examined the plain little box stroking the satin smooth, undecorated surface before twisting the lid open. Arthur gazed sightlessly into the distance, holding a woman's hand.

'My God ' Lord Burghley muttered under his breath handing the little box to Walsingham.

"God's teeth!" Walsingham looked up at Nicholas "To whom did this young man ask you to send this portrait?"

"Sir Dru Drury, via John Ashley." Nicholas could feel the heat of the fire burning the back of his legs. There was no turning back now. Either he was trusted by them or he was about to find himself on a very short trip to the Tower.

"But instead you brought this to me." Lord Burghley looked at the miniature again.

"Because of whom he resembles." Nicholas replied.

Sir Francis pursed his lips and looked into the fire, nodding slightly. Burghley coughed as if the warm wine had caught the back of his throat. Both waited for Nicholas to continue. They did not have to wait for long.

"He said he had been brought up in Enfield." Nicholas was intrigued at the muttered expletives. "and had been educated in the classics, dancing, grammar, rhetoric and swordplay. He asked me to give it to Sir John Ashley when he was next at Court, and then told me that Sir John would pass it on to Sir Dru Drury."

"Go on." breathed Sir Francis looking at Nicholas over the top of his pewter tankard and blowing on the hot wine. Nicholas did not know what else to say.

Sir Francis knew the benefit of letting silences grow. The person being questioned would always fill the gap, even someone as adept at listening as Nicholas who could work silently for hours whilst appearing to listen to his sitter's chatter.

The atmosphere in the room grew thicker. Outside, the fading feeble winter sunlight showed the cold December day was nearly over: the purple shadows within the room were growing long and dark. The fire became the glowing focus for the story unfolding in these private rooms.

"Sir Dru is part of the Queen's entourage." It was a bald statement and Nicholas threw it into the silence as an incentive for either of the two men to tell him why this courtier might be the recipient of Arthur's miniature.

"Quite so, but why should that arouse your interest young Nicholas?" Burghley ignored Nicholas's desire for an explanation and leant back making himself a bit more comfortable.

"I want to protect my Queen in case there is trouble afoot."

Walsingham sighed. There was always trouble afoot. Perhaps Hillyarde had unearthed something that neither he nor Burghley had yet heard of.

"But why this particular young man?" he asked the artist.

"Sir Francis – he resembles so much the Queen and my Lord Leicester that someone might try and use him for bad mischief. I spend my whole life looking at people's faces and he is as like a pea in a pod to them." Nicholas's reply was quiet, but his words seemed to still the air in the room making the atmosphere more tense.

Burghley drew in a deep breath, rose, went to the closed outer door of his apartments and locked it.

"And have you any reason to think there might be trouble afoot?" he asked as he settled himself back in his chair.

"Young Arthur said he was about to go abroad; to the Low Countries and he wanted his guardian to have a remembrance of him in case he did not return."

"Hmm… any more than that?" Sir Francis asked.

"My Lords" Nicholas addressed both men "if I see a resemblance, then sooner or later, someone else will."

Both men exchanged looks. Burghley raised his left eyebrow in thought. The firelight flickered on the faces of the three men. Their voices had been so low, no one would have been able to detect their conversation had they tried to listen at the door.

"Arthur told me that he was born in 1561." Nicholas continued.

Burghley nodded and Nicholas wondered if he was agreeing with him, or just indicating he should continue.

"And so that would make him," Nicholas paused as he calculated Arthur's age "twenty three?"

Burghley appeared to be only slightly interested, but Nicholas caught the surreptitious look he cast in Walsingham's direction.

"My lords, I was a very young man in 1561, but even I heard the rumours about the Queen and Lord Leicester. If others think that this man is an heir to the throne of England, and if our enemies abroad get hold of him, there could be much danger to the Queen's life. I for one, do not wish this to happen."

The two most powerful men in England looked at each other. It was Sir Francis who spoke;

"And do you have any evidence other than an uncanny resemblance to the queen and Leicester, for this man being who you think he is?" his voice was barely a whisper. Sir Francis did not look at Nicholas, but gazed into the fire. Nicholas shifted on his stool and sipped his drink. There was a hint of menace in Walsingham's question. Nicholas looked at Burghley, who was regarding at him with a quizzical expression. Nicholas coughed nervously.

"As you know, many years ago I painted two large portraits of the Queen that were designed to be hung as a marriage diptych. She wanted to be shown wearing her Pelican and Phoenix brooches and in her best gowns with her best jewels. At the time I painted the pelican portrait, I thought it was because she was under considerable pressure to marry and this was her way of saying that she was sacrificing her womanly desire to have children by remaining single, because she was already married to the people of England. Using the Pelican for the symbolism it carries, would ensure everyone would understand her message."

"Go on" Lord Burghley coaxed. Nicholas swallowed some wine to moisten his throat.

"As for the phoenix portrait, well, I assumed it was her personal statement of survival. Elizabeth had, after all, managed to survive her sister's reign and when she came to the throne, the phoenix was her statement of how she rose from the ashes of a problematic era."

Nicholas paused for any comment from his audience.

"And" Burghley invited him to continue. Nicholas could not read either man's expression. He took another sip. The wine was warm and spicy, but not as good as Alice's.

"What if someone else comes to the same conclusions that these are evidence for a royal birth?" he asked.

"How so? So far this is purely speculation." This time is was Sir Francis prompting him to continue. Nicholas swallowed involuntarily suddenly feeling as if he were a nut in a tightening nutcracker, but he was so far down the line of explanation he could not stop.

"The pelican is always understood as the emblem of the mother who will sacrifice herself for her own children by pecking her breast in order to provide the blood on which they can feed. It has been a religious symbol of self sacrifice for hundreds of years." Nicholas paused.

"Continue…" Burghley said.

Nicholas wanted one of the two men to say something to him, but all they did was lead him on to reveal more of his theory. "What if Elizabeth would not marry in order to protect a child she knew already existed, this could be a form of self sacrifice and very much along the lines of the pelican mother protecting her brood."

Burghley nodded. His expression was unreadable. Nicholas took another sip of his drink noting it was now tepid and slightly sour.

"Legend has it that there can only be one phoenix at a time and it appears that the Queen will die without an heir. But what if a child is hidden away, growing up and being educated. Presumably this child would have as much a claim as others. If this were so, then the phoenix portrait is a statement that the Tudor line is not going to die out with the death of the Queen."

Nicholas stared into the flames. He now thought his theory sounded fantastical and he wondered whether he was just trying to find evidence that did not exist. Neither man sitting either side of the fire was either confirming or denying anything Nicholas said.

"And then there is his name" Nicholas continued quickly, "Arthur: the name of the king who was once the saviour of England and in time to come, according to legend, will come again to England's aid when her need is greatest. Rex quondam, rex futuris – the once and future king. You have to ask yourself: Is the real reason why the Queen is so fond of the Arthurian legends because she knows there is an heir hidden away?"

The ash logs had burnt right down, leaving a deep bed of glowing orange embers. The room was very comfortably warm, but, even so, Sir Francis pulled his robes across his knees as if to ensure no finger of cold would find its way to chill his body. Burghley leant forward and threw another log on the fire sending a shower of sparks up the chimney.

"Nicholas," the old man turned his head so he could see Nicholas's expression. "Sir Francis is right. This is purely circumstantial speculation. Have you told anyone of your thoughts?"

"No, Lord Burghley." He had thought for a long time before coming to see the Queen's most trusted servant, but had concluded that the dangers of not telling Lord Burghley outweighed the dangers of revealing his thoughts. Nicholas knew he was playing a dangerous game, but then life was dangerous and sometimes it was necessary to take risks to protect the ones you loved.

"Good….. Good." Burghley said nothing more for a few minutes. Walsingham sat looking into the fire. "Say nothing to anyone …." Burghley finished. Nicholas needing no command on this score, nodded and rose to leave. The tiny box sat on the table. He reached for Arthur's portrait. Walsingham sat watching him. Nicholas looked at the image briefly before replacing the lid, screwing it down tightly and replacing the box on the table.

"Nicholas," there was a sinister note in Sir Francis's voice "about the motto? Was it of your own devising?"

"No, Sir Francis. It was Mr Southron's own invention."

Sir Francis nodded, tapping his lips with his fingers. "Thank you."

Burghley rose and escorted Nicholas across the rooms.

"Come and see me at New Year, Nicholas and, in the meantime ...." Burghley left the sentence hanging and tapped the side of his nose indicating Nicholas should stop nosing around in affairs that did not concern him. Burghley unlocked the door to his inner office and escorted Nicholas to the outer door.

Outside it was freezing cold and Nicholas pulled his cloak up tightly around his ears. The door closed quickly and quietly behind him. He heard the key turn in the lock thankful that he was on the outside. He sat on the stone bench wondering why Sir Francis had asked him who had thought up the motto. Aghast, he realised perhaps Sir Francis had immediately understood the allusion to Atticus and thought that if he had composed the motto, it was his way of revealing Arthur's parentage.

It was time to head for the safety of home, but, despite the dangers of telling Lord Burghley and Sir Francis about Arthur, he was glad the miniature was now with them.

As Nicholas made his way back to Gutter Lane, he could not help pondering what the two men might be talking about. They had not rejected his ideas out of hand, merely told him that the evidence was circumstantial speculation, but their reactions had been strange. If there was no mileage in his theory about Arthur, then surely they would have laughed at him and sent him packing. If Arthur were who Nicholas thought he was, then it was more than likely that Lord Burghley and Sir Francis knew all about him. Perhaps Lord Burghley had arranged for Arthur to be brought up by the mysterious Mr Southron. If so, then Levina must have been part of the conspiracy because she could be relied on to observe and record a child's progress.

He had not told the two men about the curious images of Mary and Elizabeth in the P's. If they knew these were there, they might just ensure that the front sheets of the Plea Rolls for those two particular law terms just disappeared. Alice was right, he should stop being so curious. It was far too dangerous.

24th December

"Oh my God!" Alice gasped and clutched her swollen belly. "Nick, the pains are coming quicker ...... "

Beads of sweat broke out on Alice's brow and her eyes were pinched with pain.

"I'll send for the midwife" he whispered "and your sister."

Alice smiled weakly as he left the room in search of Molly. Each labour had been considerably shorter than the one before. She thought she would be delivered in just a couple of hours at the most and her back ached worse than ever. It was a deep gnawing pain at the base of her spine and she hoped it would soon pass. Walking helped so Alice walked up and down their bedroom.

A tighter band of pain grabbed her round Alice's belly and a warm trickle of fluid flowed down her legs. Her waters had broken. This baby would not be very long in coming.

"Oh Nick," she gasped as another contraction gripped her and she grasped the upright of their bed "...do hurry."

The sound of feet running up the stairs heralded Nick's return. Alice was hunched over, trying to breathe through the contraction. He blenched as he saw the puddle on the floor and hoped that the midwife would soon be there.

"Come on Alice, let me help you on to the bed." Nicholas half lifted Alice on to the big bed and settled her against a big pile of cushions. "Let me rub your back."

Alice whimpered. There was nothing she could do but breathe through the pain. Nicholas was squeamish and hated the sight of blood, but there was nothing she could do about that.

It was only some minutes before the bedroom door opened and the midwife came and took charge.

"Come Mr Hillyarde – this is woman's work. I'm sure your wife doesn't want you around now."

Heaving a sigh of relief and after giving Alice a swift kiss, Nicholas fled upstairs to his eyrie to await the arrival of another Hillyarde and to pray for Alice's safe delivery. He would have to concentrate on something else in the meantime and his thoughts returned to Arthur Southron.

He stoked the fire and settled down in his chair, wrapped in a fur to keep out the December chill. Thomas Bodley's knowledge was the key. The parallels to Elizabeth and Dudley were there. Like Cicero and Atticus they had been childhood friends and similarly, one of Cicero's female relatives had been married to Atticus's brother. Dudley's brother Guildford had been married to Jane Grey, and was not she a cousin of Elizabeth's? It was not quite the identical relationship to Atticus and Cicero, but Nicholas thought it sufficiently similar for the parallel to be deliberate.

More importantly Atticus was a knight and, specifically, a Horse Master. The first position that Elizabeth had awarded Dudley immediately she came to the throne was that of Master of the Queen's Horse. Therefore, was Arthur's motto a subtle way of telling the world that he was 'of, by, with and/or from the love of the Queen's Master of Horse'? Therefore the hand he held was not that of a beloved mistress, but that of his mother who was the Virgin, unmarried Queen of England? That explained Arthur's suggestion that the lace on the lady's cuff be painted in black and white. Arthur had said, at the time, that he thought it balanced the image, but these were also Elizabeth's colours.

Any scholar with a profound knowledge of roman society might be able to decipher the apparently meaningless motto but would they get the chance to see it? Since Arthur had commissioned it as a remembrance for his guardian it was unlikely to be seen by many, because, presumably, the guardian knew of Arthur's parentage and would keep the portrait hidden away. Perhaps the portrait was eventually destined for Elizabeth, or Dudley?

Nicholas was pleased he had painted another miniature of Arthur whilst his memory of the man was still fresh. It had been this second portrait he had given to Lord Burghley the previous day. The first portrait was the better of the two and it was safe upstairs in his workroom. He sat back musing that if Arthur, Elizabeth and Dudley were ever in the same room, then it would be obvious they were related. No wonder Arthur was going away. He wondered what the young man was doing now and where he was.

And what of Burghley and Walsingham. He had been surprised at their reactions. Nicholas felt guilty because he had betrayed Arthur's instructions. Levina had drilled the need for discretion regarding a client's wishes into him, but, in this instance Nicholas felt justified in behaving as he had. Did he regret going to Burghley? No, his loyalty to his Queen outweighed any loyalty to a client who may, or may not, be related to her.

Nicholas wondered whether Arthur's trip had anything to do with either of the great men. It would be typical of Burghley to know of the boy and then find him a job. Burghley could hide a bastard heir in a foreign place to keep him out of the reaches of those in England who might use him for their own plots. If, in the meantime, Arthur became troublesome, he was abroad and much easier to dispose of. Arthur Southron would be just another victim of circumstance. This was just the sort of subtle play that Burghley would engineer so no finger of blame could point back to England.

A pained wail rose from below. Nicholas winced. Poor Alice, this labour was proving difficult. Normally, she was quick to deliver, but tonight this baby was taking its time. Nicholas stoked the fire again and threw on another log and prepared for a long night.

Alice's cries made him consider Arthur's birth. He could not help himself; his curiosity kept returning to Arthur and the Queen. How had Elizabeth hidden her pregnancy? Had she been so strapped into her corsets that she just looked as if she were getting pudgy? Who might be able to tell him if the queen had ever been fat? But this question that would be too dangerous to find an answer to.

But how had she coped with the pain of child birth? Elizabeth was a terrible hypochondriac and made a huge fuss of something as simple as a hangnail or a turned ankle, not to mention headaches. And where was this child likely to have been born? Perhaps it had been Hampton Court, which was far enough away from the City to avoid the summer plague, or had it been Greenwich, or perhaps the hunting lodge at Enfield. So, who had taken the baby and had he been taken immediately he was born? Alice always cooed and cried over her babies until Nicholas felt quite left out, but he was getting used to playing second fiddle to the newest member of the Hillyarde family.

Had Elizabeth been able to greet her son like this? Had she been able to hold him close, count his fingers and toes and kiss his eyes and ears? Had she been able to tell him how much she loved him, just like Alice did, every time? Had she ever had the chance to hold her son and remember the smell of her personal miracle of life?

How could any woman cope with such a cruel severing from the child she had carried in her belly for so many months?

What did some women compare giving birth to? Nicholas wracked his brains until he remembered what Alice had said. "Passing the Pikes". It was a saying she used for coming through the dangers of childbirth safely. Evidently childbirth was thought to be as dangerous as battle and was a statement of surviving the enemy lines of pikemen. Now she had given birth so many times she likened it to shelling peas and said the pikes were merely the sticks they climbed up.

And what of Arthur's father? Had Dudley gone through these dreadful waiting hours, hearing his loved one's cries as she endured the agony of childbirth? Had he stayed nearby, to be close in case Elizabeth asked for him?

Had Dudley expected Elizabeth to marry him in order to legitimise their son? But the Queen had not married Robert Dudley and had continued to dance to the diplomatic tune of various marriage proposals with foreigners. Her flirting and dalliances were never more than a political tease, unless she was dancing, or flirting with Dudley, then the atmosphere became charged with passion. Nicholas had watched her doing the international marriage dance for these past twelve years and, whilst these quadrilles appeared serious, he knew that she led all her suitors a merry dance.

Nicholas leant back and tried to put himself into their place. Arthur's birth had to be kept a secret. Elizabeth would have had to remain silent not only all her life, but also during the birth. The first was comparatively easy, but how had she stifled her cries of pain during labour? Who might have been there? Who would have taken the baby to the wet nurse? There would have had to have been a wet nurse because it would have been impossible for a new born child to be kept secret at Court. They made too much noise.

Had Elizabeth been able to hold Arthur just once? Had she been able to cuddle her new-born son before saying goodbye?

And what of Dudley? Had he felt that rush of amazement at his beloved's ability and courage to produce a beautiful baby? Had Dudley watched mother and son and felt that deep love and desire to protect them as they both lay exhausted?

Perhaps Dudley had felt the same pang of jealousy Nicholas experienced each time another Hillyarde came into the world. Nicholas smiled as he remembered how Alice looked at her newborn babies in a way that she never looked at her him; total amazement, adoration and pure unconditional love. Had Elizabeth done the same? How had she endured the pain of giving up her child immediately in order to protect him, herself and her country. Nicholas hoped that she had been able to have some moments to gaze into her son's eyes, nuzzle his hair and kiss him gently, before handing him over to his future protectors.

Nicholas doodled on a piece of paper. Levina? Sir Dru Drury? The Ashleys? Lord Burghley? These were all those who Elizabeth would have trusted enough to protect her son. Elizabeth was an enigma, an impression she deliberately cultivated often asking her audience 'was she not a weak woman?' They would agree, and then, when she had entranced her audience, she would tell them that her heart was that of a man and they would then praise her courage, flattered that she was wise enough to consider whatever it was they wanted her to. She was subtle and would lead her audience down the path she wished them to go. Elizabeth was far from weak, but he wondered whether her ability for dissembling had been brought about not only by her childhood experiences, but also for the necessity of keeping a very precious personal secret?

Nicholas's thoughts turned to whether there was any other evidence for a clandestine royal birth, apart from the image in the 'P's'?

The Tudor colours were green and white, so why had Elizabeth chosen black and white? Why change? Green was the perfect foil for her pale skin and red hair. Elizabeth liked to reinforce the idea of dynasty so it was puzzling why she had chosen to change household colours rather than remain with the traditional Tudor green and white. Visually, the effect was dramatic and, since her household were all dressed in black and white, they were a perfect foil for the magnificent Queen in her fabulous gowns, thus making her appear even more glorious by contrast.

Perhaps there was a more subtle reason? The colours could relate to her being a woman and monarch and was a quiet way of saying that that everything about her was black and white, with no shades of grey. He chuckled at that thought. If there was one thing Elizabeth was not, it was black and white. She dealt in subtleties which were definitely many varying shades of grey.

Elizabeth's symbols were deliberately suggestive of her character. The thrifty squirrel bolstered her reputation that she ran a tight ship where national finances were concerned. Some critics called her miserly, but the royal purse had much to cover and these people probably had no concept of just how expensive it was to maintain a royal Court. But was there an alternative meaning to her squirrel?

A squirrel hid its winter store of food in many places, often not appearing to remember where. Did the Elizabethan squirrel hint at a hidden cache containing a Tudor heir?

When Nicholas had first painted Elizabeth's miniature he had used the Tudor rose and the iris as emblems of England and France, which Levina had interpreted as being far more complex than he had intended. As a result of that little miniature he had then been asked to paint the two larger portraits of her wearing the phoenix and the Pelican because he was young and new to the Court, so unaware of the early rumours of her reign? If so, had this been because his being asked to paint these images would not raise any questions about why Elizabeth wanted these portraits with these emblems, which might have been the case if it had been Levina who had painted them? Had Levina's excuse that she could not paint larger portraits been real? If not, then what hand had Levina had in this commission and why?

He had requested private sittings with Elizabeth so had he, unwittingly been an unsuspecting support of this conspiracy. Levina had taken his request even further and not allowed anyone near him or his rooms whilst he had been painting. Had this been at Elizabeth's request or was Levina protecting her protégé? Perhaps she was protecting both of them? If Levina had known about a baby, had she also been part of the conspiracy to hide the child from view.

Nicholas would not get any sense out of his idle speculation, so he turned to the concept of the bejewelled symbols themselves. She would wear them as a subtle message that everyone could negotiate as much as they liked, but she was not marrying. Was the Pelican mother symbolising Elizabeth's broken heart of not being able to acknowledge her son publicly?

Popular belief was that she had adopted the Phoenix because she had survived being declared a bastard and eventually come into her inheritance, just like a phoenix rising from the ashes. If Arthur were her son, it was logical that Elizabeth would choose a Phoenix emblem. He was the phoenix and, like the Arthurian legend told, coming to England's aid when everything supposedly lay in ruins. No wonder the Arthurian legend was one of Elizabeth's favourites. If Arthur existed then all the Court entertainment based on the Arthurian Court was actually laying clues that there was an Arthur, who would come again at England's hour of need and fulfil the legend – rex quondam rex futuris, the once and future king.

Nicholas shook his head in disbelief. It seemed so obvious when you actually started to look at things from a different viewpoint. But were these hidden meanings or the meanderings of his vivid imagination?

He used similar concepts himself, often for the same reasons – a public image with a secret message for those in the know. And who had taught him this? He smiled, he was back with Levina.

Dudley might be Elizabeth's favourite and possibly her soulmate, but she was well aware of his ambition. No wonder he had married.

He and Alice no longer questioned the fact that Arthur Southron was the illegitimate son of the Queen of England and the Earl of Leicester. Nicholas shook his head to clear the horrified realisation that, no matter how true this might be, to even consider it was treason. He risked his life and that of Alice and perhaps even those of their children with all of this speculation and investigation.

A scream split the night. Nicholas froze. Something was badly wrong. Jumping up, he threw open his study door and ran down the stairs two at a time.

Alice's sister Sarah opened the door just as he got to it. Her face was white and grim. Seeing Nicholas she burst into tears.

"Alice …" he whispered "is she all right?"

Sara nodded, but could say nothing. Nicholas pushed into the room. The room smelled of blood and sweat. Blood soaked towels lay on the floor. Alice was rocking backwards and forward in bed clutching a bundle and keening. The midwife was trying to wash her face.

"No, no, no…" Alice moaned.

Nicholas turned to Sara. "What happened?" he whispered.

"The baby strangled itself with its cord. There was nothing we could do. He was a beautiful boy, with blonde hair," she sobbed "but he's dead. He never even breathed!"

Nicholas felt so guilty. If he had not told Alice about his thoughts about Arthur then perhaps their baby would have lived.

This was all his fault and now they would have to have bury this son who had never even had a chance to smile. Nicholas wept. His son would be called Nicholas, as a reminder that all his idle speculation had brought about this disaster.

Alice extended her arm to him and Nicholas walked tentatively towards her. Her hair was plastered to her head with sweat and her hand was clammy to his touch. Tears streamed down her face and she sobbed as if her heart would break.

"Oh Nick, he was so beautiful …"

Nicholas looked down at his son's face. He had a perfect cupid bow mouth, button nose and a fluff of blonde hair. His eyes were closed, but somehow Nicholas knew that they would be blue, just like his mother's. Nicholas sat on the bed and put his arm around Alice's shoulders, holding her close as she sobbed. Tears ran down his cheeks. He could not bear the thought of losing her too.

"It's my punishment for thinking ill of God's anointed." he thought.

Nicholas stood as the priest intoned the words of the funeral service. Outside St Vedast's Church icy flakes blanketed the world in a carpet of white. All the world was withdrawn against the winter chill and he was here, in a cold church, his still born son being laid to rest in the cold earth without having drawn a single breath. The bleak weather matched his heart. It was so unfair that this child, who had been so robust in the womb, should be strangled by his own cord at the moment of his birth. Alice was lying inconsolable at home and he was sure it was his punishment for daring to suggest that God's anointed Queen had committed the sins of lust and adultery and borne a son. Unbidden, Arthur's face rose in Nicholas's mind and he prayed he was safe.

"In sure and certain resurrection ..." the priest's voice intoned and Nicholas's attention returned to his son as the tiny body was laid to rest beneath the cold marble slab of the church floor.

The sad little service came to an end and the congregation filed out. Nicholas had not even noticed his brother John, or his sister-in-law Sarah. Both of them gave him a hug, incapable of any words of sympathy. Nicholas gave a weak smile.

"Thank you for being here, Sarah;" Nicholas took her hands in his. They were cold despite being tucked inside her sleeves. "Would you be so good as to go to Alice?" he asked. Sarah nodded and Nicholas noticed that her eyes were red rimmed with recently shed tears. He felt he would snap if he stayed around all these well meaning, but doleful, relatives.

"If you don't mind, I think I need some time on my own."

Nicholas turned on his heel and walked away heading for the river, snowflakes swirling around him covering his footsteps so it was as if he had never been there.

1585

January

Nicholas had to present Elizabeth with a gift to celebrate the New Year. It would be easy to stay at home and avoid all contact with the rest of the world, but he could not afford that luxury. Life was never easy and he had to ensure that any future royal patronage remained his.

Alice was at least now out of bed, but she had become a ghost of her former self. She sat on the settle next to the fire with Little Lettice nestled against her, just gazing into space and bursting into tears at the slightest thing. When they were together in bed she would sob her heart out on his shoulder as silent tears slid down his own cheeks on to her head, making her hair damp.

Alice knew he had to leave her to attend Court today. His best doublet and shirt had been all beautifully laid out and she helped him dress.

"Does the Queen know?" she asked, her voice barely more than a whisper. Nicholas felt even more wretched because he had not told anyone of their news. He assumed people would just know because bad news had a way of travelling.

"I don't know," he replied "I assume not."

Alice sighed and sniffed. "Good luck, Nick. I hope she likes your present." and patted his chest.

Nicholas took her hand and held it to his lips. "I shall be back as soon as I can get away, but it might take longer than I would want." Nicholas kissed his wife gently. Alice tried to smile.

"Cook and Molly are downstairs if you need them. They will look after you." Nicholas hoped Alice would let Cook pamper her. Cook was worried that her mistress would fade away as she had hardly eaten since Christmas Eve. They all hoped the children would occupy Alice, but Nicholas worried that this might not be enough to chivvy her out of her melancholy.

The City bustled with life and a thaw had set in, making the streets a sea of slush and mud. The Maydenhead seemed an island of gloom amidst an ocean of life. Nicholas had remained inside since the funeral but, once outside his home, he felt better. The noise and bustle cheered him up as he walked to the Palace of Westminster.

He made his way to the great hall where musicians were playing a volte. Dancers twirled around and Nicholas spotted the Queen being lifted high by Dudley. He smiled a sad smile as he stood by the door to the great hall, watching the revelry and quietly enjoying the music. It was good to know that some things did not appear to change.

"Ah, hum"

A senior page stood to one side, coughing to attract his attention. Nicholas did not recognise the boy.

"Mr Hillyarde?"

"Yes." Nicholas waited for him to continue.

"My Lord Burghley asked if you could spare him a few moments."

Nicholas sighed and wondered what he wanted then followed the page to Lord Burghley's private chambers.

Burghley was on his own, seated at his desk and writing rapidly across a large piece of paper. The desk was neatly stacked with papers and a fire crackled in the grate. Candles bathed the room with a warm light and Nicholas stood waiting for the great man to finish writing.

Burghley placed his goose quill at the top of his desk, stood up and grasped the younger man's hand in his own.

"Ah, Nicholas, my deepest condolences. How is Alice?" Burghley's words confirmed that Nicholas's sad news had reached the Court.

"Thank you, my Lord. Alice does as well as she can."

"Sit down, sit down." Burghley indicated a chair next to the fire and settled himself in the other before continuing the conversation.

"Have you had any further contact with Mr Southron?"

Burghley's direct question caught Nicholas by surprise.

"No. Not since the day I finished the portrait and he asked me to deliver it."

"Hmm. Thank you."

Nicholas knew better than to ask why.

"And Mr Bell? Have you seen anything further of him?"

"No, none at all, not since the Throgmorton affair. Is there a connection?" Nicholas asked the question before thinking through the possible consequences.

"Not that I know of. Do you think there might be?" Burghley asked.

Nicholas sighed. Why could he not keep his mouth closed.

"No, and I have no idea why I asked the question."

Burghley smiled. "New years sometimes bring new plots. If you hear anything, my door is always open ...." Burghley left the sentence unfinished.

It was Nicholas's turn to smile. There was not much that did not reach Burghley's ears. He probably knew exactly how many portrait commissions he had undertaken, those that were still pending and for whom. There had been little time for painting with the winter light so bad, and anyway, Nicholas was just not in the mood.

"I hear the Queen is enjoying the New Year revels." Nicholas commented. The music was distant.

"Ah, yes, almost like old times. I have told her your news, so she is aware." Burghley sighed remembering Christmases long gone, then continued " Elizabeth would like you to see her away from the dancing. She didn't think you would want to be caught up with all the Court jollities. Perhaps you would like to go to her private rooms and, no doubt, she will be along soon."

"Thank you, Sir William,"

"Nicholas, you do much good and the Queen is very grateful. She would not want you to think she is unheedful of your sadness."

Nicholas nodded. Burghley might appear to be ruthless and forbidding, but the great man had experienced his own share of sadness and worry and had been saddened to hear about the Hillyarde still-birth.

Nicholas made his way to the Queen's private apartments via the back stairs and corridors, thus avoiding contact with any members of the Court. A guard stood outside the door, but let him in quietly closing the door behind him. Nicholas realised the man must have been expecting him because no-one would normally be allowed to wait in the Queen's private apartments.

The sun had not yet set, but even so the room was almost in darkness with the only light as the dark red glow from the banked fire. Henry VIII, Jane Seymour and Henry's parents looked down at him. It was a very great privilege being allowed to wait there alone. Confident he would hear the Queen and her herd of women approaching long before they entered, he allowed himself to sit by the fire to wait. The warmth of the room and the luxury of being alone lulled him to sleep, something that had been lacking for some days.

He snapped awake and froze as the click of the door closing brought him back to consciousness but it was someone leaving, not entering. Somebody had tucked a cover round his knees which meant somcone had been in, seen him and been solicitous enough to make sure he remained snug, but he had been in such a deep sleep he had never heard the stranger enter nor felt the cover being tucked round him. He wondered who it was and considered getting up and looking down the corridor, but his exhaustion was such that he remained seated and fell asleep again.

A little later, as anticipated, Nicholas heard the laughter of the Queen and some of her ladies coming down the corridor some seconds before she entered her rooms. He wondered briefly why it was that women seemed to chatter aimlessly about absolutely nothing all the time. Their voices babbled like a small stream swollen by the spring thaw, but their noisy approach enabled him to be standing and fully awake by the time Elizabeth entered. He heard the guard snap his heels as he came to attention just before the handle turned and the door opened. Elizabeth swept in with three of her ladies and none of them seemed surprised to find him there. Nicholas swept a bow.

"My, Mr Hillyarde, I hope you are now well rested?"

Elizabeth's question embarrassed him. Had it been the Queen herself who had put the cover over his knees? Nicholas flushed deeply; he would probably never know the answer and he was not going to embarrass himself further by asking.

"Your Majesty, you do me a great honour allowing me to wait for you here, and thank you, I am much refreshed."

Elizabeth smiled at him and shooed her ladies away, who drifted over to sit on the window seat. Elizabeth took the right hand seat next to the fire and indicated that Nicholas should sit on the other.

"Nicholas" Her tone was gentle and the use of his first name surprised him; she had not called him this since he had painted the Phoenix. " I was greatly saddened to hear of the death of your son." Elizabeth paused, as if trying to find the words to say something further.

"Your Majesty, ..." Nicholas's voice caught in his throat. He was trying to make the right sort of reply, but his emotions were still too raw. Whatever he was attempting to say next came out as a sob. The Queen leant forward and patted his arm.

"I know how hard it is to lose someone close, but to have to say goodbye to a child when they have only just been born is unimaginable." she murmured sympathetically.

"Thank you, Ma'am. You are very understanding and Alice too, will be most touched by your concern." Tears started to slide down his face so, to try and regain some composure, Nicholas brought out the New Year's gift he had designed and made for her. A gold trinket box sat on his hand as he knelt and offered it.

"This gift comes as a token of my esteem for you, your Majesty. The children instructed me to fill it with your favourite sweetmeats. Your god-daughter has your liking for these, and was unable to eat her supper because she had eaten so many."

Elizabeth smiled with delight knowing that little Elizabeth liked the same almond paste sweeties as herself.

"Thank you, Nicholas. I shall enjoy these." She said popping one into her mouth. "I hope to see you back at Court, but at the moment it is your family who needs you."

The Queen stood and Nicholas scrabbled to his feet and made a deep bow. Elizabeth patted him on his shoulder, then turned and left the room with her ladies, the golden box still in her hand.

For a few minutes Nicholas sat and thought about their meeting, then gathering his cloak about him, made his way out of the Palace and home. He was certain that it was because of his speculation about Arthur Southron, that God had decided to punish them by taking little Nicholas, but despite the possibility that this was divine retribution, he could not help asking himself what did Elizabeth mean when she had said that she could not imagine what it would be like to lose a child? Was she sympathising with him because she knew what he was suffering?

1586

The King's Head was one of the more prosperous ale houses catering for rich merchants. The food was good and the drink even better. Marcus had finished for the day and was pleased to be able to spend some time with his famous artist friend so the two men were sharing a fine claret and some delicious roast beef.

"How's Alice faring?" Marcus enquired hesitantly.

Nicholas took a sip of his claret and rolled it round his mouth savouring the delicate flavours of the grape.

"Well Marcus, I have good news. Alice is expecting again. She seems to be completely recovered from the melancholy of last year and she is blooming. I've forbidden her to do anything and, as far as possible, I try and satisfy her every whim, which is one of the reasons why I wanted to see you."

"Nick, this is marvellous news. Penny will be thrilled as we've both been very worried."

"Thank you, and I hear you've been blessed with a daughter."

"Now that's gossip for you. She was only born yesterday and yet you already know!"

"Marcus, you should know by now that our wives have a far better information system than even Walsingham or Lord

Burghley." Nicholas smiled at his friend, "I propose a toast to the new Mistress Teerlinc. May she have a long, healthy and prosperous life." Both men raised their goblets and clinked them together.

"To my daughter." Marcus replied; both men drank.

"After the past year, it's good to have something to celebrate, Marcus. I feel as if I've been living a dreadful dream. At times I wondered whether I was losing my mind and so shut myself away."

"I know. Several times I called to see you, but young Lockey told me you were not to be disturbed."

Nicholas nodded. "'tis true. I lost myself in my work, which, thankfully, still seems to be popular. Tell me what's been happening, bring me up to the minute with all the news."

"Indeed, you must have been in the doldrums if you missed all the news from the Low Countries!"

"That I have, but I do know that Leicester is in the United Provinces with his step-son, young Robert Devereux."

"Aye, that he is and rumour has it Dudley is making a fine mess of things. The Lady Letitia has been banned from joining him and has to stay in England."

Nicholas chuckled at this news.

"Marcus, that will upset her mightily and no doubt, Elizabeth enjoyed making her remain behind in England."

"That might be so, but now Antwerp is in Spanish hands, it is no easy matter. Some of us will be investing in this next expedition Raleigh is sending to the New World."

"No doubt you will be hoping for new fancies with which to tempt the fat burghers of London?"

It was Marcus's turn to chuckle. "That's quite so. I gather the furs from the New World are of a very great quality."

"Don't tell Alice, as she will want whatever is the most expensive!"

Marcus was relieved to see his friend quite back to his old self.

The door to the street opened and two elegantly dressed young men entered, calling loudly for ale and food.

"Marcus, are you expecting, or know of any cargoes of oranges that may be due?"

"Oh dear, Alice craving again?" Marcus laughed. Every time Alice fell pregnant she seemed to have more and more expensive cravings. Luckily, his Penelope had not been so demanding and only ever wanted to eat apples.

"'friad so. Usually it's strawberries, but this time it's oranges. So can you help?"

"It just so happens that an Italian trader docked this morning and I know he had a mixed cargo. Give me ten minutes and I'll be back with something to tempt Alice's delicate palette."

Marcus left Nicholas nursing the jug of claret and observing the newcomers. The two young men were in deep discussion. Nicholas envied the casual elegance of the taller blonde man. He had an elegance in the way he moved, sat, even picked up his wine. Everything was done with a dancelike grace as if he were more used to dancing attendance at Court except Nicholas could not remember ever having seen him there. His face was familiar. The other man seemed gauche and cumbersome by comparison and his movements suggested he had experienced a life considerably more adventurous than dancing attendance on elegant members of society.

The door opened again and James Bell entered and made his way directly to their table. Bell did not notice him seated in the corner and Nicholas moved slightly so that he was out of their direct line of sight. Another man, much older and walking with a gait suggesting he spent time at sea, joined them some minutes later.

"Buongiorno, Antonio. Com estai?" The newcomer greeted the blond man and held out his arms. The blonde man stood and the two men embraced Italian style then, to Nicholas's amazement, James Bell and the Italian greeted each other like long lost friends. The Italian was not particularly tall, but had a presence that was as large as his rich, dark voice.

"Bello, Bello, Luigi." Bell replied as effusively, if not as loudly, as the Italian. "Come sit down, join us and tell us your news." The rest of the conversation died away to a murmur and Nicholas could not hear any more, but he had seen enough to pique his curiosity.

After a further ten minutes Marcus returned, beaming with smiles.

"Well, you, or rather Alice, is in luck. I've sourced a box of oranges and these will be delivered direct to Gutter Lane this afternoon."

"Marcus, Alice will be forever in your debt as I told her that it was very unlikely anyone would have anything remotely resembling an orange at this time of year. How much do I owe you?"

"If Penny and I can do anything to make sure that Alice keeps well, then it is our delight to give her a box of oranges."

"Thank you very much. I know she will be very grateful. As you can probably imagine, we are very concerned that all should go well with this pregnancy. She has been so melancholic for so long that I can deny her nothing."

"Well then, Nicholas," Marcus said "I propose another toast, to Alice's health."

Again the two men clinked goblets and drank to Alice Hilliard's continuing good health.

After a while the two men went their separate ways, Nicholas deciding to slip out of the side door as he had no wish to be seen by Mr Bell.

William Davidson was hard at work when Nicholas entered Lord Burghley's offices.

"Good-day, Mr Davidson." Nicholas greeted the cleric.

"Good morrow, Mr Hillyarde." Davidson replied as he lay down his goose quill. Robert Beale looked up and smiled a welcome before returning to his document.

"Tell me, Mr Davidson; is either Sir Francis or Lord Burghley available?" Nicholas felt jittery. Seeing Bell had unnerved him.

"You seem a trifle troubled, Mr Hillyarde, is anything wrong?" William Davidson was curious as to what had disturbed the artist.

"No, no, nothing in particular, but I would be grateful if there was the chance of a quick word."

William Davidson rose and knocked on the door to the inner sanctum, pressing his ear to the wood. At some unheard response he turned the handle and stuck his head round the door. Nicholas did not hear what was said, but Mr Davidson turned and smiled at him.

"Go in." Davidson held the door wider so Nicholas could enter the room.

"Nicholas, take a seat." Sir Francis gestured to the opposite side of the desk. "What brings you to my door today?"

Nicholas waited until the door was closed.

"Sir Francis, do you remember asking me to let you know if I saw James Bell again?" Nicholas asked as he made himself comfortable.

"Indeed, I do." Sir Francis waited for his visitor to continue.

Nicholas folded his hands together and took a deep breath. "I've just come from an alehouse in the City where Mr James Bell was meeting with some others."

Sir Francis sat with his hands hidden in the sleeves of his gown and nodded, as if to say 'continue'.

"They were young, good looking men; well dressed and clearly of property. It might not be anything, but they were joined by an Italian."

"Were you able to hear anything of what was said?" Sir Francis asked.

"No. Only when the Italian came in and greeted them loudly, Italian style." Nicholas continued.

"Did you recognise him?"

"No. Only Bell, and the blonde man whom I think is Antony Babington, but I haven't seen him since '78."

Walsingham nodded. "So, Mr Bell is back in London." Sir Francis mused.

"He seemed to know the Italian well because they greeted each other like long parted friends. Sir Francis, it may be nothing, but I felt you should at least be aware that Mr Bell was in London."

"hmm." Sir Francis tapped his lips whilst he thought. "Nicholas, thank you. As ever, my door is always open." Sir Francis leaned back and smiled at his visitor.

Nicholas was anxious to get back home now he had delivered the news of Mr Bell's appearance in the City.

"Sir Francis, I hope I haven't wasted your time."

"Good heavens no. All information is useful, even though it may not appear so at the time."

Nicholas closed the door quietly behind him. Whenever he visited Sir Francis, he always felt relieved to leave. He mused on what it would be like to be on the wrong side of this man and shuddered. The Throgmorton episode had demonstrated just how Walsingham's network could infiltrate everywhere, even foreign embassies.

In the outside office a man stood studying the large map of Europe pinned to the wall. The stranger turned and Nicholas recognised him as one of the men from the tavern. The man did not appear to recognise Nicholas, which came as a relief.

"Mr Maude" Nicholas heard Davidson address the stranger "you may go in now."

"Thank you." Maude disappeared into Sir Francis's office.

Clearly this was one of Sir Francis' spies. Nicholas wished he could talk this all out with Alice, but she had made it very clear that she did not want, ever, to go through another birth like the last one. She was convinced that losing little Nicholas was a punishment by the Almighty, so her husband would just have to keep his thoughts to himself.

Nicholas walked home mulling over what the various connections between Sir Francis's spy, Maude, Mr Bell and Babington might be. Sir Francis had a spy network second to none, but it was not often anyone came across any of Walsingham's men face to face.

Nicholas was still grappling of what might be afoot by the time he had reached home. He found a very excited household exploring the contents of a large wooden crate containing several dozen oranges, tissue wrapped bundles of dried figs and half a dozen bottles of claret. Alice was sitting with a small pile of orange rind at her feet.

"Now you just take it easy, mistress" Cook told her "You eat any more of them there oranges and you just might give yersell the belly ache."

"Oh shut up, Cook." Alice chided "Try one, so you know just how delicious they are. Here take this peel and boil it up with some sugar. Perhaps we can make it taste less bitter."

Nicholas smiled. His wife looked beautiful despite the orange juice dribbling down her chin. Alice pulled another orange apart and fed a segment to Little Lettice who took it gingerly between her pudgy fingers and sniffed it before putting it into her mouth.

"Yeuk," Lettice spat it out and threw the remaining segment at her mother. "Horrid, mummy. It's euky!"

"Well, if you don't want it Lettice, then I'll eat it." Alice popped the remains of the segment into her mouth. "Nicholas, where did these oranges come from? Cook says Marcus sent them over?"

"You were very lucky; these are just landed from Italy. Marcus did indeed send them, as a gift for you."

"And I just love these dried figs with all their tiny seeds. There's a note from Marcus to say not to eat too many of these, but Penny recommends them for when or if, my stomach turns solid."

Nicholas picked up one of the figs and sniffed it, then nibbled the edge to test its palatability, then finding it still quite juicy, finished it. Alice sucked a segment of orange dry of juice.

"Marcus sent you some bottles of claret." Alice reached for another orange, peeled it and stuffed yet more of the fruit into her mouth.

"The claret is so I can get to sleep without you disturbing me every time you turn over!"

"Perhaps so, my darling husband, but it makes you snore like a pig!" Alice laughed at him.

Summer

Nicholas was kept busy all summer with commissions. He saw Bell several more times in the City, but it was always in the distance. He learnt from Robert Beale that Mary Stuart was now in the charge of Sir Amyas Paulet and, not only had her gaoler changed, she had first been moved to Tutbury Castle, then Chartley Manor.

Tutbury was a dank, stinking and crumbling castle and, despite its forbidding aspect, not that easily secured. Nicholas could almost hear the loud moans Mary would have made about how badly she was being treated. Presumably, the fact that it was far more easily defended was why she had been moved to Chartley, which was comparatively less moist than Tutbury.

Nicholas remembered Sir Amyas Paulet as a dour, strict Puritan who would have no sympathy for his Catholic charge. Mary would have a much harder time under Paulet's eye. No doubt she would be complaining that Sir Amyas was of insufficient status, being only a Knight, and that she should be housed with someone of much higher rank as would be more fitting as 'keeper' of an anointed queen.

There were rumours that Mary had been caught communicating and collaborating with proven traitors. It was well known Sir Francis had long thought Sheffield far too comfortable a prison and the Throgmorton affair provided the perfect excuse for a change of both residence and gaoler for the Scottish Queen.

Nicholas considered Elizabeth was far too soft concerning Mary Stuart. Surely she could see that Mary would be the focus of every Catholic plotter across Europe, let alone England. He sighed, remembering how Mary had complained to him that her health was delicate and affected by being unable to exercise. He had long thought it would be so much easier if Mary would do everyone a favour and succumb to that delicate state of health. Unfortunately so far she continued to live, despite her protestations of suffering from a weak constitution.

Nicholas pondered on why fate had thrust him into the murky world of spying. Would this have been the case if Lord Burghley had not offered him a place in Sir Amays's entourage in Paris? Probably not because, if he had remained in England, he would not have been in Jersey in '78, so he would not have met Mr Bell.

Despite the young man's promises of contacting him, Bell had never sought him out. Nicholas often wondered why the man had even spoken to him at all. It had been an odd encounter, but then Bell had been talking to a man he had recognised as being in the retinue of the Duc de Guise and he still wandered what a member of the Guise household had been doing in Jersey. The only reason that Nicholas could think of for the man being in Jersey was to spy, but it still did not answer his question of why Bell had approached him or what Bell was doing with Guise's man, in the first place.

Since then de Guise had been proven to be part of the Throgmorton plot. Thanks to Robert Beale, Nicholas was able to dismiss some of the more outrageous gossip that had come his way for what it was – pure speculation. Bell had evaded arrest then but now he had re-appeared it was apparent Bell was connected with the Scottish queen rather than Throgmorton. Throgmorton was now dead and the French Ambassador had been replaced. In France, Bernadino De Mendoza had returned to colder climes as the Spanish Ambassador to the French Court. Therefore, the only connection he could see between Bell and London was Mendoza and Guise

There had been the case of Dr Parry in the same year, and Parry had been executed for his plotting against the Queen. No-one in Sir Francis's office had told Nicholas of any link with Bell. All of a sudden London seemed to be a noxious mixture of spying and counter-spying and it did not feel healthy.

August

London was sweltering in the early morning August sun. Alice had taken the children to stay at her father's country house and Nicholas was on his way to join them. He had decided to get a boat, which would save him the tedium of having to ride the twenty or so miles. He did not like boats, even river boats, but they were quicker than horses and far more comfortable.

The noise of the docks was an assault to his ears and he longed for the quiet of the country. Brandon kept a good table and harvest time was always fun. The children loved it and he was keen to get join them.

The wharf was abnormally crowded.

"Stand back, stand back." A burly man pushed the crowd back as two other men pulled a naked corpse up on to the landing stage.

"Poor sod." A woman said to no one in particular.

"Probably murdered for 'is clothes." Offered another.

Nicholas pushed his way to the front. The corpse was a man of above average height, with a ring of lank mousy hair around a balding pate. There were no bruises on his back, just a very small incision slightly to the left of his spine that looked like a slim dagger wound. A well dressed man knelt down and prised the edges of the wound open.

"Whoever did it knew what they were doing'." He stated clinically.

"Why, what is it?" someone asked.

"It's a glass dagger." The man explained. "Been snapped off at skin level." He paused. "Nasty. ... very nasty. Smacks of very dark deeds."

"'ere, d'you suppose he's some'at to do with that traitor Babington? I 'ear 'es been took up near St John's Wood. Skulking in some woods hiding from the Queen's men who want him for plotting 'agin her."

"Tell me what's happened?" Nicholas asked of one of the women standing next to him.

"Well, I 'eard there were arrests this morning of some Cafflic gentlemen plotting to murder the Queen and put Mary

Stuart on the throne. Some say we would all have become good Cafflics. Antony Babington and 'is friends was up at St John's Wood, hiding near the Bellamy's estate and the Bellamy's are known Cafflics they are." The woman was relishing repeating the morning's gossip.

The body was turned over and Nicholas looked into the sightless eyes of James Bell. For the men on the dock there was no way to identify the naked body. There was no decomposition suggesting the murder was recent.

"As I said before, poor sod." The first woman spoke again. "well, it don't look like he wore a wedding ring, so he's probably not got a family waiting for 'im."

Nicholas pondered on just who had killed James Bell? Had it been coincidence Bell had been murdered at the same time as Babington and his cronies had been arrested or had he been murdered for his fine clothes? If the latter, perhaps Bell had been murdered by a creditor who had taken anything of value as payment, but if the former, had Bell been murdered by one of Walsingham's agents, or by one of the plotters? Whatever the reason Nicholas knew he should tell Sir Francis about Bell's death before continuing on to Kent. Walsingham's London house in Seething Lane was near and if Walsingham were not at there, he would leave a sealed message.

The door to the Walsingham's City house was opened by a short stout woman.

"The Master's in 'is study. Wait here and I'll ask if he 'as a minute." The stout woman disappeared through a doorway.

Nicholas stood in the hall admiring portraits of Sir Francis' wife, Ursula, and his daughter, Francis.

"Nicholas, come in" Sir Francis stood in the doorway to his study. Nicholas made himself comfortable on a chair on the other side of a desk piled high with papers.

Sir Francis waited for Nicholas to speak.

311

"James Bell has been murdered."

"Are you sure?"

"Sir Francis, whilst I'm not good at remembering names, I never forget a face. It was Bell, despite his being as naked as the day he was born. I'm probably the only person in London who could identify him without papers."

"Quite so." Sir Francis was amused by Nicholas's professional arrogance. The sketch Nicholas had given him nearly a decade before had been remarkably accurate.

"How did he die?" Sir Francis asked

"A single thrust in the back with a thin glass blade that had been snapped off at the hilt leaving just a small slit in the skin." Nicholas shuddered involuntarily remembering the inch wide slit just below Bell's shoulderblade.

"Ah, the glass stiletto so beloved of the Venetians. Sounds more like a ritual murder avenging betrayal, than a casual murder." Sir Francis leant back and smiled. It was as if the spymaster's soft spoken observation were his thoughts rather than an explanation.

"Whoever did it knew what he was doing, Sir Francis. At least Bell won't be popping up every now and again."

"Indeed. His demise will be a relief to us all."

"It might be he owed money, but somehow, I don't think that was the case." Nicholas paused, but the spymaster's face gave nothing away. "A woman down at the docks spoke of Anthony Babington being found in woods in St John's Wood and being arrested for plotting to assassinate the Queen, free Mary Stuart and put her on the throne. Is this so?"

"Yes, quite true and, Nicholas, as we speak, the plotters are on the way to the Tower. No doubt Mr Topcliffe will discover what else Babington and his friends planned."

Nicholas shuddered at the mention of the new questioner at the Tower. It was rumoured Topcliffe took such great delight in his job that he preferred it to sex. Some whispered that he derived ecstatic sexual satisfaction from hearing the screams of his victims. If this were true, Babington was to be pitied.

"However, in view of the lack of evidence regarding Mr Bell's demise we shall never know why he has been murdered, or by whom. Thank you, Nicholas. Be assured, your information has been well used."

"Thank you, Sir Francis." Nicholas rose to leave, eager to be on his way.

Nicholas left Seething Lanes with feelings of dread and pity for those now in the Tower. Bell's death was no coincidence. First of all, there had been the Italian spy he had seen in inn and then again later in Walsingham's office. Had he murdered Bell? He, of all people, would know whether Bell was a traitor. The manner of Bell's death spoke of the neat tying of loose ends without the messiness of a trial. Bell had been a small cog in a much bigger wheel and a quick dagger in the back was a neat way of disposing of a small problem.

On the trip down river Nicholas had time to think about what might now happen to Mary Stuart. That would all depend on what the new queen's questioner found out from Babington and his friends, and what further evidence Walsingham had against them? As long as Mary lived, it was inevitable there would be plots to free her, which meant that eventually someone would make sure she died. If she died in suspicious circumstances it would be seen as an act of regicide and Elizabeth would be the prime suspect.

What if Mary died suddenly, especially if it looked like natural causes? She was, on her own admission, in 'delicate health'. How would England convince the world her death was not deliberate? The whole Catholic world might unite and move against England.

What was Mendoza plotting at the French Court? Was he trying to forge a Spanish alliance with France? Was it possible Mendoza was negotiating for money and support for a joint army to invade England and put Mary Stuart on the throne? It would not be the first time he had been involved in a plot like this. Had Elizabeth's support of the Protestants in the United Provinces so angered Philip that he was prepared to invade England and place Mary Stuart on the English throne?

Whatever was happening on the international stage, Nicholas hoped it would not lead to war, but something would have to be done about Mary and he wondered what Walsingham and Burghley were plotting. All Nicholas wanted was to live in peace.

20th September

"Alice, I forbid anyone to go to St Giles in the Fields today."

Alice was coaxing the knots out of little Lettice's blond locks.

"Nick, it's too late. They've all gone except Molly."

Nicholas took a deep breath. He had hoped to stop the household going to see the Babington executions.

"Where are the children?"

"They're with Molly, who's making gingerbread men with them."

"Good, good. I don't want a repeat of the last time. Daniel had nightmares and none of us got any sleep!"

"Nick, what have you heard?"

Nicholas sat down beside his wife. Four year old Lettice held out her arms for her father to take her on to his knee, eager to be away from her mother's comb.

"Daddy, what's a hanging?"

"Why do you want to know."

"Rowland says he wants to see the hanging."

Nicolas sighed and looked at Alice for support. Alice just smiled.

"Lettice, it's when very bad people are punished for their crimes."

"What happens?"

Alice put her hand up to her mouth to smother a smile. Nicholas frowned and looked at his wife as if to ask why he had to explain this.

"Bad people are hanged by their necks until they are dead."

"That sound horrible, so why was Cook and Rowland wanting to go?"

"I can't answer that, perhaps you should ask them."

"I did, and Cook said to ask you."

Nicholas groaned, then paused to gather his thoughts. "Lettice, sometimes bad people do things that are so bad they have to be punished and sometimes," he paused again "sometimes, the authorities want to make an example out of the bad people to make sure other people won't do the same things, so they make the punishment very bad and very horrible."

"What a 'thorritys'?"

"Well, it's those who make the rules."

Lettice looked at her father very seriously. "Is the Queen a 'thorritys'?"

"Lettice, not exactly. It's very complicated, but she rules the country with the help of various people, and they are the ones who make the rules, with her guidance."

"So will the Queen do the hanging?"

"Lettice, that's enough questions." Alice was trying hard not to laugh at Nicholas squirming under Lettice's questioning.

"Mummy, when you and Daddy are cross with Daniel and Francis will you have a hanging?"

315

"Oh sweetheart, no, of course not. Hanging is only for very, very bad people."

"So what have they done to get hanginged?" Lettice looked very serious.

"Well, some very naughty men were plotting to kill the Queen and put someone else on the throne."

"Why?" Lettice was not going to let the subject go.

"Because they thought the Queen should be replaced by someone called Mary."

"So who made the Queen?"

Nicholas sighed wondering how to explain the concept of Divine Right to a young child?

"God."

"So why doesn't God do the hanging?"

Alice burst out laughing. "Lettice, that's enough questions."

"Well, if God made the Queen, why doesn't he do the hanging if he doesn't want Mary to be queen?" Lettice asked.

"I think it's very much more complicated than that ..."
Alice did not get any further as Daniel burst in, with his siblings only a few seconds behind.

"Those are my gingerbread men, Daniel, give them back." demanded Elizabeth.

"If you don't behave, Daddy's going to have a hanging!" Lettice shouted at her siblings.

"Enough!" Nicholas handed his small daughter back to her mother. "Back to the kitchen. I'll take the plate, thank you."

"Daddy," Lettice called. Nicholas turned as he held the plate above his head and shooed his children out of the room. "Daddy, can I be queen?"

Nicholas blew her a kiss, then shut the door behind him.

It was evening before Nicholas and Alice had a chance to speak alone.

"Nick, have you spoken to Cook since this morning?"

"No, and I thought supper was very poor tonight?"

"She's very badly shaken by Babington's execution. Was there some reason why you wanted to stop everyone going?"

"Yes. Beale told me there were orders to make sure that Babington suffered a very long and painful death. Has Cook said anything?"

"Only that she thinks it was a wicked thing to see. She keeps shaking her head and muttering under her breath."

"I couldn't get anything out of the Rowland either. He was very subdued and shaken. Alice, I hope the savagery of these hangings wasn't a direct order from Elizabeth. I understand she's very shaken by this plot coming so quickly after the Throgmorton and Parry affairs. "

"Nicholas, could we not talk about today's hangings. It might affect the little one." Alice rubbed her rounded belly. She was seven months pregnant with her seventh child and was still a lovely looking woman.

14th October

The makeshift Court was gathering in the hall of the bleak castle of Fotheringay. Nicholas sat in the minstrels gallery and watched as the commissioners came and took their seats, or stood exchanging words with one another. He was pondering what Robert Beale had told him the previous evening.

When Mary had been told of the charges she had argued that Elizabeth had no right to try another sovereign princess. Beale had taken theatrical delight in mimicking, in a falsetto French accent, how Mary had cried out that she would have none of 'zees' and 'zat she was no subject and would prefer to die a sousand dess zan acknowledge 'erself so'. Nicholas wondered what a 'dess' was, then realised Mary was saying 'deaths'! It had been pointed out to her that in England under Elizabeth's jurisdiction, anyone, princess or otherwise, was subject to her laws. Sir Christopher Hatton had been the one who had finally persuaded Mary to present herself by telling her that, if she continued in this vein, they would try her 'in absentia'. Mary had realised non appearance would only further prejudice the Court against her.

Nicholas surveyed the scene below. Lord Burghley wanted everything recorded and it was his job was to make a visual record of the scene. A fire had been lit, but even so, Nicholas felt cold and hoped Sir Francis would not take a chill.

A throne with an elaborate cloth of estate had been provided for Elizabeth, but Elizabeth would not be attending. The throne was a symbol of her authority at a trial her Commissioners were conducting in her name. As Elizabeth's representatives, these Commissioners were there to dispense her justice. A chair had been provided for Mary, which instead of an ordinary wooden one, was draped with red velvet and looked quite regal. Instead of facing the empty throne, it faced Lord Burghley. Nicholas wondered why this chair had been allowed to become so throne like.

Nicholas could see Robert Beale moving around below. The thirty six queen's commissioners sat on two settles against the walls of the Great Chamber. The seven judges, two lawyers, two doctors of the civil law, Elizabeth's Attorney General, her Solicitor General, her Notary and her serjeant at law sat in the well of the Court. the Knights' bench was crosswise and Knights Mildmay, Acroft, Hatton and Sadler had their backs to him. Nicholas did not envy them their job.

Their purpose, some might call it a trick, would be in carrying out both a trial and execution without appearing to make Elizabeth complicit. Beale had whispered that there was evidence that Mary had asked for foreign aid and Nicholas wondered if this would be proved to be through Ambassador Mendoza.

Nicholas wondered, not for the first time, which side had ordered Bell's death. Had the order come from France, or had it been on orders from Seething Lane. Either way, Bell was dead and had been buried in an unmarked grave. No-one knew his identity, no-one that is except himself, Lord Burghley, Walsingham and Bell's executioner.

Marcus had said that Philip II was becoming increasingly angered by the raids on Spanish shipping by the likes of Hawkins and Drake. Philip now called Drake 'El Draque'; Nicholas smiled at the thought of his friend being likened to a Dragon. The antics of Drake and the other privateers might anger Philip, but would the Spanish king be sufficiently irritated to declare war on England. Further rumours suggested a Spanish navy was being mustered and that as many as one hundred and fifty warships were moored in Cadiz. The execution of a Catholic queen might give Philip the excuse to mount an invasion.

What would the French do? French factions had been proved to be at the hub of at least two conspiracies to free Mary. Might they might be persuaded to ally with Spain? He knew Elizabeth well enough to know that she would not want war with anyone. The Netherlands fiasco was costing the country far too much and was gaining nothing.

Evidently the King of Scotland had written and reassured Elizabeth she could be sure there would be no army coming south against her should she need to 'deal' with Mary Stuart. It transpired that James VI had no love for his mother. But would this lack of filial love still carry weight if Mary were executed? Perhaps filial duty might suddenly sprout new loyalties with the English throne as the prize for James's new found filial feelings?

England had to remain a peaceful and tolerant land, which meant it was inevitable that Mary would be found guilty.

However, there would have to be sufficient evidence to convince everyone of her complicity in order to avert a foreign invasion or civil war, or worse still, both.

Walsingham and Burghley would never have allowed this trial to take place if there were any doubt as to the outcome and absolutely sure that everything presented was, to all the world, genuine.

Then there was his own family. Nicholas did not want Alice worried so very near the end of her pregnancy. This trial had to be over quickly, so he could be home before the baby decided to appear.

As well as those officials and nobles who had to be here, there was a group of carefully selected onlookers to witness the day's proceedings. Everyone was dressed in thick robes against the chill which pervaded the hall despite the fire. The witnesses talked to each other in muted voices. Nicholas wondered what was going through Sir Francis's mind and how Lord Burghley would conduct the day. Sir Francis had been in poor health for some time and William Davidson had been appointed Assistant Secretary only two weeks beforehand. Nicholas watched Sir Francis take his seat on the cross bench, together with the other knights. There was no doubt about it, dressed in his official gown, the great man looked even more sinister than usual.

The door at the end of the room opened. A hush fell as Mary Stuart entered and surveyed the ranks of commissioners and witnesses. She limped and appeared to have great difficulty in moving to the chair set for her. Nicholas recognised her women and her steward, Melville. She paused for maximum dramatic effect.

"Alas! 'ere are many councillors, but not one for me." She bemoaned in her heavily accented English. Nicholas snorted his disgust. Did the woman not know that anyone accused of treason was not entitled to legal representation? They had to speak for themselves.

The years of confinement had made her even more stout than he remembered and she appeared defiant. She looked around and for a minute Nicholas wondered whether she would sit on the throne, but she was ushered towards the prepared chair. His initial sketches showing how the room was set out and who was seated where on the dais were done allowing Nicholas time to concentrate of the proceedings.

Sir Thomas Bromley, rose:

"The most high and mighty Queen Elizabeth, being not without great grief of mind, advertised that you have conspired the destruction of her and of England and the subversion of religion has, out of her office and duty lest she might seem to have neglected God, herself and her people, and out of no malice at all, appointed these commissioners to hear the matters which shall be objected unto you and how you can clear yourself of them and make known your innocence..."

Nicholas took up his pen and sketched the faces of the witnesses. He found it difficult to listen to what Sir Thomas was saying and work at the same time so he gave up listening to the preamble and concentrated on making individual sketches of each of the commissioners. He would make a fair copy of the whole scene later and give each commissioner sufficiently individual features for them to be recognised.

"Madam, you have heard why we have come here; please listen to the reading of our commission. I promise you that you shall say all that you wish." Sir Thomas concluded.

Nicholas was sketching quickly and missed the first part of Mary's reply "... by my replies to all ze world, that I am not guilty of zis crime against the person of ze queen, which it seems I am charged."

The trial then got underway and Nicholas wondered what might appear in the P of the roll for this law term.

Mary droned on with long speeches in answer to the questions put to her.

"I knew not Babington" Mary denied. Nicholas sat up. Here was as direct link with Bell. He listened as Mary continued. "I never received any letters from 'im, nor wrote any to 'im. I never plotted ze destruction of the queen. Eef you want to prove it, zen produce my letters signed wiz my own 'and."

A hush fell over the court. The serjeant at law stood smiling.

"But we have evidence of letters between you and Babington."

Mary looked at him as if he were of no consequence.

"If so, why do you not produce zem? I have ze right to demand to see ze originals and ze copies, side by side. It is quite possible zat my ciphers 'ave been tampered wiz by my enemies. I cannot reply to zis accusation wizzout full knowledge. Till zen, I must content myself wiz affirming solemnly zat I am not guilty of ze crimes imputed to me."

Nicholas sat back. Mary had to be admired for her sheer gall in denying any complicity.

"I declare formally zat I never wrote ze letters zat are produced against me. Can I be responsible for ze criminal projects of a few desperate men, which zey planned wizzout my knowledge, or participation?"

Would she accuse Walsingham or Burghley directly?

"Madam" Nicholas could not see who had spoken. "These letters were found amongst your own papers."

Mary was caught in her own lie.

"It may be zat Babington wrote them – but let it be proved zat I received zem. If Babington or any others affirm it, I say zey lie openly. Ozzer men's crimes are not to be cast upon me. A packet of letters, which 'ad been kept from me almost a whole year came to my 'ands about zat time, but by whom it was sent, I know not."

Nicholas smiled. She was guilty as charged. He leant forward to follow the events unfolding before him. Mary continued

"If Babington really confessed ze sings, why was 'e put to death wizout being brought before me so I could confront him?" Mary paused and looked around accusingly. "It is because such a meeting would 'ave brought to light ze truth." Her tone was stern and accusatory.

Mary then changed tactics.

"I 'ave, as you see, lost my 'ealth . I cannot walk wizout assistance, nor use my arms and I spend most of my time confined to bed. Not only zis but, zroughout my trials, I 'ave lost ze use of my memory, which would 'ave aided me to recall zose zings which I 'ave seen and read and which might be useful to me in ze cruel position I find myself." Nicholas thought she looked remarkably healthy.

"Not content with zis, my enemies now endeavour to complete my ruin, using against me means which are un'eard of towards persons of my rank and unknown in zis kingdom before ze reign of ze present queen and even now not approved by rightful judges…"

Nicholas was irritated by her wheedling attempt to gain sympathy for what she saw as persecution so stopped listening and started thinking about what she might be trying to gain. Certainly she had been held under house arrest, but these conditions could never have been considered arduous. The Earl of Shrewsbury had spent a small fortune looking after his 'guest' and Nicholas had seen for himself that her conditions at Sheffield had been more bordering on luxurious. This latest move to the old dank castle of Fotheringay was far more of a prison, but considering she had been caught plotting treason, he thought she was lucky she was not languishing in the Tower. The problems of keeping this queen captive were, in his opinion, more a figment of Elizabeth's imagination. The longer Mary was allowed to live, the more she had become a focal point for conspiracies. This had been demonstrated by how young Babington had become ensnared in this latest plot and Nicholas wondered just how that had come about, and how Bell had been involved.

Beale had told him that when she had arrived here, Mary had not been forcibly confined and had been quite free to move around the castle until today, so her speech was a demonstration of her histrionics and bending of the truth.

"Look here, my lords." Mary took a ring from her finger and waved it at her judges "See zis pledge of love and protection which I received from your meestress – regard it well." She continued holding the ring for all to see.

Nicholas had to admit that Mary had a great sense of theatre. She was still playing for sympathy, but her audience was not to be moved. Her own letter to Babington was read out and it concluded with her own written plea: *Fail not to burn this privately and quickly.*

Mary burst into tears, whether they were tears of frustration, despair or anger was unclear, but she continued to defy the evidence and pointing directly at Walsingham and accused him of forging the evidence.

"It ees easy to imitate ciphers and 'andwriting, as has been lately done in France by a young man who boasts zat he is my son's brozzer, by ze name of Ballard. I fear zat all of zis is ze work of Monsier De Walsingham. I am certain he 'as tried to deprive me of my life and my son of 'ees."

Nicholas snorted. This was an act of pure desperation.

"But, Monsieur Walsingham" Mary continued, still waving her finger at the spymaster "I zink you are an 'onest man and I pray you say in ze words of an honest man whezzer you 'ave done so or not!"

"As to Ballard" Mary continued "Information 'as reached me from France zat he was a very firm Catholic and that he wished to serve me but I was also told zat he 'ad great intelligence with Monsieur De Walsingham and zat I must be on my guard …" Nicholas pondered the question of Ballard's identity. He had not heard of this man and it sounded much like James Bell, but now Bell was dead it no longer mattered whether they were one and the same man, but he would have liked to satisfy his curiosity all the same.

Mary continued "I protest zat I never even zought ze ruin of ze Queen of England and zat I would a hundred times razzer 'ave lost my life than see so many Catholics suffer for my sake and be condemned to a cruel death zrough hatred to my person."

Lord Burghley jumped to his feet spluttering with indignation. Nicholas could not quite catch what he was saying because everyone started talking at once. It seemed that Burghley was denying that no-one, loyal to Elizabeth, had ever been condemned on religious grounds. Mary was accusing him of lying and saying that, on the contrary, she had read accounts of these condemnations.

Walsingham entered the verbal fracas attempting to answer her accusations against him. An expectant hush fell over the onlookers. Finally, these two antagonists were face to face.

Walsingham bowed in Mary's direction, which surprised Nicholas. Sir Francis was according Mary a respect he thought was far from deserved.

"I protest that my soul is free from all malice. God is my witness that, as a private person, I have done nothing unworthy of an honest man and, as secretary of State, nothing unbefitting my duty." Sir Francis paused a bit longer, took a deep breath and look directly at the Scottish Queen. "You have been told that I wish you ill; that I have often said things to your disadvantage; that I have confessed myself to be your enemy. No. Even that I planned that the death of you and your son should happen on the same day. But, I assure you that I bear no ill-will to no one. I have attempted no one's death."

The Court held its breath as Walsingham and Mary gathered themselves for their next verbal skirmish.

Walsingham continued "I am a man of conscience and a faithful servant to my mistress. I confess that I am ever vigilant regarding all concerning the safety of my queen and country. As for Ballard, if he had offered me his assistance I could not have refused it, and should have probably rewarded him. If I had any secret dealings with him, why did he not declare them in order to safe his life?"

Perhaps this was the closest Nicholas would get to finding out who had murdered Bell. If Ballard and Bell were one and the same, then Walsingham had ordered his death.

Whilst it appeared that Sir Francis was justifying what had happened and his own part in it, Nicholas appreciated his use of double speak. Walsingham's words completely unnerved the Scottish queen.

Mary sat crying. "Spies" she sobbed "are men who dissemble one zing and speak anozer. I would never make a shipwreck of my soul by conspiring ze destruction of my dearest seester."

Nicholas nearly laughed out loud at her hypocrisy. The serjeant at arms banged his staff on the floor and adjourned the proceedings until after the midday meal. Nicholas tidied up his various sketches and went to find something to eat.

That afternoon the confessions of Mary's cipher clerk and her secretary were read out. Mary stood up, their evidence clearly knocked her confidence, but she faced her accusers bravely. .

"Ze majesty and safety of all princes falleth to ze ground if zey depend upon ze writing and testimony of secretaries." Mary's tone was tart, but she did not deny that the letters were real. " I delivered nothing to zem but what nature delivered to me, zat I might at length recover my liberty.

I am not to be convicted by my own word or writing? If zey have written anything which may be hurtful to ze queen, my sister, zey have written it wizout my knowledge. Let them bear ze punishment of zeir inconsiderate boldness. I am sure, if zey were 'ere present, zey would clear me of all blame in zis cause. And I, if my notes were at 'and, could answer particularly zese zings."

At this point Nicholas decided that he had heard enough. In his mind, any further evidence was window dressing. Mary was guilty and that was an end to it.

Nicholas showed Beale his sketches over dinner.

"Nicholas, these are just perfect."

"You do realise they are purely preparatory. I will do a fair copy on my return to London and let you have them immediately."

"Well, Nicholas, returning to London will be sooner than you might think."

"How so." Nicholas was perplexed.

"We've had word from the Queen that she wishes to be consulted before a verdict is reached. We will continue the trial until tomorrow lunchtime and then return to London."

Nicholas groaned. He sympathised with Beale. Elizabeth was prevaricating and this would infuriate her commissioners. He was glad that all he was doing was sketching the scene for the records.

"So what happens now?"

"Nicholas, I have no idea." Beale paused to think "but I assume the trial will be reconvened in the Star Chamber."

"Will Mary be present?" Nicholas wondered whether Mary's complaints about her accommodation had been acted upon and she would accompany them to London, Elizabeth having decided that Mary would be better under her own eye at Court.

"I should think not. Walsingham won't let her outside Fotheringay. Elizabeth's decision is just another one of her delaying tactics and he is beside himself with fury." Beale spluttered.

"I'm relieved." Nicholas offered.

"He believes Elizabeth will never allow us to convict Mary." Beale continued.

Nicholas raised his eyes to heaven. "I suppose it's to do with Mary being an anointed queen?"

"Correct. Like herself, Mary is God's anointed representative and, because of their mutual 'divine right', Elizabeth does not want to be accused of condoning regicide."

"What did Walsingham say when he received Elizabeth's command?"

"It was unprintable!" Beale snorted in sympathy "so we return to London the day after tomorrow and, presumably, at the end of ten days we shall reconvene."

"If that's the case, and it's all the same with you, Robert, I can't see that my services are required any further here, so would like to get back to London as soon as possible."

Robert Beale frowned "Don't you want to see how it all unfolds?"

"Any other time, yes, but my wife is about to give birth and after the last time, I want to be there."

It took a few seconds for Robert to remember that Nicholas had lost his last baby at birth.

"Of course. Forgive me, Nicholas, I had quite forgotten."

"Will you need my services for the hearing in the Star Chamber, Robert?" Nicholas asked.

"No, no, dear boy. Sir Amyas will keep Mary here, under close guard. We won't require any further images." Beale paused and thought a minute "well, not until the execution."

Alice produced a bonny girl on All Hallows Eve and announced she was to be called Penelope.

"Penelope has orange hair, father. Do you think it's because mother ate so many oranges?" Daniel observed; he too had developed a liking for oranges during Alice's pregnancy. Nicholas had wondered whether the baby would appear in the world coloured bright orange because Alice had eaten such a vast quantity of the fruit and was relieved it was only the baby's hair that appeared to have been affected. Baby Penelope was a good baby and her birth had been quick and easy.

After the initial excitement of Penelope's arrival subsided, Nicholas produced a fair copy of the events at Fotheringay that had to be delivered to the Court at Richmond. Normally Elizabeth stayed at Whitehall when Parliament was in session and he wondered whether her choice of palace well outside the City of London had anything to do with Mary's trial.

Robert Beale was delighted with the sketch. "The Queen may never ask, but just in case she does we can show her who was there and where they sat."

"Robert, I completely understand. It's better to have this rather than be caught out should the queen ask for details."

"Likewise when Mary loses her head." Beale took a deep breath "Walsingham wants you there."

"So, whatever happens and whatever Elizabeth says, Mary will die."

Beale nodded in affirmation. "It's only a matter of time, but Elizabeth will agree and she will sign the warrant."

Nicholas nodded. He had never witnessed an execution.

"Eventually," Beale continued "but that could be months away. However, Mary's guilt is confirmed. You should have stayed for the second day."

"Surely it was only ever just a matter of form? Mary was never going to be found anything but guilty then or, at worst, a later date."

"Quite so, but she decided to accuse Burghley of being her enemy." Beale waited for Nicholas's reaction.

"I didn't think she was that stupid. An accusation like that is only going to antagonise the most powerful man in the land, which doesn't seem a very good strategy to me."

"Quite so." Beale nodded in agreement.

"How did Burghley respond?"

"Burghley told her 'No', implying he wasn't her enemy, but then continued that he was 'an enemy to the queen's enemy'."

Nicholas snorted in derision, admiring phrasing. "I suppose after that, the trial 'adjourned' in accordance with her Majesty's wishes? Can't Mary see that the verdict is a foregone conclusion?"

"She's now playing the Catholic martyr and she's been comparing her trial to that of Christ's! Nicholas, it's worse than a bad play. You should read the transcripts of what happened. It is a shame we can't ask Dudley's players to perform this comedy. However, Walsingham is very concerned that Elizabeth will continue to use the excuse that Mary is an anointed queen to delay ordering the death sentence. Her argument being that since Mary, like herself, is ordained by God, no one has the right to sentence a queen. "

"Surely Elizabeth cannot be that lily livered. She's never liked the woman who's been a thorn in the royal side ever since she came south of the border. Mary was caught conspiring to have the queen murdered and will continue to do so unless she dies."

"I quite agree, but Elizabeth sees it differently from all of us. We will never understand why, because we are not a monarch. However, Walsingham has written to Leicester asking him to apply pressure to get Elizabeth to make the necessary decision."

"Walsingham must be desperate. You didn't tell me what he said when he was told of Elizabeth's shilly-shallying?"

"I can't remember exactly what it was, but the jist of it was that Mary, despite being ordained by God, was a wicked ungrateful creature, who would probably continue to live despite all the evidence, because her majesty will not look after her own safety and have Mary beheaded, which would see an end to the affair."

"Well that's fairly clear, but I still find it interesting that Walsingham wrote to Leicester."

"As you so rightly observed. Writing to Leicester does indicate Walsingham's frustration and desperation. Whatever Leicester either manages to do, or not, let's hope he will, at least, bring some pressure to bear so Elizabeth will at least issue a proclamation announcing the verdict of the Chamber. However, I'm sure she will do nothing until absolutely necessary."

November

Nicholas sat wishing he had made a copy of the sketch he had given to Beale. In the last month Mary's trial had commenced, then adjourned and then heard in the Star Chamber. Parliament had finally been told of Mary's complicity in the Babington plot, and now the Members were calling for Mary's head. One of the Member's had called her 'the daughter of sedition, the nurse of impiety, the handmaid of iniquity'. Parliament was baying for blood, but still Elizabeth resisted the obvious solution.

The bells under the top steps tinkled their warning giving him just enough time to put his drawings away before the visitor entered the room.

"Congratulations Nicholas. Another fine daughter and a red head, just like our queen." Marcus shook Nicholas by the hand. "My Penelope is delighted you want her to be godmother; 'tis an honour."

"Thank you, Marcus. I'm just relieved this birth all went well. Alice is positively blooming and quite back to her old self. She's taking life easy and Molly and Cook are making sure she doesn't do too much. Come, let me pour you some ale - to wet the baby's head." Nicholas poured two tankards, handing one to Marcus.

"I don't suppose you've heard the latest news?" Marcus asked. Nicholas raised his eyebrow in silent question, and waited for Marcus to continue. "I understand Elizabeth has asked Parliament to find some way of making Mary secure, thus obviating the necessity of an execution."

Nicolas groaned and shook his head.

"Sometimes I don't believe how blinkered she can be!" Marcus continued. "If Mary's not executed she will be the focus for every Catholic plotter in England and Elizabeth will never be safe."

"Marcus, I totally agree, but have you about thought why she asking this?"

"I can only assume she hesitates because of her mother." Marcus stretched his legs in front of him and looked at Nicholas questioningly.

" So, despite all the evidence, you think Elizabeth feels the charges against Mary appear fabricated and she is protecting her from the ultimate sanction?" Nicholas realised he had an opportunity to quash some of the more elaborate rumours circulating about Mary's trial.

Marcus nodded his agreement.

"But, and this is only a suggestion," Nicholas continued "what if, at a later date, Parliament turned against the Crown? It seems to me that Elizabeth is frightened that the Members would use the precedent of Mary's execution to condemn an unpopular monarch."

"That's ridiculous. The woman has been proved to be plotting against the queen and is up to her neck in deceit and treason."

"Marcus, you may think it's an impossibility, but I've learnt that nothing's impossible if those in power so wish it."

"That's a very twisted thought. Elizabeth is very much loved by her people and they want Mary dead." Marcus paused, contemplating what Nicholas had said. "Do you really believe that's her reason for delaying the inevitable.?"

"Far more likely than any sentimental thoughts about something that happened when she was a child. Elizabeth was only three years old when her mother was executed so she probably doesn't even remember her. Certainly, this may play some part of it, but it will not be the main reason."

"So are you suggesting that Elizabeth doesn't want to be compared with her father and accused of callously executing an inconvenient family member?"

"Marcus, again that's a possibility. However, Elizabeth is far too canny to let sentiment cloud her judgement. Mary might be a relation, but Elizabeth has no fondness for her at all. I know, I've seen her when one of Mary's many letters has been delivered. She disdains to read it and leaves it unopened, giving it to Burghley or Walsingham to do with as they see fit. I believe she would much prefer to ensure her continued safety from any

Parliament that might wish to rid itself of an unpopular queen. Put yourself in her place – think how she must feel hearing Parliament demanding the head of an anointed queen. Don't forget the time she spent in the Tower when her sister thought she was plotting against her. I understand her rooms overlooked the site of mother's execution. For a young woman, that must have been quite an experience. Just the thought of Parliament baying for Mary's blood must terrify her."

"Hmm, that does sound plausible. But can't she see she has to be strong, therefore she needs to sign that death warrant? Not only would the people see that Elizabeth is a strong queen, it's what they want."

"Marcus, again cast your thoughts a little wider. It's not just the will of the people that has to be taken into consideration. If you were the kings of France and Spain what would you do if a Protestant English monarch executed a Catholic queen?"

"Ah," Marcus thought for a minute. "Now I see where you're taking me. You are thinking Spain and France might just be tempted to put aside their differences and mount a joint campaign against England; but wouldn't an outside force be more likely to come from Scotland because James wanted to avenge the death of his mother?"

Nicholas nodded in agreement. "You can never rule out James, but I doubt he could convince his nobles to join him because they would have to put their hands in their purses. Most of them have no love for Catholics. However, whatever we might think, it isn't going to make an bit of difference to the outcome. I believe Mary will die, but I'm not sure how. The simplest solution would be for her to die of natural causes."

"Do you mean poison her?"

"No, I do mean natural causes. If she were to die in suspicious circumstances, then I think we might well have James jumping our borders demanding justice for his dead mother."

"But if Mary were to die in her sleep, that would look just the same as suspicious circumstances. You would need for her to die in public, without any knife, musket or other weapon near her."

"Quite so Marcus, and the likelihood of that happening is as remote as either you or I changing the colour of our skin." Nicholas paused, pulling his thoughts into order. "What I am sure of is that Elizabeth will find a way of ensuring she is not implicated and until she's figured out a way to make sure that the world will understand this, Mary will stay alive and well in Fotheringay. However, since we cannot change what will happen, perhaps I can divert you a little."

Nicholas went to pick up a small velvet pouch lying on his desk.

"These are for Penelope - a birthday gift from her god-daughter?"

Marcus pulled open the drawstrings and tipped a pair of coral earrings into his cupped hand. Picking one up between his forefinger and thumb, he held it to the light. The finger of coral dangled from its gold mount and small diamonds glinted in the firelight.

"My, my Nick. This is indeed a generous gift."

"Marcus, I have to tell you that if it weren't for your wife, I do believe that my Alice would still be grief stricken, even to the point of insanity. It is our little Penelope's way of saying thank you for all your Penelope's constancy and friendship making it possible for her to be born safely." Marcus looked at his friend not knowing quite what to say. He had no idea that Alice had been so bad nor the role his own wife had played in her recovery.

"With Alice now safely delivered," Nicholas continued "I feel a great weight lifted from my shoulders. I have my dear Alice back and a beautiful new daughter. What man could wish for more?"

"So you haven't heard the other news?" Marcus paused and Nicholas looked puzzled. "Sir Philip Sidney has been killed in action?"

"No" Nicholas was aghast "that's dreadful news. What about Lord Robert and young Essex?"

"As far as I know, Nick, they are both in health."

"This is a great blow for the English. Young Oliver, - you remember my young painter apprentice?" Marcus nodded. Nicholas went to his shelf and took down a small painting, handing it to his friend to examine. "He painted this cabinet miniature of Sidney leaning against a tree as his final 'master' piece for me. Sidney was a very attractive man, very much one of the better additions to the Court and will be much missed." Nicholas continued. "And then there is his wife, the fair Frances. What do you think will become of her, Marcus?"

"No doubt she will return to her father's." Marcus was quite surprised at Nicholas's shock.

"But Walsingham's in poor health. How did Sidney die?"

"Foolishly, he decided not to wear his leg armour going into battle and was hit in the thigh by a musket ball. Evidently the wound turned gangrenous and he died on the 17th October. Leicester's not covered himself in glory during his time in the Netherlands, so, from the little I know, I assume Elizabeth will use Sidney's death as an excuse to haul Leicester home where she can keep an eye on him."

"Elizabeth wanted to recall him when he first accepted the Governor Generalship of the United Provinces. She was furious with him because it implied she agreed to England having sovereignty over the United Provinces, which she didn't, plus it meant Leicester, in his role of Governor General, could act with impunity on her behalf. She was furious! If that wasn't a provocation for a declaration of war by either France or Spain, then nothing was. However, the French are currently too concerned with their own problems of succession, but don't think the threat has gone away. I think Sidney's death is more useful than you think, tragic though it is."

"How so?"

"Because his death will give Elizabeth an excuse to withdraw our troops, who in turn will bolster our own defences and give us time to plan a defence against a foreign invasion."

"Do you really think that'll happen, Nick?"

"Do you truly believe it won't – if not immediately, but when the French have stopped fighting each other they will ally with the Spanish and come against us. They will have the blessing of the Pope and perhaps even some of his money?"

The blood drained from Marcus's face as the implications of what Nicholas was saying sank in.

"You really believe Philip will launch an invasion?"

"Why not? English meddling in the Low Countries must have angered him greatly and he appears to have a determination to make England Catholic again. What I can't understand is why he hasn't used either excuse for launching a war so far!"

"Have you spoken about this with Alice?"

"No. I have no wish to upset her and the Spanish are not yet knocking on our doors."

"That may be all well and good for you. I've got ships out there, and investments to think about."

Nicholas chuckled.

"I know you and Drake, and the other merchants are all hand in glove. You can't seriously expect me to believe that you haven't considered war with Spain?"

"No, but I hadn't thought that they might ally with France, then you bring the Pope into the equation, which suggests a whole new scenario. But why the Pope?"

"Have you forgotten that Elizabeth was excommunicated by him and remains so?"

337

"Yes, I had, and thank you for that reminder. It makes me feel so much better!" His use of irony masked the depth of shock at what Nicholas had said.

"Will you discuss this with Penelope?"

"Would you rather I did not, my friend?"

Nicholas nodded. "Let's not worry our wives until there is more definite news. They will only worry unnecessarily."

24th November

"Cook, what's all the noise in the street."

"Mr Nicholas, it be ever such good news."

"How so," Nicholas could hear all sorts of shouting, but could make no sense of it.

"Well, the street crier is calling that Mary Stuart is to be executed. There's a bonfire in Smithfield later."

"Indeed Cook, if everyone is going to Smithfield, just make sure everyone is not too late to bed."

"Thank you, Mr Nicholas." Cook's delight in Mary's guilt astonished him, but her pleasure in the news showed just how much the people wanted the Scottish Queen's head. Marcus was right about the people, but Nicholas knew it was going to take more than Parliament declaring Mary guilty to get Elizabeth to sign the death warrant. If her behaviour throughout the trial was anything to go by, Elizabeth would try and delay this for months

1587

1st February

"**M**r Nicholas," Molly stuck her head round the door to the workroom. Nicholas looked up from supervising the setting of some sapphires in an oval frame.

"What is it, Molly?"

"Mr Beale wants to see you," Molly paused "… privately, and 'e said it were urgent."

Nicholas frowned. Wiping his hands on a cloth he left his apprentice, Rowland, to finish setting sapphires.

Robert Beale stood warming his hands at the fire. He looked stern and businesslike and Nicholas wondered what was afoot.

"Robert, how nice to see you," he started.

"Quite so Nicholas, but I need to talk to you on an urgent matter." Beale raised an eyebrow as if to underline the fact. All it did was make him look ridiculous, which made Nicholas want to laugh.

"Come, it's probably more private in my room at the top of the house." Nicholas was able to cover his momentary lapse of manners by leading his visitor to his eyrie. The bells tinkled as they walked over the top steps.

"These alert me to anyone coming up the stairs," he explained.

"Ingenious, Nicholas, and I'm very grateful for your foresight, for what I have to discuss must be kept absolutely secret."

Nicholas closed the door and lit the fire laid ready in the grate. The kindling was dry and he added a few pieces of dry ash wood as the fire caught, then added more logs until a merry blaze began to take the chill off the room. Nicholas offered Robert Beale a chair next to the fire and, as his guest made himself comfortable, took the one opposite.

"Nicholas, Sir Francis has asked that you prepare yourself for a ride to Fotheringay"

"So Walsingham's back at Court?"

"No, Sir Francis is still recovering from his malady and is currently at Barnes. As to whether or not her Majesty has signed the warrant, when I left Greenwich probably not, but William Davidson had been summoned by her Majesty and told to bring it with him. The minute she signs he will hand it to Lord Burghley. You must be at Fotheringay to make a record of the execution, in exactly the same manner as the trial."

Nicholas gulped in horror. "What if Elizabeth changes her mind?"

"If we move fast enough, by the time that happens it will be too late."

"Burghley is obviously determined to leave nothing to chance." Nicholas paused. "But how come Elizabeth has decided to sign now? Has something happened? I thought that perhaps with Mary's delicate health … " Nicholas let the sentence drift away into silence.

Beale's face was grim. "I too would have preferred that Mary might, as it were, succumb to natural causes, but I understand that, despite it being suggested that Mary might just 'die', certain individuals do not have the stomach to carry out this task."

The situation was fraught with the possibilities of misunderstandings. Nicholas wondered how he and Beale would fare should Elizabeth turn on any one who had been involved in Mary's execution in any way at all. Just being there might inflame Elizabeth against him and he did not want to lose either her patronage, or her friendship.

"How do you feel about your involvement, Robert?"

"Like you, apprehensive, but my duty to my Queen is to protect her at all costs and I pray that if she takes against me, she will see that I was acting according to my oath under the Bond of Association."

Nicholas nodded his agreement.

"Even so, Elizabeth's reaction to this might be like nothing we have ever seen, so I might just send Alice and the children, to stay with her father."

"No!" Beale almost shouted his refusal "Nicholas, do nothing that is in anyway out of the ordinary. Does Alice normally go and stay with her father in February?"

"Er no, but why not?"

"Sir Francis wants everyone to act as normal. It must not appear as a conspiracy against the Queen."

"Hmm." Nicholas tapped his fingers against his lips. He could see the merit in this. If it looked as if there were a conspiracy of the Queen's advisors and their underlings, Elizabeth might just have their heads. "It looks as if we have no choice!"

"I feel as uncomfortable about this as you, but it is better that the Scottish queen is relieved of her head. If she lives, one day one of these damned plots will be successful and I, for one, do not wish to live under the yoke of a Catholic monarch."

"So when do we ride?"

"Be prepared to travel at dawn. It will be a hard ride."

"Is Lord Burghley coming?"

Beale laughed.

"Oh, come, my friend. Do you think Burghley is that stupid?"

"No, indeed. If Elizabeth has truly signed that warrant, his disappearance from Court would be just too coincidental, but I would lay money that Elizabeth tells Davidson not to hand the signed copy to anyone."

"My thoughts exactly, Nicholas, but perhaps these are best kept to ourselves for the time being."

Beale rose to leave.

"Until tomorrow, Nicholas. It's momentous times we live in and sometimes I wish I did not work quite so closely with those who guide this land."

Nicholas smiled. "Robert, I agree. As exciting as it is to be close to the Court, sometimes, just sometimes, I long for a simple life."

"Until tomorrow, Nicholas. Be at the stables at Seething Lane at dawn. Don't come down. I'll see myself out."

Beale turned and ran downstairs leaving the little bells tinkling in his wake.

Nicholas sighed and put together new sketchbooks, red chalk and silverpoints to take with him.

8th February

Once again Nicholas was seated in the minstrels' gallery looking down into the great hall of dank and gloomy Fotheringay Castle. It was seven in the morning and the light was poor. He quickly sketched the room. A twelve foot square stage was draped with black fabric with a knee high rail round three sides. The surface was strewn with straw, but what drew his eye was the wooden block, very obviously very new as the wood was very bright and unstained.

Their party had arrived the previous day and been greeted by Sir Amyas Paulet and Sir Dru Drury. Seeing Sir Dru, Nicholas wondered if Burghley had ever handed over the little miniature of Arthur. He realised he should not have been surprised at Sir Dru's presence. The knight had been a loyal and trusted member of the Queen's household for many years. It was clear that only those trusted by Elizabeth were here at Fotheringay.

They had ridden north with Henry Grey and George Talbot, the Earls of Kent and Shrewsbury. Together with the two Earls, Beale had handed various written instructions to Sir Amyas and then told Mary her fate, giving her the night to prepare herself. Nicholas was glad he was only an onlooker and not actively involved. Believing she was a traitor was easy, but being a witness to her execution was proving extremely difficult. It would be his hand that recorded this event; it would be his hand that detailed just how you execute a queen.

Despite his reservations, Nicholas was finding the mechanics of the event gruesomely fascinating as he sketched out the details of the hall and just who had been allowed in. Nicholas looked at those who had been allowed in to witness the event and sketched various interesting faces. He wondered about their motives in being here today. Were they there to satisfy their own curiosity or were they demonstrating their loyalty to Elizabeth; were they there to satisfy their own blood lust or perhaps wanting to be part of history. Considering Sir Francis's almost manic desire for secrecy, it was strange that, in addition to those in the hall, there was close to a thousand people standing in the freezing cold outside in the castle's lower bailey. They would not even see the event, so it made little sense for them to be there.

Bull, the official execution and his assistant, had arrived at day break. As far as Nicholas knew, the castle had been locked since his and Beale's arrival the night before and Bull and his assistant had been the only people allowed in until now, which meant that the crowd outside must have been there since the previous night. If that were the case, they had been remarkably quiet.

Nicholas watched in grim fascination as Bull, now dressed in his black masks and gown and white apron, removed his axe from a box and sharpened the blade on a whetstone. Bull propped the weapon against the rail and stood waiting, standing with his arms crossed. Reflected flames flickered on the polished blade.

Shortly after eight o'clock the door opened and Mary entered the great hall accompanied by the two Earls. He recognised Andrew Melville, her steward and her ladies, Jane Kennedy and Elizabeth Curle. There were other men with them but Nicholas did not recognise them.

Mary appeared quietly composed. He noted she was dressed in black satin gown with a bodice of crimson velvet and her hair was covered by a white cap. Her women were red eyed and he could see Mary also had been crying. She climbed the scaffold slowly.

Beale stood and read out the death warrant to Mary and the assembled company. Nicholas could clearly see the Great Seal dangling from the ribbons. The Great Seal he had designed. The queen might have signed the warrant, but without the Seal being attached, this execution could not happen. He hated the thought that something he designed was so crucial to this grisly event.

The words proclaiming her death did not seem to affect Mary at all and she appeared almost cheerful. She looked around at all those who had come to see her last moments on earth. Having cast her eyes around the hall and examined the great and the good standing below her, she looked up at the minstrels' gallery and, for a moment, Nicholas looked straight into the eyes

344

of the Scottish Queen. She smiled. Nicholas sat back feeling physically sick.

The Protestant Dean of Peterborough droned words Nicholas knew were meaningless to her and managed a smile when she interrupted :

"Mr Dean! Trouble not yourself nor me, for know zat I am settled in ze ancient Catholic and Roman religion and in defence thereof. I mean, by God's 'elp, to spend my blood."

The Dean gave up trying to save her soul and took to praying, but she interrupted him again, this time reciting her Latin prayers. Tears coursed down her cheeks and her six companions joined their voices to hers, drowning out that of the Dean. Mary slipped to her knees and continued in English:

"… Christ's afflicted church: for an end to 'er troubles and for my son, zat 'e might truly and uprightly be converted to ze Roman Catholic church."

Nicholas blinked at her reference to her son, James. Beale had told him it was extremely unlikely that Scotland would make anything other than a token complaint at Mary's execution. Nicholas wondered if there were secret negotiations about his position should Elizabeth die childless. Nicholas shuddered at this thought. How callous the minds of kings.

Nicholas turned his attention back to the hall below.

"… and for ze Queen Elizabeth, zat she may long and peacefully proper and serve God aright."

Mary knelt, clasping her ivory crucifix to her bosom, begging the saints to intercede on her behalf and that God would, in his mercy and goodness, avert his plagues from 'zis silly island'.

Nicholas snorted. The Earl of Kent leant forward demanding:

"Madam, I beseech you: settle Christ in your heart and leave the addition of these Popish trumperies to themselves."

345

The whole event was in danger of becoming a farce. Mary deliberately ignored him and continued with her prayers.

Bull and his assistant stepped forward and knelt before her to ask her forgiveness for what they were about to do.

"I forgive you with all my 'eart, for I 'ope zat zis death shall give me an end to all my troubles."

The two men stood up. Mary wore a gold Agnes Dei medallion round her neck which, according to tradition, Bull could claim as his, but Mary smiled at him and Nicholas heard her tell him that it would be given to one of her women as a gift.

Aided by her women she proceeded to disrobe until she was stripped to her petticoat. Mary stood dressed in head to toe in scarlet satin.

"My God," he thought *"Beale's right, she's turned her execution into a one act play!"*

Nicholas saw her lips move, but was unable to make out what she was saying. Mary knelt on the cushion in front of the block. Jane Kennedy stepped forward and taking out a white cloth she first kissed it then folded it into a neat triangle and tied it as a blindfold across her mistress's eyes. Mary reached up and patted the woman's hand then groped forward, all the while intoning

'In te Domino confide me confundar in eternum'.
Nicholas wrote the words in his sketchbook.

Mary's hands found the twelve inch high block and bent forward laying her neck in the hollow, her hands first resting on the block either side of her head; then she stretched her arms out sideways and called out

"In manus tuas, Domine commendo spiritum meum."
There was no need to translate. Everyone in the room recognised the words "Into your hands Lord, I commend my spirit!"

Later, Nicholas could not remember if she had called out once, twice or even three or four times, but he knew he would always remember the silence when she finished.

George Talbot signalled to the axe man. The solid Bull hefted his axe high above his head and swung it down. The blade bounced off the knot of the kerchief; Mary whimpered, but remained motionless.

Bull swung again, this time the blade sliced through her neck almost to the front, but her head and body were still attached by a little gristle. Blood sprayed out of the neck stump briefly. Bull knelt down, changed his grip and wielded his axe like a meat cleaver to cut through the last piece of flesh. Nicholas sat numbed, bile rising up his throat and he swallowed hard, trying not to be sick.

Mesmerised he watched as Bull stood up, bent down and picked up Mary's severed head by her hair. The head dropped from Bull's grasp and bounced on the floor, leaving the shocked man holding only a red wig. The nearly bald head rolled across the scaffold and came to a stop. Glazed eyes looking up directly at the minstrel's gallery. Mary's lips continued to move, but her eyes no longer held the unvoiced question as to why he was there.

"So perish all the queen's enemies." The voice of the Dean of Peterborough broke Nicholas's trance. George Talbot was sobbing. Considering the Earl's long relationship with the late Scottish Queen this came as no surprise.

"Such be the end of all the queen's and the Gospel's enemies." the Earl of Kent replied.

Nicholas turned his back on the scene below and quickly filled in the details on his sketch. The little narrative was to be read from top left where he showed Mary entering with her two gentlewomen, the two earls seated on the scaffold, four further nobles to the back of the hall and the crowd. He did not show the beheading. There was no need to embellish what was already sufficient to record the morning's events and he felt so nauseated he could not have brought himself to draw Mary headless even had his life depended on it.

Young Henry Talbot was to deliver all the official documents to London. Nicholas did not envy young Talbot his job, and quickly finished filling in the missing details so Beale could include the sketch in the official bundle. It had been a grim day and it was not yet lunchtime.

The mood of the crowd was sombre as Nicholas made his way to where Beale was gathering his papers.

"Robert, I shall return to London with young Talbot."

Beale nodded. He was very pale and Nicholas wondered if he too was feeling ill.

"Quite so; quite so." Beale looked at the figures on the paper, glad to have something to focus on. "It's a good sketch, Nicholas. Well done."

Nicholas put his hand on Beale's shoulder, neither man knowing quite what else to say.

April

As expected, Elizabeth exploded with fury when she heard that, despite her orders to delay the execution, Mary had lost her head. Davidson was languishing in the Tower and Lord Burghley at his house in the country. It was two and a half months since Nicholas had been at Whitehall and he was not sure who he would be able to see. If Beale were still at his post it would suggest that Elizabeth was focusing her fury on those she considered immediately responsible. Sir Francis was still at Barnes, suffering from his recurrent malady and so far, it did not appear he had been a focus of the queen's ire.

However, it seemed there were fresh problems looming. The City was full of rumours and gossip about Spain. The whole of London knew that Drake had gone to sea and the rumours were that he was hunting Spanish gold in Spanish ports. Another story was that the Spanish were massing an invasion fleet to come against England and wreak vengeance for Mary's death. Since both these stories felt as though they might be founded in fact, Nicholas wanted to see if Robert Beale knew whether there was any substance to them. He just hoped Beale was still in office.

Nicholas found all the clerks very intent on their work. Beale look haggard and worn.

"Ah Nicholas. How good to see you."

"Robert, how does life fare for you?" Nicholas was shocked by the secretary's appearance. He had lost weight and looked ill.

"Considering events, not so bad. . . now. Lord Burghley will be back soon, I'm sure. Elizabeth cannot let him stew in the country with what we now know is happening in Spain."

"Would this have anything to do with Drake's departure?"

"It would have everything to do with that." Beale ran his hands through his hair and leant back in his chair

Nicholas waited for him to expand on this statement. The careworn man stood up.

"Come, Nicholas. Let us walk together in the sunshine. Storm clouds are gathering and we may not have the chance to do so for some time."

Nicholas had walked from the City under a cloudless sky so either Beale was being poetic, or he thought the weather was on the turn. They took a walk round a garden where the low hedges were neatly clipped into an elegant design. Tiny daffodils nodded in the breeze and the willow trees were hazy with a hint of green as they began to unfurl their new leaves. It had been a long, cold winter and it lifted their spirits to see spring returning. A heron skimmed the treetops heading for the river.

Beale shut his eyes and turned his face to the sun taking a deep breath as if inhaling the fresh spring air would somehow renew him. Nicholas was amazed at how the fresh air brought the colour back to Beale's cheeks.

"Well, so far Nicholas, we haven't lost our heads!"

"No, but Davidson's still in the Tower."

"Quite so. Poor man; when Elizabeth heard the news from Fotheringay she wanted his head parted from his shoulders immediately." Nicholas waited for Beale to continue. "It was a bad day for all of us. From your spot in the minstrels' gallery, did you see Mary's dog hidden under her skirts?"

"No" he shook his head. "In fact I didn't even know she had one."

"Someone had given her a sky terrier, but you didn't see it on the dais at all?"

"Robert, if I'd seen it, then others would have too. Why do you ask?"

"We'd had strict instructions that everything was to be burnt so there was absolutely no chance of any of her followers turning anything into a relic." Beale continued. "When Bull and his assistant went to move Mary's body, the terrier was hidden under her skirts. As Bull lifted the body the damn dog appeared as if by magic. Poor thing was terrified and ended up covered in her blood. It was all a rather unpleasant find and the poor dog needed a very good bath."

Nicholas pulled a face. Luckily he had not seen this, neither had he heard about it until now.

"But we've had news from Spain that is far worse." Beale was clearly glad to have someone to unburden himself to.

"Go on." Nicholas wondered what trauma Beale was going to reveal.

"Philip is gathering a great armada and we understand he intends to move against England."

350

Nicholas shuddered. So that particular rumour was true. "Because of the events at Fotheringay?"

"No, I don't think so." Beale shook his head. "Our agents have been keeping an eye on things for the past year, and Philip has been steadily increasing the number of ships and supply vessels of his fleet. At first I thought it must be to do with the protection of Philip's treasure ships coming across the Atlantic since Drake, Hawkins, Frobisher and Raleigh are all ensuring that England's coffers are benefiting from Spanish gold."

Nicholas smiled. The privateers liked nothing better than to relieve a Spanish ship of its cargo.

"Unfortunately," Beale continued "we have received information that this is not the case. As you probably know, the Spanish are having some success against us in the Low Countries. For some time Philip has been gathering land forces there under the Duke of Parma, and now we've learnt that he is to mount an Armada against us and with this army available just across the Channel, it doesn't take a genius to realise that England is in grave peril."

Nicholas nodded as all his worst fears were confirmed and waited for Beale to continue.

"We need more reliable sources of information rather than having to rely on intermittent information gleaned by our merchants. Ever since Philip imposed a trade embargo on English merchants, up until recently, our reliable information sources have been a bit thin on the ground."

"So, how come you now have a reliable source?" Nicholas was not sure where Beale was leading him.

"In short, an Italian in Madrid."

Nicholas wondered if the Italian was the same informant he had seen in Walsingham's office. Perhaps it was the same Italian who had wielded the Venetian stiletto and murdered James Bell.

"Drake has sailed to see if there is any truth in the rumours."

"Knowing Drake, I don't suppose he will limit himself to gathering information! He'll grab any opportunity to tweak Philip's nose and if that depletes the size of this navy, then all well and good."

Beale smiled. "You may also have heard that Elizabeth has sent a ship after him, to make sure he doesn't do anything that will spark a war."

"If Drake's already left Plymouth then it will be like finding a needle in a haystack? How on earth will anyone find Drake's small fleet on the Atlantic ocean, let alone stop him doing anything provocative! An empty gesture for the benefit of the Spanish spies back here at Court!"

"Quite so, Nicholas. We can but wait to see what occurs?"

"Do you really believe Philip will move against England?"

"I do, and so we must prepare for the worst!"

"What are you planning to do, Robert?" Nicholas began to feel queasy.

"I'm thinking I might go to the country if it looks as if Parma's forces are likely to land. If I were you, I would give some deep thought to where you might take your family."

"Has there been any hint as to where he might land?"

"Not so far as I know, but then I'm here and Walsingham is in Barnes, and Burghley is still in the country so I have no idea of any of the very latest intelligence. Leicester does not see it fit to confide in me!"

"So her Majesty is still not having anything to do with those who were at Fotheringay?"

"Nick, that might be the case, but I believe she ignores my existence. Whether it has anything to do with Mary's execution, or not, these offices still need to function and they won't do it without someone being here. Elizabeth knows that so perhaps she chooses not to see me."

"If you were in Parma's position, where would you choose to land?"

"Hmm, I'm no soldier, but strategically, I would want to make as quick a strike against the queen as I could, so somewhere upstream from the mouth of the Thames, so I could take London."

"Is the Queen preparing to leave London?"

"I know as much as you do, regarding her Majesty's plans."

"Hmm" Nicholas wondered what he should do. He did not like the idea of his family being in London should the Spanish invade. Whilst he was not an official member of the Court, he was close to the Queen and should Parma take London he would prefer it if Alice and the children were somewhere safe from marauding Spanish soldiers.

"Robert, if I hear anything I will let you know."

"Are your sources reliable?"

"Sometimes the traders and merchant men are as good as Walsingham's network and, at the moment, they're all you and I have as a source of information until such times as things return to normal."

May

"Master Teerlinc is not due back until later, Mr Hillyarde."

"Thank you, do you know what time?"

The clerk shook his head. "He's meeting with some of his captains. An Italian trader docked this morning and all of them will be down at The Anchor trying to learn more."

"He did have news of Drake?"

"Indeed, Mr Hillyarde. Sir Francis darted in to Cadiz and I gather set light to several of Philip's ships. Evidently the King of Spain is in a state of apoplexy as much of his Armada is gathered there. What I don't know is just how much damage this has done and that's what they're all a dither to find out at the Anchor."

Nicholas had so far ignored any of Alice's gossiping, but now there was new information he had to make some decisions about where to send the family.

The Anchor was crowded.

"Can you tell me where Master Teerlinc is sitting?"

The landlord tossed his head indicating the backroom. "He's in there with the Italian captain."

The inn was heaving with men and rumours. Despite, or perhaps because of, the atmosphere of subdued anxiety, the landlord was making a good living.

A group of men were listening intently to what the Italian had to say. Nicholas recognised some of the merchants and one or two of the sea captains then spotted Marcus sitting at the back.

"… and Sidonia is definitely in charge of Philip's Armada. If you are right, Drake's actions will delay the ships sailing, so I don't see any threat will appear for some time."

"Teerlinc, I agree. All the same, I'll sail '*The Lady Penelope*' well to the North and come down the coast of the New World, into the Caribbean." Marcus nodded and wrote something in his notebook. Nicholas did not recognise the speaker.

"And what about you Captain Black?"

"As you know, I'm due to sail to Genoa, so I'll go well West to avoid any Spanish shipping, then slip through the Straits of Gibraltar."

"Thank you Capitano Cioncolini," Marcus turned to the foreigner "you have given us much information, which is much greatly appreciated."

Nicholas coughed to get the Marcus's attention.

"Ah, Nicholas. Come, join us. Let me introduce Capitano Cioncolini. He's fresh from Spain with news that Drake has caused mayhem and havoc in Cadiz."

Cioncolini had one of those faces which had seen far too much sun. Nicholas was reminded of the Italian he had seen in Walsingham's office three years.

"Do you know where Sir Francis was headed after his mission at Cadiz?"

"No, but the treasure ship, the San Filipe, is due into Cadiz shortly. He may well have gone after her."

Nicholas smiled. Drake would be unable to resist such a prize.

"If he has, Captain Cioncolini, I'm sure he'll return as soon as he's filled his holds with Spanish plunder."

A murmur of amused agreement rippled through the room.

"A toast to Drake's safe return." Marcus raised his tankard.

June

"Mr Hillyarde, the Earl of Essex is here."

"Thank you Molly. Show him to the parlour and bring us some claret. Tell the mistress to join us."

Nicholas cleaned his brush and removed his painter's smock. The second Earl of Essex, young Robert Devereux, needed to be scrutinised by Alice. Perhaps between them they could work out just who his father was.

Downstairs, the young Earl had made himself comfortable in Nicholas's chair.

"Ah, Hillyarde." The Earl remained seated as Nicholas entered the room. "I trust you are not too busy. By the way, my stepfather sends his best wishes."

"I trust my lord Leicester is in good health?" Young Devereux was arrogant and Nicholas did not like him.

"He is to return to the Low Countries tomorrow, despite finding the advancing years are making his joints stiff." Devereux paused "which is why he has resigned his position as Master of the Queen's Horse, in favour of me."

Alice entered, followed by Molly carrying a tray of refreshments. Nicholas could hear his wife talking quietly, glasses being filled, the door close then Alice standing next to him.

"My Lord, may I present my wife."

Finally, Robert Devereux had the grace to stand and bow.

"Delighted, Madam. The Earl of Leicester has told me of your generous hospitality and ..." Devereux lifted Alice's hand to his lips " ... your beauty."

Alice blushed, flattered by the young man's blandishments. Nicholas felt a pang of jealousy seeing Alice blush and fumble like a young maid.

"My Lord Essex," Alice fluttered "to what do we owe the pleasure?"

"Mistress Hillyarde, I desire your husband to paint one of his little portraits to commemorate my being appointed as her Majesty's Master of Horse."

Nicholas smiled. Robert Devereux might be good looking, but all his flattery was transparent and purely so he could have his own way. However, this commission would give him the opportunity of studying this young man's face closely and perhaps see whether Alice's theory had substance. One family resemblance was already clear, Robert Devereux had the Knolly's chin.

"I thought perhaps I should be dressed in a doublet of black and white, and looking pensive, perhaps with some roses around the edge of the portrait." Devereux waved his hand making strange circles in the air as he described his vision

"The colours of the queen's livery, and you captured in constancy by the stems and thorns of the eglantine showing your loyalty to the queen."

"That's quite so." Devereux turned " Do you not think it appropriate, Mistress Hillyarde?"

Alice smiled "My Lord Essex, the word picture sounds exquisite, and I'm sure her Majesty will be charmed by your demonstration of loyalty. Perhaps some poetry …"

"My, that sounds a laudable idea. Do you have any verses in mind?"

Alice blushed. "I'm sorry, my education doesn't extend to poetry or recitation. However, I'm sure my husband will be able to suggest something suitable."

"Well, Master Hillyarde this sounds the start of a veritable masterpiece. When can we start? Now perhaps?"

"Do you have such a costume in the queen's colours?"

"Ah, quite so." The Earl thought or a minute "I have such a one, but not with me."

"No matter. If you bring it with you, shall we say, the day after tomorrow. And between now and then, perhaps you could give thought to a suitable motto."

"I shall present myself tomorrow two hours after sunrise, so with such an early start we shall be soonest finished."

"Then I look forward until tomorrow my lord." Nicholas was punctilious with his manners.

Devereux downed his wine and left. Nicholas shut the door left open by the new Master of the Queen's Horse.

"Well, Alice, what think you of Walter Devereux's offspring?"

Alice gave Nicholas's question a few minutes thought. "So you don't think he's Dudley's son, then?"

"Alice, that's not what I asked."

"Well, I don't think he's a Devereux."

"Because he has the arrogance of a Dudley?"

"Perhaps. His behaviour is as I remember Dudley as a very much younger man, when he came to my father's."

"Just because he has similar high handed traits does not make him a son of the Earl of Leicester."

"Quite so, Nick, but why would Leicester give his position as Master of Horse over to a stepson? Why not resign and leave the Queen to appoint someone new. Surely Leicester would have some say in who was appointed, but Devereux seems to want us to think Leicester made sure the position went to him."

"Ah, yes. I was too busy looking at his face. That poses a conundrum."

"So, husband, you don't think Dudley is his father."

"I never said that. He has the Knollys's chin, but I couldn't say with certainty I see much of Dudley in him. I agree there's something about him across his eyes, and yes, he has all the arrogance of a Dudley, but so do a lot of young men, and you cannot be suggesting they all come from Leicester's loins?"

Alice giggled. "Nick! Why would I think that? Dudley has never behaved improperly towards me, so his reputation could just be gossip. Beside, I thought young Robert quite charming."

Nicholas sniffed. "And another thing. I quite clearly said I would see him the day after tomorrow, not tomorrow."

"True, but that's just the sort of thing Dudley does to you every time he commissions something!"

"Devereux's behaviour still doesn't prove he is who you think he is."

Robert Devereux appeared two hours after sunrise the following day. Nicholas had already sketched a few ideas, using a slightly larger oval than usual to accommodate a full length figure. The painting could still be held in the palm of the hand, but could also be hung on a wall. To give the young Devereux an air of nonchalance and daydreaming Nicholas had decided he needed something to lean against. At first he had thought about having his client leaning on his elbows and gazing out of a window, but these sketches had not been very successful. Then he had looked out of the window and seen one of the apprentices leaning against the door frame and the boy's casual air of insouciance had inspired him.

"Here are some preliminary ideas, my lord. Have you had any further thoughts about a motto?"

"Ah yes, Dat poenas laudata fides!"

Nicholas raised his eyebrows. If that was what his client wanted, then who was he to comment.

"Mister Hillyarde, I like these ideas, particularly since I will be one of your rare full length paintings."

"If I could ask you to stand like so." Nicholas raised his elbow and leant against the tree trunk trying to look suitably lovesick.

"I'm impressed you've gone to the trouble of procuring a real tree trunk. How about I lean against it like this, and place my hand over my heart so." Walter leant against the tree and crossed his legs.

"Lord Devereux, that's perfect. Stay there and I shall sketch in the details." Nicholas's brush flickered quickly over the surface of his vellum and he soon had the Earl's outline perfectly placed. " The eglantine poses a difficult problem. If it's all the same to you, I shall put that in after I have finished your portrait, so it lays over you entwining you as you suggested."

"Excellent, and how long do you estimate this will take?"

"Provided we have no interruptions, three to four days." The young man nodded his acceptance even though Nicholas could sense his desire for it to be finished sooner. "I'm interested in why you want a full length portrait."

"I've seen the one you painted of Sir Christopher Hatton and wanted one like it."

"Ah, the one I painted celebrating his appointment to the position of Chancellor."

"That's the one I saw, but I want something a little bigger, but not so large it cannot be held in the hand."

Despite the larger size and the work it entailed, Nicholas was as good as his word and three days later, 'Dat poenas laudata fides' was finished and delivered. Alice called it 'The Young Man Amongst Roses'.

"What is it about the Dudley men liking obscure Latin mottoes, Nick. What does Dat Poenas etcetera, mean?"

"If you believe the Earl's Latin translation, he says it means My praised faith procures my pain!"

"That's as bizarre as Arthur's 'Attici Amoris Ergo'. So do you have a theory about Robert Devereux's praised faith and what pain it is that it has bought?"

"Only he knows, and I have no desire to ask him, Alice. It's his business."

"Well, if you are not interested in his motto, having spent considerable time in his company, who do you think his father might be.?"

"I only ever saw Walter Devereux from a distance so I couldn't say for sure whether Devereux was, or was not, his father."

Alice snorted with derision "I suppose you are now going to say that you can't say for sure that Dudley is his father, either?"

"Quite so, my lovely wife. However, he does have many of Dudley's mannerisms. I believe the most telling evidence for Dudley being his father is nothing to do with whom young Devereux resembles, but Dudley's obvious affection for the young man and ensuring he takes over as Master of the Queen's Horse."

"But what if young Devereux was the best man for the position?"

"Alice, the Queen is always very taken with good looking young men, so it might just be so, but it does seem a very curious coincidence. Devereux is very high in the Queen's estimation, mainly because of Dudley and Dudley is very happy for him to be there. Now that's the action of a father, wouldn't you agree?"

In his opinion, Devereux did not resemble Robert Dudley as much as Arthur did. However, he certainly favoured his mother in behaviour and somewhat in looks.

1588

June

"Alice," Nicholas took his wife's hand in his own. "Alice, I want you and the children to go to Exeter."

"Nick, I'm not leaving you here."

"Alice, we know the Armada is on it's way and I've been told Sidonia is planning to pick up the Duke of Parma's army in the Low Countries. If Parma's troops are going to land, there is intelligence it will be somewhere along the Thames and I don't want you, or the children, exposed to any danger."

"Nick." Alice shook her head. "Nick, I can't do it. I can't leave you, and if we were to go, why Exeter?"

"Alice, I've told you. London won't be safe. If the Spanish come, then it will be as an invading army and you've heard the stories of what invading armies do to women and children."

"But Elizabeth won't let that happen."

"She may not have an option if Drake and the navy doesn't stop Philip's Armada."

"What is the navy doing? Where are all our good sea captains when we need them?"

"Alice, don't try and change the subject. You and the children will travel down to Exeter overland and that's an end to it."

"And what if I refuse."

"You won't because you want the children to be safe and not end up speared on the end of a Spanish pikestaff, or worse, picked up by their legs and their heads smashed against a wall."

"Nick. Stop it" Alice had her hands over her ears. "We'll go. You don't have to say anymore. But you have to come to?"

"I can't."

"Why not? You can't let us to travel to Exeter on our own. And you can't stay here. You're too close to the queen and if the Spanish find you, it will be you at the end of a Spanish pikestaff."

Alice walked to the window and watched the children playing in the garden.

"We will be taking Cook and Molly with us. Your father can't be expected to put us up, so we will have to take a house, and since I cannot do all that on my own and look after the children, you will have to come with us. And that's another thing, what are you going to tell the children? You've always said we would face everything together."

"That they're going to stay with their grandfather and nothing else. There's no need to frighten them with stories of what might happen if you stay in London."

"All right, I'll go, but not just yet."

July

"The beacons are lit – The Spanish are coming!" A boy was running through the streets shouting the news. "The beacons are lit. Prepare for invasion."

It was a blustery day and it seemed as if the weather were determined to push the Spanish closer to London as fast as possible. Rumours flew and the people's fear was tangible.

"Nick, the queen is staying in London so I'm not leaving you!"

"But Alice we agreed ..."

"That was last month and I don't want to leave you. If the queen is going to stay, then so will I."

"You will be much safer in the country." Nicholas was not quite shouting, but his tone was stern.

"Piffle! Nick, I'm not leaving you. You've always wished your father hadn't sent you to Geneva and by sending us away you're doing just the same thing. I'm not going anywhere!" Alice stamped her foot.

"Where's your father?"

"He's staying too. He has no wish to live under Spanish rule, but he's said he's not going to run and hide. We will put our trust in God. He will see England stays safe"

"Well, it seems that between you, you have me boxed into a corner. I will branded as a bully or a coward if I insist you leave London. We can but wait and see whether our navy manages to defeat Philip's Armada." Nicholas wished he had her faith. In his experience God had a strange way of suddenly changing things just when you thought everything was going your way.

August.

There had been little news of what was happening in the Channel except that again Drake has used fireships and had scattered the Spanish fleet. There were rumours they were trying to regroup further up the English coast and everyone prayed the weather would hold against them and the navy would protect England.

Nicholas was at a loss as to what to do. Should he over-rule his wife and insist they go down to the country, or should they wait and see what happened. Troops were being mustered at Tilbury in case Parma's troops were going to invade and evidently the queen was determined to lead them.

Should he join up? He was forty one years old and had absolutely no ability with a sword or any other weapon. The last time he had thrown a punch in anger had been when he was twelve. As an adult, the most aggressive thing he had ever done was throw a paintbrush across his workroom in frustration. He knew he would be of no use, but he did not want Alice to think him a coward.

Marcus had formed a squad of his own men, given them weapons and armour and, as far as Nicholas knew, they were with the army at Tilbury. Young Lockey had joined Marcus's men, but he had always been a bit of a scrapper and well able to look after himself in a brawl.

The days passed and the tension grew as the City waited for news of any sort. There were wild rumours, but these just made everyone more fearful.

"Daddy," Lettice was trying to attract his attention. "What will happen if the Spanish come?"

"Oh Lettice, let's hope it won't come to that."

"But Daddy, if they do, will the Queen hang them?"

Nicholas picked up his daughter. "We can only wait and pray they don't come, Lettice. Where's your mother?"

"She's gone to Aunt Sarah's and Daniel, Laurence and Francis are sharpening the knives with Cook, just in case."

So the City waited and finally the news came that the Spanish were on the run with the English navy in hot pursuit.

September

"Nicholas, please sit down." Nicholas had never seen Lord Burghley look so concerned. Sir Francis was resting his elbow on the arm of his chair, holding his head.

"We have grave news." Burghley paused and took a deep breath. "The Earl of Leicester is dead."

365

"My God;" Nicholas felt sick with shock. He had known Robert Dudley since his first days in London. "Lord Robert was on his way to Buxton to take the waters, was he not?"

"Indeed." This time it was Sir Francis who spoke. "He'd stopped at Woodstock and died there."

The import of their news sank in slowly. Despite everything, Elizabeth still adored the man. Dudley had become quite portly in recent years and she had teased him that he should dine on only the leg of a wren, but, despite her waspish teasing, their affection for each other was still palpable after all these years.

"How is the Queen?" Nicholas had the terrible thought perhaps these two men might want him to break this news to her.

"We've not long heard, so Elizabeth does not yet know and, since receiving the news from Buxton, we've had further news from Spain." Lord Burghley's voice was grave.

Sir Francis turned and looked at Nicholas. Walsingham had deep shadows under his eyes and his complexion had a distinctly yellow hue. "The young man you know as Arthur Southron has been at Philip's Court for some time." His voice was soft and low.

Nicholas swallowed and waited. Both Burghley and Sir Francis were silent as if waiting for the other to speak.

"Nicholas," Sir Francis paused and took a deep breath "we heard this morning that he too is dead."

"How? …. Why?" Nicholas asked in a barely audible voice, unable to take in what he had just been told.

"Evidently he died in his sleep." This time it was Burghley who spoke.

"But he was a young man … in his prime!"

Burghley smiled a rueful smile. "We received news of Arthur's death just half an hour after the news from Buxton."

"Sir Francis, from our conversations I understood Arthur was joining the English army in the Low Countries, so why, or rather, how did he end up in Spain?"

"Nicholas, we have no idea. We understand he was shipwrecked of the coast of Northern Spain and arrested as an English spy. There he made a wild claim that he was Arthur Dudley, son of Elizabeth I and the Earl of Leicester and so was taken to Madrid where Philip questioned him closely." Sir Francis explained.

"Are you sure it was Arthur Southron making this claim?"

"Nicholas, of that fact, we are certain. He was carrying papers in the name of Southron. However, Philip was sufficiently convinced by his story to give him an allowance and a place at Court." Walsingham's voice was barely audible.

"Was he openly referred to as the Queen's son?"

It was Burghley who answered. "He took the name of Dudley, and it appears that Philip accepted him as such. Perhaps Philip thought he had a sufficient likeness for the claim to be sound."

"People always see what they want to see." Sir Francis snorted.

"The Arthur I knew was a fit and healthy young man, so had the shipwrecked injured or made him ill?" Nicholas asked.

"Not as far as we know." Burghley replied.

"Nicholas," Sir Francis's voice was soft and low "your loyalty is much appreciated and will not be forgotten."

"My Lords," Nicholas stood up, feeling very shaky. "As ever my lips are sealed. When are you telling the Queen?"

"We cannot delay too long, but with the Queen in such good spirits I hesitate to be the bearer of such bad news, but I cannot delay for much longer."

"Lord Burghley," Nicholas rose and bowed to the old man, then turned and bowed again, "Sir Francis, I do not envy you this day."

"So, Alice," Nicholas watched as a jackdaw settled on the chimney opposite the window in his attic workroom, "it appears Philip was sufficiently convinced by the story that Arthur was Elizabeth's son, to have him poisoned as an act of revenge for the drubbing his Armada got at the hands of the English navy. That way he rid himself of an unnecessary expense, delivered an emotional body blow to his enemy and deprived England of a possible heir to the throne."

Alice let out a sob. "Oh Nick. To lose both your lover and your son in one day …"

Tears coursed down Alice's face.

"Alice" Nicholas hugged his wife close to his chest. Alice sobbed uncontrollably against her husband's chest. "Alice, hush. You'll be ill if you continue like this."

"Nick, Elizabeth has been so strong all these years and, in one day, she's lost everything she's ever loved."

"Sh, I thought you never wanted to hear about Arthur again."

"Not wanting to hear doesn't mean I've never thought about him" Alice paused to sniff "and poor Elizabeth. Imagine what she's been through. All her sacrifices - never being able to hold your only child, not even being able to be in the same room just in case someone, seeing you with a red-haired child, made all the sort of assumptions you did not want them to make. And what about Dudley? Nick, I know he was ambitious and self-seeking, but he had to watch Elizabeth flirt with various marriage prospects for years, right under his nose. He was an attractive man, so why wouldn't he take every opportunity to bed a wench if they offered. Perhaps he married Letitia to make Elizabeth jealous."

"Alice, I don't think the queen was ever jealous of Dudley's quick tumbles, but I agree Letitia was a different matter. Come, dry your eyes. The children will wonder why you've been crying."

"Do you know how the queen has taken the news?"

"No, my lovely wife, I don't. I left Burghley and Walsingham in their office. They may still be there for all I know."

"Nick …" Alice paused, "Nick, would you give Elizabeth that portrait of Arthur you have?"

Nicholas frowned in thought. "Are you thinking Elizabeth would want a memento of Arthur?"

Alice nodded. "I would if I was her and we don't know for sure if Burghley ever gave Arthur's guardian the one you gave to him."

"I'll give it some thought; but I won't promise anything."

Nicholas cradled the first portrait of Arthur he had painted, in his hand.

'Attici Amoris Ergo, - by, with, from, of or perhaps, through, the love of Atticus'. Was this really a very obscure motto masking a cryptic reference to parentage?

The information Burghley had given him had not, if Nicholas were completely honest, confirmed his theory. Burghley and Walsingham had only repeated what Arthur had claimed at the Spanish Court. That in itself was strange. Why had they told him anything at all. Nicholas smiled, despite Walsingham and Burghley's ambiguous statements, there was still the visual evidence on the Plea Rolls hidden deep in the archives. But, whatever the truth, it no longer mattered. Arthur was dead.

Nicholas picked up his pen and dipped it in gold ink.

Later, seated in front of his workroom fire, Nicholas handed Alice a small plain turned box.

"Oh, Nick," Alice's eyes welled up with tears "1588 – you've added the year the King of Spain killed the heir to the English throne." Alice paused to wipe her eyes and blow her nose. "Do you really think Philip murdered Arthur because we beat his Armada?"

" It appears Arthur's death may well be Philip's act of revenge, but who's to know? Sir Francis, Burghley, Ashley, Sir Dru Drury, Elizabeth and possibly Dudley's brother Ambrose, the Earl of Warwick, and they're not going to tell the likes of us." Nicholas paused, thinking. "Alice, didn't Robert and his brother Ambrose fight under Philip?"

"It wouldn't surprise me."

"I'm sure they did. I'm sure they joined the Spanish army after they were let out of the Tower, as a way of showing their allegiance to Mary and her new husband. In which case, if Arthur had known this, he might have thought he would be welcomed at the Spanish Court because of his father's and uncle's previous service."

Alice nodded. She was still cradling Arthur's portrait in her hand.

"You poor darling," she murmured. Nicholas was not sure if she were talking to him or the portrait. "you never had a chance."

"What do you mean, Alice."

"Arthur might have been taught all the Greek and Latin tutors could teach him, and how to fence, dance and make impressive speeches, but did he ever have anyone to tell him silly stories about pearls being frozen droplets of moonbeams, or that ostrich feathers are the feathers from angels' wings? I'm sure Elizabeth and Dudley loved him dearly, but they weren't even able to acknowledge his existence, let alone give him a cuddle."

Nicholas kissed the top of his wife's head. The children were all safely asleep and he wondered how he had ever had a life without them. Their noise and chatter filled the house and he loved them all, even though they cost him a fortune and peace and quiet was an occasional luxury. Alice could never abandon any of the children to someone else's care so how had Elizabeth been strong enough to do just that, or was Arthur's likeness to the queen just the workings of his imagination and everything else merely coincidence?

1603

Midday 24th March

Robert Cecil sat admiring Isaac Oliver's portrait of the queen wondering if the symbolism was not too obvious. Elizabeth looked down at him portrayed as the exquisitely young Astraea, the Just Virgin in a Golden Age. Cecil smiled as he thought about the network of agents who were shown as symbolic eyes, ears and mouths on the queen's skirt. Without their information England would not be as safe as it was now.

The Queen held a rainbow and the words *Non Sole Sine Iris* had been inscribed above it. 'No rainbow without the sun'. The rainbow was the bridge between heaven and the queen, who had succeeded to the throne by divine right. Now she had crossed that bridge and was, he hoped, in heaven having left England a peaceful and prosperous nation.

He reached forward and picked it up the ring lying on the blotter. The shank was very worn and it had been necessary to cut it in order to remove it from the queen's finger. He could not remember a time this ring had not been on the queen's hand. Examining the entwined ER under a hand lens, he realised there was a hinge so he gently squeezed the single pearl opposite and the entwined letters rose slightly. Cecil raised the tiny lid and Anne Boleyn and her daughter Elizabeth looked at each other.

It was not a ring of state so Cecil put it in away safely in his drawer deciding this was something the young King James of Scotland did not need to inherit.

*

The streets had few people in them. Those who had ventured abroad looked sad and many looked as if they had been crying.

Inside the Goldsmith's Hall Nicholas stood in front of the large portrait of the queen he had painted only a few years previously. Despite not liking painting these big portraits, this part of the agreement for the renewal of his lease had given him the opportunity to honour the three people to whom he owed everything - Levina Teerlinc, Robert Brandon and the Queen.

Using Levina's sketches for the tiny Coronation miniature England's Virgin Queen sat dressed in her gold coronation robes embroidered all over with Tudor roses, holding the orb and sceptre with her glorious hair cascading down her back. It had not been possible to set a diamond on the orb as in the miniature, but despite the lack of diamond sparkle, this portrait was magnificent.

Nicholas took the black silk from his satchel and draped it over the frame. The age of Gloriana was over.

Let me not to the marriage of true minds

Admit impediments. Love is not love

Which alters when it alteration finds,

Or bends with the remover to remove:

O no! it is an ever-fixed mark

That looks on tempests and is never shaken;

It is the star to every wandering bark,

Whose worth's unknown, although his height be taken.

Love's not Time's fool, though rosy lips and cheeks

Within his bending sickle's compass come:

Love alters not with his brief hours and weeks,

But bears it out even to the edge of doom.

    If this be error and upon me proved,

    I never writ, nor no man ever loved.

Sonnet CXVI

William Shakespeare

About the Author

Melanie Taylor was born in Pinner, England in 1953 and brought up on the Channel Island of Jersey. On leaving school she attended the local secretarial college. With secretarial skills learned, London beckoned and Melanie returned to England.

After marriage, children and divorce, in 1999 she saw an advert for part-time degrees at Kingston University in her local newspaper and enrolled to study The History of Art, Architecture & Design, graduating in 2005. Redundancy and an inheritance gave her the luxury of studying full-time for her Master of Arts degree in Medieval & Tudor Studies at the University of Kent, Canterbury.

Melanie now lives in Surrey and lectures in art and social history.

Selected Bibliography:

Images:

Portraits by Hilliard referred to in the text.
Unknown Lady: Fitzwilliam Museum, Cambridge.
1572: Levina Teerlinc: Bowhill House, Collection of the Duke of
Buccleugh.
1577 Two miniatures of a boy previously thought to be self
portraits: Bowhill House, Collection of the Duke of Buccleugh
1572: Elizabeth I: Miniature dated 1572. National Portrait Gallery,
London www.npg.org.uk Ref: **NPG 190**
The Phoenix Portrait: National Portrait Gallery, London. On Loan
to Tate Britain
The Pelican Portrait: Walker Art Gallery, Liverpool.
1576: Robert Dudley, Earl of Leicester: Victoria & Albert Museum:
Ref: **E1174-1988** c 1571-74. Also National Portrait Gallery,
London. Ref. **NPG 4197.**
1577 Self Portrait: : Victoria & Albert Museum, London. Ref
P155.1910.
1578 Alice Hilliard: Victoria & Albert Museum, London. Ref P.2-
1942.
Mary Queen of Scots:: The Royal Collection; Also Victoria & Albert
Museum Ref: P.24-1975.
1581 Sir Francis Drake: National Portrait Gallery, London
1581 The Drake Jewel: Victoria & Albert Museum, London
Sir Walter Raleigh:
Young Man Amongst Roses:: Victoria & Albert Museum, London
Ref. P.163-1910
1588 Attici Amoris Ergo: Victoria & Albert Museum, London,
www.vam.ac.uk **Ref. P.21-1942**

Miscellaneous Images referred to in the text.
Lady Jane Grey: Yale. US. (Previously thought to be of Princess
Elizabeth, but redefined as being of Lady Jane by Dr David
Starkey, in 2007).
Coronation Miniature: Levina Teerlinc, Private Collection, image
from Wikipedia.

1520 Treaty between France & England (illuminated): National Archives, Kew, Richmond, Surrey. E30/1109

Coronation Portrait: Anon. Tudor Section, © National Portrait Gallery, London.

The Rainbow Portrait: Isaac Oliver/Marcus Gheerhearts the Younger, Hatfield House, Herts.

Sketch of those present at the trial of Mary Queen of Scots: Anon, © British Library.

Sketch of those present at the execution of Mary Queen of Scots. Anon, © British Library.

Coram Rege Rolls illuminated Ps for the whole year of 1561 pen & ink. Photographs of the relevant terms are available by email from Melanie.V.Taylor@gmail.com

Accession Roll September 1553 KB27/1168/2 National Archives, Kew..

Document series consulted at The National Archives, Kew

C47 – Chancery Miscellanea c 1216-1702.

C66 – Chancery & Supreme Judicature : Patent rolls 1201-1600

E 36 – Exchequer: Treasury of Receipts: Miscellaneous Books : Edward I – George II.

E 30 – Exchequer: Treasury of Receipts: Diplomatic Documents c1100 – c1625.

E 101 – Kings Remembrances: Accounts Various c1154 – c1830.

E 315 – Court of Augmentations: Predecessors & Successors: Miscellaneous Book c1100-c1800.

E 323 – Court of Augmentations: Treasurer's Accounts 1536 – 1834.

E 403 – Exchequer of Receipts: Issue Rolls & Registers c1216-1834.

E 405 - Exchequer of Receipts: Jornalia Rolls; Tellers Rolls, Certificate Books, Declaration Books & Accounts of Receipts and Issues 1283 – 1835.

KB 27 – Coram Rege Rolls : Proceedings for the Kings Bench. (Years examined 1546 – 1565).

LC 2 - Lord Chamberlain's Record of Special Events.

PC - Records of the Privy Council and other records collected by the Privy Council Office: 1481-1987.

SP 12 - State Papers Domestic, Elizabeth I 1558-1603 .

Westminster Abbey Library

Westminster Cathedral Treasure No. 7: The Crampe Ring Manuscript (kept at Westminster Abbey Muniment Room)

WAM LXXXVI: Charter for the re-foundation of the monastery of Westminster.

Modern prints of prime source literature

Alberti, Leon Batista; *On Painting*; Translated by Cecil Grayson; Penguin Books Ltd., Harmondsworth, Middx., England, Penguin Books Inc., 3300 Clipper Mill Rd, Bellhouse, Maryland, USA; Penguin Books Pty Ltd., 762 Whitmore Rd., Mitcham, Victoria, Australia; Penguin Books (Canada) Ltd, 47 Green Street, St Lambert, Montreal, PQ, Canada; Penguin Books (SA) PTY Ltd, Gibraltar House, Regents Rd; Sea Point, Cape Town, SA; 1st translated for Phaidon Press 1971; this edition for Penguin Classics 1991.

Anon; *The Arte of Limming*; London; 1573. (Reprinted 1588).

Castiliogne, Baldessar: *"The Covrtyer of Count Baldessar Castilio"* Printed in London by Wyllyam Seres at the sign of the Hedgehog; 1561.

Cherry, John, Editor; *Medieval Love Poetry*; British Museum Press; A division of the British Museum Co Ltd., 38 Russell Square, London WC1b 3QQ; © 2005.

Durer; Albrecht; *Albert Durer Revived: Or a Book of Drawing, Limming, Washing or Colouring of Maps and Prints"*; printed by I Dawks for John Garrett, London; 1652 (translated from the original German printed 1528).

Elizabeth I; Collected Works; edited by Leah S Marcus, Janel Mueller, and Mary Beth Rose; The University of Chicago Press, Chicago 60637 & The University of Chicago Press Ltd., London © 2000 by The University of Chicago.

Hilliard, Nicholas; *A Treatise Concerning the Art of Limning, together with A More Compendious Discourse Concerning Ye Art of*

Liming by Edward Norgate; eds. R. K. R. Thornton & T. G. S. Cain; Mid Northumberland Arts Group, Northumberland in association with Carcanet New Press, Manchester; 1981.

Lomazzo, Paulo: *Tracte containing the Artes of Curious Paintinge Carvinge & Buildinge;* translated into English by R. H. a student of physik; 1598.

Melvil of Halhil, Sir James; *Memoires;* ed George Scott gent; printed by E. H. for Robert Boulter at the Turks Head in Cornhill against the Royal Exchange, 1683.

Ovid; *Metamorphoses*; transated by A. D. Melville, Oxford University Press;. Great Clarendon Street, Oxford OX2 6DP; Athens, Auckland, Bangkok, Bogotá, Buenos Aires, Calcutta, Cape Town, Chennai, Dar es Salaam, Delhi, Florence, Hong Kong, Istanbul, Nairobi, Paris, Sao Paulo, Shanghai, Singapore, Taipei, Tokyo, Toronto, Warsaw with associated companies in Berlin, Ibadan. published in USA by Oxford University Press Inc., New York; 1986.

Spenser, Edmund; *The Faerie Queen;* edited by Thomas P Roche Jr with the assistance of C Patrick O'Donnel Jr., Penguin Books Ltd., London WC2R 9LI, England; Penguin Putnam Inc., 375 Hudson Street, New York N010014, USA; Penguin Books Australia Ltd., Ringwood, Victoria, Australia; Penguin Books Canada Ltd., 19 Alcom Avenue, Toronto, Ontario Canada N4V 3BR; Penguin Books India (P) Ltd., 11 Community Centre, Panchsheel Park, New Delhi 10 017, New Delhi, India; Penguin Books (NZ) Ltd, Cnr Rosedale & Airborne Road, Albany, Auckland, New Zealand; Penguin Books (South Africa) (Pty) Ltd., 24 Sturde Avenue, Rosebank 2196, South Africa; 1978.

The Bible, The New Revised Standard Version; Mowbray, Villiers House, 41-47 Strand, London WC2N 5JC, 1994.

Turbeville, George; *The Noble arte of venerie or hunting*; held in the Huntingdon University Library.

Vasari, Georgio; *Lives of the Artists*; translated by Julia Conaway Bondanella & Peter Bondanella; Oxford University Press, Clarendon Street, Oxford OX2 6DP; New York, Athens, Auckland, Bangkok, Bogotá, Bombay, Buenos Aries, Calcutta, Cape Town, Dar es Salaam, Delhi, Florence, Hong Kong,

Istanbul, Karachi, Kuala Lumpur, Madras Madrid, Melbourne, Mexico City, Nairobi, Paris, Singapore, Taipei, Tokyo, Toronto, Warsaw & associated companies in Berlin, Ibadan,; 1st published as a World's Classics paperback 1991, re-issued as an Oxford World's Classics paperback 1996.

Walpole, Horace, *Anecdotes of Painting in England* collected by the late Mr George Vertue: Vol 1; printed by Thomas Kirgate at Strawberry Hill, MDCCLXV 2nd edition; British Library CW330642426.

Washington, Peter, editor; *Love songs & Sonnets*; Everyman's Library Pocket Poets; Published by Alfred A Knopf; © Everymans Library 1987.

Xenephon; Heiro www.mirrorservice.com (5/07/2006)

Secondary Sources

Anderson, Janice; *Illuminated Manuscripts*; Todtri Book Publishers, P.O. Box 572, New York, NY 10116-0572; ©1999.

Auerbach, Erna; *Tudor Artists*; University of London; The Athlone Press, Senate House, London, W.C.1; 1954.

Auerbach, Erna; *Nicholas Hilliard*; Routledge & Kegan Paul Ltd; Broadway House, 68-74 Carter Lane, London, EC4; 1964.

Brown, Michelle P., *Understanding Illuminated Manuscripts: A Guide to Technical Terms*; The J Paul Getty Museum & The British Library Board, 96 Euston Road, London, NW1 2DB; 1994.

Chadwick, Whitney; *Women Art & Society*; Thames & Hudson; 30 Bloomsbury WC1B 3QP; ©1990 and revised edition 1996.

Coombes, Katherine; *The Portrait Miniature in England*; V&A Publications, 160 Brompton Road. London SW3 1HW; 1998.

Doherty, Paul; *The Secret Life of Elizabeth;* Greenwich Exchange; London; © Paul Doherty 2006.

Duffy, Eamon; *The Stripping of the Altars*; Yale

University Press, New Haven and London; ©1992 2nd edition ©2005.

Edmond, Mary; *Hilliard & Oliver: The Lives & Works of Two Great Miniaturists*; Robert Hale, London; 1983.

Elton, George R; *The Tudor Constitution*: Documents and Commentary; The Syndics of the Cambridge University Press; Bentley House, 200 Euston Road, London N.W.1; American Branch, 32 East 57th Street, New York 22, New York; West African Office: P.O. Box 33, Ibadan, Nigeria; 1960.

Fumerton, Patricia & Simon Hunt (eds); *Renaissance Culture and the Everyday*; University o f Pennsylvania Press, Philadelphia, Pennsylvania 19104-4011; © 1999.

Fumerton, Patricia; *Cultural Aesthetics*: Renaissance Literature and the Practice of Social Ornament; University of Chicago Press, Chicago & London; 1991.

Hibbert, Christopher; Elizabeth I: *A Personal History of the Virgin Queen*; Penguin Books Ltd, 80 The Strand, London WC2R ORL, England; Penguin Putnam Inc, 375 Hudson Street, New York, NO10014, USA; Penguin Books Australia Ltd, Ringwood, Victoria, Australia; Penguin Books Canada Ltd, 10 Alcorn Avenue, Toronto, Ontario, Canada M4V 3B2; Penguin Books India (P) Ltd, 11 Community Centre, Panchsheel Park, New Delhi - 110 017, New Delhi, India; Penguin Books (NZ) Ltd, Cnr Rosedale & Airborne Road, Albany, Auckland, New Zealand; Penguin Books (South Africa) (Pty) Ltd, 24 Sturdee Avenue, Rosebank 2196, South Africa; First published by Viking as The Virgin Queen: The Personal History of Elizabeth I 1990; Published by Penguin Books 1992; Reprinted by Penguin Books as Elizabeth I: A personal History of the Virgin Queen 2001; © Christopher Hibbert 1990.

Howarth, David; *Images of Rule: Art and Politics in the English Renaissance, 1485-1649;* Macmillan Press Ltd., Houndmills, Basingstoke, Hampshire RG21 6XS; 1997.

Kempers, Bram; *Painting, Power & Patronage*; Penguin Group; Penguin Books Ltd, 27 Wrights Lane, London W8 5TZ England; Penguin Books USA Inc., 375 Hudson Street, New York, New York 10014, USA; Penguin Books Australia Ltd, Ringwood, Victoria, Australia; Penguin Books Canada Ltd, 10 Alcorn Avenue, Toronto, Ontario, Canada M4V 3B2; Penguin Books (NZ) Ltd., 182-190 Wairau Road, Auckland 10, New Zealand; First published in Dutch under the title Kunst, macht en mecenaat, 1987; This English Translation first published in English by Allen Lane, 1993; Published in Penguin Books 1994.

Loades David; *Elizabeth I The golden reign of Gloriana*; The National Archives, Kew, Richmond, Surrey TW9 4DU, UK. 2003.

Matthew, David; *The Courtiers of Henry VIII;* Eyre & Spottiswood (Publishers) Ltd; 11New Fetter Lane, London EC4; 1970.

McKendrick, Scot; *Flemish Illuminated Manuscripts 1400-1500*; The British Library, 96 Euston Road, London, NW1 2DB; 2003.

Murrell, Jim; *The Way Howe to Lymne; Tudor Miniatures Observed*; Victoria & Albert Museum; London; 1983.

Reynolds, Graham; *English Portrait Miniatures*; Press Syndicate of the University of Cambridge; The Pitt Building, Trumpington Street, Cambridge, CB2 1RP; 32 East 57th Street, New York, NY 10022, USA; 10 Stamford Road, Oakleigh; Melbourne, 3166, Australia; First edition published by A & C Black, 1952 this edition published in 1988.

Smeyers, Maurits; *Flemish Miniatures*; Brepolis, Uitgeverij Davidsfonds/Leuven, Leuven; Blijde-Inkomststraat 79-81, B-3000 Leuven© 1999.

Starkey, David, editor; *Henry VIII: A European Court in England*; Collins & Brown; Mercury House, 195 Knightsbridge, London SW7 1RE; This edition was published in 1991 by BCA by arrangement with Collins & Brown.

Starkey, David, editor; *Rivals in Power*, Macmillan London, 4 Little Essex Street, London WC2R 3LF and Basingstoke; 1990.

Starkey, David; *Elizabeth;* Vintage; Random House, 20 Vauxhall Bridge Rd, London SW1V 2SA; Random House Australia (Pty) Limited, 20 Alfred Street, Milsons Point, Sydney, New South Wales 2061 Australia; Random House New Zealand Limited, 18 Poland Road, Glenfield, Auckland 10, New Zealand; Random House (Pty) Limited, Endulini, 5A Jubilee Road, Parktown 2193, South Africa; First published in Great Britain by Chato & Windus 2000 and by Vintage 2001.

Strong, Roy; *Gloriana: The Portraits of Queen Elizabeth*; Pimlico; Random House, 20 Vauxhall Bridge Road, London, SW1V 2SA; Random House Australia (Pty) Limited, 20 Alfred Street, Milsons Point, Sydney, New South West 2061 Australia; Random House New Zealand Ltd, 18 Poland Road, Glenfield, Auckland 10, New Zealand; Random House South Africa (PTY) Limited, Endulini, 5A Jubilee Road, Parktown 2193, South Africa; First published Great Britain by Thames & Hudson; London 1987 and Pimlico edition 2003.

Strong, Roy; *The Cult of Elizabeth*; Pimlico; Random House, 20 Vauxhall Bridge Road, London, SW1V 2SA; Random House Australia (Pty) Limited, 20 Alfred Street, Milsons Point, Sydney, New South West 2061 Australia; Random House New Zealand Ltd, 18 Poland Road, Glenfield, Auckland 10, New Zealand; Random House South Africa (PTY) Limited, Endulini, 5A Jubilee Road, Parktown 2193, South Africa; 1999.

Strong, Roy; *The English Icon: Elizabeth & Jacobean Portraiture*; The Paul Mellon Foundation for British Art 1969; 38 Bury Street, London, SW1 in association with Routledge and Kegan Paul Limited, Broadway House, Carter Lane, EC4; 1969.

Strong, Roy; *The English Renaissance Miniature*; Victoria & Albert Museum; 1983 and revised edition 1984.

Walker Richard; *Miniatures*; National Portrait Gallery; Publications; National Portrait Gallery; St Martin's Place, London WC2H 0HE; © National Portrait Gallery, 1998.

Watkins, Susan; *In Public and in Private: Elizabeth I and her World*; Thames & Hudson; 30 Bloomsbury Street, London, WC1B 3QP; © 1998.

Wenzler, Claude; *The Kings of France;* Translated by Angela Moyon; Editions Ouest-France; 13 rue de breil, Rennes; 1995.

Williams, Neville; *Elizabeth I;* Sphere Books Ltd; 30/32 Gray's Inn Road, London WC1X 8JL; 1975; © George Weisenfeld & Nicolson & Book Club Associates, 1972 and Cardinal edition published in 1975.

Williams, Neville; *Henry VIII & His Court*; Sphere Books Ltd; 30/32 Gray's Inn Road, London WC1X 8JL; First published in 1971 Great Britain by Weisenfeld & Nicolson Ltd. Cardinal edition first published in 1973.

Williamson, George C.; *How To Identify Portrait Miniatures*; George Bell and Sons; York House, Portugal Street, WC; 1904.

Williamson, George C; *The Miniature Collector*; Herbert Jenkins Ltd; 3 York Street, Saint James's, London SW1; MCMXXI.

Winter, Carl; *Elizabethan Miniatures*; Penguin books, Penguin Books Ltd, Harmondsworth, Middx, England; Penguin Books Inc, 3300 Clipper Mill Rd, Bellhouse, Maryland, USA; Penguin Books Pty Ltd, 762 Whitmore Rd, Mitcham, Victoria, Australia; Penguin Books (Canada) Ltd, 47 Green Street, St Lambert, Montreal, PQ, Canada; Penguin Books (SA) PTY Ltd, Gibraltar House, Regents Rd; Sea Point, Cape Town, SA; First printed 1943; this edition revised and reprinted 1955.

Exhibition Catalogues

Strong, Roy; *Artists of the Tudor Court: The Portrait Miniature Rediscovered 1520*; Victoria & Albert Museum;

London; 1983.

Foister, Susan; *Holbein and the Court of Henry VIII*; The Queen's Gallery, Buckingham Palace; 1978 – 1979.

Kren, Thomas & Scot McKendrick; *Illuminating the Renaissance: The Triumph of Flemish Manuscript Painting in Europe*; Getty Publications; 1200 Getty Centre Drive Suite 500, Los Angeles, California, 90049-1682; © 2003 J. Paul Getty Trust.

Lloyd, Stephen; *Portrait Miniatures from the Clarke Collection*; Trustees of National Galleries of Scotland; 2001.

Doran, Susan and David Starkey; *Elizabeth*; National Maritime Museum, Greenwich; 2003.

Articles

Auerbach, Erna; *"Illuminated Royal Portraits"*; The Burlington Magazine for Connoisseurs; 1951; Vol 93 No. 582; pp 300+302-3.

Auerbach, Erna; *"An Elizabethan Illuminated Indenture"*; The Burlington Magazine for Connoisseurs; 1951; Vol. 93 No. 583; pp319-321 + 323.

Auerbach, Erna; *"Portraits of Elizabeth I"*; The Burlington Magazine for Connoisseurs; 1953; Vol 95 No. 603; pp 196-205.

Auerbach, Erna; *"Anglo-Flemish Art under the Tudors"*; The Burlington Magazine for Connoisseurs; 1954; Vol 96 No. 612; pp 86 + 89-90 + 95.

Auerbach, Erna; *"Some Tudor Portraits at the Royal Academy"*; The Burlington Magazine for Connoisseurs; 1957; Vol 99 No 646; pp 8-11 +13.

Bergmans, Simone; *"The Miniatures of Levina Teerling"*; The Burlington Magazine for Connoisseurs; 1934; Vol 64 No 372; pp 232-233 + 235-6.

Drigsdhal, Eric; *"The Grimani Breviary & The Iconograhical Heritage in Ghent"*; Royal Library of Belgium Brussels; Nov 2002;

Foister, Susan; *"Tudor Miniaturists at the V&A London"*;

385

The Burlington Magazine for Connoisseurs; 1983; Vol 125 No. 967; pp 622 + 623-636.

James, Susan and Jamie Franco; *"Susannah Horenbout & Levina Teerlinc: And the Mask of Royalty"*; Jaarboek-Koninklijk Museum Voor Schöne; 2000; pp 90-125.

Hervey, Mary F. S; *"Notes on some Portraits of Tudor Times"*; The Burlington Magazine for Connoisseurs; 1909; Vol 15 No. 75; pp 151-5 + 158-160.

King, John N; Queen Elizabeth I: *"Representation of the Virgin Queen"*; Renaissance Quarterly; Spring, 1990; Vol 43 No. 1; pp 30-74.

Orth, Myra D; *"A French Illuminated Treaty of 1527"*; The Burlington Magazine for Connoisseurs;1980; Vol 122 No. 923; pp 125-6 + 139.

Saxl, F: *"The Power of the Name?"*; Journal of the Warburg Institute; Vol 1, No 1 July 1937; p73.

Schlosser, Julius; "Two Portrait Miniatures from Castle Ambras"; The Burlington Magazine for Connoisseurs; 1922; Vol 41 No. 235; pp 194-5 + 197-8.

Strong, Roy; *"The Leicester House Miniatures: Robert Sidney, 1st Earl of Leicester and His Circle"*; The Burlington Magazine for Connoisseurs; 1985; Vol 127 No. 991; pp 694 + 696-701 + 703.

Weale, James W H; *"Simon Bennink, Miniaturist"*; The Burlington Magazine for Connoisseurs;1906; Vol 8 No. 35; pp355-357.

Weale, James W H; *"Levina Teerlinc, Miniaturist"*; The Burlington Magazine for Connoisseurs; 1906; Vol 9 No. 40; p278.